SARAH DREHER

SOLITAIRE AND BRAHMS

NEW VICTORIA PUBLISHERS

Published by New Victoria Publishers, Inc., a feminist literary and cultural organization, PO Box 27, Norwich, VT 05055-0027

1 2 3 4 5 2001 2000 1999 1998 1997
Printed and bound in Canada

Cover painting by Elaine Frenett

Library of Congress Cataloging-in-Publication Data

Dreher, Sarah.
   Solitaire and Brahms : by Sarah Dreher.
      p. cm.
   ISBN 0-934678-85-5
   1. Lesbians--Fiction.   I. Title.
 PS3554. R36S65 1997
 813' . 54--dc21   97-19545
                                                CIP

For Liz, Fayal, Jeannette, Alice and Pat
the women who kept me alive

Other Titles by Sarah Dreher

Stoner McTavish

Something Shady

Gray Magic

A Captive In Time

Otherworld

Bad Company

Shaman's Moon

Lesbian Stages

Chapter 1

The one thing Shelby Camden had always known about herself was that there was something about herself she didn't know. Sometimes she thought she had known it once but forgotten it. And sometimes she thought she had never known it, but was always on the edge of knowing. Sometimes it felt like an animal of a strange and frightening nature, one that would draw strength from daylight and so had to be kept in the darkness. Sometimes it felt like a friendly thing, perhaps a hidden talent or skill, one that would give her a great deal of pleasure. Most of the time it was a secret box that might be opened one day— if she could, if she wanted to, if she dared, reach in her pocket and find the key. But until she did...

She leaned back against the celery green Naugahyde sofa and watched a small gray and black bird as it pecked at a tightly-wrapped maple bud. A goldfinch, still in its winter plumage. The day was as gray as the finch. The days were always gray in March. March in New England was the other side of November. It gave you more to look forward to than November, but lasted twice as long. The sky dripped—not really mist, not really rain, but a compression and congealing of soggy air that coalesced on anything it touched. A single droplet cut a channel down the picture window.

Inside the editorial offices of *The Magazine for Women*, the radiators chugged and clanged but couldn't make headway against the creeping, bone-devouring dampness. Shelby pulled her attention away from the window and glared across the coffee table at the rubber tree plant that languished in the far corner of the waiting room. Rubber tree plants always struck her as annoyingly artificial, with their dark green glossy leaves and arched limbs like department store mannequins. They never bloomed, as far as she knew, and she'd never seen a new branch or bud. They never quite lost all their leaves, only an occasional pitiful dry one, which wouldn't fall while you were watching but liked to greet you in the morning with all its dead-leaf-from-the-rubber-tree-plant pathos. They did this just often enough to make you think you were doing something wrong, and should water it less or feed it more, or maybe prune it. But if you took action on its behalf, the next day it would look exactly the way it had the night before. And it would have dropped exactly one leaf.

Rubber tree plants were very popular, and Shelby hated them.

Good God, she thought with a twinge of self-disgust, listen to you. She'd be twenty-five years old next week. She had a Master's degree in journalism, just as she'd always planned, and an apartment of her own in a large, old and slightly spooky house on a quiet, tree-lined street, just as she'd always hoped. She had

1

friends, and a job with a popular and respectable magazine that was sold on newsstands, not in grocery stores, and could be found in most libraries, and she'd probably be promoted to assistant editor within the next six months. And here she was taking offense at rubber tree plants.

She glanced across the room toward the door to David Spurl's office, where the editor's private secretary sat like a concrete Chinese dragon on guard and tapped away at her typewriter. Miss Myers was an enigma. If she had a life outside the office, a first name, a family, a pet, even a pet peeve, no one had ever discovered it. If she had ever been young or foolish, there was no one around who had witnessed it. She never took a day off and was never sick. There were no photographs of loved or admired ones on her desk or tucked into the corner of her blotter. She ate her lunch in the lunchroom, but always sat alone and reading a paperback book, sipping her tea and nibbling delicately at bits of lettuce and tuna salad. No one had ever been able to get a peek at the paperback book.

Once, feeling sorry for her, Shelby had invited her to join their table. Miss Myers had merely glanced up, murmured, "Thank you, no," and dismissed her by turning her head away.

Miss Myers was there when they arrived in the morning, and still there when the offices closed at night. She might be potted behind her desk like the rubber tree plant, slipping into a coma through the passing night hours, gray-streaked hair forever gray-streaked, wearing the same modest dark and flowered dress, just a touch of lipstick, a dab of powder, no rouge, hands poised above the typewriter keys, fingers delicately arched, nails filed and polished to perfection...

Or maybe Spurl crept back in after the offices were closed, while Miss Myers waited in black lace panties and garter belt, and they made wild, abandoned love while the rubber tree plant dropped its solitary leaf.

From behind her desk, Miss Myers glanced up at her and briefly smiled. Well, she didn't really smile. "Smile" implied an act of volition. In Miss Myers' case, the smile was a random and unwilled act, an autumn cloud drifting across the face of the moon.

A smile happened to Miss Myers, Shelby thought.

She realized she envied the woman, in a way. A smile happening took no decision, no force, no planning or intention. It happened whether it was expected or not. Some days Shelby thought the energy required to smile would be too much for her.

Smiling was mandatory in Shelby's world.

The keys of Miss Myers' typewriter rose and fell in perfect cadence, a well-trained army. The platen slid along at a constant speed. You could probably fine-tune a motor to the intervals between strokes. Now and then, Miss Myers paused to proof her typing, scowling at the words as if defying them to display a blemish. If she found one—Shelby had witnessed this once, and it had struck terror into her heart—Miss Myers ripped the page from the typewriter, tore it to shreds, and dropped the offending item into the waste basket. No easy solutions for Miss Myers, no indeed. Miss Myers obviously felt that anyone who relied on White-Out or other modern conveniences was of low moral character and unworthy of the privileges and responsibilities granted to *superior* human beings. Sometimes Miss Myers would look up suddenly, her eyes

2

sweeping the room with a piercing, wary expression as if searching for disorder. Finding no rebellious inanimate objects—animate objects knew better than to rebel against Miss Myers—she'd give a satisfied nod and go back to work. Her fingers never broke stride.

The rubber tree plant caught Shelby's attention again. She scowled at it. Too bad Miss Myers didn't disapprove of this monster. It would go the way of errant commas and misplaced hyphens.

They were just that self-satisfied, rubber tree plants. And they were everywhere. Like those wax-encrusted Chianti bottles they all had back in college. Tall-necked, green, round-bellied things, dressed up in terribly cute little baskets. She'd even saved one after an evening of pizza, herself—"*Everyone*" did, her roommate insisted—although they galled her.

Sometimes, when she took a dislike to something for no reason—it had happened with paper napkins for a while, and stuffed celery—she ended up feeling sorry for the poor thing which hadn't done anything, really, to deserve her animosity. That hadn't happened with Chianti bottles; they had sinned by being too rigorously popular. And it hadn't happened yet with rubber tree plants.

Miss Myers was still tapping and dinging away, getting those letters and words and punctuation marks in line. She was just the kind of woman Shelby's mother had said Shelby would turn into, when she'd found out Shelby had applied to graduate school. Naively, Shelby had hoped Columbia's prestige would count for something in Libby's social-climbing eyes. It hadn't.

Libby had raved for a while, and there were some pretty unpleasant, silent dinners at the Camdens,' but eventually she had calmed down. Calmed down, not to be confused with coming around. She'd probably never come around. A career was a Sure-Fire Dead End on the Marriage-Go-Round as far as Libby was concerned, and the Marriage-Go-Round was the only thing that counted in this life. Journalism wasn't *quite* as Disastrous as—God Forbid—Science, as long as it didn't lead to Unfeminine Activities such as reporting on Wars and Crime and Juvenile Delinquency. But it was Pretty Bad.

Libby was fond of capitalizing her words. Shelby could hear them when her mother spoke. Sometimes parts of her periodic letters were in all caps. Bits of advice, mostly, followed by DO NOT FAIL TO DO THIS—usually referring to sending thank-you notes or birthday cards to relatives, especially those on her father's side of the family. Which was a little strange, considering that Libby and Thomas had been happily divorced for years.

Silence had fallen. Miss Myers had abandoned her typewriter and was standing by the filing cabinet. Shelby made a mental note to tell the lunch bunch that she had actually witnessed Miss Myers away from her desk during working hours. Only very fortunate persons were privileged to see Miss Myers away from her desk during working hours. It was thought among Shelby's fellow senior readers to be an omen, a sign that one was destined for greatness.

Shelby didn't feel destined for greatness. What she felt destined for was sitting forever on Naugahyde couches in waiting rooms, grinning like an idiot at every human being who came within view. That was what people like her—young, probably-about-to-be-successful women—did.

Thinking about killing themselves certainly wasn't what people like Shelby

Camden did.

There it was, another one of those thoughts that popped into her head without warning or permission. It was happening more and more lately—words appearing uninvited and unexpected, as sudden as snakes.

Maybe I'm developing a multiple personality, like Eve White and Eve Black.

But if she were splitting into a one-woman group, someone would have noticed and spoken up. She could count on that. In Shelby Camden's life, people noticed and spoke up.

She noticed she was chewing her lip. Great. Probably chewed off her lipstick. Shelby took a deep breath and steeled herself. "Excuse me," she said to the formidable Miss Myers in what she hoped was a self-assured voice, "I know I'm a little early. Do you think I have time to wash up a bit?"

Miss Myers paused, hands hovering above the file drawer. She seemed to do a quick calculation. A brisk nod. "You have time, if you don't dawdle."

She hadn't dawdled since she was five, if then. No one had ever accused Shelby Camden of dawdling. Not even on her way to the dentist, which was certainly an appropriate time to dawdle. If there was one thing that could be said of Shelby Camden, it was that Shelby Camden did NOT dawdle.

She walked briskly down the hall to the ladies' room.

The offices of *The Magazine for Women* were in an old, creaky, weather-beaten brick building that was slowly being strangled by an eerily healthy Boston ivy. The building had recently held a book bindery. Before that, it had been a private school, and before that a creamery. With each new incarnation, the inside had been remodeled, scraps of its former identity left here and there like scars. The latest renovation had brought the Naugahyde sofas in the public rooms, and picture windows that looked out-of-place from the street, chopped out of the brick and ivy. The editorial offices were high-ceilinged, with dark book shelves and stuffed leather chairs. Masculine. The readers' room was like a school library, large, with heavy wooden desks spaced just far enough apart to offer some privacy. Its floor was made of narrow hardwood slats that had begun to curl at the edges and squealed pitifully when you walked across them. The lunchroom was light and smelled of brown linoleum and old ice cream.

The ladies' room was different. The ladies' room had kept its schoolish institutional flavor, with a tile floor and gray walls, and stalls with green metal doors. As if whoever had designed the rest of the building had overlooked, or didn't want to get involved with, the ladies' room.

Shelby liked the ladies' room. She suspected she was the only person who had ever liked that room, or who ever *would* like it at any time in the foreseeable future. Its musty sterility reminded her of the common bathroom back in college, where you had to yell a warning before you flushed the toilet or whoever was in the shower would be scalded to death, and where Pru Richey—the scholarship student from Appalachia—used to sit late into the night playing her dulcimer.

She dug into her handbag for her lipstick, and glanced at herself in the mirror. The room's dim, quivering, fluorescent lights gave her a washed-out appearance, brown hair gone mousey, hazel eyes gone flat. Her skin, pale enough after another New England winter, had taken on a blue-grey tinge.

I look dead, she thought.

She felt a heavy pressure behind her eyes.

Oh, God, not another headache. Not now. Not when I have to see Spurl about…whatever it is I have to see Spurl about.

What did he want to see her about, anyway?

Spurl, Spurl, Spurl. Friend of the working girl.

She browsed through her actions for the previous week. Couldn't find anything she'd done wrong or overlooked. Hadn't been too pushy, or too timid. Kept up her end of the conversation in the lunchroom . Hadn't communicated with any writers without her Assistant Editor's OK. No major social blunders. Her mother would be gratified.

The ladies' room smelled of old showers and wet wool.

She touched the shiny metal frame that ran around the mirror, avoiding eye contact with herself. She knew she was delaying the meeting, that she was a little bit apprehensive. But not dawdling. She was always a little apprehensive dealing with Authority Figures, as they called them back in Sociology 101.

Good old Sociology 101, with balding Professor Jannings of the baggy sweaters with the leather elbow patches. Professor Jannings smoked a pipe. He really did. Smoked a pipe and paused to relight it whenever he was working up to a profound thought. Professor Jannings was a bit of a fool, who fancied himself a character in a British novel, a college-level Mr. Chips. But Professor Jannings held the power of pass or fail, so it didn't matter how much of a fool he was, he was an Authority Figure.

This isn't college, she reminded herself firmly, no grades or term papers or extra points for class participation. This was Real Life, with or without Libby's capitals. It only felt like college.

Shelby ran her hands through her hair, brushing the soft brown waves away from her face. She sighed and left the ladies' room.

The door whooshed shut behind her.

Miss Myers had returned to her fortress and was typing away, stiff and expressionless. Shelby crept to her assigned place on the sofa and stared out the window. It had started to rain. The bird had left.

She heard the typewriter go silent and glanced up. Miss Myers gave her a curt nod, meaning she could go in now. Shelby wondered how she knew; she hadn't heard the intercom, or a door opening, or anyone yelling from the Inner Sanctum. Maybe Miss Myers and Spurl were psychically connected, Siamese twins who thought as one, separated at birth.

She took a deep breath and stood. Her fingertips tingled with anxiety.

As she started into the office, Shelby felt a light touch on her arm. She looked down.

Miss Myers smiled up at her. A purposeful smile, not a random one, complete with eye contact. "I think you'll be pleased," she said.

"*You* have got it *made*," Connie squealed. Connie always squealed when she was excited. Sometimes the prospect of it made Shelby think twice before telling her exciting news.

"I don't know, Con. He didn't say any…"

"He didn't *have* to. You get the glad hand from Myers the Mannequin, you're in like Flynn."

"She only smiled…" Shelby began.

"Does Mount Rushmore smile? Does the Statue of Liberty smile? I'm telling you, two weeks, a month max, you're an assistant editor." She gave Jean a look across the table, demanding agreement.

Jean looked back in an apologetic way.

Shelby wanted to go home.

Connie wouldn't approve of that thought. No way.

Connie Thurmond had an enthusiastic nature and large, very white teeth. Movie star teeth. Connie thought she looked a little like Gloria DeHaven. It didn't matter that DeHaven had larger eyes, a smaller nose, fuller lips, and brown rather than blonde hair. Connie saw the resemblance, and that was all that mattered to her. Connie had a firm, unshakable belief in her own particular view of reality. The whole rest of the world, including the four billion Chinese or whatever, could disagree with her. The whole rest of the world would be wrong.

Shelby picked at her chicken salad sandwich and tried to think of a way to change the subject. Connie was probably right, she was on her way, but she didn't want to think about it. It was too much of a…of a…well, just too much. "Maybe."

"What did Spurl say, actually?" Lisa asked. Lisa Marconi—whom Connie had immediately and predictably nick-named Macaroni—was skinny and angled and accident-prone and always in motion. She leaned forward eagerly, the corner of her scarf trailing in the mayonnaise on top of her canned-pear-and-lime-Jello salad.

"He wants me to train a new reader."

"There you are!" Connie snapped her fingers and scanned the table triumphantly. "What'd I tell you?"

"It doesn't necessarily mean anything." The headache she was nursing had moved front and center.

Connie rolled her eyes and sighed heavily. "It *means*," she said with infinite and weary patience, "you're being primed for a move, and the new girl's your replacement."

"It means I'm being watched, I suspect."

"For God's sake, Camden…"

Let it go, she told herself, unless you want to spend the rest of your lunch hour arguing.

Because this kind of argument was exactly what Connie liked best, one that could get heated and stubborn and wasn't about anything that could possibly matter to anyone.

"You're probably right," she said agreeably, ruining Connie's lunch.

She realized then why she still thought so often of college. It was because nothing had really changed. The people she shared her work with and ate lunch with and relaxed with on the weekends were nearly identical to the people she had studied with and roomed with and eaten with back then. There had been a Connie, only her name had been Suzanne, nicknamed Sukie, and she even had the big teeth (wealthy Philadelphia teeth, Shelby called them). There was a Lisa, *aka* Maggie, who was from Oklahoma and didn't notice that the Sukies looked

6

down on her, laughing at her behind her back and showing their big Philadelphia teeth and Ipana-pink gums. And there was a Jean, Nancy in those days, who hovered around the edges of the group and was always quietly serious.

"Oh, Gawd, Sheffield!" Connie wailed. She was staring at Jean's lunch. "What's *that* stuff?"

"It's called tabbouleh," Jean said, her face reddening a little. "I found the recipe in a cook book. It's really good. Want to try it?"

"It looks *disgusting*. Like something from the slums of India."

"It's no worse than that Jello thing we're eating," Shelby observed.

"So she might as well eat what we have."

Jean had put down her fork and was looking at her hands.

For God's sake, Jean, stand up for yourself.

Sometimes she wanted to grab Jean by the shoulders and give her a good shake. She was too deferential, too soft. People like Connie could chew her up and spit her out. Not out of cruelty—she couldn't imagine Connie being deliberately cruel—but Connie was congenitally insensitive and needed to be reminded of the limits from time to time.

Shelby liked Jean. She didn't really know her well, even though she'd been at the magazine for two months now and had lunch with them every day. Jean faded into the background, which wasn't hard with Connie and Lisa around. But she seemed to fit in. Marginally.

She remembered the day she'd met Jean. She'd forgotten her lunch money, and gone back to her desk for it. The readers' room was silent and empty except for the dust motes that slid and danced down a winter sunbeam. And there she'd been, sitting at her desk—where she'd been all morning, only no one had taken the time to notice.

Jean had spread out a paper napkin for a place mat, and was eating some strange, yellowish, lumpy-looking gruel-like substance from a cottage cheese container. As she reached into her brown paper bag and pulled out a bottle of orange juice, she glanced up. Her eyes met Shelby's. She glanced down.

"Well, hi," Shelby said, and hoped she didn't sound as guilty as she felt. She started to say, "Don't you want to join us?" but realized it would sound as if she thought the fault were Jean's rather than her own. All of their collective own, really, the way all fifteen readers had jumped up the minute a distant chime announced the cafeteria was open, and stampeded down the stairs like cattle, never giving a thought to the new reader. She could say, "I'm sorry, I completely forgot about you because my head was in this unusually intriguing story I've been reading…," Or she could come clean and say, "I'm an insensitive clod, I hope you won't take it personally," which would be the most accurate…

"Is something wrong?" the woman was asking.

"No, I…uh…" She stuck out her hand. "I'm Shelby Camden."

Jean took it and shook it. "Jean Sheffield. We already met. This morning."

"Right," Shelby said heartily, feeling foolish now as well as guilty. "Listen, do you prefer to eat alone, or…?"

Now Jean looked as flustered as Shelby felt. "Not really…but…"

Their mutual discomfort stretched until Shelby heard herself laugh. "This is a ridiculous. I'm a jerk, I apologize, come with me, and what is that you're eating?"

7

"Polenta," Jean said as she stuffed the napkin and spoon into the brown paper bag. "I found the recipe, but I don't remember where. Maybe on the bus or something. Want to try it?"

Shelby looked down into the cottage cheese container and lost her nerve. "Later, maybe." It smelled like corn, and had streaks of something resembling ketchup running through it. Shelby was reminded of Port Salut cheese. She grabbed her wallet from her desk drawer.

Later it was discovered that Jean could play bridge, which made her a valuable addition to the lunch bunch, since their previous fourth had gone off to get married. This meant she was also included in after-work and weekend activities. Shelby was glad for her company. Connie was always chattering and laughing, because she wanted the attention. Lisa was always chattering and shrieking because that was how she was. Shelby was always chattering because it was expected of her. Having quiet Jean on the periphery was like having a Guardian Angel. When everything got to be too much, Shelby could exchange sympathetic looks with her.

Sometimes they went to Jean's apartment for a quick Friday evening cocktail, since she lived in West Sayer, just a few blocks from the office. But her place was small and dark and full of old furniture, which Connie claimed gave her claustrophobia. Shelby liked it.

"So what we ought to do," Connie was saying, "is have a party."

"A party?" Shelby asked.

"To celebrate."

"Celebrate?"

"You."

Shelby laughed. "You'd have a party to celebrate waking up in the morning if you could."

"So?"

"So if you want to have a party, have a party. But don't use me for an excuse. It's too much pressure."

Connie rolled her eyes. "Camden…"

"I mean it." She was surprised at the irritation in her voice.

"You know you're going to get the promotion."

"No, I don't know it, so just stop pushing, ok?"

"Sheesh," Connie grumbled as she turned back to her lunch. "What a grouch."

Now she'd done it. Now she'd probably end up not only agreeing to have the damn party, she'd end up having it at her apartment, just to prove she wasn't a bad sport. She was fed up with parties. She was fed up with activities. Every weekend it was something—a concert, a movie, theater. Active, busy social life, as they said in the magazines. Today's up-and-coming young woman leads an active, busy social life.

Trouble was, today's up-and-coming young woman just wanted to crawl into bed and pull the covers over her head for about a hundred years.

"Is Ray working this weekend?" Lisa asked.

"I don't think so," Shelby said. "Unless something came up."

"Hope he's not planning on a good time," Connie grumbled. "The mood you're in…"

She could feel herself losing control. "Connie…"

Jean leaned forward suddenly, breaking between them. She flashed a shy smile. "Salt?" she said, and pointed to the shaker.

Shelby handed it to her.

"Thanks. You look pale. Do you have a headache?"

As a matter of fact, she did. By now it had grown to a real brain-squeezer. She nodded.

Jean rummaged in the college book bag she always carried as a pocket book, and pulled out a bottle of aspirin. She passed it to Shelby.

"Another headache?" Connie said, all concern now. "Well, no wonder you're in such a funk."

She felt a flare of anger and was about to snap at her when Jean stepped softly on her foot. She settled for, "Guess so."

"You really should see a doctor, you know," Lisa said, as she scraped the remnants of the Jello from the lettuce leaf. "You get them a couple of times a week, don't you?"

"She's engaged to a doctor," Connie said.

"He's not a doctor yet, and we're not engaged yet."

"Matter of time on both counts." Lisa licked the Jello-mayonnaise mixture from her fork. "What does he say about it?"

"Not much." She wasn't about to confess she hadn't told him. She didn't know why she hadn't, and it was bound to be construed as an act of treason.

Connie leaned back in her chair and tossed her napkin onto her plate. "Well, back to the salt mines. Hand of bridge first?"

Shelby shook her head. "Sorry, I have to clear up that pile of manuscripts."

"Do it tomorrow."

"The new girl's coming tomorrow."

Lisa and Connie exchanged a look. "Maybe we can grab a drink after work…" Connie stared pointedly at Shelby. "…if you're not too busy and important to drink with your old friends."

Shelby drew a very deep breath.

Connie flapped a hand at her. "Joke, joke." She gathered up her tray. "Talk to you later."

She marched off, Lisa trotting along beside her.

"She's in rare form," Jean said as she watched them go.

"Did you do that on purpose? With the salt?"

Jean smiled. "I'll never tell."

"Well, you saved my life."

"Wonder what's gotten into her," Jean said. "Professional jealousy?"

Shelby was surprised. "Connie? She's just Connie."

"She's usually a little more subtle."

"Yeah." She rubbed at her forehead, just above her nose where pressure was gathering.

Jean looked at her, a serious and worried look creasing the skin at the corners of her eyes. "The headaches are bad, aren't they?"

Shelby felt herself go defensive. "Sometimes. Not often. It's just tension."

"Tension?"

"And sinus," Shelby said quickly. "No big deal. You live in New England, you get sinus headaches. It's a fact of life."

"In other words," Jean said kindly, "butt out."

"I'm sorry. I didn't mean it that way."

"Sure, you did. You hate all this attention."

"I guess I do. I don't know why."

"Probably something deep and neurotic."

She smiled. "Neurotic and incurable."

"No doubt about it," Jean said. She forked her tabbouleh. "Terribly sad about Shelby Camden, really. She was quite a pleasant person, before the trouble started."

"Well," Shelby said, "you know how it is. Once the trouble starts…"

"It just never ends."

Shelby laughed. "What's gotten into you today?"

"You mean because I'm not sitting quietly with my hands folded and my knees together?" Jean glanced around. "Are the nuns watching?"

"You're Catholic?"

"My parents are. But I lapsed, except I never caught on to it enough to have anything to lapse from. The only lasting influence they had on me was the book bag. Nuns really know how to carry stuff."

"From carrying the world's sins and sorrows."

Jean made a face. "Are you going to take that aspirin, or did I attract attention for nothing?"

"Yeah, sure." Shelby shook a couple of pills from the bottle and washed them down, glancing at the woman who sat beside her. At lunch Jean rarely said more than "Please pass…" and "Thank you." At their regular bridge games, her conversation was limited to play-relevant statements like "three no trump" and "nice play, partner" and "down one, doubled and redoubled." Once, during a particularly clever and risky finesse, when she had captured Lisa's trump king, she had said, "Got you, you little devil." Shelby had remembered it because it was so unusual. And she hardly ever made anyone laugh.

"You're looking at me funny," Jean said.

"I'm not used to you…well…"

Jean gave a mock-serious frown. "I'm not on drugs, if you're wondering. At least I don't think I am."

"That never occurred to me."

"I did take them, once, for a while. Dexamyl. Back in college. My roommate's father got them for us. I don't know where. We didn't ask. We took them to study for finals. That stuff can really focus your attention. Trouble is, you can't unfocus."

"I get that way when I'm tired," Shelby said. "Particularly if I'm driving the car. I'm falling asleep at the wheel, but I can't stop. Some day I'm going to drive straight into the Atlantic Ocean."

"Except you don't feel tired. You feel great, like you could do anything. Excuse me, 'as if' you could do anything. But it turned on my roommate. She was flying, and all of a sudden the bottom fell out from under her. Depressed, but she couldn't calm down. We had to take her to the infirmary. We were afraid she'd kill herself. After that everyone was awkward around her. She left school before the end of the semester." Jean took a swallow of water. "Certainly helped her pass her finals, didn't it? I can't believe I was that stupid only three years ago."

Shelby hesitated. "Did you...I mean, were you awkward around her?"

"Not really. Maybe a little. I'm not proud of that. But she had gone a little strange, too, in that time. She wouldn't let anyone mention what had happened. Not even me. I did try, but she changed the subject. I guess that hurt my feelings."

"I can imagine," Shelby said.

"Most people were perfectly happy not to talk about it, except behind her back. They probably thought it was catching."

"It might be. Are you sure you're not on drugs?"

Jean balled up her napkin and tossed it at her. "No, I'm not on drugs. If I'm running on like a fool, it's just that you're easy to talk to."

Shelby felt a flare of self-consciousness. "I wasn't fishing for a compliment."

"I know that," Jean said. "But it's true. What's also true, and maybe odd, is that this is the first time in two months Lisa and Connie have left us alone."

"I made her mad," Shelby said.

"You should try it more often."

Shelby sipped her coffee. "Don't you..." She tried to think of how to phrase it. "Don't you like Connie?"

"Sure, I like her. It's not as if she's nasty or unpleasant...well, maybe a little unpleasant sometimes, but who isn't? She's just a bit much once in a while, if you know what I mean."

Shelby knew exactly what she meant.

"I think her heart's in the right place," Jean went on. "And I think she'd be loyal to you..."

"You do?"

Jean nodded. "She likes you. She's like a mother hen, and you and Lisa are her brood." She laughed a little. "I'm getting there. Give me another couple of months. She's still trying to figure me out."

"To be perfectly honest," Shelby said, "so am I."

"Me, too," Jean said with a sigh. "I'll probably spend the rest of my life trying to figure me out. Now, there's a depressing thought."

"The trouble with life is, it doesn't come with an owner's manual."

"It'd be unintelligible and inaccurately translated from the Japanese."

According to the large, round, serviceable brown and white school house clock with the striking black Roman numerals that hung on the cafeteria wall over the steam table, it was time to get back to work. Shelby was sorry. She was actually enjoying a conversation. It had been weeks, months...maybe forever...since she'd enjoyed a conversation. But there were all those manuscripts.

Jean was packing up her lunch things, putting her fork and spoon on the tray to be taken to the busing station. She hesitated before covering the cottage cheese container that held her tabbouleh, and offered it to Shelby. "Last chance."

"Thanks," Shelby said with an involuntary shudder. "I think I'll pass."

"Don't blame you," Jean said as she covered the container and put it in her brown paper bag and rolled the top shut tight.

Nearly everyone had left. The cafeteria workers, gray women with gray hair plastered to the sides of their faces in perspiration-wet curls, were clearing away the leftovers. "Tomorrow's chef's special," Shelby said, and nodded toward the steam table. "I'm beginning to understand why you bring your lunch."

"I do it to get attention," Jean said without a moment of hesitation. "And to annoy Connie."

Jean had deep brown eyes with little flecks of gold surrounding the pupils. She'd never noticed that before.

"You're a phenomenon," Shelby said with a laugh.

"Yeah. Party this weekend, do you think?"

Shelby shook her head. "I don't know. I really don't feel like it, but Connie…"

"Whatever Connie wants, Connie gets," Jean said. "Well, boola boola." She pushed back her chair and started for the door. "See you around the campus." She turned back. "Congratulations again, by the way. You must be excited."

She started to say, "Not really." But she was expected to be excited. Everyone expected her to be excited. Even Jean.

"Sure," she said.

She tried to concentrate, but her mind kept wandering. The stories she was reading were pretty bad. She had to smile at herself, remembering how she'd once believed this job would give her the chance to read hundreds of well-written, interesting pieces of near-literature. It had taken exactly one week for her to realize she'd been mistaken on that count. Oh, now and then there was a gem buried deep in the coal pile. But for the most part the writing was terrible, awkward, trite, stilted, predictable…The saddest were the stories that were submitted with such hope, almost with a prayer. The most annoying were the terrible ones whose authors' overwhelming, self-righteous egos pushed themselves at you from the pages. She particularly enjoyed rejecting those. With a form letter, no personal touch.

If she really was going to be an assistant editor, she probably wouldn't see too many truly bad stories any more. They'd be weeded out before they got to her. She'd miss that. "Truly bad stories I have read" was always a useful conversation-filler.

Things might really be different, after all. Maybe Connie was right. Maybe they wouldn't have so much in common any more.

The way home to Bass Falls led through seven miles of cornfields. Not cornfields now, of course. Now they were seven miles of dark, wet earth dotted with last year's rotting stubble. There was still a little pale blue sky in the west, visible in her rear-view mirror. The days were growing longer. Before she knew it, she'd be driving home in the light, even if she stayed in West Sayer for a drink after work. Soon the fields would take on a mossy green look, ready to be broken by the plows. Then the air would be heavy with the rich brown odor of ripe, damp earth. She'd feel better then. She always felt better when the days were longer and she could smell the earth.

She stopped by Zgrodnik's Market to pick up something for dinner. "You oughta get a dog," Jeff said as he measured out the hamburger into a red and white checked cardboard boat.

Shelby leaned against the counter and studied the boxed cake mixes in the next aisle. "Why do you say that?"

"Well, for one thing, they're good company. For another…" He ripped a sheet of butcher's paper from the heavy roll and wrapped it around her meat. "…I need more outlets for these bones."

She glanced around as he indicated a corrugated cardboard box resting on the floor behind him. It was filled to overflowing with scraped bones, glistening with shreds of blood and fat.

"One day's collection," he said ruefully. He handed her the package of meat.

Shelby took it with a laugh, and started to turn away.

"Hey," he said, calling her back. "They rent that empty apartment in your house yet?"

"Not yet."

He shook his head in a worried way. "I don't like it."

"It's perfectly safe, Jeff."

"Ground floor, nobody but you."

His concern touched her. "There are three other apartments," she said, trying to reassure him.

"Not on the ground floor."

"And the ghosts. Don't forget the ghosts."

"Listen," he said, "we take our ghosts seriously up here. Now, I haven't heard anything too bad about that bunch over your way, but you never know when something might strike 'em wrong."

"I've never heard a peep or a moan out of them."

"And they're not going to protect you if someone breaks in. That's why you need a dog."

"I *don't* need a dog. Good grief."

Jeff shrugged. "Stubborn, just like your whole generation."

Maybe I *should* get a dog, she thought. She juggled her groceries and mail in one arm and struggled to unlock her apartment door.

The silence greeted her. Some days she welcomed the silence. Other times, like today, solitude brought loneliness in its wake. Today's loneliness had a gray feel to it. Like an oily mist. She'd have a useless evening tonight, restlessly watching television for a few minutes, then trying to read, going back to the television, wanting to call someone, not being able to think of anyone she really wanted to talk to…frittering away the time until the eleven o'clock news came on and she could kiss another day goodbye.

A dog might be nice. A dog would meet her at the door with a happy tail and adoring "what did you bring me?" eyes. Maybe it would even chew on the furniture while she was away, or knock over a house plant or two, or ruffle up a rug. Anything, just so the apartment didn't look exactly the same when she came home as it had when she'd left. She could take the dog for walks. It would like walks. On days like today, when she didn't know what to do with herself, she could take it for several walks.

But it's not fair, Shelby thought, to let a dog love you when you're going to kill yourself.

Chapter 2

She tossed her keys on the telephone table, closed the door with one foot, and struggled to the kitchen with the groceries. Dropping the bag to the counter, she threw her coat on a chair and opened the refrigerator. The freezer compartment was growing a thick beard of frost; time to clean it again. She pulled out an ice tray and hipped the door shut. Yanking the handle on the metal tray divider, she splintered the cubes into dagger-like crystals that froze to her fingertips as she scooped them into a glass. She turned down the freezer control and put the tray back, divider and all. That would have given her mother fits. Libby didn't believe in returning half-empty trays to the freezer, and certainly not with the dividers in them. Libby didn't believe in sloppy housekeeping of any kind. Which was probably why Libby had a full-time maid.

Scotch over ice wasn't a ladies' drink, but there were no witnesses. Shelby carried her glass to the living room, flipped on the television, and threw herself onto the couch. Most evenings she would have changed into slacks and a casual shirt first, but tonight that felt like one activity too many. Tonight she'd put up with the discomfort of her tight skirt and garter belt for one half hour longer.

Chet Huntley and David Brinkley were on, looking solemn. Maybe Russia had invaded. Shelby took a sip of her drink. About-to-be-successful young career woman relaxes at home after a busy and fulfilling day at the office.

No invasion. In fact, there was very little of consequence going on anywhere, according to NBC. The Kennedys were entertaining—what else is new? Speculation on whether Jackie would repeat her Tour of the White House. More speculation on the meaning of Secretary of Defense McNamara's admission last week that, not only were U.S. pilots flying combat missions over Vietnam, but "a few" ground troops were "exchanging fire" with the Viet Cong. Repetitive grumbling from cigar smokers and sellers over Kennedy's embargo of all products, including tobacco, from Cuba. Dr. Martin Luther King, Jr., speaking in a small Alabama church, some unpleasantness afterward. No surprise, meriting only fifteen seconds of coverage.

Not much real news, a lot of "What if?" items. Judging by what the news media covered, the human race preferred to live on hope and dread, preferably dread, at least twenty-four hours in advance. If the reporters were limited to reporting only events that had actually taken place, there'd be no news at all.

As for twenty-four hours in advance, she supposed she should think about tomorrow and the new girl, if not the implications for her skyrocketing (ha, ha) career. She was only a little nervous. She had a pretty good idea what to do and say, she'd been through it herself and not too long ago. The kid would be either a joy or a horror. She wondered which she'd been for her senior reader. Probably neither, probably just your average, garden-variety eager-learner...

Now there was an endless cigarette ad on the screen. Some pseudo doctor in a white coat, extolling the virtues of taste. She thought about getting up and changing channels, but felt too lazy. She reached for her mail—magazines, catalogue, a note from her graduate school roommate, ads, requests for contributions. Typical Tuesday haul, full of the clutter that didn't move over the weekend and hadn't been sorted by Monday. She set Helen's letter aside for later. Helen had gone from graduation to marriage to motherhood, and the living room drapes. They didn't have much in common any more.

She missed the old days with Helen, when they'd been united in rebellion against the safe, secure—Helen added "smug"—lives they'd been brought up in. Rebellion consisted of dressing in black and creeping down to coffee houses in the Village to listen to the Beat poets read their largely-incomprehensible works to the accompaniment of bongo drums and the incense of marijuana. They played at being bored and "cool" in classes. Identity crises were all the rage, and they spent endless hours discussing "Who Am I?" At one point, inspired by J. D. Salinger, they'd even considered dropping out of graduate school to find themselves, but lost their nerve.

Odd, how two short years and different lives had separated them. But maybe, once Shelby was married and had a child of her own, they'd be close again. She could imagine how Helen, with her quick wit and dry humor, would describe the perils of motherhood. Her initial letters had been filled with outrageous observations and painfully funny anecdotes, but lately she'd seemed tired, flat, and all the things they'd poked fun at before had become deadly serious to her.

Did marriage do that to everyone?

Huntley and Brinkley were about finished. Reluctantly, she unfolded herself from the couch, drained the last bit of melted ice and weak scotch from her glass, and turned off the television.

She pictured Ray in his tiny, sterile Cambridge apartment with antediluvian tea and coffee stains in the chipped porcelain sink, the crack that ran diagonally across the living room wall, the smell of old dust and radiators. He'd be leaning forward now to turn off his TV. Standing. Running his hands through his curly red-blonde hair. Lifting his aluminum TV dinner tray from the bricks-and-boards coffee table. Walking to the kitchen, tossing the fork into the sink, the tray into the paper-bag-lined step-on can. Getting a drink of water in a jelly glass—probably the one with the Tom and Jerry design—leaning against the sink for a moment in a satisfied way. Walking back to the living room, checking his watch. Picking up the phone. Dialling.

Shelby counted off eight seconds, seven for the phone number, one for toll-call access. Her hand hovered over the phone.

It rang.

"Hey, babe. How's tricks?"

Shelby gritted her teeth. Once, just once, couldn't he find a different way of greeting her? "I'm fine, how are you doing?"

A short, waiting pause. "Something wrong?" he asked at last.

"Not at all. Why?" She knew why. She hadn't said, "Fine by me, how's by you?" Their passwords.

She could see his hesitation and then shrug as he decided to let it go. "No reason. You sound tired."

"I guess I am, a little. It was a long day. How was yours?"

Rustling in the background. He'd be stretching out on his couch now, slipping off his loafers, settling in for a long talk. His head propped on one wooden arm of the cheap, second-hand furniture ("Motel Modern," he called it. Shelby had termed it "Midwestern Mother-in-law"), his large feet dangling over the other end.

"Long enough."

Abrupt. He was indulging himself with a minor pout. Shelby sighed a silent sigh. "Anything new in exotic illnesses?"

"Nope. Anything in the publishing world?"

"No. Well, yes. I have to break in a new girl tomorrow."

"Is that good news or bad news?"

"Good, I guess. I'm probably moving up in the world. Breaking in a new reader's usually the last step before assistant editor."

"Hey!" She could hear the creak of the sofa as he stretched. "Way to go, gal. When will you know for sure?"

"When and if Spurl makes the decision. Keep your fingers crossed."

"No luck involved," Ray said. "Anything they give you, you've earned."

"Thank you."

"It's the truth."

Shelby had to smile. Ray was like a personal cheer leader. "There's talk of a party this weekend. To celebrate. I'm going to try to get them to turn it into a welcome party for the new girl."

"Get who?"

"The lunch bunch. You know. Connie, Lisa, Jean."

"What day?"

"Saturday."

"Aw, damn it..." He was running his hand over his jaw. He had five o'clock shadow. It made a little scratchy sound in the phone. "I just let Paul talk me into taking over his shift in the E.R. I'll see if I can switch it back. He's pretty strung out, though. It's been Reefer Madness around here all week..."

"Don't bother. We'll make it a hen party."

"You're sure that's ok with you?"

"Positive." She was a little surprised at how sure she was. "It'd probably be easier on the new girl, anyway."

"Yeah," he grunted, a laugh in his voice. "Us guys are damn intimidating."

"That you are, Dr. Raymond Curtis Beeman."

There was a brief pause. "Hey, Shel?"

"I'm here."

"Do you ever have...well, doubts about me, us?"

Did he? Was he? She felt a prickle of anxiety. "I don't know what you mean," she said cautiously.

"I keep shit hours. We can't plan ahead because they might tell me to work...hell, it's not much fun."

"There'll be plenty of time for fun down the road. And for planning ahead.

16

Unless there's something you're not telling me."

"Like what?"

"You're switching your specialty from endocrinology to obstetrics."

"Shucks," he kidded. "You guessed." She could hear more rustling. He was sitting up. That meant he'd let her go…she corrected herself…he'd hang up soon. "Don't panic, kid. I may be tired, but I'm not crazy."

"Well, you should know, Doc."

More rustling. Now he was standing. In a second his voice would take on that distant tone that said his mind was on his studies. "Know what, Shel?"

"No, what, Ray?"

"I think I'll marry you."

"Not until you ask me first."

"I'm asking."

"Not over the phone, you're not."

He chuckled. "You're a hard woman, Shelby Camden."

"Oh, go study."

"Keep Friday night open, ok?"

"I thought you had to work."

"Only on Saturday. Call you tomorrow." It was a statement, not a question. For some reason, that irritated her.

"Shel?"

She snapped her attention back to the phone. "Yeah, OK, tomorrow."

"Love 'ya, babe."

"Love you, too." The line went dead as he hung up.

Shelby put the phone back on its cradle and poured herself another drink.

Tonight's loneliness was like the fog. Gray, damp, cold. It made a sound of empty tunnels. Shelby stood by the window, looking out toward Pleasant Street beyond the deep front yard. A street lamp glowed wetly, the light glistening on the thick trunk of the maple tree that stood by the brick walk. A car crawled past, its tires spewing water and winter grit.

She thought of the things she could do with her evening—the television shows she might watch, the books she should read. She could even work on one of the short stories she was writing and promising herself she'd finish some day. But she kept on standing there, looking out at the night.

It wasn't good to wrap herself in loneliness this way. She should do something to bring light and warmth into the apartment. A fire in the fireplace?

She glanced down at the wood box. It was nearly empty. No kindling, no pieces cut for burning, just the two unsplit logs she was planning to use as primitive andirons. She'd have to go out to the shed. Slip into comfortable clothes and mud-proof shoes, grab a coat, and go.

She couldn't bring herself to do it.

At least she'd managed to read and critique one story before it was time to sleep. Shelby placed the manuscript and notes on the bedside table, flicked out the light, and burrowed down beneath the heavy comforter. Cold dampness and oily yellow-silver light oozed through the partially open window. The high ceiling reflected and deepened the silence in the room, turning it in on itself.

She pushed back the blankets to free her head from the sound of her own breathing, and the slow throb of blood pulsing through her veins. Outside, leaves had collected in the gutter, clogging the downspout. Mist percolated through soggy, rotting organic matter. Drops fell as steadily as a ticking clock.

She found herself missing the college boys who'd rented the apartment down and across the hall. They'd been pretty decent neighbors, polite and helpful. Students at the local science and engineering branch of the University, they had considered her an "older woman," placing her safely beyond the category of sexual prey. Except for an occasional weekend blast, they had spent most of their time studying. Then, just after Christmas vacation, something changed. The stereo blared day and night. There were beer cans in the garbage nearly every day, not just on weekends. Finally she had run into Dan by the trash bins, struggling with a torn paper bag that leaked bottles and empty Cheetos sacks. As she helped him clean up the mess, he told her they hadn't made the grade point average to stay in second semester, so they were living out the thirty days notice they'd had to give the landlord. They'd probably go into the army. On March 1 they were gone, quietly and without fanfare, vanished into the late winter snow fog.

The water dripped. The silence echoed. Her breathing was like waves breaking slowly, rhythmically. She shifted her position, and heard the rustle of sheets. It grated on her nerves.

It was going to be a long night.

* * *

They called her at eleven. The buzzing intercom shattered a thought she'd almost captured. She hadn't had many this morning, and now, just when she was about to have one...

Nerves. In spite of herself.

One of these days she'd have to get around to growing up.

Shelby gave her hair a tidying push, and tried to walk steadily and casually to the door. Lisa winked at her as she passed her desk. Connie flashed her the OK sign, thumb and forefinger pressed together to form a circle. Rolling her eyes, Jean shot her a sympathetic smile.

The stairwell was gray and smelled of dampness. Climbing, Shelby heard the measured ring of her footsteps on concrete. A steady, relentless clang, clang, clang. Like a march step played out on water pipes. Or the slamming of jail cell doors.

I ought to be excited, she thought. Why can't I get excited?

The fire door groaned shut behind her. The hallway ahead was long and empty. Brown linoleum, here and there a bit of green grit, the sand-like substance the janitor put down to gather up dust. Shoulder-high white walls topped with glass, and from behind the glass the sound of phones and typewriters. Names neatly lettered on the doors: Art Editor; Fiction Editor; Advertising Editor; Food and Home Editors.

The door at the end read "Editor-in-Chief." Behind its frosted, dimpled glass David Spurl and Miss Myers and the new girl awaited. She touched the knob, aware of the tarnished brass rubbed shiny where hands had gripped it. Turned it, and winced at the metal-on-wood clunk. Took a deep breath and went in.

"Ah," said Spurl as she came into the office. "Shelby Camden, Penny Altieri. Penny, this is Miss Camden."

Shelby reached out to shake the girl's hand, and stopped half way, surprised. She'd expected someone younger than herself, by two years anyway, but Penny Altieri was almost a child.

Or maybe it was just the way she wore her blue-black hair, long and gathered into a loose ponytail. Or her face, small and soft around the edges like a baby's. Most likely it was her eyes. Penny Altieri had the largest, roundest, deepest brown eyes Shelby had ever seen on a human being. It made her look frightened and trusting, all at the same time.

"Miss Camden will show you around," David Spurl said in his dismissive voice, as if he had something vitally important to do. Shelby knew, it being Wednesday, that what he actually had to do was meet his pals from the local newspaper for lunch and drinks at the Downtown Grill. He held out a manila folder filled with manuscripts. "Walk her through a couple of these. Have Miss Myers put you both down for an hour with me tomorrow morning."

"Tomorrow morning?" Shelby flipped through the folder and raised one eyebrow. "You want us to stay up all night doing this?"

"We'll make it late tomorrow morning, all right?"

Shelby shook her head slightly and muttered, "Slave driver."

As usual, that pleased him. "Absolute faith in you." He reached behind him for his jacket, then noticed he was wearing it and grinned sheepishly. Shelby hadn't seen David in a jacket since her first day here. He preferred the casual but hard-working look of loosened tie and rolled-up sleeves. Greeting new readers was one of his few official, formal functions.

"'Late tomorrow morning.' Famous last words," Shelby murmured to Penny.

Spurl stuffed papers into his brief case, looking at his watch. He snapped the case shut and heaved it from the desk.

Shelby reached for the door. David Spurl stretched past her to pull it open, creating confusion, a jumble of shuffling feet and multiple "excuse me's." She was always doing that, reaching to open a door instead of waiting for the man. She supposed it was the four years spent in a women's college that did it. At Mount Holyoke you were expected to open your own doors.

They all piled gracelessly into the waiting room, stumbling against Miss Myers' desk. The Dragon glared at them as if they had sworn in church. Even David Spurl was intimidated. Muttering about "'portant meeting," he swung his briefcase clear of their heads and made a dive for the door.

"MIS...ter Spurl," Miss Myers honked, "you have calls to return before you leave."

"Miss Camden, Miss Altieri, tomorrow, eleven a.m.," he said through the narrowing gap of the closing door. The leather soles of his cordovans slapped the linoleum.

Miss Myers snorted heavily.

Penny caught Shelby's eye and crossed herself.

"Eleven tomorrow," Shelby confirmed with a little choke of dangerous laughter, and pushed Penny ahead of her through the door.

Penny leaned against the sink and peered into the mirror, her dark hair falling loose around her shoulders.

Shelby splashed water on her face. She glanced up. Penny was studying her. "Something wrong?"

The girl shook her head and brushed at her hair. "No, I was just wondering…"

"Wondering?" Shelby reached for a paper towel.

"If we'll get along."

"I don't know why not. Unless you have some terrible secret…like you're a Russian spy or something."

Penny forced a slight smile. "No, I'm not a Russian spy." She hesitated, clearly having more to say.

"Go on," Shelby said gently. "It's OK. I don't bite."

"Well, it's really silly, but…"

"OK."

"But…oh, darn, I just feel so out of it."

Shelby squeezed the girl's shoulder. "You *are* out of it. It's your first day here. I felt out of it for at least six months."

"I *always* feel out of it." Penny gave an unhappy little laugh. "I don't mean to sound pathetic. It's just that I'm never sure what the rules are."

"The rules?"

"Of etiquette. The norms. The accepted behaviors."

Shelby realized she was standing there with an idiotic, puzzled look on her face and a damp paper towel in her hands. It smelled like old newspapers and sawdust. She wadded it up and tossed it in the bin. "I don't know," she said. "I guess everyone makes a mistake from time to time. Around here we worry more about our grammar than our etiquette."

"It can be really serious," Penny insisted. She reached into her handbag and pulled out a lipstick. "There are things, if you get them wrong, you can end up in a mental hospital." She faced the mirror to apply her make-up and glanced at Shelby's reflection. "Like shaving your legs."

"Shaving your legs," Shelby repeated.

"In France, no one shaves their legs. But here, if you go to a psychiatrist and your legs aren't shaved, they think you're schizophrenic." She waved her lipstick in the air. "And this. In America, women freshen their lipstick at the table in restaurants all the time. If you did that in Europe, they'd lock you up."

"I'll try to remember that," Shelby said. "You've made a study of such things?"

"I've *had* to. I think I've lived about a million different places. You never know when you're going to do something, totally innocently, that'll offend the entire population." Penny closed her lipstick, dropped it back into her purse, and blotted her lips on a scrap of tissue. She turned and grinned. "You think I'm a real case, don't you?"

Actually, she had been right on the verge of thinking that. She lied and said, "Not at all."

"Not at *all*?"

"Well, maybe that was a little strong."

"My father's with the government," Penny said. She pulled out a brush and went to work rebuilding her ponytail. "The Diplomatic Corps. We'd spend a year in one country, then he'd get transferred to another and we'd have to learn a whole new set of rules."

"That must have been hard," Shelby said.

"The Middle East was the worst. I didn't understand anything there, and it was the place where mistakes were most likely to be fatal. They dismember you for all sorts of things. Especially if you're a woman. I liked Africa, but it's starting to boil over. They sometimes look for people without families to go there now. Or the families stay home, but mostly they don't like that. They need the wives for entertaining, so they try to send them where entertaining still goes on. But not Africa."

Shelby leaned against the wall and crossed her arms over her chest. "Sounds as if you've had an interesting life."

"Oh, God, yes." She tugged loose hairs from her brush and dropped them into the trash bin. "It's had its good points and bad points." She looked at Shelby with large, sad eyes. "The bad thing is, you never get to really know anyone. At least, you learn not to get to know them, because you might like them, and the next thing you know you've been transferred and you never see them again. I hated that part. I used to pray my father wouldn't make the transition from the Eisenhower to the Kennedy administrations, so we could all come back here and settle down, but he was posted to the Philippines. My mother went with him, but I didn't want to."

Shelby nodded. "It can be hard, living that way."

"I guess so, but it's all I've ever known. Growing up in one place, where you know people and they know you for long periods of time, maybe your whole life...that could be terrifying, too."

Let me tell you about it, Shelby thought. "If we hurry," she said, "I can show you the place before lunch. That way you can meet people one at a time, and won't be mobbed in the lunchroom ."

"Sounds great," Penny said. She twisted her hair back into the ponytail and secured it with a rubber band. "Though being mobbed in a lunchroom would be a new experience. I've been in mobs on trains and buses, even marketplaces, never lunchrooms." She dropped her hairbrush into her purse and gave it a firm snap. "'Whither thou goest,' as they say." She pulled open the door before Shelby could reach it, then stood back to let her go through.

Just the way they taught us to do for teachers back in boarding school, Shelby thought. Except she was being held for this time, not holding. It gave her an odd feeling, as if suddenly, without warning or preparation, her place in the world had changed. From student to teacher, from kid to adult, from...

She wasn't sure she was ready for all this responsibility.

Penny did all the right things. She showed enthusiasm with Connie, looked Jean in the eyes while she shook hands. She joked a little with Lisa, and—accidentally?—at lunch managed to knock over the salt shaker. Shelby wondered if she came by this skill naturally, or if her years as a diplomat's daughter had trained her to sense, without even thinking about it, exactly what would please people the most.

When she said she played bridge, Jean caught Shelby's eye and mouthed a silent cheer. Shelby knew exactly what she meant. With five players, someone could get a lunch hour off once in a while. And Connie would never opt out. That left four of them to rotate through three openings. With luck, they might even get two days some weeks.

By mid-afternoon, Shelby felt as if her brain had been washed, rinsed, mangled, and hung out to dry. Penny had questions about everything she noticed and everyone she met.

Did certain groups of people always sit together at lunch, and why?

Some had come to the magazine at the same time. Some shared marriage and/or career goals.

Had all the women at the magazine already decided between marriage and career?

Most of them.

Was it a requirement?

Probably not.

If you planned to marry, were you dead in the water, career-wise?

Not really.

Probably?

Probably.

What had brought Shelby and Jean and Connie and Lisa together?

Shelby, Lisa, and Connie started at the same time, Jean played bridge.

Contract bridge or auction?

Contract.

Who was the best player?

Depended. Connie took the most risks, Jean's bidding was reliable, Lisa was best on defense—though she sometimes discarded the card next to the one she'd intended to discard.

How about yourself?

Steady. Not flashy, but usually make the bid. Might try a finesse if it can be set up in advance.

Does Miss Myers like you?

She doesn't like anyone.

When they finally got around to doing some real work, the day was half over. Light faded from the windows. Desk lamps went on, then off as the other readers finished their work and left. One by one, the desks were vacated. The echoes of their own voices grew sharper in the hollowing room. Connie wanted them to go out for drinks, and Penny seemed about to accept but Shelby put her foot down. "We have more to do," she said firmly. "There'll be plenty of time to get acquainted later."

Connie grumbled and went away.

"Did you want to go?" Shelby asked, having second thoughts and feeling a little guilty for having been so pushy.

"Good grief, no," Penny said. She ran her hands over her very own, uncluttered desk, and fingered the edges of the growing stack of read and evaluated stories. "Let's keep the momentum up. How many more?"

Shelby counted. "Four. At the rate we're going, another hour."

Penny scanned the nearly-empty room. "This place is giving me the willies. Want to go over to my apartment? It's just a couple of blocks."

22

Shelby thought about it. It was quiet here. They could finish faster. And she'd always felt comfortable in the readers' room at night, after everyone had gone. When the radiator hissed and the night pressed black against the windows. She liked to sit at her desk, in her tent of light, and think or daydream. Sometimes she spent a couple of hours working on her own writing.

But maybe tonight wasn't a night for staying. Maybe tonight was a night for getting to know each other, and if Penny felt uneasy here… Besides, she was curious about Penny's apartment. From what one day had told her, Penny was a young woman who took her cue from other people, shifting constantly like water, to fit the contours of whatever container she happened to find herself in. Without anyone around to give her signals, what kind of container would she create for herself? What things had she chosen to surround herself with? Whose pictures were on the walls and bureau? When your life was rootless, you probably carried your roots with you, the way traveling salesmen carried photos of their wives and children.

But it would add at least an hour to the day, which meant that she wouldn't be there to take Ray's call.

Well, she wasn't married to him yet. Let him wonder for a change.

"OK," she said. She closed her notebook and capped her pen and stuffed the unread stories into her briefcase. "We have to promise ourselves we'll finish these. No horsing around until work's done. All right?"

"Yes, Mother," Penny said with a laugh.

The apartment surprised her. She wasn't sure what she'd expected—small, exotic items, maybe, memorabilia from the countries Penny'd lived in. A painting or two. Wall hangings or a rug. Pottery, figurines. At the least, posters. But there was nothing. Penny's apartment defined "bare."

It wasn't even an apartment, really. One large room divided into sections. A living area with a sleeping loft. A half-wall separating that from a wide hall that served as dining room and entry. A stove, sink, and refrigerator crammed into what looked like an oversized walk-in closet. The only door other than the entrance led to a tiny bathroom containing an ancient ball-and-claw footed tub, a rust-stained basin, and a toilet with a cracked tank lid.

Penny took her coat and hung it in a niche under the loft and offered her wine. Shelby accepted. If it had been her place they'd gone to, she realized, she'd have felt compelled to make a joke about it, or apologize for the "genteel squalor," or otherwise show embarrassment. But Penny was unapologetic, and apparently unaware of her surroundings.

She curled up in the corner of a Salvation Army Contemporary sofa with drooping springs and hard, threadbare upholstery. There were no pictures, either. Or magazines. Or junk mail tossed carelessly on the coffee table. The curtained windows looked down onto West Sayer's main street three floors below. The sidewalk was nearly deserted. The few people still abroad walked with shoulders hunched around their ears. Though the sky was clear and black, a gray mist hung near the ground. The road surface glistened.

"What's wrong?" Penny asked as she handed her a stemmed wine glass.

"Nothing." Shelby felt herself blush with awkwardness. "I was just wondering, how long have you been here?"

"A week. I wanted to get settled in before I started to work. So it wouldn't be so hectic."

So she already *was* settled in. Shelby said, "Oh."

"There *is* something wrong. I can tell."

"Nothing's wrong. It's just that...well, your place is so...kind of unlived in. I mean, it's really nice..." she added quickly. "But it made me curious."

Penny put a plastic tray of cheese and crackers down on the coffee table and looked around, seeming a little surprised, as if she hadn't noticed it before. "I guess you're right. I should have more stuff, huh?"

"Maybe a few pictures, some *things*. You know, to make it look like home. To make it look like you."

"Things. Sure, I guess I could find some things."

Shelby realized what she was doing. "Oh, God," she said in horror, "I sound just like my mother. I'm too young to sound like my mother."

Penny gave a little uncertain laugh.

She hurried to change the subject. "Did you go to college in the U.S.?" she asked.

"Only my last three semesters. Mostly I went to American Universities—Beirut, Istanbul, wherever we happened to be. Most of my credits transferred to Northwestern. That was convenient, but sometimes I wish my parents weren't quite so cautious. They were afraid something earth-shaking might happen to me in the countries' regular universities."

"Was it dangerous for a young woman? The places you lived?"

"I thought so at the time," Penny said, offering Shelby a cigarette.

Shelby declined.

"But now I wonder," Penny went on as she lit up and tossed the burnt match into a tuna fish can on the floor, "if I wasn't just buying into my family's way of seeing things."

Shelby nodded and looked for a place to put her wine glass. No end tables, and the tray of snacks took up what passed for a coffee table. She settled for the moth-eaten rug.

"The furniture came with the apartment," Penny said. "*That's* not my fault."

"I could tell. It's just like mine." Her mother had objected to her renting furnished, but Shelby told her apartments were hard to come by, and she was lucky to get this one. Little by little, Libby was replacing the furniture with tables and chairs and lamps she thought were more "appropriate", but the old stuff wasn't entirely gone yet.

"Know what I'll bet?" Penny asked as she curled up in the other corner of the couch and sipped her wine. "I'll bet there are these huge secret department stores where landlords do all their furniture shopping."

"There are," Shelby said. "It's called the town dump." She took a cracker. "Over in Bass Falls, dump picking is a time-honored Sunday activity."

Penny raised one eyebrow. "In Bass Falls? From what I've heard about Bass Falls, it isn't a dump-picking kind of town."

"It's a social thing. People meet each other at the dump. If you're running for Select Board or Town Meeting, you might as well forget it if you don't put in at least one Sunday picking."

"Americans," Penny declared with a shake of her head, "have such weird customs."

They laughed together and sat for a moment in easy silence.

"We did good work today," Shelby said. "I take that back. *You* did good work."

Penny looked at her with those big eyes. "Really?"

"The way you pick things up, you'll be a senior reader in no time."

Penny sipped her wine. "I'm supposed to be your replacement, aren't I?"

"What makes you think that?"

"Connie sort of accidentally let it drop."

"Connie never sort of accidentally lets anything drop. She planted it."

"Why would she do that? To make trouble?"

Shelby considered that and rejected it. "She probably just wanted you to know she's the one to come to for gossip and information."

"Do you mind?"

"Mind?"

"That I might replace you."

Shelby laughed. "I assume I'm moving up, not out." She looked at the hobnail ceiling fixture that hung in the middle of the room.

Penny followed her gaze. "I think I saw that light somewhere just the other day. I think it was in the S&H Green Stamp catalogue." She gave a plaintive little sigh. "I really want this job to work out."

"You'll be fine," Shelby said. "I can tell."

"It'd be nice to stay somewhere long enough to collect Green Stamps."

"Uh-huh. What would you get with them?"

"Dishes. I've been living off paper plates. And I want a step-on can for the garbage."

"Speaking as an old, long-settled lady," Shelby said, and stretched one arm across the back of the couch, "let me give you some advice. Step-on cans are definitely overrated."

"I don't care, I want one. Nothing says 'home' like a place to put the garbage."

"That sounds like a metaphor for something."

"It does, doesn't it?" Penny tilted her head against the back of the sofa. It rested on Shelby's hand. She didn't seem uncomfortable with that. "May I ask you something?"

"Sure."

"You don't have to say if you don't want to."

"All right."

"Well…" Penny hesitated. "You're sure it's all right to ask?"

Shelby tugged at the younger woman's hair. "How do I know, for Pete's sake? Ask the question."

"OK. Do you…do you think they'll like me? There," she added quickly, "I asked."

"Of course they'll like you."

"You're sure?"

"More than sure. I know."

Penny glanced at her. "How?"

"Connie passed the word when you weren't looking."

Penny's face broke out in a grin. "No kidding."

"No kidding. So you can stop worrying."

"Who was worried?" the girl asked. Then she bit her lip. "You don't think someone'll be jealous, do you?"

"I can't imagine it."

"I'd hate that, if someone got jealous because you all like me."

Shelby laughed. "Penny, is there anything in the world, anything at all, that you don't worry about?"

Penny looked over at her, eyes sparkling. "I don't worry about the weather much."

"You live in New England now. Weather's one thing you *should* worry about."

"Are you hungry?"

"I will be, by the time we finish these stories."

"Promise?"

"Promise."

"I can't cook for us. At the moment, I only have one pot."

"You're impossible." She retrieved her hand and picked up the folder. "You criticize, I'll take notes."

When they had finished and eaten at the diner across the street, and Shelby had made the trip to Bass Falls, it was nearly bed time. She wasn't sleepy, but it was too late to call Ray. Too late for anything but the news on television, and the eleven o'clock news was usually an endless parade of school board meetings and the retirements and installations of local priests and bishops. Weather reports which, at this time of year, were completely predictable. Spring training with the Red Sox. Followed by the inanity of Jack Paar. She thought about reading, and couldn't bear the sight of one more printed word.

Which left a bath and bed. She could deal with that. She ran the water hot, added some lavender bubble bath to counteract the odor of greasy food that always hung around one like an aura after eating at the diner. Sliding down into the steaming water, she felt her muscles relax and realized for the first time that she was exhausted. Exhausted from tension, and trying to make the day go smoothly, trying to make everyone comfortable, to explain how the office worked and how to criticize a story and what the editors wanted and...

She went over it in her mind. Except for awkward moments of little importance, it had gone pretty well. If there was one thing Shelby Camden could do, it was make things go well.

Chapter 3

The promotion came through on the last day of March. It was a Friday, and raining.

Above the lunchroom's hum and clatter Shelby heard her name, and there was Lisa swirling toward her like straw blown in the wind, like a storm-whipped willow, all bones and interminable motion. Her elbows grazed the backs of chairs. Her hips skimmed table-tops. Her curly black hair bounced and flew.

"Shelby!" the other woman squealed, and grasped Shelby in a jerking, puppet-on-a-string embrace. "It's just *that* great!"

Shelby forced a smile. "Thanks."

"We want to know *everything* Spurl said. In massive detail." Lisa tossed laughter to the ceiling. It burst and tinkled through the room, and she swirled back to her table.

Shelby watched her go, touched. Lisa was incapable of real envy. Other people's triumphs were her delights. Other people's victories brightened her days. She would be unreservedly, genuinely happy for Shelby's success, because she liked her friend and wished her well.

As she neared the table Connie jumped up and took her tray. "So you *do* still want to eat with your old friends after all," she said with an edge.

Shelby glanced at her sharply, feeling her familiar instinctive caution. "We've already plowed this field, haven't we?"

Connie laughed, a fraction of a second too slowly, a shade too lightly. Or so it seemed. "You know me," she said, tossing it off.

Shelby slid the plates from her tray and placed it on the nearby stand. She raised her perfectly square serving of firmly packed, congealed macaroni and cheese and peered at it from the side. "Now I know why I think I'm still in college. It's the institutional food."

"Food," said Connie, "is putting it nicely."

"Weren't you just *floored* ?" Lisa squeaked.

"I guess."

"Really?" Connie raised one eyebrow in Lisa's direction. "We knew it was coming. It's never been any secret what David Spurl thinks of Shelby Camden."

There it was again, a subtle innuendo. Or was it? Shelby looked at her questioningly. "What he thinks?"

"Greatest thing since the printing press." Connie chuckled in a good-natured way. "And always modest." She turned to Jean with a condescending smile. "Aren't you going to congratulate her?"

Jean blushed. "Yeah, I…"

"She already has," Shelby said. It wasn't true, but it would drive Connie crazy. Shelby usually tried not to bait Connie. It caused prickly energy in the room. But today she couldn't resist. "I told her earlier."

"Oh?" said Connie tightly. She turned to Jean. "How come you didn't say anything?"

"She asked me not to," Jean said.

Connie looked back and forth between them.

Now Lisa was talking, oblivious to the undercurrents. "We have to do something to celebrate."

Another party. Oh, God, another party. This was getting as bad as the Thanksgiving-to-New Year's Eve Fest-a-Thon. And this one would be even worse than most. Connie'd invite the entire office, at least everyone between the editors and the janitorial staff. She'd probably invite Miss Myers. She'd probably rent the American Legion Hall and invite everyone she'd ever met. Her entire high school graduating class. And all their relatives. Everyone Shelby'd ever mentioned, whether Shelby liked them or not. Connie'd been working up to a Real Blast for weeks, ever since The Camden Birthday fell on a weekday and Shelby convinced them to keep it simple. You could see it in her eyes. She was restless and a little feisty, like an alcoholic about to fall off the wagon.

"Come over to my place tomorrow night," Shelby said quickly and firmly, in what she hoped was a No Nonsense tone of voice. "Ray's not on call this weekend."

Connie shook her head. She knew if they had a party in Shelby's small apartment, the guest list would be limited. "That's not right. *We* should do something for *you*."

"You would be. Save me the drive."

"Great," Lisa said. "I'll come early and help."

Shelby shuddered inwardly. Out of the frying pan, into the fire.

"Better lock up the good china," Connie said. "Here comes Hurricane Macaroni."

Lisa looked hurt but tried to pass it off with a smile.

At least Connie hadn't volunteered. But Connie wouldn't volunteer. Connie'd work her tail off for an event the size of a Presidential Inauguration. But, in Connie's own words, she didn't "sweat the small stuff." Which was OK, really. Small stuff in Connie's expansive hands could very quickly become big stuff.

"Let me do it," Jean said. "I have to be in Bass Falls, anyway."

"That makes sense." Saved again. "Lisa, do you want to join us?"

"Thanks, I'll pass."

"Early afternoon?" Shelby asked Jean. "It'd give us time to shop."

"Great."

Connie and Lisa exchanged what were obviously meant to be quick but significant looks and brief nods.

Jean didn't seem to notice.

"Dinner party?" Lisa asked. "Or after?"

If they came for dinner it meant more work. It also meant they'd leave earlier. "Dinner."

Jean pushed her chair back. "I have to go. Appointment with my senior reader." She piled up her dishes and stood, looking at Shelby in a noncommittal way. "Talk to you later?"

"You bet."

Jean hesitated. "I'm really glad for you, you know."

"I know. You said."

Balancing her tray on one arm, Jean slipped her book bag over the other shoulder and picked her way through the lunchroom crowd.

Lisa watched her enviously. "Do you think she used to be a waitress?"

"If she was," Connie declared, "she didn't get tips for her personality."

That made Shelby angry. "What's your problem with her?"

"No problem," Connie said. "She's just really quiet. Isn't she?"

"Yes, she's quiet."

"I wasn't *judging* her. I was just stating the obvious."

Let it go, Shelby told herself. "Where's Penny?" she asked to put the conversation on less touchy ground.

"The Boston workshop, remember?" Connie managed to make even *that* momentary forgetfulness sound like a breach of morality.

"I thought that was next week."

"Well, it isn't," Connie said smoothly. "It's all she's talked about. Her first workshop. A kind of rite of passage." She smiled. "But you've had a lot on your mind."

"True," Shelby said. "I have." She'd have to think up something for Penny in honor of the occasion. She remembered how excited she'd been at all the firsts. First pay check, first story to be printed that she'd sent forward, first workshop, first convention. It made the job seem almost real. It made growing up seem almost real.

"So," Lisa said, and leaned forward eagerly, "do you get your own office?"

"Part of an office, really. A desk. But it's better than being in the Pit with the men. I'm sharing the room with Charlotte May."

"Uh-oh," Lisa said. "Fashion. You'll have to be careful how you dress."

"Better still," Connie said, "watch how *she* dresses and report back."

Shelby grinned, glad to be on smooth ground, glad they were all going in the same direction again, the way friends should. "Anything in particular you want me to find out?"

"A girdle," Lisa said. "See if she wears a girdle with her panty hose. I say she doesn't."

"I say she does," Connie said. "Don't ask," she added to Shelby. "She might not tell you the truth. Personal observation, preferably with supporting photographs."

"How am I going to do that? Follow her into the stall in the ladies' room? She's hardly the type to prop her feet on the desk so I can peek up her dress."

"You'll think of something," Connie said. "I have great faith in you." She turned to Lisa. "Five bucks?."

"You're on," Lisa said.

They shook hands across the table.

"This is great," Shelby said with a laugh. "Now, whoever offers me the best bribe wins."

Connie looked at her in genuine surprise. "You? Take a bribe?"

"No way," Lisa said.

"What?" Shelby said in mock horror. "I have a reputation for honesty? No wonder I'm always in trouble." She took a bite of macaroni and cheese, then poked it with her fork. "They could stuff sofa cushions with this food item."

"Are you nervous? About the job?" Lisa asked.

Shelby exercised her jaw on the macaroni for a moment. "A little, I guess."

"How come?" Connie asked. "If anyone knows what they're doing, you do."

"Thanks for the vote of confidence."

"It's true."

Maybe. But there was more than that involved. She'd be making decisions. Not final decisions at first, but her opinions would carry more weight, and sooner or later... Decisions about whose work got published. Decisions about who was 'good enough' for *The Magazine for Women.*

"Honest," Lisa was saying. "You have the instincts."

She wished they'd stop. Enough attention. She wanted to pretend nothing had happened, that everything was the way it had always been and in a minute Connie would crumple her paper napkin, toss it on her plate, and say, "OK, who's for bridge?"

Instead, Connie said, "Come on, Camden, you know you're hot stuff."

"I'm not, Connie. I only..." know there's more to getting ahead than bridge and parties, she thought.

"What's wrong?" Lisa was asking.

"Wrong?"

"You look as if you don't feel well."

Shelby forced a laugh. "I forgot where I was for a minute, and let myself taste the lunch. Bad idea."

"I guess we don't have to worry about you serving macaroni and cheese Saturday night," Connie said.

"You *never* have to worry about that."

"Listen," Connie said in a lowered voice, although no one in their vicinity was showing the slightest interest in their conversation, "about Saturday. When you get together with Jean...well, this is just great. It's the perfect time for a little chat."

Shelby was puzzled. "Little chat?" She hated the expression "little chat." In Connie's vocabulary, that usually meant big trouble.

"About her..." Connie paused pointedly, "...problem."

"Jean has a problem? What? Is she pregnant?"

Lisa jumped in, leaning across the table conspiratorially. "She's really a sweet person, but so *withdrawn.*"

"Yes," Shelby said. "Sometimes."

"Well, we have to *do* something about it."

"We do?"

"She's obviously unhappy," Connie pointed out. "I'm sure she feels she doesn't fit in. She doesn't, of course, but nevertheless... She talks to you. You could encourage her to make more of an effort."

"I'm not sure that's a good idea," Shelby said. "Who are we to say she's unhappy?"

30

Connie spread her hands.

"You could listen harder," Shelby suggested.

"Oh, really," said Connie.

Shelby sighed.

"She has to learn," Connie insisted. "The whole world isn't going to accommodate itself to her shyness."

"I could try," Shelby said.

Connie folded her napkin and placed it carefully beside her plate. A bad sign. Her face took on a resigned, determined look. "All right, if you don't want to do it, I will."

Which would be the worst thing that could happen. Jean might seem all right with how she was, but criticism was criticism, and never nice to hear. Besides, Shelby sensed in Jean a vulnerability that could leave her very, very hurt. It was Connie's style to wade in with the best of intentions and leave carnage in her wake.

"Never mind," Shelby said. "I'll see what's up." She glanced around the table and counted heads. Good news. Only the three of them. "No bridge today, I guess."

* * *

It was cold on Saturday. Depression moved through her consciousness like an oily fog. She was going to have a headache any minute. The thermometer hovered above freezing, but a damp wind blew from the east, searching out cracks and door sills with icy fingers. Shelby knew the chill deep below her skin, knew she wouldn't be warm again until the wind died. Beyond the walls a light drizzle turned now and then to pellets of snow, then back again to rain. Tree limbs, bare against the flat gray sky, were softened and dripping in the curtain of mist. Looking like black skeletons, the trees clung miserably to the earth.

She turned from the window and gazed without passion around the living room. On days like this she was always drawn to the thought of small dark places with heavy drapes and old chairs that seemed to reach out and wrap you in their softness. There should be a roaring fire and a glass of sherry and the smell of apples faintly in the air. There should be the sound of a clock ticking in the hallway, and a dog stretching and sighing before the fire.

This house had once had rooms like that. A massive, red brick building with weathered trim, it had endured behind its iron spike fence for a hundred and fifty years, and would probably endure a hundred and fifty years longer. Giant maples shaded the porch, and deep within the recesses of the house the hidden hallways and closets and carved oak woodwork held secrets.

Her apartment had been the original living and dining rooms, but only the fireplace and high ceilings remained. The owners had knocked out and rebuilt walls, installed plumbing, scraped and enameled over shiny varnished woodwork, and carpeted old floors. Shelby had painted the walls an unbroken chalk white, had hung a few abstract paintings. Her mother was steadily replacing the landlord's eclectic taste with Danish Modern. She knew her friends enjoyed her apartment and found it comfortable. For herself, she regarded it with indifference and thought at times, on days like this, of small dark places and soft, worn couches.

At least she could have a fire. The wood was damp, but caught and burned smokily, and as she dressed she could hear the soft hiss and pop of the steaming logs. When Jean came and saw it her eyes went wide with delight. "Oh," she said simply. "A fire."

Shelby smiled. Jean's hair was wet, and clung to her face in sodden clumps. Her eyes were hazel and deep, and sparkled in the dim light. She was tall but not overly thin, and standing there with the rain dripping from her coat, clutching a paper bag and gazing ingenuously into the flames she seemed as delicate as a fawn.

Suddenly Jean remembered herself, and ducked her head in embarrassment. "I'm sorry," she said, holding out the package. "Here."

"What's this?"

"Just some stuff I made. Cookies." Jean shrugged. "You know…not for tonight…for you."

Shelby was touched. "Thank you," she said, and felt inadequate. "It was sweet of you."

Jean fidgeted uncomfortably. "Tell me what to do."

She closed the door. "Sit down. Dry off. We have plenty of time."

"Know what I'd have done today if I were you?" Jean asked. "I'd have called everybody and told them I had the flu and just curled up in front of the fire with a ghost story."

"I was thinking the same thing." The afternoon was quiet, the fire warm and comforting. But in a few hours the room would be heavy with small talk and cigarette smoke, and everyone would be straining to be funny and clever until they had drunk enough to think they were funny and clever without straining. The fire would die unnoticed, and after it was over she would probably go out for a cup of coffee or a drink with Ray while the apartment aired, and then come home and drop into bed too tired to hang up her clothes or wash the glasses, and tomorrow would wake to the smell and taste of stale liquor.

"Listen, if you want to play hooky, I'll go." Jean started to get up. "I won't tell. I can make up illnesses; it'd make you sick just to listen."

Shelby touched her hand. "I'm only kidding. By the time I made all those phone calls, the day'd be over, anyway."

"I could do it. You can be too sick."

"I appreciate the thought, Jean," Shelby said with a smile. "But I do want to do this."

"I don't know, it seems to me this is a party by default."

Shelby held out her hand for Jean's coat. "You might be right."

"Why are you doing it?"

She turned away quickly and hung the coat over the back of a chair in front of the fireplace. "I want to, really. I'm just in a mood."

"What can I…?"

"Nothing," she said. "I like to suffer."

The other woman held up her hands. "I make it a policy never to interfere with suffering." She sat more easily on the couch and curled her legs beneath her.

This was all right. In fact, it was nice. "How about it, coffee or tea?"

"Coffee. But don't we have to shop or something?"

"It won't take long." She went to the kitchen and plugged in the coffee pot.

"I already made the list," she called into the other room. "All we have to do is pick things up."

"God, you're independent," Jean said.

"Am I?" She reached for cups, then changed her mind and opted for left-over-from-graduate-school mugs.

"I came here to help you, and you've done all the hard part."

"The hard part?"

"Making the lists."

The coffee perked and bubbled and smelled wonderful. Shelby leaned against the entryway and looked into the living room. "I guess independence comes from living alone."

"*I* think it's a character trait," Jean said. She ruffled her hands through her hair, sending droplets of rain flying. "I'm trying to develop it, but I'm not sure it's a good one."

Shelby smiled. "Is Barry coming tonight?"

"I hope not. We broke up."

"You did? When?"

"Last weekend."

"Whose idea was that?"

"Mutual. I think." Jean shrugged. "It just kind of petered out. It bothered me a little, but not as much as I thought it would."

"Why didn't you say anything?"

"To the lunch bunch? Give me a break."

"To me."

Jean combed her hair into place with her fingers. "There wasn't much of a chance, really. You've been pretty busy."

"Not *that* busy. You could have gotten my attention at work, or called me here…"

"I did, but your line was tied up."

"You called once?"

"I tried at least three times, at least half an hour apart."

Shelby frowned. "When was that?"

"Tuesday, I think."

Tuesday. Of course. Tuesday night her mother had gotten back from that late-winter cruise to Bermuda and had kept her on the phone endlessly with stories of every shipboard event, every person she'd met, every…

As she recalled, Shelby had listened politely, the TV on and the sound turned off, and polished off at least two scotch and sodas.

"It was Libby," she said.

"I figured something like that. Anyway, it didn't matter." She looked at her. "Honest, Shelby, it didn't." Jean hesitated. "May I ask you something personal?"

"Sure," she said with more enthusiasm than she felt.

"Sometimes it seems as if—well, you're not real pleased with the promotion."

Shelby felt herself withdraw. "It's fine, really."

"Really?"

She wanted to tell the truth, but the truth was Jean was right. Oh, she was glad, in a way. But not the way she'd expected to be. Sometimes the thought of it made her tired.

You couldn't go around telling people that. It was crazy.

"It's a lot of responsibility," she said. "Terrifying."

Jean nodded. "Sticking your head over the edge of the foxhole."

"Exactly. You never know what might be flying around out there."

The coffee was ready. She pushed herself away from the wall, poured it, added a teaspoon of sugar to Jean's.

OK, the opportunity had presented itself. They had time, and the mood was casual. Not that it made it any easier. Not that she wanted to do this at all.

She got out a plate and carried the mugs to the living room and put them down and reached for the cookies. "There's something I have to talk to you about," she said as she arranged the cookies on the plate.

The silence in the room went cold.

Shelby glanced up. "Come on, Jean, I'm not going to bite."

"OK," Jean said stiffly.

"We're friends, aren't we?"

"Yes."

"So don't be afraid of me."

"It's not you," Jean said. "It's that 'have to talk to you' thing. It's all too familiar, and never good news."

Shelby had picked up a cookie. She put it down. "Look, don't make too much of this, but…I mean, it's not a criticism…" The words felt like stones in her throat. "Help me out."

"Go ahead and talk," Jean said quietly and tightly. "It's your dime."

She took a deep and slightly exasperated breath. "All right, it's about how you're so quiet when we're all together."

"I thought that didn't bother you."

"It doesn't, not really. I just wish…well, is there any way we could make it more comfortable for you?"

Jean hunched her shoulders with an ironic smile. "Well, I figured that was coming, sooner or later."

"Please," Shelby said, "don't do this."

"I just don't have anything to say."

"But you do. When we're alone it's easy for us to talk. You're smart, and fun." God, that sounded condescending. "I like talking to you."

"Thank you," Jean said tightly.

"Jean…"

"By the time I have something to say in a crowd, the conversation's changed."

"So change it back. Nobody else cares about changing the subject. You don't have to be brilliant."

Jean looked at her, her eyes hurt and angry. "This isn't fair, Shelby."

"I know it isn't…"

"I thought I was safe with you."

"It is. This wasn't my idea."

"What, you're doing Connie's dirty work now?"

She wanted to stop this. Wished she'd never gotten into it. Serious damage was being done, and she wasn't handling it well. She should have told Connie to mind her own business, to take her concern and shove it, to…

"You just said you didn't mind, how I am."

"Oh, Jean, I don't," she said. "I really don't. I just thought you were unhappy."

"Sure, I'm unhappy, sometimes. But I've tried to change. I can't, that's all. There's something missing in me."

"It's just a trick, making conversation," Shelby heard herself say, and was surprised at the edge of anger in her voice. "You don't have to give a damn what people think. They're going to think what they think no matter what you do. It doesn't matter who you are or what you're doing, they only see themselves. If they say you're too quiet, it's just because they want more attention from you. If you make noise, and stop now and then to let them make noise back, they'll think you're wonderful."

"Shelby," Jean said.

"Conversation's easy. Just make fun of something or someone." There was bitterness in her voice. "Be critical. That always impresses them. That makes you look good."

"Shelby," Jean said again.

She caught herself, realized she was on the verge of raving and she wasn't altogether sure of what might come out.

She tried to smile. "You're right, I'm doing Connie's dirty work. I like your quietness. I like you, and I don't care how you are in public. I'm sorry. I shouldn't have done this."

Jean glanced down at her hands, frowning a little.

"What are you thinking?"

"I never realized," Jean said, looking up directly into her eyes, "that you're afraid of her, too."

Shelby was stunned. "Well," she said shakily, "you have to admit she's a force to be reckoned with."

Jean laughed a little, things all right on the surface. But Shelby couldn't shake the feeling she'd betrayed Jean, and that it had driven a wedge between them.

* * *

She knew, by the way Ray parked the car and turned off the motor and left the key in the ignition that he wanted to talk. Oh, God, she thought. Not tonight, please not tonight.

The party had gone well. Lisa and Connie and Penny and their clutch of boyfriends had arrived together. Then Ray. Then Libby, late as usual, after declaring as usual that she might not be able to make it, cuing Shelby to express disappointment and beg her, as she always did. Then going on to declare she was too old for Shelby's friends and probably bored them. At which point Shelby was required to say, "No, they really like you, it wouldn't be the same without you." Which was true, it wouldn't be the same and they did like her, and saying it always worked. Libby could be charming and slightly risqué, the kind of qualities people liked in a mother. She was always interested in what "the kids" were up to, asked lots of questions, listened intently, and fractured the current slang in an endearing manner.

Libby arrived in her light wool Davidow suit and bouffant Jackie Kennedy hair style, too young for her but everyone told her how wonderful she looked. Bearing cheer and her famous silver decanter (she called it her "jug") of whiskey sours.

Dinner had been mushroom caps and lobster tails and peas cooked in lettuce leaves, with a touch of nutmeg. She'd gotten the recipe for the peas from Betty Crocker, but she doubted anyone would know. Her friends tended to divide their culinary efforts between TV dinners and *The Joy of Cooking*. Betty C. was too middle-of-the-road.

They sat around after dinner while Libby told cruise stories, the same cruise stories Shelby had already heard. Not that she minded. It gave her a chance to relax, to recover from the relentless attention that had come her way over the meal and the relentless attention she'd had to pay to everyone else, and to become intimately acquainted with this evening's headache. All in all, it was a pretty successful time, and she might have almost enjoyed it, if Jean had ever looked her way.

Ray was wound up now and talking non-stop, about his favorite topic, the evils of drug use among the 'beatniks' as he called them. Ray didn't approve of the new drug culture. Drugs made people messy and difficult to deal with. And it was getting worse, he said. Even adults, who should know better, were gobbling up something called LSD and claiming to find the meaning of life in a raindrop.

Mystical experiences. He gave a sharp, contemptuous laugh. It sounded like spitting.

Shelby thought she wouldn't mind having a mystical experience herself. The sooner the better.

He wouldn't notice if her thoughts wandered. He demanded nothing more from her than an audience. But her eyes were burning, her face felt hot, her skin so sensitive that even her soft cotton dress grated like sandpaper. Half-turned toward her, Ray draped one arm carelessly over the steering wheel and cushioned her neck with the other. In the glow of the street light, his angular features were softened, the creases that ran both ways diagonally from the corners of his mouth shadowed by darkness. His hair and eyes, vivid in daylight, seemed to blend with the shadows. Shelby could feel his hand moving back and forth, back and forth over the curve of her shoulder. The gesture annoyed her, but she knew he did it unconsciously.

The car clock ticked. Fine mist fell through yellow circles of light that hung suspended in night beyond the dampened windshield. In the car the air had turned cool, and Shelby shivered, while Ray's voice rolled on, and on, and on, rumbling in her ears, her headache throbbing to the rhythm of his words.

"So what do you think, babe?" he asked.

She'd been drifting. She didn't know what he was referring to. "I don't really have an opinion," she said. "What do *you* think?"

"I ask you to marry me, and you don't have an opinion?"

Oh, God. "I mean," she said quickly, "I just got promoted, and you're not through your residency. It seems sort of, well, premature."

Now he was annoyed. "I'm not talking about a wedding next week. But we could announce the engagement, couldn't we?"

"What if there's a war?"

He looked at her as if she were slightly insane. "There's not going to be a war. What's with you tonight?"

"I think I don't feel too well."

"Too much to drink?"

"No, just not well."

He was silent for a moment. She could feel his disappointment. "I guess you don't want to talk about marriage, then."

"I want to talk about it, Ray. Just not tonight."

"All right." He lapsed into silence.

She'd hurt his feelings. She hadn't meant to do that.

She took his hand and brushed her cheek against it. "I'm sorry. I know I'm cranky. It's just that people have been talking at us all night. I'm worn out from it."

He squeezed her hand. "It's OK, Shel. I didn't realize." He slipped his arm around her shoulder and pulled her to him.

Reluctantly, she let her head rest against his neck. He held her.

After a moment it felt good. If they could just sit like this for a while... Ray was strong, protective. For now she was safe, though she didn't know from what. "We should do this more often," she said.

He kissed the top of her head, then tilted her face upward and kissed her mouth.

She forced herself to kiss him back.

He didn't even notice she didn't mean it.

Of course she meant it. She loved Ray. She just didn't happen to feel anything at the moment.

There were a lot of moments when she didn't happen to feel anything.

He was kissing her again. Harder.

She followed his lead. It was an act.

His breath turned shallow and quick.

Shelby wanted to run. She made herself stay with him.

"Forgive me," he murmured. "I'm a clod."

"What?"

"I should have realized this was what you wanted."

She felt tears spring into her eyes. It isn't what I want. Jesus, can't you tell? No, he couldn't tell. Not if she didn't tell him.

But she couldn't tell him.

Now he was touching her breast, fumbling with the buttons on her dress. Her body wanted to go limp. Lifeless. She couldn't let it.

You can do this, she told herself. You've done it a hundred times before.

She was swept with a wave of loneliness so terrible she wanted to die.

"I love you," he whispered, and slipped his hand beneath her skirt.

"I love you, too."

It didn't mean anything. Or she didn't know what it meant. But she was expected to say it. She hated herself for saying it.

Hated herself.

But maybe, when he said it, it wasn't anything more than it was when she said it.

Maybe.

If it wasn't, he wouldn't be grabbing at her. Or she'd be grabbing at him. Wouldn't she?

She pulled his shirt out from beneath his belt. As if she couldn't reach his skin fast enough.

Ray sighed and shuddered when she touched his nipple. "Oh, Shel..."

She pressed against him harder, and felt his body tighten. Something strange and warm ran down her face, and she realized she was crying.

He didn't notice.

"Oh, God, I love you, babe," he said again.

No. You don't love me. I'm sitting here crying, and pretending to want you, and feeling absolutely nothing. If you loved me you'd know that.

"Well," she heard her mother say in her head, "if it isn't one thing with you, it's another."

It won't always be like this, she told herself. When we're married. When we've gotten to know each other better. When we're settled into a life together, instead of this hit-or-miss way of being. Then I'll love him. Really, I will.

Then he'll really know me, too. After we've been together for a while. He'll know when I'm crying, and when I'm pretending. It'll be all right then.

It won't be so lonely then.

He was becoming aroused. His body felt heavier, stronger. He pulled at her clothes, trying to touch her everywhere at once.

She had to get out of the car.

"Ray," she said softly, "we can't do this here."

He went limp for a second, then pulled back. "What?"

"We're right in the middle of the street."

"No, we're not. We're in my car."

She tried to keep her voice light. "Someone could see us."

"It's the middle of the night... Who's going to be driving around at this hour?"

"We were."

He sighed heavily. "OK, we'll go inside."

"You have to work tomorrow. You'll be a wreck. Probably make a fatal mistake and the hospital will be sued."

He was silent.

"Come on, Ray. We can do this...another time." Take a rain check, like at a baseball game. Later we'll have a double header.

Now she honestly did feel sick. "I have to go in."

Even in the dim light she could see his wounded look.

"OK," he said in a flat voice, "if you really have to."

He waited for her to deny it, but she opened the door and got out. She leaned toward him through the window and gave him a quick, sisterly kiss. "Call me tomorrow?"

"All right."

She started up the walk. For a split second the street was quiet and then she could tell, by the way the car motor roared, that Ray's bewilderment had turned to anger.

She didn't care. All she wanted was to be alone.

38

He wouldn't wait for tomorrow. She knew that. In an hour and a half, two hours at the most, the phone would ring.

Shelby checked her watch. After midnight.

The fire had dwindled down to hard, charred knots of log that wouldn't burn. The wood box was empty. It was cold and damp in the apartment. She thought about closing the flue, but the ashes were smoldering, creating all kinds of opportunities for death by asphyxiation.

Tempting, but not well thought out.

She put the screen in front of the fireplace and changed into pajamas and got a paper bag to empty the ash trays. She washed the worst of the dinner dishes. That made it one-fifteen. The television showed nothing but test patterns.

One-twenty. She thought about putting a record on the player, browsed through a few albums. But he might hear it in the background and think she was having a good time without him and his feelings would be hurt. She didn't want to hurt him. Ray was a good man, one of the best she'd met. It wasn't his fault she was irritable and strange.

The phone rang at one-twenty-two. She grabbed it on the first ring. "Honey, I'm sorry," she said.

"So am I. It was lousy timing."

"It's not your fault."

"Yeah, it is. This was your night. I shouldn't have pushed on the marriage thing."

She perched on the back of the couch. "That wasn't it. I just wasn't feeling well."

"Shel, you should have said earlier."

"It was dumb. Just another one of those headaches."

A brief pause. "What headaches?"

Damn. She hadn't wanted to tell him. "I get headaches now and then. It's nothing. Probably the weather."

"God, babe, how's a person to know what you need if you never let on?"

Lovely. That's twice in one day I've been accused of being overly self-reliant. "It's not a big deal," she said. "If I don't pay any attention to it, it goes away."

"Kind of like yours truly," Ray said wryly.

"Huh?"

"It was a joke, OK?"

"OK."

"So how about *you* set the date for me to propose?"

Shelby let her eyes drift shut wearily. "I don't think I can make that kind of decision right now, Ray. I have a lot on my mind. This new job's going to take a lot of getting used to."

"Shel..."

"I mean it. I want to do it well."

"It isn't going to matter in the long run. As soon as we're married..."

No. She wasn't going to have that discussion tonight. Not tonight, not tomorrow night, not for a long time.

"Honey, it's late and I can't think straight. Can't we talk about this some other time? Please?"

She heard him light a cigarette. "You're right. How about you come in here Tuesday? We'll go some place special for dinner. Maybe come back here after."

She didn't want to, didn't want to, didn't... "Fine. Tuesday."

"Meet you at the bus?"

"Fine."

"Sweet dreams, babe."

Her dream wasn't sweet. Something was outside the window. She could see the shadow of it, a large and shaggy, cloud-like mound, cast by moonlight on the opposite wall. A bush, maybe. But it was too solid for a bush, especially now, when there were no leaves. She thought about getting up to take a closer look, but some intuition, some warning in her mind told her to stay still and small. She watched.

The object, if it was an object, swelled. An appendage of darkness sucked itself out of the body and stretched toward the window. There was a scratching at the screen.

Frozen, Shelby stared at the shadow. The dark mound began to change, to form itself into something human but not quite human. It made a snuffling sound, as if sniffing for a way in. She looked toward the window. The screen bulged. Moonlight brightened through a narrow slit that grew longer, and longer...

Shelby opened her eyes, heart drumming like sleet on a tin roof. A dream. It had been only a dream. But the fear still drifted around her. She fumbled for the bed lamp, pressed the switch...

And found herself back in darkness, with the moonlight shadow of the creature even larger and closer.

This is a dream, she shouted to herself, and forced herself awake. The shadow was gone. Exhausted from the effort, sweating from fear and exertion, she lay quietly listening to the silence. She took a deep breath and let herself relax.

The shadow was back. And now the window was opening, slowly, carefully, as if the creature hoped to surprise her asleep.

A dream, a dream, it's only a dream. She reached for the lamp. Light flooded the room. The banging of her heart was palpable. She wouldn't let herself fall back to sleep. She'd get up and go to the bathroom, splash water on her face, maybe turn on the radio, walk around. Anything to stay awake.

With a ripping sound, the shadow creature split the screen and slid into the room. It moved in a flowing, viscous stream down the wall, across the floor. She tried to get out of bed and run, but she couldn't move. At the foot of her bed it stopped, pulled itself once again into solid form, this time with features—a flattened nose, heavy eyebrows, gaping bottomless mouth, red glistening eyes...

Shelby screamed.

It came out more like a grunt than a scream, but it awakened her into darkness. She grabbed the lamp, pressed the button. This time she really was awake. The room was the same as it had always been, window off the foot of her bed to the left. The screen was intact, the window closed. No shadows on the opposite wall, only her bureau and mirror. Bedside table with the file folder of stories and her blue pencil. Max Lerner's *America as a Civilization*, her guaranteed put-to-sleep book since graduate school, lay open on the floor.

Carefully, certain she'd be thrown back into the dream any minute, she slipped out of bed and tiptoed to the bathroom. She turned on the light. No goblins in the shower or the tub. Nothing strange in the medicine cabinet. Shelby glanced at herself in the mirror. "You look like the wrath of God," she said aloud, and ran cold water and buried her face in her cool, wet washcloth.

"Well," she said, "that's the last time I cook something out of Betty Crocker." Which suddenly reminded her of Ebeneezer Scrooge trying to pass off Marley's ghost as undigested beef.

Shelby peeked at the clock on top of the stove. Three a.m. Perfect, just time enough to finally get back to sleep before she'd have to get up.

Then she remembered that tomorrow was Sunday, and she had no plans.

She searched through the medicine cabinet for something to help her drop off, to take the edge off her nerves. Aspirin was iffy. Sometimes it worked, sometimes it didn't. But there was a pack of dramamine. If it made her sleepy enough to nearly miss planes, it ought to put her to sleep now. She swallowed one, and carried a second with a glass of water to her bed, just in case.

Chapter 4

When did it turn so complicated?

Shelby let the Entertainment section of the *Boston Sunday Globe* slip to the floor and sipped her coffee. The apartment was still a mess, furniture all out of order, overlooked plates lurking in surprising places, stale glasses making rings on the coffee table, on the top of the TV set, on the phone stand. She didn't care.

When they had first started going out, while Ray was still in medical school, it'd been fun. They'd both been dating other people, and their times together had been easy. Gradually, the other people had dropped out, until it was just the two of them. Somewhere along the line, their friends had started to see them as a couple. She wasn't even sure when it had happened. Now it was assumed, if they were invited anywhere, it was Shelby and Ray.

Maybe that was the trouble. Maybe they had become too twisted up in each other's lives without thinking about it, because lately it seemed they were always pulling in opposite directions.

They'd been thrown together without either of them making a decision, like tree branches entangled in a flood.

Ray was asking for a decision now.

Except he wasn't asking for an "if" decision, he was asking for a "when" decision. But surely he'd thought about it. Surely he'd sat down and asked himself if Shelby Camden was the woman he wanted to marry.

She wondered if it had been that clear-cut. Straightforward, yes or no, up or down. Or had it come with conditions—*if* she lets her hair grow or promises never to let her hair grow, *if* she agrees to have two children in the next five years, *if* she quits her job?

And what about yourself? she wondered. Do you want to be Mrs. Dr. Raymond Curtis Beeman?

"Sure, why not?" she heard herself say out loud.

Why not? Because "why not" is a hell of a reason to get married, that's why not. Of course you want to get married, she told herself firmly. And you want to get married to Ray. Ray is, in Connie's terms, "the greatest."

Do you love him?

She went to the kitchen and poured another cup of last night's coffee.

I must love him, she thought as she sipped the bitter liquid. He's a good person. I feel safe with him. I like the way we look together. We're easy with each other. I can see us growing old together.

We already *have* grown old together. We're comfortable. Like a pair of well-loved, well-worn slippers.

42

God, I'm twenty-five years old and thinking as if I'm eighty.

But where's the excitement in it? The anticipation? The passion?

In the movies there was always excitement. Romantic stuff. Ray seemed to feel romantic.

Shelby didn't know what that was, to feel romantic.

That was only what the movies showed you. Nobody knows what you really feel. Maybe Ray's just expressing what he thinks he's supposed to feel, the way they show it in the movies.

It must be nice, to feel the way they did in the movies. If they did. If anyone did.

But somebody must. Somebody makes up the things you see in the movies. They must get it somewhere.

It didn't make any sense, thinking like this. It was morbid, and probably just the remnants of a hangover.

She was always thinking too much about things. Everyone said so. Sometimes they didn't even say it, just stared at her with that "I can't believe the way your mind works" look.

Get up. Move around. *Do* something.

She wished she had someone to talk to. Someone who'd understand this, and help her understand it.

Not a shrink. She pictured a short, balding middle-aged man with glasses who'd take notes and say "uh-huh" now and then. He wouldn't know what she was talking about.

Or he'd have her committed to a hospital for the hopelessly deficient.

And then they might as well commit Libby, too. Libby would go totally off her rocker.

Libby wouldn't have to know.

Libby knows everything, sooner or later.

She needed someone who'd been there, a sister, someone who'd know what was happening to her. Someone who could explain, or help, or at least be kind. The tears were starting up again, pressing against the backs of her eyes.

And there was a feeling, distant, circling toward her like a hungry shark.

Fear.

No, she thought. I will not sit around and be maudlin.

She put her coffee cup in the sink and went in search of leftover party debris.

The living room still smelled of stale cigarettes. She'd opened the windows, but the outside air was so heavy it simply lay there. A draft would help. A fire would set up a draft.

This is a good thing to know, Mrs. Dr. Raymond Curtis Beeman. A good little housewife should always know how to do important things like remove the cigarette odor from a room.

The wood box was empty, of course. And yesterday she'd noticed there were no more split logs in the shed. Chances were, no one had split any. Since the students had left, the apartment house was very short on log splitters.

Not to worry. Mrs. Dr. Raymond Curtis Beeman was the best log splitter in Suburbia.

The shed was fragrant with the clean smell of cut wood. Her old jeans,

43

which she kept tucked away almost guiltily in the back of her closet, were soft against her legs. Metal struck logs with a satisfying "thunk." The wood fibers cracked with a twisting sound as the logs split, and odors of pine and dried cherry drifted through the sawdust.

It felt good to do this, to feel the axe weight in her hands, to feel the power in her arms as she swung it overhead and down. No thinking while you split wood, either. Focus and concentrate. Set the log. Swing. Strike. Separate the two halves clinging together by their fibrous threads. Stack the split halves.

Get a rhythm going. Set…swing…strike…separate…stack.

Set…swing…strike…separate…stack.

Set…swing…strike…separate…stack.

Mrs.… Doctor…Raymond…Curtis…Beeman.

She missed, hitting the log on its outer rim. It tumbled over. "Shit," she muttered, and bent to right it.

"Need a hand?"

Shelby started and looked up. Someone was standing in the doorway, leaning against the frame. A woman, a silhouette against the misty gray glare.

Leaning, Shelby thought. People lean in that casual, comfortable way when they've been standing there for a while, watching.

She felt her face go hot. She had a pretty good idea what she looked like, hair in her eyes and chips of wood clinging to her sweater like weed seeds. The sneakers—oh, God, the beat-up sneakers—and the torn jeans… She started to cram her hands into her pockets self-consciously, forgetting she was holding the axe. The tool clunked to the floor.

"I'm sorry," the woman said. "I didn't mean to scare you." She laughed a little. She had a nice laugh. "Actually, I was watching, which is rude, of course. But I couldn't help myself." She indicated the wood pile with a flick of her wrist. "You do that very well."

"Thanks." Shelby ran a hand through her hair casually, hoping she could rearrange herself without appearing to. Some of the wood chips transferred themselves to her hair.

The woman pushed away from the door and stepped inside. She picked up the axe. "Want me to cut a little?"

"It's OK, I'm finished, but thanks." She wished the woman would face the light so she could see her. She couldn't even tell how old she was.

"Let me give you some help with carrying." The woman bent to pick up an arm load of split wood. "I assume you're going to take it inside and burn it, or are you just working off steam?"

"It isn't necessary, really." Shelby grabbed at a log, and felt a splinter slip into the squishy part of her palm.

"Least I can do," the stranger said as she piled the wood high in the crook of an elbow. "After scaring you."

Shelby picked the splinter out of her hand. "You didn't scare me," she said firmly.

The woman glanced at her. Shelby faced down her backlit shadow with her best noncommittal look. The woman shook her head and went back to lifting wood. "Off on the wrong foot," she muttered. "Definitely the wrong foot."

"Who *are* you?" Shelby heard herself ask bluntly.

44

"I'm sorry. Fran Jarvis. And you are?"

"Shelby Camden."

"I thought so." Fran made a gesture to reach out to shake hands, realized she was holding the wood, and settled for a shrug. "I just moved in across the hall from you."

"Oh!" Shelby said with a little too much enthusiasm. "That apartment's been empty for weeks."

"Is there something I should know? Like rats in the walls? Or a grisly murder happened there and the body was never found but there's a strange odor emanating from behind the bathroom wall?"

Shelby grinned. "I don't think so. The whole house is sort of haunted, but it's not personal."

"Well," said Fran, "thank God for small favors—which, of course, is the only kind God does." She tilted her head to one side. "You ready to go in, or do you have another project out here?"

"Ready." She gathered up the remaining wood, made one final swipe at the chips in her hair, and set the axe in the chopping block.

The outside light was blinding after the dimness of the shed. They were halfway across the yard before she could see clearly. Fran strode on a little ahead of her. She was about Shelby's height, with light brown hair cut short and slightly wavy. She was wearing brown wool slacks and a caramel blazer and penny loafers. Standard late winter New England dress. Not much of a clue to personality.

Shelby still hadn't seen her face.

The mud squished around her sneakers. It smelled like decaying earthworms. The grass was brittle, and looked as if it would never green again. Bare roots, twisted by frost heaves, pushed out of the ground under the maples.

"It was spring when I left Washington," Fran said over her shoulder, as she slogged across the soggy yard. "It disappeared somewhere in northern New Jersey. On the Garden State Parkway, I think."

"Is that where you're from? Washington? D.C.?" She wanted to walk faster, to catch up with her. But the ground was treacherous. She knew she'd throw herself off balance and land face down in worm-scented mud.

"Visiting," Fran said. "I've been making my way up from Texas. How about you?"

"I've lived in Bass Falls about three years, since graduate school. But I'm a native New Englander. Andover. Outside of Boston."

"Dyed-in-the-wool Yankee?"

"I guess so."

They had reached the house. Fran pulled the wooden storm door open with two fingers, then stood back to use her body to hold it.

"Thanks," Shelby said as she stomped up the steps. She looked up into Fran's face.

She was about Shelby's age, maybe a year younger or older, it was hard to tell. Soft features, high cheekbones, and the most amazing eyes Shelby had ever seen. Blue, but not the light blue of most blue eyes. Fran's eyes were deep, darkening to indigo near the irises, eyes within eyes.

Cornflowers, Shelby thought.

45

And nearly tripped over the sill.

"Careful," Fran said.

She pulled herself together and backed through the inside door, holding it for Fran. "That's my place," she said, and nodded toward her open door.

"I figured," Fran said.

"You did?"

"There are only two apartments on this floor. The other one's mine."

Now Shelby felt like a total fool. "You may not believe this," she said, "but I'm rumored to have an I.Q. in triple digits."

"I believe it."

"I'm even allowed to live here without supervision."

"Well, I shouldn't be," Fran said as she looked down at her mud-caked shoes and the tracks she'd left on the hall carpet. She stepped out of her loafers and kicked them to the side.

"Don't worry about that. When it dries, it vacuums right up."

"Assuming one has a vacuum."

"I do." Shelby led the way into her apartment and tossed her logs into the wood box. "What were you doing out there, anyway? Exploring?"

"Being nosy." Fran lowered her wood to the hearth. "I was tired of my own company, and your door was open so I knew you were around here somewhere so I came looking." She brushed the sawdust from her hands into the fireplace. "I stopped in here first—didn't come in, just made polite noises." She looked around. "Nice place you've got here."

"'We like it,'" Shelby quoted.

"Gordon Jenkins, *Seven Dreams.*"

"*Manhattan Tower,* I think. Maybe *Seven Dreams.* I always mix them up. Care for coffee?"

"If it's not too much trouble."

"No trouble at all. Shove the papers aside and have a seat."

When she came back into the room with the coffee and cream and sugar and Jean's cookies on a tray, Fran had taken off her jacket and was on her knees in front of the hearth, nursing the first tiny flames of a fire.

Shelby watched her for a moment. She liked the way the woman's hands moved, surely and firmly, like an artist's hands.

"You're staring," Fran said, back to her. "I can feel it."

"Well, you stared at me."

"True." She tossed a few wood splinters to the fire.

"You do that very well," Shelby echoed Fran's earlier remark.

Fran laughed. "I've had some experience."

"In Texas?"

Fran turned and looked at her with those amazing eyes. "Texas?"

"You said you were from Texas."

"I was in Texas for a while. Actually, I'm a native of California."

"Nobody's a native of California," Shelby said, and handed her a mug of coffee. "Around here, we say the first real sign of spring are California license plates. Transplants coming home to visit."

Fran laughed again. Her laughter reminded Shelby of a cello. "Spoken like a true easterner." She set her coffee aside and fed a few larger twigs to the flames.

46

Shelby watched her.

"What are you *staring* at?"

"Your hands," Shelby found herself saying. "The way you use them. Kind of like an artist, or an auto mechanic."

"My God," Fran said, and held her hands up and looked at them.

"I don't mean that in a bad way. Did you ever notice how really good mechanics use their hands? There's something almost holy about it."

"I never thought of it like that, but I know what you mean." Fran slipped her hands into her back pockets. "Unfortunately, now that you've pointed this out, I will never again be able to use my hands in public."

"I'm sorry," Shelby said.

"Maybe, if I stick my finger in a light socket, I'll experience a kind of electroshock therapy and forget you said it."

Shelby laughed and went to Fran and pulled her hands from her pockets and pressed them together between her own. "That's enough. I'll feel terrible."

Fran glanced over at the fire. "I'd better put on a log," she said as she gently extricated her hands. "Don't want all my skill and expertise to go up in smoke."

Shelby groaned and rolled her eyes. She settled on the sofa. "Are you sure it's not *Manhattan Tower*? The cocktail party sequence? Or was it the *Seven Dreams* cocktail party? Some cocktail party, anyway."

"Actually, no, I'm not sure." She tossed more sticks on the fire and added a couple of logs. "I have the record… Cancel that. If it's in my apartment, it's gone for good."

"Need some help settling in?"

"Another time, thanks. I've spent the last four days in a rental van with that load. I'm not interested in relating to it at the moment."

"You drove up here yourself?"

"Sure." Fran took a cookie.

"Was it hard?"

"Not as hard as unpacking's going to be. I can't believe how much *stuff* I had stored."

"If your place is a mess and you don't want to deal with it," Shelby said, "I could offer you the bed or the couch. Granted, the apartment smells like a dead party, but…"

"That's OK. I think I can find a bed, two came with the apartment."

"I have extra sheets."

"I'm used to roughing it, but thanks."

Shelby laughed. "And people criticize *me* for being too independent."

"Do they?" Fran asked, and looked straight at her with those cornflower eyes. "You, too?"

"Constantly."

"Isn't it annoying?"

"It certainly is."

"Maybe we could start a club for independent women," Fran said.

Shelby shook her head. "Too independent for clubs."

Fran sat on the hearth and faced her and wrapped her arms around her knees. "Birthday?"

"What?"

"The party. Was it your birthday?"

"No, it was…" She felt herself turning self-conscious again. "Actually, we were celebrating because I…well, I got a promotion at work."

"Congratulations," Fran said. She cocked her head to one side. "You don't seem overjoyed."

"Well, I'm glad, of course." Shelby thought about it. "I guess I have mixed feelings. I mean, I'm glad but not as glad as I thought I'd be." She frowned. "That doesn't make any sense, does it?"

"Sure," Fran said enthusiastically, but she had a strange look on her face. A half-embarrassed sort of look. The sort of look people get when they're lying to be polite.

Shelby laughed. "I hope your line of work doesn't require acting. You don't do it very well."

"I know," Fran said with a heavy sigh. "It limits my opportunities. So why the mixed feelings?"

"Well… It's not that I don't want it. Not that at all. It's… I guess I thought it would make more of a difference."

"Ah," Fran said. "Kind of like Christmas."

"Christmas?"

"You never feel quite the way you thought you would. It can even be all right on the surface, but something's always a little flat." Fran shrugged. "I guess it just doesn't live up to its advertising." She glanced up at Shelby with a sudden uneasy look. "I'm sorry. I hope I didn't offend you."

"Offend me?"

"Talking about Christmas like that."

Shelby laughed. "But you described it perfectly."

"Christmas was sacred in my home," Fran said. "Even the name was sacred. My mother once threatened to throw me out of the house for saying Christmas didn't live up to its advertising."

"Mine would, too. Did she ever?"

"Throw me out of the house? Not really."

"Sort of?"

Fran nodded. "Sort of. I needed to be on my own. Sometimes it's like that. What kind of work do you do?"

"I'm with *The Magazine for Women.* I'm what they call a reader." She caught herself. "Or was. Now I'm an assistant editor. We decide what articles and stories go into the magazine from the ones the readers pass along to us. Not the final decisions, those are made by the editors. I'm in fiction."

"I'll bet you have to be careful about your English."

"I should," Shelby said. "Though sometimes, after work hours, I have an overwhelming desire to say things like 'ain't.'"

"I seldom want to say 'ain't.' I heard enough of it in the Army."

Shelby looked at her. "You were in the Army?"

"Nobody ever believes a woman could possibly *want* to be in the Army," Fran said with a sigh. "Not even the Army."

Shelby wanted to ask her what it was like, but that seemed kind of trite. "Do you think we'll have a war?"

"We're *always* about to have a war, aren't we?" Fran said. She tossed a scrap of wood onto the fire. "This is a bloodthirsty country, but they'll have to have the next one without me."

"I take it you weren't too crazy about it."

Fran gave a little gesture of dismissal. "Parts of it were OK. Parts of it were great. Parts of it were God-awful."

"I don't believe I could stand it," Shelby said. "It seems so...controlled."

"It is, but you get used to that. After a while you even start to like not having to think or make decisions. Until you join the Army, you don't know how much of civilian life is made up of decisions."

"I think I do. When to get up, what to wear, whether to stop for gas now or wait until after work, and what would be the consequences of either course of action. What to eat, what to say, whether to get married..."

"You've got it," Fran said. "I hope I can adjust. I'll probably just sit on the edge of my bed waiting for someone to tell me what to do."

"If I don't see you for a few days," Shelby said, "I'll come in and order you to get up."

"Thank you."

"Listen, tell me if this is too personal, but...well, why *did* you join the Army?"

"Most people want to know that—with varying degrees of horror. Even the Army wanted to know. You'd think they'd have been satisfied to get me, wouldn't you?"

"So why did you?"

"The reasons change. I guess I'm not really sure, myself. For the experience. For the G.I. Bill. To do something different. Mostly I suppose I wanted to get away from home."

"Because of your attitude toward Christmas?"

"Something like that. My family and I are basically incompatible," Fran said. "I suspect I was left on their door step by invaders from Mars."

"Lucky you. There's no question in my mind that I was born into my family. There's no way out."

"Join the Army," Fran said with a sudden smile. "You'd be amazed at the number of people who won't speak to you after that."

Shelby laughed. She sipped her coffee. "Why did you leave?"

She took a long, thoughtful moment to answer. "It was time," she said at last. "They wanted me to..."

She reached for the word. Something she'd heard in World War II movies. "To re-up?"

Fran looked at her with surprise. "Re-up?"

Shelby felt herself blush. "God, that sounds stupid. I was trying to be cool."

"It was very cool," Fran said, and tried not to laugh, and failed. "Why would you want to be cool?"

"To impress you," she began, and knew immediately she'd just made it worse. "I do that with everyone. It's a habit."

"Well," Fran said, "in that case I'll try not to take it personally."

Shelby buried her face in her hands. "I can't believe I'm doing this."

"Doing what?"

"Making a fool of myself. If this were your apartment, I'd leave in disgrace and never come back."

"Then I'm glad it's yours."

Shelby looked at her.

"I mean it," Fran said.

She found herself feeling shy. "Thank you. So…uh…what are you doing in New England?"

"College." Fran reached for another cookie. "I have about two years to go to finish up. I was in pre-med, which makes it absolutely amazing that the Army assigned me to the medical corps, since they usually give you what you're least interested in or qualified for. I guess it keeps us humble. Anyway, now I'm not sure I want to stay with that. I'll look around a little, I guess. Nothing but opportunities ahead, right?"

"Right," Shelby said.

"That's why I came early. To get a job, and sort of wander around the University and see what looks interesting and what I have to catch up on and what I can maybe test out of."

"You're going to have a busy few months."

"I'm used to being busy." She looked around the apartment. "Hey, why don't I help you with KP? At the risk of being rude, it looks as if you could use some."

"I can do it later. You're probably tired."

Fran got up. "The only thing I'm tired of is sitting." She reached a hand down to Shelby. "Come on. Let's see if I remember how to act in a civilian kitchen."

She didn't realize how late it was until she heard the phone. They'd cleaned up the party debris—which Shelby kept apologizing for, until Fran said she couldn't possibly understand the meaning of "mess" until she'd seen the inside of an enlisted men's rec hall. They'd considered going out to dinner, but rummaged through the refrigerator and decided there were plenty of leftovers to satisfy.

Fran told about her Army days. Shelby found herself fascinated and horrified to about equal degrees, but for the most part couldn't imagine having the courage to join the Army in the first place. She could just hear what her parents would say.

"If they're anything like mine," Fran said, "their nastiness would reach levels previously unknown to humankind."

Shelby folded her dish towel. "What did yours do?"

"Well, since I already had a rough idea of the depths to which they could sink, I made sure I was on the base, in barracks before I called and told them. They tried to get me out, but I was over legal age so they couldn't touch me. Mostly they were restricted to threats and name-calling. But I'd grown up with that, and it was safe in the Army. Believe me, if someone wants to get to you there, even on the phone, it can take an act of Congress."

"Now that you're out, will they try to find you?"

Fran shook her head. "They pretty much gave up on me. We don't even exchange Christmas cards. I suspect they're just glad I'm out of their life."

"Does that bother you?"

"Only on Hallmark card occasions." She smiled to herself. "But then it's not my real family I miss, it's some kind of ideal movie family I never really had. I mean, how can you *really* miss a bunch of people you left home to escape?"

"Why did you leave…" Shelby began to ask, and that was when the phone rang. "Damn," she said. "It's Ray." She started for the living room.

"Who's Ray?"

"My…uh…boyfriend." She glanced back. "Fiancé, almost. I guess."

Fran just raised one eyebrow in a quizzical way.

"Hey, babe," Ray said.

"Hi," Shelby said.

"How're you doing?"

Since yesterday? "Fine. How about you?"

"Good. Listen, that was a great party, wasn't it?"

"Yes, it was."

"But not as great as Tuesday's going to be."

Tuesday? Oh, God, Tuesday. Tuesday they were going to discuss getting engaged. Or get engaged. Or something. She hoped he wasn't going to make it a party. Anything but a party. "Ray, you're not planning anything lavish for Tuesday, are you?"

"Not lavish, just special. Cocktails at the Carousel, dinner at the Copley. Sound good?"

"Sounds wonderful," she forced herself to say. "I'll have to make it an early night, though. Work on Wednesday."

"I know. Unless you want to…" He chuckled suggestively. "…stay over and call in sick from here."

"Oh, sure." Shelby put on her best teasing voice. "And just what are you trying to do to my good name, Dr. Raymond Curtis Beeman?"

"Once I get you in my power, my sweet," he said, and she could almost see him twirling his invisible moustache, "your reputation will be as naught."

"Listen," she said quickly, "I have company right now and…"

"You have company?"

"The new tenant, across the hall. I'm helping her get organized…"

"Oh."

"So I have to get back to it. I'll take the bus in and meet you at Park Square. Or would you rather I drove?"

"Take the bus," Ray said. "If you miss the last one out, I can run you home."

"Good. See you at seven. Love you."

"Love you, too, babe."

She hung up the phone.

"Did something happen?" Fran asked as Shelby entered the kitchen.

"No, why?"

"The last time I looked like that, I was on my way to a root canal."

Shelby poured herself another cup of coffee. "He wants me to come in to Boston Tuesday."

"Is that a problem?"

"He wants to discuss getting married."

"That's a problem, all right."

Shelby loaded her coffee with sugar.

"Go easy on that stuff," Fran said. "You'll never sleep tonight."

Shelby tossed her spoon into the sink. "I never sleep, anyway."

"Why not?"

Too busy listening to my heart beat, she wanted to say. Too busy contemplating suicide. Too busy being depressed, or angry, or...

"Look," Fran said, "it's probably none of my business, but...well, when a girl gets engaged, isn't there usually a whole lot of squealing and shrieking with joy?"

"We're not engaged yet," Shelby pointed out.

"I've seen a lot of women on the brink of engagement, and you strike me as a few points south of ambivalent."

Shelby ran her hand across her face. "I'm just tired."

"Is that my cue to leave?"

She didn't want her to go. "No, please." Shelby sipped her coffee and tried to think of something that would explain her mood. "I guess I feel pressured. There've been a lot of changes lately. The promotion..." Which he probably hates. "Learning a whole new job..." Which I probably won't be allowed to keep. "I feel as if I need some breathing room."

Fran touched the back of her hand with a fingertip. "If you ever need to let off steam, I'm right across the hall."

"Thank you," Shelby said. She gave a little smile. "You know how men are. Once they get an idea in their heads, they shift into overdrive and plow forward."

"I know," Fran said.

"And I'm the type that likes to settle in and feel comfortable with things before they start changing." She shrugged. "We'll probably be good for each other."

"Or kill each other," Fran said.

Shelby laughed. It felt good to be able to laugh about this. It felt good to *talk* about it. "The thing that *really* drives me crazy is that he's so precise. He calls me every night. At exactly the same time. I can set my watch by it. I *have* set my watch by it. I don't know if he wants me to marry him because he loves me, or because we've been going together for two years, and that's when we should start making plans."

"What does he do?"

"He's a doctor. Well, almost. This is his last year of residency."

"I guess precision is a good thing in a doctor. And a tax accountant. Is it what you're looking for in a husband?"

"I don't know," Shelby said. "I never gave it much thought."

Fran gave her that quizzical look again.

"I know. I should. One of these days."

"Sounds like a good idea to me," Fran said.

"Maybe I'm too young to get married."

"Maybe you are. How old are you?"

"Twenty-five."

Fran nodded. "Definitely too young."

"How old do you think a person should be before they get married?"

"Ninety," Fran said.

Shelby laughed. "I take it you don't think a lot of marriage."

"It's OK, if you're the type."

"Are you?"

She seemed to hesitate. "Not at the moment. But I'm not the one who's about to get engaged."

"Yeah." Shelby took a swallow of coffee and stared down into the cup. "I wish I knew what to do."

"Well," Fran said, "as Davy Crockett once said, 'Be sure you're right, then go ahead.' "

Shelby had to laugh.

"I'm sorry," Fran said, running her hands over her face. "I've spent too much time around the Alamo. Tell me something. Is there anything you don't have mixed feelings about?"

"Very little. How about you?"

Fran stretched. "Actually, things are always disgustingly clear for me. Too damn clear. I'd welcome a little ambivalence."

"You're welcome to some of mine." She was beginning to feel depressed. "Can we talk about something else?"

"To be perfectly honest," Fran said. "I'm just about to become obsessive about unpacking. Since you've provided me with this delightful caffeine buzz, I should go put things away."

Shelby pushed back her chair. "I'll help you."

"Thanks, but I haven't known you long enough to let you see me obsessive." She looked up at Shelby and smiled. "Nothing personal, but I'd really rather be alone. I have to make the place mine, and I can only do that if I do it myself."

"I understand," Shelby said. She walked her to the door. "I'll help you another time, OK?"

"No doubt about it." Fran draped her blazer over one shoulder. "It's been real, as they say."

"I appreciate the hand with the mess."

"I appreciate the dinner. And the company."

Shelby smiled. "I have to tell you this. When I realized you'd been watching me, out in the shed...well, for a moment there I was really embarrassed."

Fran cocked her head to one side.

"At being seen," Shelby said. "The way I was brought up, nice girls don't chop wood."

"What do nice girls do," Fran asked, "if they're lost in the wilderness? Freeze to death?"

"Nice girls don't go out in the wilderness without nice boys."

"Poor nice girls." She reached for the door knob. "So I guess I don't have to worry about you being too nice."

"Probably not," Shelby said. "And we already know you're not too nice, what with your military career and all."

"Correct." Fran opened the door. "Thanks again, and if you need anything, you know where to find me."

"And you me." She laughed. "You know, we might be the two most *help-ful* people on the face of the earth."

Fran reached over and rested her hand on Shelby's arm. "Could be. Goodnight, Shelby." The door closed behind her.

* * *

"Well," Connie said over coffee on Monday morning, "you must have had quite a time after we left Saturday."

Shelby added milk to her coffee. "What?"

"You're positively *glowing.*"

"I am?"

"You are."

She felt her face grow pink.

Connie noticed it. "Hah!" she said, and grabbed for Shelby's left hand. She looked down, then up again, puzzlement slipping over her face. "Where's the ring?"

"There's no ring," Shelby said, and extricated her hand from Connie's.

"In that case," Connie said, giving Lisa a nudge in the ribs with her elbow, "there much be another reason for that glow." She almost leered. "Come on, Shel. Tell all. With details."

"There's nothing," Shelby said firmly. "Ray stayed for a little while after you left, we talked, and he went home."

"Oooh," Connie said, and rolled her eyes. "You *talked.*" Her glance demanded that Lisa and Penny and Jean back her up in the teasing.

Penny and Lisa grinned. Jean looked at the floor.

"We had an argument."

"Oh, no," Lisa said.

"It was an argument. Not the end of the world."

"Did you make up?"

"Yes, Lisa, we made up." Your dreams are safe, she thought. The world is the marvelous, romantic, picture-book place you want it to be. Life according to *The Magazine for Women.*

"Listen," Connie said. "Want to flick out tonight?" It was Connie's way of inviting them to a movie.

Shelby shook her head. "You'll have to go without me. I promised the new tenant I'd help her move in." Which wasn't a *total* lie. She'd promised *herself* she'd help Fran move in.

"You mean they finally rented that apartment?" Lisa asked. "Who is it?"

"A woman about our age. I only spent a few minutes with her."

"What's she doing here?" Connie wanted to know.

"Finishing college."

"Where's she from?" Penny asked.

She found herself not wanting to tell. As if she were protecting Fran from them. "She didn't say."

"Well, what *did* she say?" Connie demanded.

"She said 'hello.'"

Jean took a large swallow from her coffee mug, but not before Shelby saw the smile that trickled over her face.

54

Shelby quickly looked away from her. Meeting Jean's eyes right now could lead to a serious breakdown into conspiratorial giggles.

"Other than that," Connie pressed on in an unamused tone, "what did she say?"

"Nothing, really. We discussed the weather, I offered to help her unpack, she refused. She offered to help me clean up, I accepted. End of story." She turned to Jean. "I need to go over some stuff with you. About that last story you sent on. OK?"

"Sure," Jean said. "Want to do it now?"

"I'll come along," Penny broke in. "I'll bet I'd learn something."

Penny was still being the eager beaver. In the weeks that she'd been there, she'd dogged Shelby's footsteps, asking questions, probing into the why's and wherefore's of every editorial decision Shelby made. If Shelby was busy, or beginning to appear frayed, she transferred her attention to another of the lunch bunch. She was like a mental street-sweeper, sucking up every grain of information she could find. "Not this time," Shelby said. "This is simple and routine."

"We can work at my desk," Jean offered as she got up.

"All my stuff's in the office. It'd be quicker to go there." She did her best imitation of Woman Oblivious of the Tension She Has Just Created, and gave them a short smile. "See you at lunch."

She flicked the switch that turned on the fluorescent ceiling lights. Charlotte, her officemate, who was older and vividly remembered World War II and rationing, had a fetish about turning out lights. The first time Shelby had left them on, Charlotte was in such a state over it that Shelby decided it was simpler to develop the same mania than to risk her own life and Charlotte's mental health.

The office was small but comfortable. The desks faced one another, separated by a few inches. Charlotte's was directly beside the window, and covered with drawings, photographs, and layouts. On the bulletin board behind her swivel chair she had hung sketches of the new fall designs from the more conservative houses. *The Magazine for Women* shied away from the unconventional and exotic. "Elegance and good taste," Charlotte was fond of saying, "are what our consumers expect of us."

Charlotte liked to think of their readers as "consumers." Shelby pictured upper-middle-class housewives all over the country, sitting in their sunny breakfast nooks, calmly shredding and eating *The Magazine for Women*.

Her own desk was more shadowed, and stacked with manuscripts. Her telephone sat squarely on the corner of the desk. Pencils were lined up in meticulous rows beneath the reading lamp. There was nothing on her blotter, and her written notes were carefully filed in folders.

"It's so *neat*," Jean said. "You could perform surgery on your desk."

Shelby laughed a little self-consciously. "Unlike my apartment. I'm trying not to be too intrusive. After we know each other better, I'll let Charlotte see the real me."

"What's she like?" Jean wandered over to the bulletin board and studied the sketches.

"I don't really know yet. She's out of the office a lot. Very career-minded. I don't know much about her line of work, and she doesn't know much about

55

mine. I think she tolerates me."

"You need a bulletin board," Jean said.

"What would I put on it?"

"Newspaper clippings about serial killers. Do you like her?"

"Charlotte?" Shelby shrugged. "Sure. She's OK. I mean, she's not nasty or anything."

Jean finished her tour of the office and perched on the window sill. "What'd I do wrong, boss?"

"Nothing. I just wanted to talk to you…" She held up one hand quickly. "Not like the other day. I really needed to apologize again. It was a cowardly and unkind thing to do, and I feel terrible about it."

"It's OK," Jean said.

"I think it's created a wall between us. At least it seemed that way at the party. I don't want that to happen."

"Hey, I'm over it. I probably would have done the same thing in your place. Connie's a scary lady when she wants something."

"She doesn't mean to be," Shelby said. "She's just kind of single-minded."

"It's not her motives that can hurt you. It's her methods."

"I know," Shelby said. "I'm sorry."

"Please stop being sorry. You're probably just an agent of her *karma*."

"Her what?"

"Fate, destiny. It's an Eastern religious concept."

Shelby laughed. "You know the strangest things."

"Food and religion. It doesn't get much stranger than that." She looked out the window. "This is the kind of day that fools you. The sun comes out and you think it's warm, but it isn't. The air even looks cold."

Curious, Shelby went to look out. There was a crystalline clearness to the air. It made the sunlight lemon yellow. The trees across the street, the edges and windows of houses, even the cars going by seemed to have been drawn by a compulsively meticulous artist with a pin-sharp pencil. "It does," she said. "I never noticed that before."

"My trouble is," Jean said with a glance up at her, "I notice everything. It drives me crazy."

"I can imagine."

"Like during the party. You were tense from the minute Ray got there. I'm not surprised you had an argument."

Shelby felt a familiar impulse to hide. She fought it. "He wants to get married," she said. "I'm not sure I'm ready. I feel kind of…well, pushed. I mean, I do want to marry him, someday. But things are just too new right now."

"He can understand that, can't he?"

She nodded, then gave a little laugh. "But you know Ray."

"Do you love him?"

"Of course."

"Then it doesn't matter, does it, whether you marry him this year, or next year, or the year after?"

"I guess it doesn't." Shelby leaned against the wall and felt the first low hum of a headache. "But he doesn't see it that way. I'm meeting him tomorrow night, and I know he'll push for an engagement."

"So let him. You can say 'no,' or you can have the longest engagement known to mankind."

"Yeah." Shelby kneaded the back of her neck with her hand. "But you know what it means if we get engaged tomorrow night."

Jean grinned. "Sure do. Another damn…"

"*Party,*" they said together.

"I get so sick of parties," Shelby said.

"Me, too. At least *you* sometimes enjoy them. It's my idea of Hell."

"Always?"

"Usually. It's easier when your mother's there. You don't have to worry about making conversation."

"That's the truth," Shelby said with a laugh. "Once Libby gets going, you can't get a word in edgewise."

Jean jumped down from the window sill. "I'd better get the show on the road. See you at lunch."

She nearly collided with Charlotte May, who came bustling through the door in a trim light wool suit, gloves, and hat. Charlotte was a short, sturdy, no-nonsense woman in her late forties. It was a widely appreciated joke in the office that Charlotte May had two speeds: bustle and sit. She sat.

"Good morning," Shelby said as she returned to her desk. "You're looking festive."

Charlotte plucked off her hat and tossed it on the desk. She stripped the gloves from her hands. "Through no choice of my own, thank you. This is one of *those* days. Breakfast meeting, you can't imagine the quality of the food. And that is not a recommendation. Avoid the Breakstone as if your life depended on it. It does."

"I'll remember that." She leafed through her pile of folders and decided to read Penny's submissions. "Is it sunny in Hartford?"

"It is not." Charlotte reached into her desk drawer and drew out a box containing a new pair of white gloves. She placed it under her hat. "And I have to go back this afternoon for a fashion show at Jordan's. With photographer in tow. Don't ask me why, I don't know. I hope they don't give me that foul-mouthed child…what's his name…Jerry." She gave Shelby a quick smile. "What's your life like today?"

"Same as ever." She picked out a story, read a few paragraphs, then put it down. "Charlotte, tell me something. You've been married…"

"Early and often," Charlotte said.

"Well, do you think it's a good move or a bad move, as far as career goes."

"Best move a man can make, worst for a woman." Charlotte glanced up from her notes. "Why? Thinking of tying the knot?"

"Maybe."

"Then you can kiss the publishing world good-bye. They're convinced any married woman will quit in a minute to have children. No matter what you promise, they won't believe it. That makes you a liability." She tapped the desk. "This is as far as you'll go, kiddo."

Shelby frowned. "But you made editor."

"Because I'm a bully. You're a nice person, Shelby, and nice people have to run twice as fast just to stand still."

"Isn't that kind of cynical?"

"No, lamb, it's based entirely on experience." She got up and opened the window and lit a Tareyton with her silver lighter. "I've seen good women come and go in this office. Talented, smart women. And the minute they start talking about marriage…" She poked at the air with her cigarette. "…it's out with the garbage. You look around. How many married women are there in this office? Not counting the readers, trainees, and underlings. Women with a bit of power and authority."

"I don't know," Shelby said. "You. And Harriet Palmer in the Art department…"

"Widow," Charlotte corrected her.

"Mary Birnbaum in advertising."

"Divorced."

Shelby thought. "That's all I can come up with."

"That's about it." An ash fell from the tip of Charlotte's cigarette onto the bosom of her blouse. She swiped at it angrily. "Well, there's that rattle-brained redhead in Circulation, but she's the publisher's daughter and probably a spy from *Redbook*." She stopped pacing and gesturing and fixed Shelby with a hard gray-eyed gaze. "I'm not saying you're doomed. From what I've seen of your work, you *can* run twice as fast. I'm just trying to tell you, you need to think long and hard about it. If marriage is what you want in your heart of hearts, then get married and leave the rest of it in the laps of the gods. But if you want to go as far as you can in this business—and that can be pretty darned far, in my opinion—for God's sake take a long, thorough, realistic look at the situation before you make a decision." She stubbed out her cigarette and sat. "And that's the end of Mother May's lecture for today."

Shelby had to smile. There was no one she could think of who exemplified Motherhood less than Charlotte May. "Well, thanks for the advice. I really will think about it." She wanted to thank her for the compliment, too, but if she did Charlotte would probably think Shelby didn't take it seriously. "Thank you" to a compliment always had an undertone of "I know it's not true, but thank you for trying to make me feel better."

She squirreled it away, to be taken out later and enjoyed like a gift.

It was a miracle she made it home that evening. She'd been working on a headache since lunch, and by the time she left the office she began to wonder if she could drive. On top of that, the two-lane bridge across the Mashentucket River that divided West Sayer from Bass Falls was jammed with traffic. Gasoline and diesel fumes hovered over the road. At least they didn't blow their horns. Nobody blew their horns around here. After all, this was New England.

She swore as a bus cut in front of her and enveloped her in the stench of its exhaust. At the next red light, she dragged her pocketbook from the back seat and rummaged through it, searching for aspirin. She was even willing to chew them up without water if she had to. This was an emergency.

Her pocketbook wasn't helpful. Neither was the glove compartment, or the shelf behind the back seat. She searched the floor, as much as she could see without losing control of the car—not that it would matter, they were practically standing still. No luck there, either. "I'm too damn organized," she muttered.

She thought about turning off onto a side road, making a loop, and pulling into the A&P lot. But in the time it would take to do that, she could be home. Sighing, she flicked on the radio and sat back to suffer.

It was another half hour before she got to her apartment. They were driving rusty nails into her head. Flashes of light burst in front of her eyes. She went into her apartment, tossed her pocketbook and jacket in the general direction of the couch, kicked off her shoes, and headed for the medicine cabinet.

No aspirin. Nothing to substitute, either.

Shelby clenched her jaw.

A drink might help. Or it might make it worse. And she hated using alcohol for a headache. She had so many, she'd be addicted before summer.

She had to go out to the market. The thought made her feel sick in her stomach. Moving at all seemed nearly impossible. Standing still helped a little, but even turning her head set off waves of throbbing pain.

Fran. Fran would have an aspirin.

Not bothering to put shoes on, she eased her way down the hall.

"Hey," Fran said brightly. "Come on in. I'd apologize for the mess, but I don't want to draw your attention to it." She looked hard at Shelby. "Are you OK? You look as if someone punched you."

"Just a headache," Shelby said, forcing a smile. "I'm out of aspirin. Do you…"

"Sure." Fran crossed the room to an old wicker sofa covered with boxes and books and unidentifiable things. She gathered them in her arms and dropped them onto the window seat. "Sit down. Lie down. I'll be right back. Don't die on me."

Shelby lowered herself to the sofa carefully and rested her head in her hands. Focus, she thought. Focus on staying as still as you can. She heard the medicine cabinet door slam, then water running in the sink. Then footsteps. Then Fran's voice.

"How many do you want?"

She glanced up and winced as the ceiling light pierced her eyes. "Three."

Fran handed them to her and gave her the water and turned off the light. She took the glass and put it on a low coffee table. "Come on, lie down."

"I'll be OK in a minute." Shelby waved her away.

"Don't argue with me," Fran said, pushing her gently down and tucking a pillow under her head. She lifted Shelby's legs onto the sofa and found a blanket and spread it over her.

"I'm sorry about this," Shelby said.

"Close your eyes. Go to sleep if you want. I have plenty of stuff to do in the bedroom. If I make too much noise, just throw the glass at me."

It was nearly dark outside when she woke. For a moment she was disoriented—windows were in the wrong places, the couch didn't feel right, the doorway opposite didn't lead to her kitchen but to a lighted bedroom. Then she remembered where she was, and why. She lay for a moment, free of pain, reluctant to move and set it off again. In the bedroom, Fran was walking softly and rustling papers and easing drawers open and shut.

Shelby twisted her head first to one side, then the other. The headache seemed to have let up, at least for now. But she didn't want to risk sitting up too fast. She closed her eyes, languishing in the darkness and warmth and the safety of hearing Fran moving quietly around. If she could only stay like this for few hours, a few days... But from the looks of the light outside the window, it must be close to seven. Time for Ray's call.

She opened her eyes and pushed herself up onto her elbows. So far, so good. Swinging her legs to the floor, she sat up. Nothing. OK, last big trial, standing.

It was all right.

She folded the blanket and took it to the bedroom.

Fran glanced up from a box of photographs and smiled. "Welcome back."

Shelby kneaded her face with one hand. "How long did I sleep?"

"About an hour. Feel better?"

"Much. Do you know what time it is?"

Fran glanced over to the clock on her bedside table. "Ten of seven."

"I'd better go."

"That was one murderous headache, wasn't it?"

Shelby tried to toss it off. "I guess."

"Do you have them often?"

"Fairly."

"It's none of my business," Fran said as she folded a sweater and carried it to her bureau, "but I think you should have it checked out."

"I'm going to."

Fran laughed. "You are not. I can tell by the way you said it. What about Ray? He's a doctor, what does he say?"

"I haven't told him."

Fran looked at her. "You know, you're very complicated. You'll confide in me, a near stranger, but the man you're thinking of marrying..."

"I never said I was a rational human being," Shelby said quickly. She put the blanket down on the bed. "Thanks for..."

"Don't thank me. We *are* just the two most helpful people in the world, aren't we?"

"Yeah." She started to leave and turned back. "Fran?"

"That's what they call me."

"Ray's calling at seven, but it shouldn't take long. After that, would you like to get something to eat?"

"I thought you'd never ask." She looked up from the photographs. "But I have to warn you, I'm in the mood for something terrible. Is there a White Castle in town?"

Shelby laughed. "I'm afraid not."

"Dairy Queen? Burger King? Hot Dog Prince?"

"Nope."

"Peasants."

"We do have a local version of a greasy spoon. Smoke-filled, plastic hanging plants, smells like cooking oil and fish, and the upholstery on the booths is cracked."

"Perfect." Fran said.

Chapter 5

Spring was taking its own good time about arriving. Mid-April, and only the crocuses and daffodils were in bloom. Tulip buds were barely visible, tight and closed in on themselves. The goldfinches were just starting to molt their winter grays. And the old maples in front of the house hadn't even begun to put out tiny mahogany blooms.

Last night hadn't gone too badly. They'd had a couple of martinis, dinner and wine, and then dancing. Ray had brought his car, and they drove to a private spot they'd found when they were first dating, where they could look toward Cambridge and watch the headlights of the cars on Memorial Drive reflected on the Charles River. They'd both been quiet and a little thoughtful, and Shelby had been nearly asleep, her head on Ray's shoulder, when he brought up the subject of their engagement.

She'd had a moment of panic then, but forced herself to settle down and listen to him. He apologized for pushing her, and for the tension that had sparked between them Saturday. They were both working hard, he said. He knew she was under a lot of pressure with the new job, and for him life in the emergency room was a never-ending string of horrors. "There'll be other times as crazy as this in our life," he said. "It's good to learn what they can do to us now, so we'll know how to deal with them in the future."

She should have felt relieved.

"What I'm thinking," he went on, "is there's no reason to rush into this marriage. In a year I'll be through my residency. Why make it harder on ourselves than we have to?"

She couldn't believe it. She'd expected him to insist on a wedding this year, and now he was suggesting they wait...

"You're absolutely right," she said.

Ray took her hand, kissed her fingertips. "What I *would* like us to do is announce our engagement this June, and aim for the wedding in a year." He leaned forward to look into her eyes. "How about it?"

"Announce it? I thought we'd just do it."

"I think we should have a party—a dinner, at least, maybe dancing afterward. At the country club."

A lot of things suddenly became clear. "I see Libby's fingerprints all over this," she said.

"We talked about it," he said as if it were the most natural thing in the world.

"I don't know, Ray. Can't this be something we do on our own?"

He put an arm around her and pulled her close against him. "Come on, babe. We'll have a whole marriage to do on our own. This wedding business, it's all for the mothers, anyway, you know that. Be a sport." He nuzzled her ear and rubbed his cheek against hers. His beard stubble chafed her skin. "When our daughter gets married, you can run the show and be as difficult and demanding as you want."

"I guess you're right," she said. At least it would buy her a year.

She kissed him lightly on the cheek. "OK. Let's do it."

He mashed his lips against hers, pinching the skin between her teeth and his. "babe," he said, "I think I'm the luckiest man in the world."

"Me, too," she said. "Luckiest woman."

And that was that. Sitting on the bus on her way back to Bass Falls, she felt the gentle vibration of the tires against the roadway, looked at her dim double reflection in the blackened window. The bus was like a bullet moving silently and steadily through night. This must be what it would be like to be an astronaut, orbiting the planet deep in space, this feeling of completeness, of quiet solitude, of being outside of time.

A year, she thought. A whole year.

* * *

"Honest to God," Connie said irritably as soon as Penny was out of earshot. "What is her major maladjustment?"

"Whose?" Shelby looked over the cards Penny had put down and counted spades. They could make the bid, but she had to be able to finesse the queen.

"Penny's. She just stares at you with those cow eyes."

Shelby hadn't noticed. She shrugged and covered Lisa's four of diamonds with an eight from the board. Lisa must have a bunch of diamonds, or three at the least. She wasn't signalling high-low doubleton with a four. Singleton? Possible.

"Penny has a crush on you, Shelby," Lisa said.

"She's a grown woman," Connie said, and tossed down the diamond jack. "That is just so high school."

"You're imagining things," Shelby said to Lisa as she topped the jack with her queen. If Connie had the ace, she would have played it to ensure the trick. Lisa must have led away from it. She did that sometimes, breaking the rules, because it was unorthodox and occasionally fooled the competition. That meant she still had one or two diamonds. Two on the board. Shelby had three. And Connie would have two or three. Honest little devils. Shelby gathered up the trick. She'd better stay away from diamonds, at least until she had run the trump. She compared her hand and the dummy. Three spades out and jack-high on the board. Damn. If Connie didn't have the queen, they were down one.

Lisa shook her head animatedly. "It's not imagination. Look at how she follows you around. And she's always running errands for you. She didn't bring the *rest* of us anything from Boston."

"I asked her to look for that book." She could get to the board with a heart, but it was risky this early in the game.

"And I'll bet she went all over the city to find it," Connie put in.

Clubs. Penny had six to the ace/jack. Shelby had four to the king. She tossed the seven and prayed no one was void.

"Well, I think it's embarrassing," Connie said.

"I think it's cute," Lisa countered. "Second hand low." She put down the five.

OK. If Lisa had played away from her queen, the jack would take the trick. If she hadn't, if Connie had it... She glanced over at Connie, whose face was completely without expression. Connie was famous for being the most poker-faced bridge player in the lunch bunch.

Something told her to go to the ace. She did. Connie scowled and slammed down the queen.

"God, Camden," Connie said. "You are dipped in it."

"In what?"

"Luck."

"It isn't luck," Shelby said to get her goat. "It's skill."

Penny was back by the time they'd finished the hand. "How'd we do, partner?" she asked as she slid into her seat.

"Made it. Doubled and redoubled."

Penny beamed. "I knew it."

"You wouldn't have," Connie reminded her, "if I didn't have that queen of clubs bare-arsed."

"But you did, didn't you?" Shelby said with a pleasant smile. She gathered up the used cards and passed them to Penny to shuffle and reached for the shuffled deck. "My deal. One more rubber?"

"Were you out with Ray last night?" Connie asked as she arranged her hand.

"Yes."

"I called a few times. There was a concert at the University I thought you might like to go to. You didn't answer."

"I'm sorry," Shelby said. "I'd have enjoyed that."

Connie laughed. "Not as much as seeing Dr. Ray, I'll bet. What did you do?"

"Dinner and dancing at the Copley. Then the bus trip back here. It was after two before I got to bed."

"Oh," said Lisa. "You lucky dog." She passed.

"Two no trump," said Penny.

Connie scowled. "Three hearts."

Shelby passed.

Lisa passed.

Penny went to three no trump. They all passed. Connie led a high club. Shelby put down her pitiful hand with the obligatory, "Sorry, partner."

The look on Penny's face told her she only wished she'd taken a chance and forced them to slam.

"Did he ask you to marry him?" Connie asked.

"Sort of."

"Did you accept?"

"Yes."

Lisa shrieked, causing the few diners left in the room to look for the fire. "Well, when *is* it?"

"A year from June," Shelby said.

"Why so long?"

"We have a lot to do. If I know Libby, this is going to rival Elizabeth II's Coronation."

"It's going to be *fabulous*," Connie said, bouncing a little in her seat. "Presbyterian or Episcopal?"

"We haven't discussed it that far."

"I vote for Episcopal. Presbyterian churches are always drab and serviceable." Connie took a swallow of coffee. "There's something grand about Episcopal."

"I'll keep it in mind," Shelby said.

Penny was taking tricks at a steady pace.

"I can't believe you're really doing it, after all this time," Lisa said.

Shelby looked at her. "All this time? We've only been dating for two years."

"But doesn't it feel like forever?"

"Not really." But it did, a little. Because they knew each other so well, because their togetherness had become so…well, predictable.

"Ray's just the greatest," Connie said.

"I guess he is." Actually, he was. Maybe not the *greatest*, though she hadn't met a man she liked any better. Ray was intelligent, and considerate, and would never treat her unkindly. He got along with her friends, charmed her mother, and could probably stand up to her father if he had to. He had no bad habits.

What are you talking about, she asked herself, a man or a dog?

"Of course," Connie said casually, "there are *some* people who won't be happy to see you married." She cast a quick and meaningful glance in Penny's direction.

Penny didn't notice.

"Who do you have in mind?" Shelby dared her with a deliberate challenging stare.

Connie smiled. "Just people."

Penny leaned back and tossed down her last card. "Baby slam."

"Very nice," Shelby said.

"It played itself."

"Yes," said Connie. She scooped up the cards. "Macaroni's deal."

Shelby couldn't take it any more. She got up. "I just remembered, I have stuff I have to get to Spurl before one-thirty."

"Stuff?" Lisa asked.

"Work."

"If someone said 'stuff' in a story," Lisa said good-naturedly, "you'd send it back."

"I'm being lazy. Don't quote me."

"It was your idea to play another rubber," Connie reminded her.

"I forgot. OK? Forgot?" She turned away.

"Sheesh," she heard Connie say behind her. "Must be that time of month."

The more she thought about it, the more Connie's behavior irritated her. Connie had to create drama, to make mountains out of molehills, simply to spice up her life a little. She was forever looking under beds and into medicine cabinets to ferret out snippets of scandal.

A ferret was exactly what she reminded Shelby of sometimes. With her beady ferretty eyes and twitching ferretty nose and alert ferretty whiskers. Lurking in dark corners and slinking around in the places that were too small for anyone else to get into. Granted, she never gossiped outside of their circle, and her embellished stories could be entertaining. Sometimes it was even diverting to watch her hot on the trail of a rumor. But one of these days someone was going to be hurt, and Shelby was getting sick of it.

On her way back to the office, she stopped by the readers' room. Jean looked up. "How was bridge?"

"Bridge-like." She sat on the edge of Jean's desk. "Sometimes Connie makes me want to scream."

"What's she on about today?"

"Penny."

"And her famous crush on Shelby Camden?"

"Has she been talking around about that?"

"Endlessly. As if anyone gave a damn."

"Penny's *young*, for God's sake," Shelby said. "And probably a little emotionally immature. And insecure. She's going to attach herself to anyone who can show her the ropes."

Jean nodded in agreement. "Plus she likes you. Does it bother you?"

"Of course not. What bothers me is Connie."

"I suspect she's just being Connie."

"Maybe she should try being someone else once in a while. What's her problem, anyway?"

"Beats me." Jean shrugged. "She likes to pick. No nit is safe around her."

"Yeah," Shelby said.

"She can't help it, she's was born in the year of the Rat. You, on the other hand, are a Buffalo, assertive, forward-looking, and a natural leader."

Shelby laughed. "Another tidbit from your endless store of esoteric knowledge."

"My mind is like a garage, full of worthless junk that might come in handy some day."

"By the way," Shelby said, "Ray and I agreed to be engaged to be engaged last night."

"'By the way?' This is a 'by the way' thing?"

Shelby felt herself redden. "I guess. I mean, we've been talking about it so long it's hardly news."

Jean eyed her suspiciously. "Still and all, one expects a certain level of enthusiasm, doesn't one?"

"You sound like Fran," Shelby said, and was surprised to notice that she took pleasure in saying her name.

"Fran?"

"Fran Jarvis. She moved in down the hall. In the empty apartment."

"What's she like?"

"Our age. Interesting, I think. I haven't gotten to know her yet, really."

"I'd like to meet her some time," Jean said. "Unless she turns out to be creepy."

"You will," Shelby said with a laugh. "Even *if* she turns out to be creepy, probably."

Jean leaned back and sipped green tea from a cardboard container. "When's the wedding?"

"A year from June. Connie thinks we should go Episcopal because the church is more ornate."

Jean laughed. "Good old Connie. *Her* values are certainly in the right place."

"I'd like you to be a bridesmaid. Unless you turn out to be creepy."

"I'd be honored," Jean said. "Unless you turn out to have hideous taste in bridesmaids' dresses."

Suddenly the first spectacular hurdle loomed ahead of her. Maid of Honor. She was going to have to pick someone from the lunch bunch. Connie would expect to be the one, since Shelby'd known her the longest and they double-dated the most, and spent the most off-from-work time together, usually at Connie's instigation. If you asked her, Connie would assure you she was Shelby's "best friend." But right now she wanted Jean, who probably didn't expect to be asked. She wished she'd had a sister, or good friend or roommate in college to be the obvious choice, but her friends were scattered, and she hadn't been particularly clubby with her roommate, and the one friend she had really felt comfortable with had gone strange on her. There was Helen from graduate school, but they'd kind of drifted apart...

She'd always believed she was close to her friends, but when it came to something like this, she realized she didn't feel it at all. The thought stunned her. She felt a headache cranking up.

"What's wrong?" Jean asked.

Shelby forced a smile. "I was suddenly overwhelmed with complexities."

"Don't worry about it," Jean said. "Once it's under way it'll have its own momentum. Like a roller coaster."

"That's what I'm afraid of," Shelby said.

"Your mother will take care of everything."

"I'm afraid of that, too."

Jean grinned, and it struck Shelby once again that, of all her friends, Jean was the only one with whom she could be that frank. Penny would just look at her with those big eyes, and Lisa would be shocked. And Connie...

"Jean, do you think..." She was reluctant to say it, but needed to try out an idea. "Do you think Connie could be...well...envious of me?"

"I know she is."

"How do you know?"

Jean just looked at her as if Shelby were simply too naive to be believed.

"Why would she be envious?"

"For starters, you both came here around the same time, and you're moving up while she's still doing a job she considers beneath her. And now you're engaged to be engaged to a man she thinks is the crotch...excuse me, *catch* of the century. Need I go on?"

Shelby winced. "Does everyone feel that way?"

"Connie's a law unto herself. Don't worry about it. It's not your fault."

She hoped it wasn't. She hated the idea that she might have done or said something to make Connie—or anyone—envious. Envious people could be dangerous. And, besides, Shelby really got no pleasure from making someone else feel bad. Maybe she should be nicer to Connie, ask her out to dinner or something. Make her feel important…

My God, she thought, that is so condescending.

"What's up, boss?" Jean asked.

"Connie. I don't know what to do about it."

"She's having a good time," Jean said. "Don't spoil it."

"Maybe, but it's not…"

There was a throat-clearing noise from the hall. "Excuse me, *Miss* Camden." Miss Myers stood in the doorway and looked pointedly at her watch. "*Mr. Spurl* is waiting for your critiques."

"Oops," Shelby muttered. She got up to go.

Jean waved the story she'd been working on. "Thanks for your help," she said, covering. "You saved my life."

Charlotte was out for the day, attending the opening of something-or-other in Boston. Shelby was glad to have the office to herself. Even though Charlotte neither demanded nor expected conversation, it was easier to think when she was alone.

She returned a call from before lunch from her Senior Editor, who said Spurl was in a state over the missing critiques. Shelby explained that she had personally placed them in Miss Myers' loving hands only a few minutes ago. "Well," Janet said, "I guess you've had your trauma for the day."

She went through a couple of stories, sent one back to a reader with cogent comments, and put the other aside to reread later.

Today had started out a beautiful day, with a pastel sky and pastel trees and splashes of unexpected color along the roadsides. The season of dandelions and wild mustard was waning, and the time of violets and woodland geraniums and lilacs had come center stage. Then, mid-morning, the sky had closed down, bringing a gray, damp chill. There would probably be rain by nightfall.

Sometimes she wished life could be like a short story. Neat, clear, and succinct. Have a problem, in twenty minutes it's solved and everyone has—hopefully—grown a little. But real life was complex, and seldom clear, and certainly not neat. Real life was full of mud, fog, and subtlety.

What the hell was she going to do about the maid of honor situation? And that was only the beginning. Someone was bound to hate the bridesmaids' dresses, or not fit into the shoes, or be afraid she looked hideous in whatever color Shelby chose. Ray would come up with more ushers than she had bridesmaids, and they'd have to go searching frantically for another, someone she didn't know all that well, who would end up acting out hither-to-unsuspected streaks of depravity. She was going to forget to invite someone who would be offended, and hurt twenty-five feelings along the way. She would probably go for weeks without sleeping and throw up halfway down the aisle. Ray would get drunk the night before and forget to show up. Her jackass second cousin would try to throw them in the Country Club pool. The pictures would turn out to be awful—if they turned out at all—and everyone would get salmonella poisoning from the shrimp cocktail. And somehow it would end up all being Shelby's fault.

Her stomach was tied in knots just thinking about it. She wanted to run away and change her name and live the rest of her life deep in the woods where nobody would ever find her.

Marriage is going to be a snap, she thought, if I can make it through the wedding.

* * *

There was no getting around it, she had to call her mother. No doubt Libby already knew about the engagement, since she'd obviously engineered much of it. But it would look very strange if Shelby waited more than twenty-four hours to tell Mommy the good news. She hated it. Libby was going to grab this wedding and run with it like a fox raiding a chicken house. And unless she wanted to spend the next twelve months fighting with her mother, all Shelby could do was go along.

The thought of that gave the final touch to her headache. She pulled out of the traffic and headed down Maple to the A&P. The least she could do to comfort herself was stock up on aspirin.

As she wandered through the aisles wondering what to pick up for dinner, she remembered Monday night, when her headache sent her scrambling to Fran's apartment. She remembered the feeling of quiet and safety, and the comfort of hearing someone in the next room, and the peace of knowing no one could find her. It seemed a long time ago. Sighing, she plucked a box of hash brown potatoes from the shelf. Maybe, if she survived her mother's phone call, and then Ray's, she'd go give Fran a hand with her unpacking. If it wasn't obscenely late. It wouldn't be late if she didn't get into an argument. But if she didn't get into an argument she'd probably end up agreeing to something she hated.

She wondered what would happen if she left town.

"Well," said Libby, "congratulations, and I must say it's about time."

Shelby's hand tightened around the phone. "Best wishes," she said casually. "You congratulate the groom and wish the bride best wishes."

"I'm well aware of that, Miss Emily Post. In your case, I offer congratulations on seeing the light before that man got fed up and walked out on you."

"Well, I guess I did," she said, "because he didn't."

Libby's voice changed from icicle to cocoa. "I'm very, very happy for you, Shelby. Your father's going to be happy, too."

It was one of the great mysteries of her life that her mother, who had divorced her father five years ago—thereby risking a serious loss of social status—for reasons which had never been made clear to her, continued to be so concerned with what he would think. Granted, he was a frightening kind of person, but once she was out of the house he couldn't nail Libby to the wall with that cold, disapproving stare. Or maybe they just liked one another better now than they had when they were married. They didn't have the same friends any more, and didn't go to one another's family reunions—that little treat was left to Shelby—but they talked on the phone often, and sometimes went out together for dinner. And they always, always saw eye-to-eye where Shelby was concerned.

Sometimes she wondered if they were kept together by their mutual fear that she was going to do something that wouldn't Look Right. Maybe Get Her Name in the Paper. Or be an Old Maid. Or forget to write a thank-you note.

"Ray wants an engagement party," Shelby said. "At the country club."

"Really?" Libby was the only person Shelby knew who could try to sound wide-eyed with innocence over the phone.

"Yes." She stretched the telephone cord as far as it could go and barely managed to reach the scotch.

"That's a *wonderful* idea."

She noticed that her mother didn't ask her if *she* wanted it. She looked around for a glass. "So we should probably get together, the three of us, and make plans."

"Yes, we should. When were you thinking of having it?"

"Sometime in June."

"Oh, dear, June," Libby said. "The Club's usually booked solid in June. Weddings, you know."

"Oh," Shelby said, trying to sound wide-eyed herself. "I forgot." She found one, a dirty one from last night. It seemed to have contained water, not milk but she couldn't tell for sure. Well, any port in a storm. She poured herself a drink.

There was a paper-scratching Libby making notes noise from the other end of the line. "We should plan on one hundred-fifty to two-hundred guests, I suppose."

"Whoa," Shelby said. "Most of my college friends are pretty far away, and so are Ray's. We probably can't put together a party of fifteen."

"That's typical," said Libby in an exasperated tone. "What about my friends? What about your father's friends? And you have a few relatives, in case you'd forgotten."

She hadn't forgotten. She never had a chance to forget her relatives. "It's just an engagement party," she argued. "Not like the wedding reception. We don't have to invite everyone."

"Well, I wish you'd let me in on your magic secret for cutting the guest list."

She took a swallow of warm, probably contaminated scotch. "I didn't know there *was* a guest list already."

Her mother sighed. "I can see it's going to be like pulling teeth every inch of the way with you." She lowered her voice to indicate urgency and seriousness. "Shelby, this is one of the most important things you'll ever do. Years from now, you'll look back on your wedding day and everything that led up to it as the High Point of your Life. The time will Stick in your Memory Forever. Please, *please* try to make it a pleasant experience."

Her mother was right, in a way. At least it was one of the high points of *Libby's* life. No matter how much it annoyed her, she couldn't spoil this for her mother. Not when she'd been planning it practically from the moment Shelby was born. Even her graduation from college wasn't as important. And the masters' degree ceremonies were a definite low point. Libby was certain it had ruined Shelby's marital chances utterly and forever. It was surprising she hadn't hung a black wreath on the door. "You're right, Libby. I'm sorry."

"Leave everything to me, dear," Libby said happily.

"OK. Tell me what you need me to do, and I'll do it. The party doesn't have to be on a weekend, you know," Shelby went on. "Maybe the club could fit us in on a Thursday or something."

"No, this has to be super-special. There's nothing special about Thursdays. Except Thanksgiving, of course. Darling, let me get to work on this—I don't suppose there's anything I can do tonight, but first thing tomorrow morning. I'll phone you at the office."

"You don't have to do that," Shelby said. "I'll give you a call in the evening."

"I'm much too excited to wait," Libby said. "Love you, Sweetie. Kiss-kiss." She hung up.

She supposed she should call her father while she still had her telephone personality in place. Undoubtedly Libby already had, but she'd be expected to pretend she didn't know that.

She went to the refrigerator and added a few cubes of ice to her drink. She didn't want to call him. For one thing, she never knew *what* to call him. As a child she called him "Daddy." Now it struck her as babyish. "Father" sounded snooty and formal. There was no way she could think of him as a "Dad" or "Pop," much less "Papa." Even though Libby liked to be called by her first name—she thought it made her seem "hip"—that kind of familiarity was out where her father was concerned. Most people called him "Thomas." "Thomas Camden." All it lacked was a "Sir" or "Esquire." She ought to call him "Tom." "Tom Camden" had a breezy, slightly debauched sound. "Tom Camden, the town drunk."

Except that Sir Thomas Camden, Esquire, was far from being the town drunk. Sir Thomas Camden, Esquire, was an attorney, Harvard Law, and currently representing at least three major multi-million dollar corporations from his office in Philadelphia. His specialty was patent and copyright infringement, but when things were slow he would defend the companies in lawsuits brought by consumers who had been injured by products the companies knew perfectly well weren't safe.

Oh, don't start, she told herself roughly. Miss Righteous Indignation, as Libby would say.

Maybe he wouldn't even be home. Maybe she'd call three or four times and he wouldn't be there, and she could tell her mother she'd done her duty without having to talk to him.

"Hello," he said. Most people said "hello" like a question, with a rise of voice at the end. Thomas Camden said "hello" as if it were the last word on the subject.

"It's Shelby," she said. "I'm glad I caught you in."

"You won't find me out doing the cha-cha-cha until dawn at my age," he said, and chuckled a little. Which told her that his latest girlfriend was within earshot. "What's on your mind? Need money?"

"No, I just wanted to tell you...I'm engaged."

"Is that so?" His voice told her he'd already heard. "Anybody I know?"

"Ray," she said. "Ray Beeman. I've been going with him for two years."

He knew that, too, though she hadn't told him. He wasn't terribly interested in her day-to-day life, satisfied with the highlights Libby would pass along whether he wanted to hear them or not. Marriage, or the possibility of marriage, was one of those highlights.

"He's a doctor," she added.

"Beeman. Is that a Jewish name?"

"No." She wished it were. He'd probably change his will.

"Who are his people?"

"They live in Seattle. His father's in business of some kind."

"A company official?"

Shelby wanted to scream. "He went to Princeton," she said.

"Good, good."

"We're going to wait a year for the wedding, but we're having an engagement party at the club sometime in June."

"Well," he said heartily, "that's one I won't want to miss. Or weren't you planning to invite your old Dad?"

She wondered what the new girlfriend was like. In front of the last one, he'd been more formal and less jolly.

"You know you're invited," she said. She could hear the new girlfriend lighting a cigarette in the background. "Can you send me a list of the relatives you think I should ask? Or you could send it to Mother."

"You bet," he said even more heartily. This one must like things really upbeat. "Anything else I can do for you? Sure you don't need money?"

"I don't need money." She wasn't a college student any more, for God's sake. She was a grown woman. With a job. "But thanks for offering. See you soon."

As she hung up the phone, she felt like throwing things. Whether from frustration or desperation or anger, she couldn't tell. It was just all so…so…something. She drained her glass and carried it to the sink and washed it. She washed the rest of her dishes. She thought about defrosting the refrigerator. She thought about working, she thought about watching television. She swallowed a couple more aspirin. She leaned against the sink and considered taking up smoking.

The phone rang. It was Ray. His sins had caught up with him, he said, and he had to pay back three different residents by spending the weekend covering their shifts. He hoped she wouldn't mind, but they had a lifetime of weekends ahead of them, didn't they? She didn't mind. They said silly, mushy things to each other and hung up.

Shelby wondered if another couple of aspirin would make her sick.

There was a knock at the door. She opened it.

"Hi," Fran said. "I don't want to interrupt if you're busy, but I wanted to tell you I got a…" She broke off, staring at Shelby. "You look like the wrath of God. What's wrong?"

Shelby stood back and motioned for her to come in. "My family's driving me crazy."

"I think they're supposed to do that."

"I got engaged last night," she said, dropping into an armchair. "Engaged to be engaged, I mean. It's brought all the horrors out of the woodwork."

"Forgive me," Fran said as she settled onto the couch. "But are you sure it's horrors that come out of the woodwork? I always thought it was mice or termites or unpleasant people."

"It *is* unpleasant people. I happen to be related to them. Would you like a drink?"

Fran shook her head. "No, thanks. What are your horrors up to?"

"Ray and I decided we'd announce our engagement next month. Now my mother's engineering a massive, formal, humiliating party at the country club, and making me feel guilty for not wanting it. My father's impressing his new girlfriend by being relentlessly hearty and Papa-ish. And believe me, that man is no Papa."

"They sound like professionals," Fran said.

"*And,* to top it *all* off, my obvious choice for maid of honor is someone I'm not even sure I like at the moment."

"Nightmare," Fran said.

"All of which has added up to one big headache—figuratively and literally."

"Yep. You have that look."

"I should tell them to take a flying leap. God, parents. How do they manage to make us jump through hoops like this?"

"They get us when we're small."

"Yeah." Shelby ran her hand through her hair. "Enough about my exciting life. What's your news?"

"I have a job. Physician's assistant."

"That's great!"

"Well," Fran said, "it's great and it's not great. It's great to have the job, and it pays well, but it's with the Student Health Service, doing exactly what I've been doing for the last four years."

"But at least it's security while you look around."

"It is that. Shelby, have you eaten?"

"Sure."

"What?"

"Hash brown potatoes."

"That's it?"

She felt herself grow defensive. "I had all those phone calls to deal with, and I didn't feel too well." She shrugged. "Nerves, I guess."

"I think you should eat."

"I'm not hungry."

"Irrelevant," Fran said. She got up and headed toward the kitchen. "I'm going to make you something."

"You don't have to…"

"Oh, be quiet. Get out of your work clothes. I think I can handle this."

It was only canned soup and crackers, but it helped. Her headache receded. Or maybe it wasn't the food. Maybe it was having a sane conversation with a sane individual. Fran shared more Army stories. Shelby said it sounded wretched, with the hours and the lines and people yelling at you all the time and marching in rain and sleeping in mud.

Fran said it was only hard for the first couple of weeks. After that, you had no mind left and didn't care what happened to you.

Then she changed the subject. "Look," she said, "I know it's none of my business, but I really am worried about those headaches of yours."

"It's just tension," Shelby said quickly. "And fatigue. I don't sleep well. Haven't for months. Years. I think maybe it's a personality trait."

"Do you have any odd sensations, like tingling or seeing things or strange smells?"

Shelby shook her head.

"Ever feel sick to your stomach?"

"Sometimes."

"And you have them a couple of times a week?"

"At least."

"Any particular time of day?"

"No," Shelby said, and laughed.

"How long do they usually last?"

"A while. It varies."

"Does drinking help?"

"Sometimes. Really, it's just tension."

"Maybe it is, and maybe not. I wouldn't worry about it if they didn't make you sick. There could be something seriously wrong. Like early migraines, or even the start of more sinister things."

She started to toss it off, then realized her hands were shaking. She folded them, but Fran had probably noticed. "I know," she said.

"I'm surprised Ray hasn't gotten on you about it."

"I haven't told him," she said before she realized how that would sound. She wanted to stop talking about this. Right now. Every time she had to look at it, every time she went below the level of aspirin and tension, she wanted to run.

Fran's hands closed over hers. "Have you talked with anyone? Someone who could tell you what's going on?"

Shelby shook her head.

"Why not?"

Shelby shrugged.

"Afraid of what you'll find out?"

"I guess so." Be honest, she told herself. She wants to help. "Yes."

"I figured," Fran said gently. "But, Shelby, the worst that can happen is finding out what you fear is true. The best is that you'll find out there's nothing to worry about. This way you're living with the worst."

"You're very sensible."

"And probably insensitive," Fran said. "If I were in your shoes, I wouldn't want me being sensible. I'd want me running in circles and screaming hysterically."

Shelby smiled. "Don't do it. There's a two-month old baby upstairs. You *really* don't want to wake him."

"So what do you say?" Fran squeezed her hands.

"I just hate the idea of everyone knowing, and talking, and asking all the time…"

"Nobody has to know. You make an appointment with a neurologist. You find out what there is to find out, and then do whatever you want with the information."

She could feel anxiety rising.

"Do you know a neurologist?"

Shelby shook her head. The inside of her face felt brittle.

"That's no problem," Fran said. "I can get some names from work…"

"I don't know, Fran. I don't think I can cope with that right now, making appointments, going through it, on top of everything. It seems like too much."

"I'll make the appointment for you, and come with you if you want. You won't have to do anything." She released her hands. "When you're ready, just tell me. I won't mention it again, I promise."

"Yeah, but every time I look at you I'll be thinking about it."

"Well, *I* won't. The subject is closed." Fran got up and started clearing the table. "Are you tied up Saturday and Sunday?"

Shelby carried dishes to the sink. "No, Ray has to work."

"Ever been camping?"

"Only summer camp. But that was pretty fancy. Cabins and plumbing, music lessons. They didn't even have mosquitoes. Not like camping with a tent and cooking over a fire and animals crashing through the underbrush."

"Want to try it?" Fran ran hot water in the sink.

As long as she could remember, she'd wanted to go camping. Real camping. "I sure do."

"Great. It'll give me a chance to show off what the Army taught me."

"Really? You want me to go camping?"

"Saturday morning. We can come back Sunday evening."

"I'll probably be completely useless."

Fran laughed. "Beginners are excellent people to camp with."

"How come?"

"They do all the boring things and don't even know they're boring."

Shelby took the washed and rinsed the plate Fran handed her and reached for the towel. "What should I bring?"

"Just yourself. I have everything we need, compliments of Uncle Sam." She looked Shelby up and down. "Do you have any knock-around clothes, or do you always dress as if you were about to meet the public?"

"I was wearing knock-around clothes when you met me."

"This is true. It was what I liked about you right off. You should have rain gear, just in case. I haven't heard any forecasts, but I wouldn't trust them, anyway. There's a good Army surplus store over in West Sayer. I checked them out."

"I know the place."

"Just be comfortable. Especially your shoes. If you have hiking boots, fine. But don't bring new ones. Believe me, next to the Army, camping is the worst possible place to break in new boots."

Shelby smiled. She was very glad she knew this woman.

* * *

"Camping?" Connie asked with a puzzled frown.

Shelby laughed. "What, you think I'm a hot-house flower? You think I can't rough it?"

"I'm sure you can," Connie said. "You've just never expressed any interest in camping."

"I went to summer camp. I told you that, didn't I?"

"Yes," Lisa said. "But you said it was like boarding school, and you were homesick the whole time."

"Yeah, I was. But that was different, and I was just a kid." And an unhappy kid, who didn't know where she belonged but knew it wasn't with four hundred gleeful, well-adjusted girls who weren't afraid of horses and could dive like Olympians before they even got there, and who were always running around organizing chamber music ensembles. Even the little ones cared more for their violins and flutes than their pocket knives. Once, one of the other girls, someone she'd never even met, someone younger than herself, had caught her out behind the dining room, crying, and had lectured her on how she should appreciate the opportunities her parents were giving her, not sit around crying like a baby. There was only one girl in the camp who seemed to like her, but she was older and Shelby couldn't remember her name.

"So are you going with a bunch of people, or what?" Lisa asked.

"Just Fran and me."

Lisa looked terrified. "What if something happens?"

Shelby had to smile. Lisa firmly believed that the safest place to be when faced with natural disaster, civil disorder, or act of God was in the middle of a crowd.

"I guess we'll handle it," Shelby said, "or die."

"I want you to call me the minute you get back," Lisa said. "No matter what hour of day or night."

She knew Lisa was really frightened, and it touched her. "I will. I promise."

"I'm going to be a wreck the whole weekend."

"We're not leaving until Saturday," Shelby said.

"She'll be all right," Jean said to Lisa. "I've been camping. The worst that can happen is severe discomfort."

"It can't be any more dangerous than being a white girl living in Kenya during the Mau Mau uprisings," Penny said.

Shelby looked at her. "You did that?"

"For a couple of weeks, then we were called Stateside and reassigned to Europe."

"It must have been hideous," Connie said, leaning forward eagerly, loving a grisly story. "Weren't you terrified?"

"I was too young to get what was really going on. Our cook disappeared one night. My mother said she'd gone back to her village. And one of the chauffeurs was beheaded."

Lisa gasped.

"I didn't see it. I just heard about it. But I was scared enough to be glad to get out of there."

With a twinge of guilt, Shelby realized how much she didn't know about Penny. She'd meant to spend more time with her outside of work, and now that Connie had taken that ridiculous attitude about her…But the time had slipped away. As Libby was fond of saying, the road to Hell was paved with Shelby's good intentions.

"What do you *do*," Lisa asked with a little shudder, "camping?"

"I don't know," Shelby said. "Read and hike and cook over a fire, I guess."

"What if it rains?" Connie put in.

"Fran said she'd teach me to play gin rummy."

"You sit in a tent, on the ground…"

"On sleeping bags," Shelby said.

"And play gin rummy?"

"That's what she said."

Lisa shrieked and pulled fistfuls of her hair. "I will *never*," she said, "commit a sin so heinous that I'm forced to do penance by going camping."

Shelby laughed. "Lisa, you're one of a kind."

"The whole idea strikes terror into my extroverted heart."

"Well," Shelby said, "I have to admit I'm a little nervous. I don't want to make a fool of myself."

"A *fool* of yourself ! You'll be lucky to get back alive, much *less* with your dignity intact. This thing has 'fool of yourself' written all over it."

"Oh, come on," Jean said with a laugh. "It's a *camping* trip. People do it all the time."

"I don't like the woods at night," Lisa said.

"What's the matter?" Connie asked. "Afraid someone will jump out at you?"

"Yes!" Lisa insisted. "Me!"

They all laughed at that. "Lisa's a city kid," Connie explained to Penny. "She grew up in New York. When she first came here, she didn't even know how to drive a car."

"I still don't," Lisa said, "very well."

"Of all the things I associate with New York," Connie said in a teasing way, "understatement was never one of them." She pushed her chair back. "Anybody want anything from the trough?"

"Not me," Shelby said, looking down at her half-finished lunch, at the wilting lettuce and overcooked canned peas and gray-brown meat of unknown origin. "I've punished my gastro-intestinal system enough for one day." She plucked the corner of a slice of meat with her fork and examined its underside. "Have any of you seen the papers lately?"

"No," Connie said. "Why?"

She let the meat flop back onto the plate. "I wondered if there was a serial killer in the area."

Lisa shrieked and knocked over her glass of water with her elbow.

"You know," Jean said as she picked up her brown paper bag and mopped at the spill, "if word ever gets out about the cooking at *The Magazine for Women,* our credibility is shot."

"Maybe they should fire the food editor and hire you," Connie said with a wink.

Jean shook her head. "I just want to run the kitchen here. And make all you slaves eat *my* cooking."

"The magazine would save a mint on lunches," Penny said. "Everyone would bring their own."

They loaded their dishes onto trays, clearing the table for the bridge game. Shelby caught Penny's arm. "Listen, I have some shopping to do over here after work. Do you want to have a drink?"

Penny blushed deeply. "Of course. Would you like to come to my place? I'll make us some supper."

"That'd be great." Penny could go on ahead to cook, while she shopped. She didn't want anyone with her on this trip to the Army Surplus store. She wanted to be alone, to take it all in and enjoy it without being watched.

Her friends would probably be shocked. She was more excited about a trip to a camping store than she would be over the Christmas "Messiah" sing-along.

Connie was coming back to the table, cards in hand. "Bridge time," she said. "You in?"

"Sure. Just let me clear my stuff." She pulled her dishes together. "Who's out?"

"Lisa. She offered to help clean out the supply cabinet."

"There's trouble."

"Tell me about it," Connie said with a heavenward roll of her eyes. "She's such a...a..."

"Klutz?" Shelby offered.

"Klutz. Sometimes I worry about her."

"You worry about everyone, Con. Your maternal instincts are out of control."

"Well, just remember," Connie said, "Mother's Day is nearly here. Don't go to any trouble. Something extravagant will do."

"Oh, God, what am I going to get Libby?"

"Libby's easy to buy for."

"Not for me. I always get the wrong thing."

"Set a price limit and give me *carte blanche*, and I'll pick up something."

"You would? Really?"

"Easy as pie," Connie said, and snapped her fingers. "So put it out of your mind."

"I had."

"Random forgetting is not wise. Getting someone else to do it and *then* forgetting is wise."

"Yes, Mother."

"Respect and obedience," Connie said approvingly. "Excellent qualities."

"Seriously," Shelby said, "I really do appreciate it."

"I know." Connie patted her arm. "When it comes to your mother, your IQ drops fifty points." She sighed. "Next time I create the world, I'm going to do away with the whole parental thing. When it's time to breed, we'll lay eggs by a spring and wander off into the desert." She leaned close to Shelby. "By the way, you're doing a great job with Jean." She shuffled the cards. "Now, get rid of your dishes and prepare to be humiliated."

* * *

Except for the clerk with the voice that would register on the Richter scale, the Army Surplus store was everything she'd hoped. Foot lockers piled halfway to the ceiling. Cardboard boxes spilling olive drab web belts into the aisles. Metal canteens and mess kits. Compasses and knapsacks. Ammunition cases. Topographic maps. Bandanas. Boot laces. Cookstoves. Wool socks. Gas masks. Worn Army jackets, some with names still on them. Spray cans of waterproofing for canvas. Collapsible aluminum drinking cups and water purification kits. Lanyards and whistles. Tight metal cases holding water proof matches. Sentry first aid kits in red and white metal boxes. Zippo windproof lighters. Service ribbons. Handbooks teaching wilderness survival. Army shoes and paratroopers' high black boots. Trench shovels and hatchets and axes. Navy blue balaclavas. Machetes. Wood and canvas cots. Everything looked and smelled sturdy, clean, and useful.

It was a good thing she'd made a date with Penny. She might be tempted to stay here forever. Simply being here, surrounded by forbidden treasures, made her feel calm. Her mother would be horrified. Maybe she should pick up a little something for Libby while she was here. An olive drab flashlight that hooked over your belt would make a nice accessory. She could wear it to the country club. Or how about a nested stainless steel knife-fork-and-spoon kit in its own olive drab case? Always in good taste. Or a floppy olive drab fatigue hat with sewn-on mosquito netting. Or a lovely pair of worn olive drab slacks that had once belonged to a soldier who was probably killed on Guadalcanal.

She was losing control of herself, never a good idea when dealing with matters Libby-esque. Libby just didn't have a sense of humor about some things. Especially things involving her daughter doing or owning anything masculine, crude, or "unladylike." In fact, Libby would not have a happy attitude about this entire camping trip.

She ran her finger down the sharp blade of a Bowie knife. You could do serious damage with this knife. Skin a rabbit, cut branches from trees, slice meat, open a vein…

She put the knife down and found the ponchos, chose an olive drab one. She took the poncho and a knapsack to the counter and paid for them, and—telling herself it was an afterthought even though it really wasn't—picked up a Swiss Army knife. At least, with a pocketknife, she wouldn't look like a total novice.

Chapter 6

"Where's your stuff?" Penny asked as she opened the door.

"I left it in the car."

"Didn't you want to show me? Connie always wants to show everything she buys. So does Lisa. Jean doesn't, but I don't think Jean buys things. She makes them."

Shelby went to the sofa and kicked off her shoes. "This wasn't anything special. Just some rain gear."

"For the camping trip?" She poured Shelby a whiskey sour and handed it to her.

"Yep. Thanks." She took a sip. "This is great."

"It's your mother's recipe."

"My mother, the cocktail queen."

Penny poured herself a drink and settled beside her. "I hope you'll have nice weather this weekend. I haven't heard any forecasts."

"They never commit themselves this far in advance. How's it going in the readers' room?"

"OK, I guess." Penny propped her feet on the coffee table and frowned into her drink. "I miss having you there, though."

"Hey," Shelby said with a little laugh. "I haven't left the planet. My door's always open."

Penny looked at her shyly. "It isn't just because of work."

"A problem of any kind. I'm always glad to see you."

"Darn it." Penny kicked at the table and jumped up and scurried into the kitchen. "That's not what I mean." If the kitchen had had a door, she'd have slammed it.

Shelby started to get up, then thought better of it. The kitchen was tiny. She didn't want Penny to feel trapped. Trapped people often did things that were out of character and a humiliation to themselves for the rest of their lives.

"I just miss having you around," Penny said, coming back to the living room with big eyes and onion dip.

"I miss seeing you, too. Things get hectic." Shelby turned the glass in her hands. "Time gets away."

Penny looked down at the onion dip. "I don't know why I made this. If we don't have dinner soon, it'll be midnight, for God's sake."

"Would you like to go out?"

"No! I've been slaving over a hot meatloaf all evening."

"I love meatloaf."

"So you've said," Penny said with a satisfied grin.

"Uh…you didn't get Libby's recipe for that, did you?"

"No." Penny went back to the kitchen. "I've heard you on the subject of your mother's meatloaf."

"My mother has a mutant cooking gene. It's a good thing she can afford help."

She looked around Penny's loft apartment. It hadn't changed since the first time she was here. There were still no pictures, no knick knacks, no magazines or half-written letters, nothing personal. It reminded her of a freshly-cleaned motel room. "I see you still haven't finished unpacking," she said, and hoped it was tactful. "Would you like me to help?"

Penny poked her head into the room. "I'm done, but thanks, anyway."

OK. Maybe Penny preferred it this way. Maybe she felt more at home in places she could walk out of with a minimum of fuss if there was a Mau Mau uprising. There was no law that said you had to impose your identity on everything you touched.

Still, it made her feel odd.

"So," Penny called over the clatter of plates, "When do we get to meet this woman?"

"Fran? Soon, I guess. We should all do something together some time."

"Great. Although vague." She brought knives and forks and spread them out on the coffee table.

Shelby felt a prickle in her stomach at the shadow of sarcasm in Penny's voice. "What?"

Penny turned to her and smiled. "I can't wait to meet her, that's all. You seem to think a lot of her."

"I hardly know her."

"Well enough to go camping," Penny said, and smiled again.

The smile didn't fool her this time. Penny was jealous. Shelby's heart went out to her. Jealousy was such a twisting, aching kind of emotion. "It's not a big thing," she said. "I've never gone camping before and I'm curious, that's all. I'll probably make a complete idiot of myself and spend the next year trying to avoid her out of shame and embarrassment."

"Not you," Penny said. She put their plates down and went back to the kitchen for the serving dishes.

In addition to the meat loaf there were scalloped potatoes, homemade, not the boxed kind, and a salad. "How did you manage all this," Shelby asked, "in that tiny kitchen?"

"In stages. All I really had to do tonight was make the salad and defrost and heat up the other things. What would you like to drink?"

"Water, please. So you're like a Boy Scout, always prepared. Frozen meals on tap in case a group of twelve drops in."

"Hardly." Penny handed her a glass of ice water and opened a ginger ale for herself. "I've been working on it for weeks. Well, not *weeks* weeks. Maybe two weeks. I knew sooner or later I was going to ask you to dinner. I wanted to be ready in case it was a spur of the moment thing."

"I'm flattered," Shelby said.

"Good," Penny said. "I want to make you feel special."

Shelby was stumped. "You do" seemed too personal, almost seductive. And "No need, I know I'm special" was not only untrue, but just plain—well, unacceptable. She settled for the ambiguous "Thank you."

"Dig in," Penny said. "It's a long time until fall. An expression of my father's. I haven't the vaguest idea what it means. Something agrarian, probably. His grandfather was a farmer, and all the kids had to work the farm. They stayed home from school in the fall to do the harvesting, and in the spring to do the planting. It took him an extra year to finish elementary school because of it."

And Penny was off and running. For two hours, she talked about her family, the places she'd lived, the things that had happened there. At eleven o'clock, the coffee shop downstairs closed. The crashing of garbage can lids reminded Shelby that she still had to drive home, call Ray—she should call her mother, but that was one thing too many tonight—and get enough sleep to be a functional human being in the morning.

They said good-night quickly. Penny refused help with the dishes. "I've enjoyed tonight," Shelby said. "We'll have to do it again."

Penny beamed.

Mist was hovering over the corn fields, softly lit by the three-quarter moon. The trees were starkly black against a faint gray sky. A few stars penetrated the humidity with fluttering light. Shreds of yellow mist wandered through the light from the street lamps.

Shelby turned off the radio and listened to the wind blowing in the car window. She was exhausted, but it had been a good evening. She wasn't just being polite when she said she'd like to repeat it.

The thing that bothered her was, even though Penny had talked all evening about herself, Shelby didn't feel she knew her any better now than she had before.

* * *

She was waiting in the alley behind the house when Fran showed up driving a year-old powder blue Chevy Super Sport with the top down.

"Hey," Shelby said, "when did you get this?"

Fran shoved the gear into park and got out, leaving the motor running. "Wednesday. Like it?"

"Who wouldn't?"

"I saved up for this the whole time I was in the service." She picked up Shelby's knapsack and tossed it into the back with the rest of the camping equipment.

Shelby opened the passenger door and slid in. "It makes you look like Nancy Drew."

"Good." Fran got behind the wheel and tossed her a road map. "Think you can navigate?"

"I can if I know where we're going."

"This red dot," Fran said as she leaned over and pointed, "is Bass Falls. And this green one is the state forest. We have to get from A to B."

"Can do," Shelby said.

Fran put the car in gear. "My friend Anna and I used to argue about Nancy Drew and Judy Bolton all the time when we were kids. She claimed Judy Bolton was the better detective, because Nancy Drew always had all those chums helping her and a father who knew everything, but I think it was just because Judy Bolton's hair was the same color as Anna's. "

"Personally," Shelby said, consulting her map, "I think Nancy Drew was better written. There are plot holes in Judy Bolton you could drive a truck through. Turn right onto Route 8."

"Right? Are you sure?"

"Positive."

Fran pulled over to the side of the road. "Let me see."

Shelby tucked the map out of sight. "Are you going to trust me or not?"

"Yeah, sure, OK," Fran said with a nervous laugh. "I'm sorry. I just don't want anything to go wrong."

"Nothing's going to go wrong." There was a baseball cap in the well between the seats. She crammed it on Fran's head. "At least not in the map department."

Fran settled the cap onto her head and straightened the beak and pulled out into traffic. She signalled for a left turn.

"*Right*," Shelby said. "Turn *right*."

"Oops." Fran wrenched on the steering wheel and cut a sharp turn clockwise. Her back tire caught the curb for a second. She glanced over. "Seat belt."

"What?"

"Fasten your seat belt, please. If I hit a bump, I don't want you flying off into the treetops."

She snapped the buckle and pulled it tight. "We're not going to survive this, are we?"

"Probably not," Fran said. "Unless I get a grip on myself."

"Pull over."

Fran did. "Now what?"

"What's the matter with you?"

"I want everything to be perfect."

Shelby shook her head. "Everything doesn't have to be perfect. But it will be extremely imperfect if you kill us before we get there. Automobile accidents are not my idea of fun."

"Shucks," Fran said.

"So will you just relax?"

"Give me a minute." She put her hands on the steering wheel and rested her head on them and took a few deep breaths. "OK. I can do this."

Shelby laughed. "I hope so. Because if you're too nervous to put up a tent, we're going to be in serious trouble.

"Tents," Fran sneered. "I eat tents for breakfast."

"I think you eat *tense* for breakfast would be more accurate."

Fran rolled her eyes. "Oh, boy."

"Our entire civilization stands or falls on accuracy of expression."

"Should I write that down?"

"Only after the car has come to a complete stop."

"Nancy Drew's better written, huh?" Fran said. "Is that your professional judgment?"

Shelby nodded.

"Wait'll I tell Anna."

"It's a little late to settle the argument, isn't it?"

"It continues."

The day was warm, the air soft. An unusual May day of light and dryness, more like June or August. They were in open country. Fran pressed down on the accelerator. Shelby watched her. One elbow resting the window ledge, Fran held the steering wheel firmly and lightly in both hands. She drove smoothly, with a sense of instinctive competence. It reminded Shelby of the day Fran had built the fire. Again she was fascinated by her hands. They'd never be rough, or weak, or clumsy. Whatever those hands did they would do perfectly, whatever they held would be safe.

"I think you'll like this campground," Fran said. "Well, maybe you won't, but if you like camping, you should."

Shelby turned sideways in her seat so she could see her. "How come you know so much about this state when you just moved here?"

"I've been driving around sight-seeing since I got the car." She hesitated. "That's not entirely the truth. I checked it out. I wanted to be sure it was an OK place and not the back side of the town dump." She glanced over at Shelby. "You know, the perfect thing. God, I'm such a jerk."

"Want to hear, jerk? I was afraid you'd laugh at my knapsack."

"Why would I do that?"

"Because it's new."

"So?"

"So I wanted you to think I was cool and experienced."

"You already told me you'd never been camping before."

"Well, maybe I wanted you to think I was experienced at doing things I've never done before."

Fran grinned. "I think it's time to take another look at the map."

"Right on 23," she said, glancing down. "How long will it take us to get there?"

"About an hour, unless you want to stop for ice cream."

"Do you?" Shelby asked.

"Doesn't matter. How about you?"

Shelby thought it over. "No. This is a camping trip. Ice cream isn't appropriate."

Fran grinned. "That was the right answer."

"Is this a test?"

"Tests happen," Fran said. She reached over and patted Shelby's knee. "Don't worry. Another one might not happen for five years."

Five years. In five years she'd be an experienced married matron, probably with children. She probably wouldn't be working. She'd be taking care of kids and waiting for Ray to come home from the office. Serving on the hospital auxiliary, organizing volunteers and candy-stripers. What the hell was she going to do with herself the rest of the time? Redecorate the living room? She didn't care what living rooms looked like, as long as you could be comfortable in them. Leaf through magazines? Hang out by the country club pool and drink?

"What's wrong?" Fran asked.

"I was just thinking."

"Doesn't look as if you were enjoying it."

"I was thinking about the future. I can't imagine it."

"Those who can't imagine the future," Fran said, "are doomed to repeat it."

"Do you plan to get married soon, or do you want to have a career first?"

"I'm still waiting for the impulse to strike."

"I guess that was a really stupid thing for me to say," Shelby said. "How can you know that in a vacuum? Are you seeing anyone?"

"Not at the moment."

"Do you mind?"

"Not in the least."

There was a tightness around Fran's mouth. I put my foot in it, Shelby thought. She probably went into the Army to escape a miserable break-up of a heart-wrenching love affair. Nice going, Camden. "Fran?"

She glanced over. "Yeah?"

"I'm sorry."

"What for?"

"I think what I was talking about…I think it upset you."

Fran laughed. "Upset? You've got to be kidding."

"I…"

"If I were truly upset, I'd be desperately twisting that radio knob looking for Brahms."

"Brahms?"

"That's what I do when I'm upset or depressed. I play solitaire and listen to Brahms."

"Why Brahms?"

"He doesn't try to force you to feel what he wants. Not like Tschaikovsky. God help you if you don't go along with *his* angst. Mozart's too cute. Debussy's incomprehensible." She shrugged. "I guess I just like Brahms. What do you do when you're depressed?"

"I think maybe I drink," Shelby said.

"Better watch it. That stuff can turn on you." She glanced over and smiled. "As a matter of fact, so can Brahms."

"You've been that depressed?"

"I've been on this earth for twenty-five years," Fran said. "Of course I've been that depressed."

"What's the most depressed you've ever been?"

"Two symphonies, five concertos, variations on Haydn, and double-deck Idiot's Delight. How about you?"

"A pint of cheap Vodka, straight from the bottle."

Fran shuddered. "That's serious depression. What caused it?"

"Love. How about you?"

"Love."

They laughed together.

"What I could never figure out," Fran said, "is how you tell the difference between love and anxiety. They feel about the same."

They were in open country now, with fields on each side covered with the pale green fuzz of early hay seedlings. Trees were in leaf, but their color hadn't yet deepened. The air was pungent with the smell of earth. There were no more turns for several miles. Shelby leaned back in her seat and let her mind wander.

Thirty-six hours, and nothing to do in them but what was needed and what she wanted. She couldn't do anything about weddings or engagement parties or guest lists or people's feelings. No telephone, no electricity. Her mother thought she was with Ray. Ray thought she was working late to catch up with things at the office. She hoped they didn't get together and compare notes.

Now that she thought of it, that possibility burrowed into her mind with a drill of apprehension. "Oh, God," she said out loud.

"What?"

"I lied about this trip. My friends know where I am, but my mother and Ray…"

"Is either of them likely to run into your friends?"

"No."

"Then there's no problem."

"They might contact one another," Shelby said. "I told them different stories."

Fran smiled and shook her head. "What's the matter with your mother knowing? Would she try to come along?"

That almost made her laugh. "Not in a thousand years. She just wouldn't think it was the kind of thing a person ought to do. Unless they were desperate."

"Tell her you were desperate. You seem desperate to me."

"It's not funny. This could be a real mess," Shelby said, her anxiety taking a serious leap.

"Just tell everyone you told them the truth as you knew it at that time and let them sort it out."

"Maybe…"

"As long as you don't make a lot of it, they won't. You don't have to check in with your mother every time you change your plans, do you?"

"But Jean and Lisa and Connie and Penny, they know I've been excited about this all week."

Fran glanced over at her. "Have you? Really?"

"Of course. I've wanted to do this my whole life."

"Look," Fran said, "let me make a suggestion. Put the panic on the back burner, and while we're driving home we'll discuss every possible thing that might go wrong, and what to do about it."

"I could call and tell them the truth. I could swear my friends to secrecy."

Fran laughed. "*Shelby*. It's *your* life. You're going camping for one night. That's not a mortal sin."

Shelby pulled on her ear nervously. "I'm being silly, aren't I?"

"You are, a little. But you probably have a perfectly good reason."

"I doubt it."

"I see. You work yourself into a state of anxiety because you just plain enjoy it."

"Of course I do," Shelby said. "It feels like love."

The campground was tucked back in the woods deep in the state forest. Hemlocks and birch and pine and wild laurel formed wind breaks around patches of cleared ground. A stone fireplace stood near each site, and metal garbage cans with lids fastened with a chain and S-hooks. Across the dirt road, sunlight glinted on a lake. There was a slight breeze carrying the scents of earth and pine and dust. A chipmunk squeaked a warning or a welcome, and dove into the remains of an old stone wall.

Fran stopped the car. The dust caught up with them and settled around them. "Like it?" she asked.

"It's magnificent."

"There are a couple of drawbacks. We have to go down to the beach for water and facilities."

"That's not a drawback," Shelby said. "It beats hunting for a spring and digging a hole."

"Second drawback, because the park isn't officially open, there's no cut wood yet. We have to gather our own."

"I'm great with wood."

"I know, but there's not much glamour in picking up twigs."

Shelby laughed. "If I wanted glamour, I'd have spent the weekend with my mother. Stop worrying."

"OK," Fran said as she got out of the car. "You asked for it." She pointed to a large canvas tarpaulin. "Start unloading."

The tent was airy and warm and smelled like the Army Surplus store. Shelby slipped off her shoes so she wouldn't puncture the canvas, and felt the little bumps and stones of the ground beneath the floor. "We're really doing this, aren't we?" she said.

"We're really doing it." Fran went back to the car and returned with two sleeping bags and two rolls of foam rubber. "Your bed," she said, tossing one set on the ground to her left. "My bed." She dropped the other set on her right.

Shelby unrolled the foam rubber pads and spread them out side-by-side.

"If it gets cold," Fran said as she arranged the sleeping bags, "these can zip together. That way we combine our body heat. But we're talking about it going below freezing, and I don't see that happening. Did you bring a pillow?"

"I forgot."

"You can use your clothes." She ran to the car and retrieved their knap-sacks. Fran's was faded and shapeless and had "Jarvis" stencilled on it.

"Did you use that in the Army?" Shelby asked.

"Sure did. If you want, I'll mark your name on yours after we get home." She looked at Shelby and grinned. "If we survive, that is."

"We'll survive. I have no doubt about it." The whole thing had taken less than an hour, and Fran had packed the car so that every bit of equipment was available when they were ready for it. "I think you're the most organized per-son I ever met."

"No, I've made more than enough mistakes in my time." She sat down on her sleeping bag. "Try your bed."

Shelby stretched out on the sleeping bag. It was hard, but not as hard as she expected.

"If we were going to stay longer," Fran said, "I'd have had us dig hip holes under the floor. But I guess we can live with a little stiffness for one night."

"Absolutely," Shelby said. She looked back over her head at the triangular window covered in mosquito screening. She could see the sky, and clouds, and a feathery limb of the pine. "It's like living in the trees."

"I guess it is." Fran was looking at her in a lighthearted, affectionate way. "You do like this, don't you?"

"I love it." She got to her feet. "Let's finish putting stuff away and go exploring."

They unloaded the Coleman lantern and set it up in the tent. The kitchen equipment was stowed in a canvas duffel bag. Fran set the axe in a stump and found a shady spot for the water container.

"I think," Shelby said when Fran indicated they were finished, "you forgot something."

Fran looked around. "I did?"

"You know. Like—food?"

"It's in the trunk of the car. From the way the garbage can lids are fastened down, I'd guess they have bears around here. Or at least raccoons."

"Do you really think there might be bears?"

"If there are, we'll know it. They're clumsy, and they smell to high heaven. But they can rip a food chest apart faster than you can watch."

"Would you think I was stupid if I said I hope we see one?"

Fran smiled. "I'd like to see one, too. But from a distance, thank you."

They found a foot trail that wasn't too muddy, filled a canteen from the pump by the lake, and trudged off into the laurel single-file. Shelby kept her eyes on the trail, avoiding tree roots that could trip her and smooth stones she could slip off of and do serious damage to her ankles. They were going uphill at a steep angle. Her sneakers felt insubstantial and weren't doing a thing to support her. She envied Fran's scuffed, sturdy, crepe-soled boots that held her ankles and gripped the rocks and generally prevented disaster. Before they did this again, she was going to get hiking boots. First thing after work Monday. And spend at least an hour each day breaking them in. She could do that while she was talking to Ray on the phone. Maybe she should get a longer phone cord. A very long phone cord. Then she could walk, and wash dishes, and do all sorts of useful things.

She didn't notice that Fran had stopped ahead, and crashed into her.

"Oops!" Fran said. "Daydreaming?"

"Sort of." Shelby was embarrassed. And, now that she had stopped, aware that she was breathing hard.

Fran opened the canteen and handed it to her. "It's my fault. I'm leading this like a forced march. We'll rest a minute, and then you lead. I'll try not to walk on your heels."

"I'm just out of shape."

"And I'm just out of the Army."

Shelby looked around and realized they were standing in a shower of sunlight. Tall grass grew in the clearing, and an occasional pasture juniper. Buttercups sparkled in the sun, and wild violets made a white-and-purple border separating the clearing from the woods beyond. "Somebody must have farmed up here," she said. "And this is all that's left. Isn't that amazing? Whole lives, people with plans, and ideas, and fears. Families. Don't you wonder what they talked about on winter nights?"

"Do you think we could find the old cellar hole?"

"We can try." At the edge of the woods Shelby saw what looked like a fallen stone wall. "Over here," she said, and trudged across the open space.

Fran trotted after her. "What did you see?"

"The wall."

"That's a wall?" Fran looked down at the pile of large gray stones and white stones, lichens, decayed leaves and creeper.

"It was. You probably don't have stone walls in California."

"Not like this." She knelt down to examine it. "This is what Robert Frost was talking about?"

"Probably. There were stone fences like these around all the old farms."

"Didn't they have anything better to do with their time?"

"They didn't have anything better to do with their rocks. A lot of the land around here was left behind by the glaciers. Dig down and you come to bedrock pretty quickly. The farmers claim the rocks grow like potatoes over the winter and surface with the spring thaw."

"What kind of rocks are they?"

"Mostly granite and basalt. Maybe shale." She knelt beside Fran and picked up a large milky, slightly translucent stone. "This is quartz. There's a lot of it around here."

Fran took the stone from her and turned it over and over in her hands. "It's beautiful." She gazed around. "How old do you think this farm is?"

"More than a hundred years, certainly." She studied the trees. "The woods are mostly pine going to hemlock with a few maples and birches. That happens when it's been undisturbed for 100 to 150 years." She ran her hand through her hair. "High school geography. I can't believe I still remember that."

"I wonder what it was like," Fran said, still holding the stone. "Living out here. How did they survive?"

"Not easily. You should see an old cemetery. Most of the kids didn't live into their teens, and the women were worn out by thirty-five."

"And the men?"

"Most used up three or four wives."

"Why am I not surprised?" Fran said. She looked from the rock into the deep woods, then back to the rock in her hands. Thoughtfully, wonderingly.

Shelby felt a sudden jolt, as if everything in her had stopped. As if someone had punched her hard in the stomach, taking away her breath.

Fran's face was in profile. The sunlight turned the tips of her eyelashes to gold. Her short-cut hair caught the breeze in tiny feathers. Already she was beginning to tan. Her features were soft but distinct. She had turned her attention inward, as if trying to listen to the voices of the stones. But her face was filled with life. Shelby had never seen anyone so completely present.

She thought she could look at her all day. She wanted time to stop. She wanted to study every feature of Fran's face and imprint it forever in her memory.

She's beautiful, she thought.

Fran turned to look up at her, breaking the stillness, making time move on. Her eyes were deep and sea blue. "Anything wrong?" she asked.

Shelby shook her head.

"I thought maybe there was something hideous crawling on me."

"No. I just…had a moment, I guess."

Fran got to her feet. "Want to try to find the cellar hole?"

"OK."

"Are you sure there's nothing wrong?"

"Positive. This place…it just struck me. Go on ahead. I want to look at wild flowers. I'll catch up with you."

Fran wandered off, following the remains of the wall.

There were quaker ladies in bloom in the tall grass, their tiny pale blue faces following the sun. And monkey flowers. The mayflowers were beginning to open. One night they'd all bloom at once, and fill the forest with their sweetness. She'd experienced that only one time. She'd never forgotten it.

She still felt shaken by what had happened. She needed to sort it out. It wasn't that Fran was pretty. She wasn't, not by conventional standards. But there was something stunning about her face…an inner strength…clarity.

That was it. Most of the people Shelby knew had barriers around them, self-constructed out of fear or hurt or shame or the simple desire for privacy. Some were as solid as brick, others transparent like Plexiglass, some wispy and gauze-like. But they all served the same purpose…to hold something back. It wasn't secrets. Secrets were singular entities, and you decided who to share them with the same way you decided to share a favorite toy. If the other person was the crude, clumsy type who might break it, you didn't. If you knew the other was gentle and respectful, you did. It wasn't secrets people hid behind those barricades. It was truth.

At that moment, in the sunlight, Fran had no barricades.

It was an unsettling thing to see. Shelby wanted to tell her to look out, to protect herself, because the world is a hard place and you can't go around so open.

Fran probably would have thought she was out of her mind.

The one thing she was sure of was that she wanted to put down her barricades, too. Not just because the only moral response to openness is openness. But because she wanted, if only for a moment, to be like that.

It was the most frightening thing she'd ever thought of.

She heard Fran rustling through last autumn's leaves. It felt safe to go find her. Her breathing was back to normal. Her mind was working again…sort of.

She picked up a pebble to remind her of the day.

Fran sent her off to collect dry twigs and kindling, preferably pine and nothing too gnarly. It didn't take long. The woods were filled with broken branches and downed trees, compliments of last winter's ice storms. She stumbled back to camp with an armload that reached high enough to block her vision.

"Hey," Fran said with a laugh as she took the bundle from her. "Don't get carried away. You could put out an eye."

Shelby dusted the dirt from her hands. "If you're going to act like a nagging mother, I'm going home."

"Sorry. I realize you have a perfectly adequate mother who is capable of doing her own nagging." She put the sticks on the ground and began breaking them into smaller pieces. She frowned at the pile. "Are you aware that you gathered these in order of size?"

"Sure." She picked up the axe and took a few swings at the log Fran had been cutting down to campfire dimensions.

"Doesn't that strike you as kind of compulsive?"

Wood chips flew into the air as her axe made contact. "Don't talk to me about compulsive. I've seen the way you pack."

Fran began building up a tepee of sticks in a sandy space she'd cleared.

The log broke. Shelby set it up on end and split it sideways, then did a couple more. At last she stopped for breath. "Should I go cut hot dog sticks?" she asked as she reached for the water jug.

"Hot dogs are tomorrow. Tonight's going to be special. Buffalo steaks."

"Buffalo?!"

"That's what we call it. Actually, it's plain old steak cooked in the coals. Very out-doorsy."

"What about marshmallows?"

"What about them?"

"We're having marshmallows, aren't we?"

Fran looked at her. "Are you whining?"

"This is a camping trip," Shelby said. "We *have* to have marshmallows."

"We have marshmallows."

"Campfire marshmallows? In the little boxes wrapped in waxed paper?"

"And Hershey bars," Fran said. "And graham crackers. For s'mores."

"This is great." She was as excited as a kid. "I've never had s'mores."

"Never?"

Shelby shook her head. "I had an overpriviledged childhood."

"You certainly did." Fran got to her feet and loaded a couple of split logs into place. "Well, there's our first fire of the season." She tossed the matches to Shelby. "Care to do the honors?"

Shelby changed into her pajamas by the light of the Coleman lamp. The night had turned cool and damp, but it was still comfortable. She wouldn't have cared if it was miserable. It had been a perfect day. They'd stuffed themselves on steak and baked potatoes, also cooked in the coals, and marshmallows with charred skins. They'd walked down to the lake and listened to fish breaking the surface to feed. A faint light, reflected in the water, came from one of the private homes on the opposite shore. At the far east end of the lake, a nearly full moon crept over the tree tops. By the time they came back to their campsite, it was overhead and casting shadows.

She started to pull a sweatshirt over her pajama top, then remembered that it would be considerably warmer by the fire. It had burned down to embers by now, but the embers were hot. She tied the sweatshirt around her waist and went outside.

Fran was sitting on the ground in front of the tent, staring into the fire. "Anything up?" Shelby asked.

Fran glanced up at her. "Just listening to the night sounds and meditating on my sins."

"Care to talk? They say confession's good for the soul."

"No, thanks."

"I'm reputed to be a good listener. I already know more about what goes on with people than I ever wanted to."

Fran laughed. "I'll take a rain check."

"Any time," Shelby said, and rested her hand on Fran's shoulder. She felt Fran stiffen. "I'm sorry," she said, withdrawing her hand.

"You startled me."

"Do you dislike being touched?"

"Not at all," Fran said. "It's the Army experience that makes you nervous. They're very touchy about touch. By similarly gendered persons, that is."

"So I've heard," Shelby said as she sat beside her on the ground.

"Three or four times a year they cast out their nets to 'clean house' and they don't much care who they catch. They don't even need evidence to get you. Someone gets mad at you, starts a rumor, and before you know it you're gone."

"Did you ever know anyone that happened to?"

"Not anyone I knew well." She was silent for a moment. "The worst of it was, the way to get them off your back was to point to someone else. So you had women accusing each other to save their own skin."

"Why are they so crazed about it?" Shelby asked.

Fran shrugged. "They have to do something when they don't have a war to fight, I guess."

Shelby tossed a twig into the embers and watched it flare up. "It seems to me, if you don't like the service, that's a good way to get out."

"It isn't, believe me. It goes on your service record. If you're lucky, you can get a medical discharge. But it's still not easy to explain to prospective employers."

"People are so weird about things," Shelby said. "Sometimes it gives me the willies."

"I know what you mean."

She tossed another twig. "There's this kid in my office...well, not a kid, really, a young woman...no, kid. Emotionally she's still a kid. I'm her supervisor. She doesn't know the magazine business very well yet, and her family's lived all over the world, so she doesn't really know how things are done in this culture. She's kind of dependent on me right now. Understandably. But Connie...Connie's one of those people who always has to make things into more than they really are."

"I've known a few like that."

"So Connie's decided Penny has a crush on me. It puts things on a whole different level, you know what I mean?"

"Yep."

"I hate that kind of stuff."

"What if it's true?" Fran asked. She added a sprig of pine needles to the fire and watched it flame and curl.

"What?"

"That she has a crush on you."

"She might, actually. I'm trying to spend more time with her. So I won't seem so bigger than life."

"I must say," Fran said, "you have a unique way of looking at things. Most people would back off in a hurry."

"That'd be cruel. If she has strong feelings for me, and I reject her, she'd feel awful."

"I don't know, Shelby. I think your friend Penny isn't the only one who doesn't know how things are done in this culture."

Shelby sighed. "I know. Sometimes the whole world seems like a big mystery. I mean, I know the rules, and how to do the right dance steps. But there are times when it just doesn't make any sense."

"Yeah." Fran leaned back on her elbows. "I used to think I was the only person who ever thought that. But if you think it, too, maybe we're right."

"Maybe we are."

"We'd better keep quiet about it. They do terrible things to people who catch on."

"True." She was silent for a moment. "Have they done terrible things to you?"

"Some."

"I'll kill them," Shelby said.

A bit of wood flared up. The red light showed the grin on Fran's face.

"Give me their names."

"These people," Fran said, "aren't worth spending the rest of your life in jail."

"I still want to know. Names, dates, and actions."

"Some other time, OK? I don't want to think about that tonight."

"Promise?" Shelby asked.

"Promise." The fire was winking out. "I wish…"

"What?"

"Nothing." Fran got up. "Race you to the facilities."

The night was still. The moon cast faint shadows on the tent. Overhead, Shelby could see a cloud rising and falling, churning like the white caps on the ocean. A planet stood out against the cobalt sky. Her hair smelled of wood smoke, her arms of sun. The dusty, musty odor of canvas surrounded her. She was tired, wonderfully and physically tired. But she didn't want to sleep, because sleep would eat up the hours. She wanted to feel and remember every minute.

"Shelby?" she heard Fran whisper.

"I'm awake."

"What *do* you think you'll be doing in five years?"

"I don't know," Shelby said. "I probably won't be working. I'll probably have children."

"Do you like that idea?"

"What idea?"

"Children. Not working."

"I've never thought much about it until recently. Children, that is. People who really want children think about it a lot, don't they?"

"That's what I've heard."

"But it's expected."

"Who expects it, Ray?"

"He's mentioned it. But in kind of general terms. Not like he wants a son to go into his practice so I have to keep pumping them out until he gets one or anything like that. My mother will be after me, though. I know she has a deadline somewhere up her sleeve. And my father—I'm an only child, and the only chance he'll have at grandchildren…"

"It makes you sound like a broodmare."

"It does, doesn't it?"

"Kind of a lousy reason to have kids, from the kids' point of view. And from yours."

"I know."

"Will you do what they want?"

Shelby smiled wryly. "I always do what they want." She hesitated to go on, but it felt safe in the darkness. "I'm not a very strong person."

"I think you are," Fran said. A bird rustled the forest floor. "But you *are* kind of a sad person under it, aren't you?"

A flash of something like soft electricity flowed through her. She forced a laugh. "I hope not. I'd hate to be a drag."

Fran rolled toward her on her side and leaned on her elbow. Her face was soft in the moonlight. "I don't mean like that. A kind of…" She was silent for a moment, searching for words. "Something like loneliness."

Shelby felt the sharp sting of unexpected tears behind her eyes. Fear rushed in behind them. A dozen wisecracking, off-putting responses danced into her mind. She forced them down.

"Shelby?"

"I was just thinking," she said. "You're probably right, but I don't know where it comes from."

Mist was forming into droplets at the tips of the hemlock needles. It fell like slow rain onto the tent roof.

She looked at Fran. "I really don't know. That's the truth."

"Yeah," Fran said softly. She reached over and touched Shelby's hair. "I know how that is."

She felt a lone, warm tear escape from the corner of her eye and slip down her cheek. She felt Fran touch it and lift it away. She closed her eyes.

Fran's sleeping bag rustled as she lay back down. She reached out and took Shelby's hand.

It was almost too much to bear. She wanted a friendship with this woman. Not the kind of friendship she had with other friends, not the half-honest, half-hidden kind. She felt comfortable with Fran, at ease in a way she'd never known before.

It was as if, for the first time in her life, she'd met someone who truly spoke her language. It was a touch of hearts as fragile as a glass Christmas ornament. A superficial, dishonest word could shatter it. The thought of opening herself terrified her. But she knew, somehow, if she couldn't do it with this woman, she'd never be able to do it.

"Fran," she said softly.

"Yes?"

"Do you ever find yourself—not lying, exactly, but changing the way you say things because of who you're with?"

"Constantly."

"Have you ever known anyone you didn't have to do that with? You know, someone you could really tell all the things in your heart?"

"No. Not completely."

Shelby hesitated, then forced herself to say it. "I'd like...to try to be that kind of friend with you. I don't know if I can, but I want to try."

Fran was silent for a long time. "Thank you," she said at last, and squeezed Shelby's hand. "Go to sleep, Shelby."

Chapter 7

She woke the next morning to the aroma of coffee and frying bacon. She'd never awakened to smells before. It was a gentle way to come back to earth, she thought as she lay in her sleeping bag and watched hazy shadows of hemlock branches play across the side of the tent. The light through the canvas was a soft tan. There was a breeze, lifting and dropping the tent walls with a soft flapping sound, as though the tent itself were breathing. The stillness was warm and dusty. She tilted her head back and looked through the mesh window at the sky beyond the pine boughs. It was a high, hard blue.

Shelby closed her eyes again and let herself sink into gently rocking, drowsing softness. Drifting led her back to the other camp. Much too young to be so far from home. Nine years old, her first trip away and for two months, with her parents refusing to visit so she'd learn to be independent. She remembered hanging around the office day after day, waiting for a letter. Her mother's were short, hurriedly written, and superficial. Her father never wrote at all. For a while, empty and aching with loneliness, she'd convinced herself her mother would come to see her if she believed hard enough. She decided it would be the third Sunday in July, and wrote and told her mother she'd expect her that day. Then she sat back and marked off the days on her calendar and waited for her parents to come.

They didn't, of course. She'd huddled on the main lodge steps the whole day, watching other parents arrive, bringing presents and picnics, happy to see their kids, holding their daughters' hands as they strolled across the wide lawn to the lake. The girls showed off, swimming and diving from the high board. The parents applauded their own and each other's daughters. By dinner time they all knew each other. When they ate barbecued chicken and potato salad together down by the camp fire circle, it was like a family picnic.

She forced herself to smile through dinner, so no one would suspect and ask questions. But no one asked questions. No one ever asked her questions.

When they were finally on Free Time, she went deep into the woods. In the distance she could hear the high, childish voices singing around the counsel fire. "There's a long, long trail…" "If there were witchcraft…" The camp song. The sky turned cobalt blue. The stars came out. Sparks from the fire drifted into the night like lightning bugs.

She wanted to cry. She'd come out here to cry, where they wouldn't see her and lecture her and laugh behind her back. But she felt all hard and broken inside, like glass, and she couldn't find her tears.

When the moon rose, the parents left. Shelby watched them go, heard the car doors slam, saw the dust rise in their headlights.

That was a long time ago, she reminded herself. She thought instead about last night. The dying fire and the clink of stainless steel forks on aluminum plates. The light fading and winking out. A bird, startled by its own imagination, squawked and fluttered. They rebuilt the fire and made up a ceremony to honor the Forest Gods, sang silly songs and told stupid jokes and talked and sometimes just sat with the silence and the crackling fire. And when they went to bed, she'd fallen asleep without feeling alone.

Back in the woods a bird sang, a liquid, fluting sound. Hermit thrush, she recalled. Or was it a wood thrush?

Fran was moving around outside, poking at the fire, handling pots and pans.

"Wood or hermit?" she called.

"Hermit." Fran poked her head through the tent flap. "Good morning."

"It is, isn't it?" She pushed at the covers. Nothing happened. The sleeping bag had swallowed her like a cocoon. She struggled with it. "Hey."

Fran came into the tent and crouched beside her. "I closed it in the night," she said, working the zipper. "It turned chilly. You didn't even wake up."

She remembered something else about falling asleep last night. They'd talked about…important things. Fran had been… "I didn't wake up?" she said quickly, suddenly shy and not sure why. "I must have been knocked out."

"You were." Fran sat on her own sleeping bag. "I never saw anyone fall asleep so fast outside of the Army."

"It's a first for me." She stretched. "I usually spend at least forty-five minutes worrying and obsessing. I'll bet you don't."

"What makes you say that?"

"Because you seem to know what you want and where you're going."

Fran got up and reached down to give her a hand. "Shelby," she said with a laugh, "you're a lousy judge of character."

"Not so lousy." She found her toothbrush and comb and came out into the clear morning. "Do I need to wash my hair?"

"Not in my opinion," Fran said, looking her over. She brushed at an unruly strand above Shelby's ear. "There's a little loss of control here, but we won't take off points for it."

"Do they take off points for out-of-control hair in the Army?" Shelby folded her tee shirt into a pot holder and lifted the coffee pot from the cooking grate.

"No, they just hang you. Don't pour that yet. It's not done."

Shelby sniffed the coffee. "You've got to be kidding. It smells strong enough to patch a tire."

"Don't be rude. This is cowboy coffee, boiled not percolated." Fran picked up some eggshells she'd put aside, crumpled them, and tossed them into the pot.

"You're trying to kill us."

"The eggshells settle the grounds." She swirled the coffee, flipped the pot's lid and eyed the contents. "At least that's what they claim. I don't know who 'they' are and I never could tell the difference with or without." She poured coffee into a tin cup and handed it to Shelby. "Watch out for that, it's hot. The alternative method," she said as she poured one for herself, "is a burning stick thrust into the coffee. That I can recognize by taste. It gives the coffee that fine, hickory-smoked flavor. Has also been known to dispel vampires." Fran took a swallow of coffee and shuddered.

Shelby tasted hers. It was coffee all right, she had to grant it that. And clearly had wakening powers. "How long does this stuff stay in your system?"

"I believe the half-life is twenty years." She took Shelby's coffee from her. "Let this cool a little. Get washed up and think about what you want to do today."

Shelby saluted. "Yes, Sir."

Fran stared at her, and shook her head. "If you don't stop looking so damned rumpled and cute," she grumbled, "I won't be responsible for my actions."

"Is that a threat?"

Fran looked at her, a surprised expression on her face as if she hadn't planned on saying that out loud. Then she recovered. "A serious one," she said with an evil laugh. She took a step toward her, fingers outstretched. "I have a compulsion to tickle."

Shelby turned and ran down the path to the restrooms.

"I don't want to go home," she said. Night was coming down in layers of purple and gray. "I want to stay here forever."

"We can't do that." Fran dropped their plates and mugs and steel silverware into the wash basin and added hot water from the bucket over the fire.

"Why not?"

"You ate all the marshmallows."

"We'll get more."

"You'll lose your job," Fran said. "I'll lose my job. We'll run out of money. Then what'll we do for marshmallows?"

"Knock over gas stations."

"It might look like paradise now," Fran said. "But wait until July. I'll bet that beach will be jammed with housewives in bad moods, pregnant women, and screaming children with sand in their bathing suits."

They reached for the cold water simultaneously, bumping heads. "Sorry," Shelby said. She noticed a smudge of ash on Fran's cheek and wiped it off with the back of her hand.

Fran turned away quickly.

"Did I do something wrong?"

"Of course not." She held up the dish soap. "Want this? Or should we go down to the beach and wash our pots in sand?"

"Soap'll do," Shelby said, taking it. They'd be leaving soon. Fran had insisted they strike the tent and put it and their clothes and sleeping bags in the car before evening dew could form on them. All that was left of their camp—the dirty dishes, the dying fire, the washstand Fran had taught her to build by lashing branches to tree trunks... She felt her throat tighten. In two hours they'd be home. She had to call Ray, and Lisa, and her mother... Well, maybe not her mother. Maybe this time she'd just forget about it. Maybe...

An ember popped in the fire. She looked around. Fran was drying the dishes and stowing them in a duffel bag. The campsite was nearly bare. It looked empty. Worse than a deserted house, at least a house was a house whether it was empty or not, but an empty campsite was just empty.

Fran caught her expression in the twilight. She put her towel down. "We'll come back, Shelby."

"I know." This was absurd. She wanted to cry. A headache was starting.

"Come here," Fran said, taking her hand and leading her to the log by the fire they used for a seat. "Sit down." She slipped an arm around her shoulders. "Talk to me."

Shelby stared into the dying fire. "I just don't want to go back to it. My life." She gave an embarrassed cough. "This is silly."

"No, it isn't."

"I mean, it's my life, right? If I don't like it, I should figure out what I don't like and change it, right?"

"I guess so," Fran said.

She rested her elbows on her knees and folded her hands and rested her forehead on her interlaced fingers. "I really think I'm too young for it."

Fran moved a strand of Shelby's hair. "For what?"

"My job, marriage…"

"Well, hell," Fran said softly, "we're all too young for jobs and marriage. Probably always will be. But how else are we going to get marshmallows?"

Shelby sighed. "I know I'm being a baby."

"You're not. Shelby, if marrying Ray isn't what you really want…"

"I do want it. This is probably just nerves, don't you think?"

"I don't know what to think," Fran said. "But if someone pushed you onto a speeding train and it was going in the wrong direction, you *would* pull the emergency cord, wouldn't you?"

"I hope so."

"Shelby…"

She gave herself a little shake. "I'm sorry. Here we are in this beautiful place, and I'm having a great time, and I keep turning gloomy. I don't know what my problem is."

"Maybe you don't get enough time to think back home."

"Every time I try to think, my brain turns to murk." She laughed. "People tell me I think too much."

"They tell me I feel too much."

Shelby glanced at her. "I hope feeling works better for you than thinking does for me. All I get is confusion and paralysis."

"Me, too."

She found a twig and tossed it into the fire. It smoldered for a moment, then burst into flame. "Fran."

"Yep."

"This has been really special."

Fran rested her arms on her knees and gazed into the coals. "For me, too."

It was nearly dark. They ought to be leaving. Shelby tossed another stick on the fire. "Where'd you go to college?"

"Mills."

"Women's college. So did I. Mt. Holyoke. Did you like it?"

"Very much," Fran said. "Did you?"

"Yes. For one thing, we studied. We weren't thinking about boys all the time. And with none of them on campus…well, it seemed more like family."

"So did Mills. I wish I could have stayed the whole four years."

"Do you miss college?"

"Desperately, at times. Do you?"

Shelby ran her hands over her face. "I think so. It wasn't perfect, but what is? It was beautiful. There was a feeling of time and history about it. Peaceful. Except for a few of the other students, they were kind of strange. But mostly it was good."

"What was strange about them?"

"Well, not really strange, I guess. I had one friend, I thought we were really good friends, and then one day she just started avoiding me. I never knew why. I asked her once, but she said she was busy, that's all. I don't think it was the truth."

"Ah," said Fran. "Did it bother you?"

"Yeah, I was really confused."

"Does it still?"

"I wish I knew what happened."

Fran was silent.

"I must have done something."

"Maybe not," Fran said. "Maybe it was something she couldn't tell you."

"But why not? I was her best friend. She was my best friend."

"Sometimes there are things you can't tell anyone, not even your best friend. Sometimes there are things you can't even tell yourself."

"I guess," Shelby admitted. "But it hurt."

"I know." She tossed a stick on the coals. "Life gets hard sometimes."

"Yeah."

"Which," Fran said, resting her hand on Shelby's knee, "is why there is camping."

* * *

Jean caught her coming through the door of the lounge Monday morning. "So how was it?"

"Great." She shook the cold rain from her umbrella. "I loved it."

"You didn't disgrace yourself?"

"She gave me a sleeping bag."

"Is that like a merit badge?"

"I guess so." She hung up her coat. "It was so calm. You can't imagine."

Jean hung her coat beside Shelby's. "What'd you do?"

"Talked, mostly. And hiked. And ate."

"Lisa called after you called her. To let us know you'd survived."

"She's something else, isn't she?" Shelby dug her comb out of her pocket-book and tried to do something with her damp hair. "I really think she believed I was going to die."

"She kept referring to camping as an 'unnatural act.' "

"Sounds like Libby." She gave up and dropped the comb back into her pocketbook. "Except at the moment Libby doesn't seem to care what I do, she's so wrapped up in that party. When I told her, I just got one of those 'that's nice, dear' responses."

Jean handed her a Styrofoam cup of coffee. "That's great. Maybe you should take advantage of her good mood."

"Yeah." She perched on the back of a battered Naugahyde chair and sipped her coffee. "But you know Libby. Her moods come and go like fog. Honestly, how many 'plans' do you have to make for an engagement party? When the country club's handling the whole thing?"

"A mind-boggling number," Jean said. "Things you'd never even think of."

She didn't want to talk about the party, or the wedding, or any of it. By the time it actually happened, she wouldn't remember how to talk about anything else. "What did you do this weekend?"

Jean took her turn at the mirror. "Blind date. A friend of Connie's Charlie." She shrugged. "It was OK. We're going out again."

"You don't sound very enthusiastic."

"It was fine, really," Jean said. "I'm just worn out. Maybe it's too soon after Barry to jump in again." Her eyes caught Shelby's in the mirror. "How am I doing?"

"How are you doing what?"

"With the talking?"

She was caught off guard. "All right. Fine. I guess. I don't know. I thought it was natural. I mean, I thought you were just more comfortable."

Jean turned to her sharply. "How the hell can I be comfortable when I know everyone's watching me and grading me? Would you be comfortable?"

"No," Shelby said.

"So forget about comfortable, OK? I just need to know if I'm acceptable yet." She threw her comb into her purse. "Though I guess I should assume I'm getting there, since Queen Constance has judged me adequate to go out with Prince Charles' friend."

Shelby was shocked at the anger in Jean's voice. She held out a hand toward her. "Jean…"

Jean brushed her away. "Don't reach out to me. It's too humiliating."

"Jean, you know how I feel about this. I'm really, really sorry…"

"I know you are." Jean forced a smile. "I don't know what's wrong with me today. It must be that time of month."

"No. I think what I did really hurt you, damaged you, and damaged our friendship, and I hate that, and I wish I'd never done it, but I did and now I don't know how to fix it."

Jean looked at the floor for a moment, then looked up. "I'm being stupid," she said apologetically. "I'm angry at Connie and taking it out on you."

"You're welcome to take it out on me," Shelby said. "As long at you don't really believe it's me you're angry at."

"Getting me that date. It was like bestowing some kind of medal on me for being normal." She raised her hands in a gesture of futility. "Don't get me wrong. Greg seems like a nice guy, it's not his fault. It has nothing to do with him. It just all feels…well, contaminated." She faced Shelby head-on. "And don't tell me it's silly, because that's how I feel."

"Hey," Shelby said, and held up her empty hand self-protectively. "I'm not going to laugh. It's not funny, and I agree with you."

"You do?"

"Sure. I know she thinks she's being helpful. She probably figured, gee, Jean's trying so hard, we should do something nice for her, and thought she had. If you like Greg, go out with him on your own. You don't have to double with Connie and Charlie."

"This Saturday we do. It's already arranged. I don't know what we're doing, but by God we're doing it together."

She had an idea. "Listen, I've been meaning to ask you all over for the traditional first barbecue of the season. Or, if it's too cold, a picnic in the living room. I want you to meet Fran. And you haven't seen Ray in ages. He's asked about you. I won't invite Libby, so someone else will get a word in edgewise. We'll make it Saturday. That way it'll be a crowd, not like a double date."

"You don't have to do this for me."

Shelby dismissed her objections with a gesture. "I'd be doing it anyway, sooner or later. Saturday's as good a time as any. Come on, huh? Please, huh? Pretty please?"

Jean laughed. "All *right*. I'm a sucker for your whining."

"I'm very good at it."

"I'm really sick of people trying to change me," Jean said with a sigh. "I might as well go back and live with my family."

"You can't do that," Shelby said. "You'd betray our entire generation."

Jean gave her a grim smile.

"We're supposed to *find* ourselves, aren't we?"

"I was never lost," Jean said.

"Lucky you."

Her friend looked at her. "You were lost?"

Shelby shoved her hair back from her forehead. "Well, maybe not. But, to tell you the truth, this wedding thing has broadsided me."

"Yeah?"

"I want to do it," she said quickly. "Don't get me wrong. I mean, I love Ray and all, and there's no other man I want to spend my life with, but…"

Jean cocked her head to one side. "But?"

"There's a part of me—just a small part, really—that feels, well, trapped."

"Wedding nerves," Jean said. "I'm an authority on wedding nerves. When my sister got married, we practically had to drug her to get her down the aisle."

Shelby exhaled. Wedding nerves. That was reasonable, simple. Everyone got wedding nerves.

"Trouble is," Jean said, "she's been drugged ever since."

"What?" Her voice cracked.

Jean laughed. "Just kidding. She's as happy as a clam at high tide."

Shelby crumpled her empty Styrofoam cup and threw it at her.

"Why, thank you," Jean said as she caught it. "What a thoughtful gift. Want to have dinner tonight?"

"I can't. I'm 'dining' with The Mother. At The Country Club. She mumbled something about picking the theme and color scheme."

"Oh, that."

"What do you mean, 'oh, that'?"

"The color scheme. You have to decide on the color of your dress so she can order flowers to match."

"God!" Shelby groaned. "I'm going to feel like a jerk."

"This is only the beginning." She smiled at Shelby. "If you want to get off, better do it before the rollercoaster picks up speed."

Shelby slid down into her chair. "Maybe it's not too late to talk Ray into eloping."

"I thought he liked this wedding business."

"He does."

"So it's you against the world."

"Yeah."

"Leave town," Jean said.

Shelby laughed. "You're not crazy about this marriage stuff, are you?"

"Nothing wrong with marriage. I'm just against weddings." She grinned over the top of her coffee cup. "Actually, I'm trying to get out of putting on a bridesmaid's dress. I'm going to look awful."

"You won't look awful," Shelby said. "I promise I won't make you wear anything that makes you look or feel awful."

Jean got up to refill her cup and get Shelby a new one. "Have you made a decision about maid of honor yet?"

"No."

"I figured Connie."

Shelby shifted in her seat uncomfortably. "I guess she's the logical choice, but…"

"But?" Jean handed her the coffee.

"But the person I feel closest to is you."

"No way," Jean said in horror. "No way you're putting me in that role."

"You don't want to do it?"

"One, I don't want to do it. Nothing personal, I think you're great and if I ever wanted to be a maid of honor in this lifetime, it's yours I'd want to be." She shook her head. "Thanks, but I'll pass on that." She leaned against the table, facing Shelby. "And, two, if Connie thinks she ought to be maid of honor—and I'm pretty sure she does—I do *not* want to be the one to get in her way."

"If she blames anyone," Shelby said, "it'll be me."

"I might get caught in the cross fire."

Shelby sipped her coffee. "Are you trying to make it easy for me?"

"I'm trying to save both our skins. Anyway, you should have someone who's more into it. I'd support every rebellious impulse, and it would be a disaster. Connie'll keep you on the right path."

"You'd be more fun."

Jean looked surprised. "Fun? Me?"

"Yes, you."

Jean shook her head. "Well, that's a new one. Look, Shel, seriously…if you thought about this the way most people do, I'd fight tooth and nail to be maid of honor if that was what you wanted. But since we both think of weddings as unnecessary and expensive bits of theater, let's make it easy on ourselves."

"You really are an amazing woman, Jean."

"I'm going to be an amazing unemployed woman if I don't get in there. See you at lunch."

* * *

Shelby took off her pumps and slammed them into the back of the closet. Honest to God, she didn't know why they were going through this charade. Libby knew what she wanted this wedding to look like, from the engagement party to the last grain of rice, and she was determined to have her way. Discussing it was a joke. If Shelby had the good luck to think of something Libby had already decided on, it was deemed a brilliant idea. If Libby had rejected it in her own mind, Shelby had the taste of a mongrel dog. If it hadn't occurred to Libby at all, she just made a distasteful face and rolled her eyes in long-suffering impatience.

Long-suffering impatience. Wasn't that an oxymoron? Like *your* idea, and *your* wedding? Like mother love?

She slipped out of her dress and tossed it into the laundry hamper. "Making plans together." Libby had decided they should meet for dinner every Monday until all the plans were firmed up. Terrific.

She wished she could go down to Fran's room and beat on the door to wake her up and sit and bitch her head off for an hour. But it was late. She didn't want to make a nuisance of herself. Besides, she was crummy company, and she had to get up early and she knew she wasn't going to sleep at all tonight. In fact, she ought to just shower, change her clothes, and find something constructive to do until dawn.

But that wouldn't do. Not at all. One had to go through the motions. Into the night clothes, hygiene ritual, turn out the light, close the eyes...

As it turned out, she did sleep. At least enough to dream. In the dream her parents were arguing, the way they used to. She couldn't make out what they were saying, only the undertone of anger in their voices. After a while her mother's voice dropped out altogether, and she was left with the sound of her father's—a rumbling, metallic, endless, relentless, nerve-grinding, empty-freight-train sound—instructing, instructing, instructing. Until his voice became a chant, an invocation.

This is ridiculous, she thought as she looked at her tired, grainy-eyed face in the mirror the next morning. My life's made up of one-quarter guilt, one-quarter fear, one-quarter depression, and one-quarter mixed bag. At least marriage will get me out of that.

* * *

Saturday was perfect for the barbecue. Warm but not hot. Clear. According to the weather man, it would stay warm until after sundown. By then they'd have finished dinner and could move inside or go on to other pursuits. She invited the young couple with the new baby who lived upstairs, and the Misses Young, elderly spinsters who had a ground-floor apartment in what used to be the carriage house. That way, Fran wouldn't feel like such an outsider, and would have people to talk to if the lunch bunch got too in-groupy. Lisa was bringing Wayne, and Penny her latest, whoever it might be. "So many men, so little time," had become Penny's motto, though at the rate she was going through men—like an adolescent on an eating binge—sometimes made Shelby wonder if there might be more to it than met the eye. Fran said she was coming solo. She didn't say why. Shelby assumed Fran hadn't met anyone interesting yet. She'd offered to have Ray bring a date for her, but Fran refused.

Things like that, she insisted, had the potential for damaging friendships, and she valued Shelby's friendship far too much to risk it on a blind date. Shelby thought it was an interesting concept, and was surprised to find herself grinning in agreement.

Maybe, with a few strangers around, Connie and Charlie would curtail their billing and cooing a little. She wondered why it was her and not Connie who was making the first trip down the aisle. Connie and Charlie seemed to be in love—at least they were clearly in heat. Maybe they wanted to sustain those first, fine, careless raptures as long as possible.

"I don't know what the big deal is about marriage, anyway," Fran said as she helped her lug the grill up from the basement. "People should just live together, then it wouldn't get so heavy. Damn." She stumbled into the wall, scraping the knuckles of her hand. "I mean, they get that piece of paper saying the state approves of them, and all of a sudden they forget their manners and their personalities change." She put the grill down on the lawn and sucked at her scraped knuckles. "Usually for the worse. Especially the men. My own brother turned into a tyrannical maniac the day after he tied the knot."

Shelby wiped her hands on her jeans. "Probably because you weren't around any more to beat him up. Let me see that." She reached for Fran's hand.

"It's fine," Fran said, showing her. "Not even bleeding. Where did you put the charcoal?"

She pointed to the back porch.

Would that happen to Ray and her? Would he turn into a tyrant? Would she go on the Miltown circuit with all the other suburban wives? It was hard to imagine Ray changing, he was always so solidly Ray. As for herself…

"I guess that does it," Fran said, "unless you can think of something else for me to do."

Shelby reviewed what they'd accomplished. "I guess not." She glanced at her watch. "Nobody'll be here for at least an hour and a half."

"Good. I'm going to sack out."

She thought Fran looked tightly strung. "Are you nervous about this?"

"Of course I'm nervous. I'm meeting your friends, your fiancé, for God's sake. Civilians. Normal people. The situation's fraught with danger."

Shelby laughed. "Don't worry about it. You're more interesting than all of them combined."

Head cocked to one side, hands on her hips, Fran looked at her. "You know, Shelby, you're a little strange."

"I am?" She wondered how to feel about that.

Fran nodded. "Definitely, strange. See you later."

She'd have been willing to bet a month's salary that Fran and Jean would hit it off like long-lost friends, and she was right. From the moment they met they'd been talking together, bringing trays of hamburgers covered with waxed paper from the house together, tearing up lettuce for the salad together. She almost felt sorry for Greg, who stood to one side holding a beer bottle by the neck and twirling it in one hand, and watching.

Connie was watching, too. When she wasn't draped around Charlie's neck, whispering and giggling and nipping at his ear lobe. Now and then she'd glance toward Jean and Fran and get a puzzled, thoughtful look on her face, as if she saw something no one else saw, and wasn't sure she liked it. The Misses Young, on the other hand, weren't sure they liked what Connie and Charlie were doing. Shelby caught Miss Carrie's eye and smiled and edged over to her. "My friends are a little demonstrative," she said.

Miss Carrie sighed. "At our age, one can't afford to be judgmental. But sometimes I can't help it."

"Ignore her," Miss Margaret said to Shelby. "She's really a voyeur. I'm surprised she hasn't been arrested." She gestured with her head toward Fran. "That new one's a nice girl. Fixed our sink the other day, wouldn't take a cent for it. Handy as a man."

"Handier," said Miss Carrie. "And she didn't leave a mess. I swear, young people nowadays, think they're helping you and leave a bigger mess than they started with."

"They always did," Miss Margaret said. "You just don't remember."

And they were off on one of their usual spats. They were always having small, meaningless arguments. Like a situation comedy. She wondered if all people in their eighties behaved like that, or if the Misses Young were using an 'elderly ladies' stereotype to hide the fact that they'd learned some truly horrifying things in all those years and didn't want to frighten the young with them.

Shelby let her attention drift and looked around the yard.

Lisa and Wayne had noticed Greg looking like a fifth wheel, and wandered over to include him in their conversation. It gave Shelby a warm feeling. Her friends, however much they might annoy her at times, were caring, considerate people.

The screen door banged and Ray came clumping down the back porch steps, looking boyish and athletic in his madras shirt and denim shorts and Sperry Top-Siders. He saw her and trotted over and lifted her off the ground in a massive embrace.

"Ray," she said, half-joking, "people are watching."

"Frankly, my dear," he rumbled, "I don't give a damn," and kissed her hard and long.

"Ray, please," she whispered, and struggled a little.

"Ask me nicely."

Everyone was watching. She felt like a fool.

He began to dance around the patio with Shelby in his arms, spinning in fast circles and humming, "You make me feel so young..."

"I mean it, Ray."

He only danced faster. She felt helpless, as if she were caught in one of those nightmares where everything she did was slow and weak, as if she were under water.

"I'm going to throw up on you."

That slowed him down a little. "I love you," he said, pecking little kisses all over her face. "Love you, love you, love you."

That was all well and good, but she'd appreciate it more if he put her down. This manly exuberance might be a display of affection for him, but to Shelby it was a reminder that he had the simple physical superiority to do anything with her he damn well pleased.

"Hey, cave man," she heard someone say, "come here often?"

He stopped and looked down.

"So this is Ray," Fran said with a warm and friendly smile. She stuck out her hand.

He lowered her to the ground to shake Fran's hand. "I don't recognize you," he said heartily, "so you must be Fran Jarvis."

"I see my reputation precedes me. I'm the one I must be when I'm the only one you don't recognize."

Ray held up his hands in a gesture of good-natured surrender. "Whatever you say, soldier. I never argue with our boys—or girls—in uniform."

"Big, isn't he?" Fran said to Shelby. She gave Ray a teasing wink.

They both laughed.

Shelby forced herself to smile. She sensed an undercurrent that made her uneasy.

"Seriously," Fran said, dropping her bantering attitude. "I'm really happy to meet you."

"Same here," Ray said. "I hear we're in the same line of work."

"Slightly different positions in the pecking order."

"Want a beer?"

Fran nodded. "Thanks."

He reached into the galvanized tub that held the beer and ice. "Do you plan on going on in medicine?"

"I don't know." She took the opened beer bottle and nodded a thank-you. "Right now the idea makes me want to lie down, but I could just need a vacation. You must feel that way. It's been a long haul for you."

Shelby drifted away from them. She had the feeling Fran had sensed she hated being tossed around like something from the mail room, and had interrupted it deliberately. She was grateful for that. Unfortunately, Fran didn't know what she was letting herself in for, opening the door for Ray to talk shop.

"Ray's full of himself today, isn't he?" Connie said.

"He certainly is." She pretended to be delighted with his behavior. "He's been like this since we got engaged to be engaged. By the time the wedding rolls around, he'll be completely out of control. I'll have to keep him on a short leash so he doesn't run out into the traffic." She couldn't believe what she was hearing, the things she was saying. She was already acting like every suburban housewife in America.

"Your housemate seems like an interesting sort," Connie said.

Shelby felt a wall of caution go up inside her. "I guess so."

"She and Jean hit it off." She laughed. "Funny how those quiet types always find so much to say to one another."

Good observation, Shelby thought. Now let's ask ourselves why that might be.

Connie was staring over toward Jean and Greg. "What do you think? Good match?"

"As far as I can tell."

"Charlie Brown picked him out." She hung on his arm. "He has good taste."

Shelby glanced up at Charlie, who seemed uncomfortable with the whole conversation. She smiled at him. "I've always said, Charles, you have excellent taste in men." She took a step back and looked at him. His polo shirt was neatly pressed. His plaid Bermuda shorts were a little baggy. He was wearing loafers and white socks. He looked like what he was, an electrical engineer.

"Men and women, but not clothes," Connie complained. "I can dress him up fit to kill, and he still looks like a nerd." She gave him a little kiss. "Don't you, sweetie?"

"Shore dew, ma'am," Charlie said. But Shelby saw something cross his face, and it wasn't boyish good humor. He was hurt, and one of these days he was going to be hurt once too often and then he was going to get angry. She hoped Connie wouldn't be alone with him when that happened, but she really didn't want to be the one to be there. He turned to her. "Want me to start the charcoal? I think I can manage to do that."

"That would be nice," Shelby said.

He left her with Connie.

"He's such a doll." Connie said. "An unmitigated doll."

"He's a nice guy," Shelby agreed. "Look, Con, it's none of my business, but I think it kind of bothers him when you call him Charlie Brown. It makes him sound like a loser."

"Oh, it does not. He knows I'm only teasing."

She decided to let it go. Quickly she inventoried her guests. Everyone had arrived. The Misses Young were playing with the upstairs baby and chatting with the baby's parents. Penny and Lisa and Wayne and Penny's so-far-unnamed-mystery date were clustered around the beer tub, Penny and Lisa having what they had come to refer to as a half-Italian argument, which involved a lot of waving of arms and raising of voices over an issue no one really cared about. They usually ended up convulsed in laughter.

Fran and Ray were exchanging medical horror stories, while Jean and Greg listened in.

Everything under control for now. No one was looking for a drink. The plates and silverware were stacked on the table. Salt and pepper and ketchup and relish and sliced onions and cold cups for the iced tea, lemon slices, sugar, salad dressing, ice bucket full—check. Hamburger buns. Butter. Baked potatoes were still in the oven, inside. Too early for the salad, might wilt. She got herself a beer and went over to the grill.

"Hey, big brother," she said to Charlie as she perched on the rock wall that closed off one end of the patio. The name didn't mean anything. They'd started using it one night because of something they'd done that neither of them could remember, and it stuck.

"Hey, little sister." He peered at the smoking charcoal and added a squirt of starter fluid. "How's it going?"

"It's going. How about you?"

"I'm doing OK, for a jerk."

"She doesn't mean anything by it, Charlie."

He wiped his hands on a white, pressed handkerchief. "Yeah, she never means anything by anything."

Shelby couldn't think of what to say.

"So," Charlie said, "Ray's finally decided to make an honest woman of you."

"More like I finally decided to make an honest man out of him." She swung the beer bottle between her knees.

"Well, it's good news. You two are a great couple."

She looked over to where Fran and Ray were laughing together. "Yeah."

His eyes followed hers. "I like your friend, too."

"Thank you."

Charlie squeezed her shoulder. "Something bothering you, Shel?"

"Not a thing." Which wasn't exactly true. Inside her forehead, just above the bridge of her nose, she could feel that fuzzy pressured feeling that meant a headache was on its way.

Chapter 8

By the time they'd finished eating, she was afraid she couldn't hide it any more. It felt as if someone were driving an axe into her head repeatedly. Her vision was foggy, and her stomach was beginning to churn. She obscured her hands beneath the table and shredded a paper napkin and tried desperately to concentrate on any of the conversations going on around her.

She didn't want her headache to be the center of attention. She didn't want to be the center of attention at all. Gritting her teeth, she fought against the prickly pain tears that were creeping into her eyes.

Someone touched the back of her head. She turned to look up. The picnic table and bench and yard and even the sky turned upside down. She grabbed the edge of the bench to steady herself.

"I need you to help me with something," Fran said, and grabbed her by the wrist and pulled her up before Shelby could respond. "Sorry to interrupt," she said to Ray. "I don't know where anything is, and Shelby's organization defies logic."

"That's not news to me," Ray said. "Bring my cigarettes when you come back, will you, hon? I left them on the kitchen sink."

Fran led the way back inside the house and into Shelby's kitchen.

"What's the problem?" Shelby asked.

"That's what I want to know." Fran settled her into a chair. "You have a headache, don't you?"

She nodded. "Earth-shaking."

"I know a trick. It might help." Fran washed her hands at the sink and dried them on a dish towel. She put her left hand firmly against Shelby's forehead, and her right at the point where her head and neck were joined. "Close your eyes. Take a few deep breaths and relax."

She did. The darkness was soothing. She drifted into the moment. Minutes passed. The pain began to ebb.

"Any luck?" Fran asked at last.

"It's down to a low rumble."

"That's probably the best we can do for now." She lowered her hands to Shelby's shoulders and began to massage them.

Shelby took another deep breath and let herself sink into darkness again. She thought nothing had ever felt so good. She let her head rest against Fran's body. "Fran?"

"Uh-huh."

"I'm worried. About the headaches."

"So am I," Fran said.

She held her breath for a moment. "I think I'm ready for you to make the appointment."

She could tell from the slight hesitation that Fran was surprised. "I'm glad."

"Any day but a Wednesday. We have editorial board meetings on Wednesdays."

"OK."

She wanted to let it drop right there. Play it cool and casual. No big deal. But she remembered her promise to herself. "I'm scared," she said.

Fran leaned over her, slipping her arms across Shelby's chest, resting her head on Shelby's. "I know. Want me with you?"

She gripped Fran's arm in her hands. "Yes, please."

"Good."

"Don't tell anyone, OK?"

"If you say so. Not even Ray?"

"Not even Ray."

Fran made a strangling sound. "You drive me crazy."

Shelby tried to turn and look at her. Fran tightened her grip and wouldn't let her move. "What do you mean?"

"This 'don't tell Ray' stuff."

"We're going to be married in a year. I want to hang onto my privacy as long as I can."

"Shelby," Fran said with a sigh, "I like you a lot, but you're always saying things that make me want to scream."

"Like what?"

"Do you want to marry this guy?"

"Of course I do."

"Well, maybe I've been in the service too long, but it seems to me if a woman wants to marry a man, she should be counting the days. But *not* the days of freedom she has left."

"Why not? Men do it all the time."

"Women aren't men," Fran said, and went back to rubbing her shoulders. How would you feel if you thought Ray was hoarding his days of freedom."

"He probably is."

"Wouldn't it make you kind of…question things a little?"

"It's just wedding jitters," Shelby said defensively. "Everyone goes through it."

"You're not everyone, Shelby." Fran's voice was low, soft and a little sad.

"Hey, Shel." It was Lisa from beyond the screen door. "We're out of ice. Got—" She came to a stop at the entrance to the kitchen.

Fran let go of her with a brutal jerk and jumped back.

"Sure," Shelby said. "In the freezer."

She glanced over at Fran. Her face was white.

"What's going on?" Lisa asked as she dumped a tray of ice into the Scotch Cooler.

"I was on the verge of one of my killer headaches," Shelby said. "Fran fixed it."

Lisa turned to look at them. "Really? How?"

"Can you show her?" Shelby asked Fran.

Fran deliberately stepped away from Shelby. "Sure." She gestured toward an empty chair. "Have a seat."

Shelby passed them on the way to the refrigerator. "Relax," she said to Fran in a low voice. "This isn't the Army."

"The Army," Fran muttered, "can happen anywhere, any time."

"Wow," Lisa gushed when Fran had finished with her, "that's the greatest. Where'd you learn it?"

"In the Medical Corps," Fran said. Her voice creaked a little, as if she hadn't used it in a long time. "In the Army. It's a kind of…thing."

"Well, it's neat. Thanks. I didn't even have a headache and you made me feel better." She picked up the cooler.

"Let me carry that," Fran said, and reached for it. She almost ran from the apartment.

Shelby waved until Ray's car turned the corner onto Pleasant and the tail lights disappeared into the darkness. Fumbling with her lock, she glanced toward Fran's door and noticed light glowing under it. She went down the hall and knocked softly. "It's me."

Fran opened the door. She was in her pale blue and white plaid short-legged pajamas. "I didn't think you'd be in until dawn." She touched Shelby's chin. "Beard burn. I know what you've been doing."

"Listen, I wanted to apologize."

"For what?"

"Getting stubborn about the wedding. Being a brat."

Fran smiled. "You are that at times. Want to come in?"

"For a minute." As she stepped inside she noticed the solitaire game in progress. "Solitaire?"

"But no Brahms." Fran gathered up the cards. "I was just trying put myself in a mindless coma so I can get to sleep."

"You did a real snow job on Ray."

"Well, we have work in common. Makes conversation easy." She cleared a space beside hers for Shelby on the wicker couch. "Want anything to eat or drink?"

Shelby laughed. "Are you kidding? You've seen my kitchen."

"True."

"Let's get together tomorrow and split it up."

"Great."

"If you don't hear from me by noon, come check for signs of life."

Fran stretched, sliding her arm along the back of the couch. "I like your friends, by the way." She grinned self-consciously. "That was a stupid thing to say. I don't even know your friends. I met them, period."

"First impressions are important." She wondered if she could rest her head back against Fran's hand. "What did you think?"

"Well…" Fran bit her lower lip. "Well, Jean's my favorite, of course. By the way, she's still terrified you're going to ask her to be your maid of honor since you haven't gotten around to asking Connie yet."

Shelby looked at her. "You talked about me?"

"Yes, we talked about you." She ruffled Shelby's hair. "It was one topic we had in common. Don't worry, we both said nice things about you."

Shelby felt herself blushing, and grunted noncommittally.

"Lisa...well, Lisa's lively. Good heart, no kinesthetic sense."

"That's Lisa, all right."

"Connie could be difficult, but she's not subtle. If you cross her, she'll try to get back at you, but you'll always see it coming. And, just when you're ready to kill her, she'll say or do something kind and thoughtful."

"Amazing," Shelby said. "What about Penny?"

Fran's forehead wrinkled in a frown. "She's kind of like smoke. I couldn't get a handle on her."

Shelby told her about Penny's apartment, with its empty, impersonal air.

"Yep," Fran said. "I can see that. She's the one with the crush on you, right?"

"Supposedly."

"She watches you like a puppy in the pound. If you look her way, she tries to think of something to do to please you so you'll take her home."

Shelby was beginning to feel uncomfortable. "She's a kid."

"Yeah," Fran said, and lapsed into thoughtful silence.

"What is it?"

"I don't know. Something's a little off, but I can't put my finger on it. I keep wanting to tell you to be careful."

"Something about Penny?"

"Not exactly. Something about the two of you, maybe." Fran laughed and rubbed her eyes with her hand. "I don't even know what I'm talking about."

"Are you tired?"

"Getting there. It was a stimulating evening."

"What did you think of the men?"

"The men? The men are tall."

"That's your only impression?"

"When you have to bend backward to see a person's face, it makes an impression. In the Army, he'd always be in the back row."

She waited for Fran to go on. She didn't. "That's it?' she asked. "He's tall?"

Fran shot out of her seat. "What difference does it make what I think of him? I'm not marrying him, you are. What do you want me to do, drool? What do *you* think of him?"

"Hey," Shelby said, startled by the outburst. "I'm sorry. I don't know what I said to offend you, but...you don't have to get mad."

"Don't I?" Fran whirled on her. "Maybe I *do* have to get mad, did you ever think of that?"

"I only asked because he really liked you."

"Well, I'm very glad to hear that," Fran grumbled.

Shelby got up and went to her. "Fran, what's wrong?"

"Nothing." Fran ran her hands over her face. "I'm tired, that's all. I should go to bed."

"Do you want to talk about it?"

"It's nothing," Fran said, walking to the fireplace, her back to Shelby. "I'm sorry I snapped at you. I must be premenstrual."

"You were premenstrual last week."

"I get premenstrual a lot."

She looked lonely, standing there by the fireplace. Lonely and lost and too small for the room. Shelby went over to her and slipped her arms around her. "Hey," she said.

Fran stiffened. Shelby thought she was going to push her away, but then she went soft and leaned her forehead against the mantel.

Shelby pressed her face into Fran's back. "Come on, tell me what's eating you."

"Gatherings make me nervous," Fran said.

"You seemed to be doing fine."

"But I'm wound as tight as a rusty clock. The only way I get through things like that is to put it in overdrive and run on anxiety."

"I wish I'd known that. You didn't have to come."

"I wanted to meet your friends."

"You could have met them one at a time."

Fran extricated herself slowly from Shelby's arms. "I'm being ridiculous," she said. "I'll be all right in the morning."

"Can I make you a drink or something?"

"No. Drinking at a time like this is a good way to become an alcoholic."

"Do you have a lot of times like this?"

Fran glanced at her. "A fair number."

"I take it," Shelby said with a smile, "we were working up to Brahms."

"Maybe." Fran shook her head. "I really am absurd."

"I hate to do this to you, but I'm inviting you to the engagement party. You don't have to come."

"Oh, hell," Fran said, "who knows how I'll feel by then?"

She looked so tired, dark under the eyes. "Go to bed," Shelby said, and started turning off the living room lamps. "Want me to tuck you in?"

Fran glared at her. "No, I do not want you to tuck me in."

Shelby shrugged and grinned. "Suit yourself. But you don't get an offer like this every day."

"I certainly don't."

"I'll see you tomorrow," Shelby said as she went to the door, "when we pick through the garbage." She hesitated, reaching for the wall switch to turn off the last of the lights. "Sure you're OK?"

"I'm OK." Fran started for her bedroom. "Good night, Shelby."

She was late getting to the lunchroom. It had been a morning of chaos and frustration. Two manuscripts arrived without the authors' return addresses. A page was missing from a third. Penny had sent up, with a glowing recommendation, one of the worst pieces of writing she'd ever read. Charlotte had a non-stop series of appointments and planning sessions that made their office feel like an open house.

To be perfectly honest, she was worried. Though they hadn't mentioned it yesterday, she was sure Fran would be tracking down a neurologist for her, probably already had. She was obviously one of those highly-compulsive, efficient, no-nonsense, militaristic types with no consideration for anyone's feelings as long as the job gets done.

She picked up a tray and today's special, mystery meatloaf. She should have brought a bag full of picnic leftovers. Stale buns, charred hard nurdles of dried-out hamburgers, limp salad—actually, she thought as she slid a small dish of lettuce and grated carrot onto her tray—the salad that had been left in the sun for two hours looked better than the one they were serving here.

Glancing toward their usual table, she noticed that Lisa was missing. Great. That left only herself as a fourth for bridge, and she was late and in a hurry. She steeled herself for the inevitable postmortem on the barbecue. Connie started the ball rolling by awarding the Connie Thurmond Seal of Approval to the festivities. "The greatest," she said, Jean agreeing, and Penny adding a nod. "Let's play bridge."

"I can't," Shelby said. "I'm behind on everything."

"I don't believe this," Connie said. "We *waited* for you."

"I'm sorry," she said.

Penny tossed her paper napkin onto her tray. "Well, that figures, damn it." Before anyone could respond, she picked up her dirty dishes and strode away.

Jean stared after her. "What's her major maladjustment?"

"Beats me," Connie shrugged. "She's been in a mood all morning."

She was tempted to tell them about the story Penny had recommended, to see if anyone could shed any light on it. She decided not to.

"Aren't you hungry?" Jean asked.

Shelby picked at her lunch. "For this?"

"You should eat," Connie said. "You have to keep up your strength."

Strength for what? Did Connie know about the headaches? Had Fran told her? Fran wouldn't do that. Never.

She might have told Jean, who told Connie. Nonsense, Jean didn't even like Connie particularly, certainly didn't trust her. She wouldn't gossip with her. Would she?

"Hello?" Connie said, rapping on Shelby's head. "Anyone home?"

"Sorry. I was wondering what you meant by that. Keep up strength. You know."

"Unless my memory is playing tricks on me, we go to press with the August issue in nine working days. Hell time begins."

Shelby laughed with relief. "You're right. I'd repressed it."

Oh, God, what if Fran got her an appointment and she couldn't get off work? Or she couldn't get one? Or...?

"Tell me," Connie went on, "is it as crazy in your office as it is in the readers' room?"

"Crazier, I'm afraid. You have to finish by the end of this week, but that's when the real chaos starts for us. I'll probably be working nights."

Jean shook her head. "I don't envy you."

"I do," said Connie. "As long as we have to be in hell, I'd rather do it on your salary."

"Well, part of being in hell on my salary," Shelby said as she glanced pointedly at her watch, "is sometimes I have to miss these delicious meals."

"What is the message here?" Connie asked. "Is it that we should play quietly like good little girls and let you eat?"

"That would be nice."

"OK," Connie said as she pulled her cards from her pocketbook. "Three-hand rotating dummy, no bid. I'll start."

* * *

Her desk phone rang. She picked it up. "Shelby Camden."

"Hi. It's Fran Jarvis."

Her stomach gave a lurch. "Hi."

"I wanted to let you know I got you an appointment with a Dr....Kinecki...for Thursday morning."

Shelby felt cold inside. "This Thursday?" Her voice cracked.

"I know, it's really short notice, but I think the sooner we get this over with, the better."

"I guess you're right."

She glanced up as Charlotte pushed away from her desk, gathering her pocketbook and briefcase. "Albany," Charlotte mouthed silently.

Shelby gave her a wave. "Good luck."

"Did you say something?" Fran asked.

The door closed behind Charlotte. "My office mate's leaving for the day. I was just wishing her luck. She has to cover some kind of affair at the New York Governor's mansion. I don't know what."

"Look," Fran said, "if you feel you need more time, I can change the appointment. I don't want you to feel pushed."

"No, you're right." She hesitated. "Can you come...?"

"I've already found someone to cover for me Thursday."

"OK." She didn't want to hang up, didn't want to be alone with her anxiety. But there wasn't anything else to say. "Well, thanks..."

"Shelby."

"What?"

"Talk to me."

"I'm fine."

"You're not fine," Fran said. "Your voice isn't fine."

She took a deep breath. "I'm just a little apprehensive."

"Apprehensive? Or terrified?"

"Somewhere in between," she admitted.

"Look," Fran said, "I'm scared, too. But we have to be rational about this. The chances are way in your favor it's nothing. And if it's something, there are a hundred things it could be, most of them not terrible."

"I know."

"Thursday's about information. We need more information, that's all. That's what we're going to get."

"I know," Shelby repeated. She felt paralyzed and incapable of thought. There was a sound in her head like bees.

"After that, we take things one step at a time. But I really don't have a bad feeling about this."

"Good."

"When you get home tonight, we'll go over the entire procedure so you'll know what to expect. It's absolutely painless, just boring."

"Good."

"You're tuning me out. I can tell."

"Sorry."

"Well, stop it. It won't help and you'll just end up feeling alone."

She *was* alone, she realized. She'd never felt more alone in her life. She forced herself to ask, "Fran, what if it's a brain tumor?"

"I really, really doubt it. You're not dizzy, or having balance problems, or hallucinating the smell of burning rags. But if it is, we'll do what has to be done. Look, Shelby," she said in a soft, firm voice, "however this works out, I'm with you. Whatever it takes, however long it takes, I won't leave you alone in it."

Relief and gratitude washed over her. "Thank you." She laughed a little. "I think I'm a mess."

"What else is new?"

"Hey," Shelby said, "there's no need to be insulting."

"You sound better."

"A little." She looked out the window, into the branches of the maple that stood in front of the building's entrance. A robin was building a nest. "I should get back to work."

"Me, too. I'd hate anyone to bleed to death on my shift. Looks terrible on the resumé. I'll see you tonight."

"I have dinner with my mother."

"It's all right if it's late. Any time."

"OK."

"Take care of yourself, Shelby."

"You, too."

She did feel better. Talking had connected her back to herself.

Hanging up the phone, she leaned back in her desk chair and watched the progress on the robin's nest for a while. The female stayed by the half-built nest while the male brought tiny sticks and dried grasses. He'd drop them at her feet and immediately try to mount her. Mrs. Robin would shake him off, examine the building materials he'd brought, and declare them unsatisfactory. Knowing he wouldn't get what he wanted until she'd gotten what she wanted, he'd fly off to try again.

When Shelby thought about her friendship with Fran—and she found she thought about it quite a bit—it struck her as strange and possibly a little disconcerting, but not in an unpleasant way. They'd known each other three months, but enjoyed the ease and comfort of a much longer time of knowing. Though she'd been eager for Fran to meet her other friends, and though everyone had gotten along, she now realized that her friendship with Fran was something set apart from her everyday life. She really wouldn't mind if Fran didn't come to the engagement party. She wouldn't even care, really, if she skipped the wedding. Parties and rituals were part of mundane things, on the surface of life. Their friendship wasn't about all that. She wouldn't have asked her other friends to help her find out about the headaches. Not even Jean. As much as she liked her, she couldn't go crazy and start screaming with Jean. And she had the feeling she could easily go crazy and start screaming.

What if she had to go into the hospital? There'd be no way of keeping this secret if that happened. And, once the secret was out, everyone—Libby, Ray,

Connie—oh God, Connie—would have an opinion, and everyone would tell her and her doctor what to do, and do it now before you have a chance to consider it, and she'd lose the reins of her life entirely.

She shook herself. One thing at a time. At least she could have some control over things in the immediate vicinity. She reached for her phone and dialled Penny's extension.

"Everything I've touched today has gone wrong," Shelby said.

Fran handed her a soda. "Really?" She indicated the space next to Shelby on the couch. "Feel free to stretch out. After all, this is a pajama party."

Shelby swung her legs up. Fran sat in the chair across the coffee table.

"I had a meeting with my editor, which ran over, which made me late for lunch, which meant they couldn't play bridge since Lisa wasn't in today—probably hung over—and there was no one to fill in for me, who was late, which caused no end of consternation among the truly bridge-addicted, namely Connie…" She paused to catch her breath. "Then I had to meet with Penny in the afternoon because she recommended a story that was just terrible—I mean it would take first prize hands down in a contest for the worst short stories of the 1962/63 season, no, the entire decade. I made myself believe she did it as a joke, since I couldn't believe she would really like that thing, but she hadn't. Didn't. Liked it. So there we were, coming from opposite points of view, trying to reach some kind of consensus, which was impossible since we'd both chosen this particular day to be unyielding. I finally had to pull rank and reject the story. Which is what they pay me to do. So now Penny thinks I'm nasty and foolish, and I'm doubting my own judgment—if not about the story, at least about her—and I really hate these awkward, confrontational *things* we get into."

"I imagine the news I dropped on you right after lunch didn't help much."

She sipped her drink. "Yeah, I guess I was a little nervous."

"No doubt," Fran said and gave her an 'I know you're understating but I'm pretending to let you get away with it' smile.

"So then I had to spend the evening over dinner with my mother, planning The Wedding." She sighed. "The Wedding. You'd think it was a Presidential Inauguration."

"I take it you're still not in agreement on it."

Shelby laughed sharply. "In agreement? I don't even understand the damn thing. About the only thing we're in agreement on is that she knows everything and I know nothing."

Fran raised one eyebrow. "I'll bet you know more about camping than she does."

"Anything Libby doesn't know anything about isn't worth knowing anything about."

"That's *her* opinion." She smiled at her sympathetically. "You're in a mood."

"I guess so. I know it's ridiculous, but she makes me feel so stupid."

"Shelby…"

"It's as if I'm the only person in the entire world who doesn't know how to do this stuff."

"If everyone knew how to do this stuff, there'd be no market for *Bride Magazine*."

Shelby twisted on the couch and rose up on one elbow to see her. "Are you sitting back there taking notes?"

"Are you paying me forty-dollars an hour?"

"I should be." She flopped back down and stared at the ceiling. "All I do around you is spill my guts."

"Gee," Fran said, "I thought that was what friends were for. And all this time I could have been getting rich."

"I'll bet you're the kind of person everyone talks to."

"Hardly."

"Sure, you are. You probably lock your door at the end of the day so you won't have to listen to people spilling their guts at you. It's probably why you don't have a television set."

"I don't have a television set because I've just spent four years staring at television, when I wasn't soldiering. I wanted to learn to read again." She got up and took Shelby's glass and refilled it and gave it back to her. "What's the real problem, Shelby?"

She pulled her knees up so Fran had room to sit beside her. "I don't know how to do this," she heard herself say.

"Do what?"

"Life."

Fran swirled the ice cubes in her glass with one finger. "That's simple. It's always fourth down, eight yards to go. You punt."

"Don't I wish?" She was glad Fran had sat where she could see her. It made her feel less confused, somehow. "There are rules. Millions of rules. Half of them I can't remember, and half of them I can't keep."

"Don't forget, it was just people who made them, not God."

"It's people who enforce them."

She rolled the cold glass across her forehead. "I'm so tied in knots over this wedding…it's a thousand opportunities to fail."

"Does that really matter so much?"

Shelby glanced at her. Fran looked deeply serious. "It does when you have Libby for a mother."

"I thank God every morning that Libby isn't my mother. Well, maybe not every morning. But everything you've said about her reminds me of a particularly nasty lieutenant we had at Fort Sam. He'd make you eat dirt and then kiss his foot in gratitude for the opportunity to do it."

Shelby smiled grimly.

"It was the Army. You expected it. There wasn't anything personal about it. A mother's a bit more personal than the Army."

"Quite a bit." She rubbed the back of her neck. "God, I'm sick of talking about this. There's more to life than headaches and weddings."

"I didn't know that," Fran said. "What else?"

"Camping."

"Want to go again?"

"Yes."

"This weekend?"

Shelby shook her head. "I have a date Saturday night."

"We'll go Friday, and come back Saturday evening."

Date to camping she could do. But camping to date? "As soon as we can work it out, OK?"

"Very OK."

Shelby started to get up. "Sack time."

"One moment, please." Fran took her wrist. "We're going to go over what you should expect on Thursday."

She sat back down. "Do we have to?"

"Yes, we have to. Because I can see you making it much worse in your mind than it really is, and I won't allow that."

I hate this, Shelby thought as she stared at the unmoving shadow of the maple against the bedroom wall. She could get through Thursday. That was no problem. A couple of simple tests, an EEG, all of it painless. But it wasn't the pain she was afraid of. It was what it might be leading up to. There were some pretty scary possibilities, like tumors and aneurysms—though Fran was quick to assure her, if she had an aneurysm, she'd probably be dead by now, which was a comfort—and seizures and all kinds of horrors that would force her to cancel her life as she knew it and start over. But even if it was only tension...*only* tension, like being just a little bit pregnant...she knew perfectly well it wouldn't go away until she'd made some changes in her life.

Changes. What changes? Her life was fine, going along the way it was supposed to, the way she'd always planned. So where's the tension? The wedding? She'd had the headaches long before they'd even talked about marriage. The job? Sure, she was afraid of making a mistake, but she'd lived her whole life afraid of making a mistake, what else was new?

It wasn't fair. She'd finally gotten it right, finally arrived, finally made it to where she'd been trying to go since she was a child, and what was the payoff? Headaches and insomnia. If this was life's idea of a joke, it was a really nasty one.

One thing at a time, Fran would say.

Yeah, and what else was there to do in the deep, unformed hours of darkness between midnight and dawn? Especially that three a.m. to four a.m. period. That was a real killer. That was when the heebie-jeebies would get you if they ever would. When you weren't sure what time it was, or if day would ever come, or where you were or even who you were sometimes.

Fran had said they might want a sleeping EEG, which meant staying up most of the night before. No problem. She was all set to stay up three nights before, all night, beginning now.

This was terror. Pure terror. And depression. Oh, yes, let's not forget depression. How about anxiety? Or is that just terror on a smaller scale? No, terror is about now. Anxiety is about the future. Or is that apprehension? Apprehension, what a joke. Apprehension is a scraped elbow compared to this multiple-fracture, rib-crushing anxiety.

She sat up and turned on the light. Might as well read. Might as well do something constructive with all these extra hours I've been given.

Maybe Fran was still awake. Maybe they could talk or something.

Shelby slipped out of bed and out into the hall. No light showing beneath Fran's door.

Well, it was just as well. She couldn't go running to Fran with every little problem.

She closed her door and locked it, wishing she could lock out the next few days and nights. She thought about making a drink, but something told her it wasn't a good idea. Drinking to sleep could lead to side effects.

Maybe that was what caused the headaches. Maybe she was drinking too much. Maybe her sins were catching up with her...

Be real. She'd had drinks, serious drinks, maybe ten times in college, once to excess in her junior year when she'd joined some sort-of friends for an illicit bash at the state park. She'd ended up terrified of being caught and thrown into jail, maudlin about the friend who wasn't her friend any more, and sicker than a dog the next day. One of her hall mates had put her to bed, sat up all night with her, and refused to tell her—ever—what she'd said in her drunken ramblings.

In graduate school it had been wine, and not much of that. She didn't want to be cotton-headed and miss something important, especially now that everything she was studying was relevant.

She drank more now, of course. They all did. It was what career women, on their own for the first time, did. As if she were truly on her own, what with Libby checking in twice a week, keeping track of her every move. And Ray, and her friends...she was answerable to them all. That was how it was when people cared about you. You took their feelings into account, and when you had to take someone else's feelings into account you weren't really on your own.

Which wasn't such a bad thing, she thought as she forced herself to get back into bed and turn out the light. It was better than being alone in the world.

Fran was alone in the world, at least for now. In a new place, estranged from her family, separated from her friends. She'd put a life together soon, but until then...How did it feel? Did she like it? Was she lonely? Maybe she felt free. Maybe loneliness was worth that. Shelby realized she'd never asked. That was rude, as if she didn't care. And she did care. It was just that Fran always seemed so all right with where she was and what she was doing. She'd have to remember to ask.

A bird twittered, a fluting sound. Robins. Next would come the sparrows, with the pewter pre-dawn sky. Once the light started, she'd be awake for good, and she'd have to go around all day with that gritty, metallic, half-sick, half-stupid feeling of no sleep. She turned on one side, then the other, then back on her back. The shadows on the wall faded. The window glass turned gray.

"Oh, shit," Shelby said.

She got up, bathed and dressed, and went to her car. The town was eerily silent, security lights glowing dim in stores, the landscape washed with gray. Mist hung over the fields and along the creeks. An occasional light burned in a farm house kitchen, but there was no one inside. Everything was lifeless, suspended, hollow, waiting.

She drove until it was time to go to work.

Chapter 9

Fran was sitting in one of the orange molded plastic chairs in the waiting room engrossed in "Children's Activities." Shelby went to her and held out a prescription slip. "Will this stuff kill me?" she asked.

Surprised, Fran gave a little jump. She took the slip and glanced at it. "Not unless you take a bunch of them at once. It's just sleeping pills."

"Well, " Shelby said, "in that case I guess you're going to have to put up with me for a while longer."

Fran stood. "You're OK?"

"Overworked, underslept, and tense. As opposed to immature, insecure, and frustrated, which is what they called us in boarding school." Shelby couldn't help grinning. "Other than that, there's 'nothing organically wrong' with me. Wish my parents were as easy to please." She pulled her London Fog from the coat rack. There were implications to this 'nothing organically wrong' business, of course, but she'd deal with them later. For now, it was enough to experience the temporary high that came with a close call.

Turning back, she noticed Fran swiping at her eyes with her sleeve. "Hey, are you crying?"

"Outside," Fran said with a glance in the direction of the receptionist.

"Meet you there." She went to the desk to deal with insurance.

Fran stood in the parking lot, leaning against the car. The morning's drizzle had given way to gray skies and an unseasonable damp, biting wind that felt and smelled as if it had blown across a thousand miles of ice. It tossed the tips of Fran's hair. They sparkled like dew in a slanting beam of watery sun. Waxed paper wrappers skittered across the parking lot. Last winter's salt and grit, kicked up by swirling eddies of wind, whirled and fell and scoured at the parked cars.

"For Pete's sake," Shelby said, "it's a Montreal Express. Get inside before you freeze."

Fran slid into the passenger seat. Shelby started the motor and turned on the heater. "You realize," she said, "we're not going anywhere until you tell me why you were crying."

"I'm just relieved." She rammed her hands into her cardigan pockets. "I was afraid they'd find something really terrible wrong with you."

"I never knew you were worried."

"You were scared enough for us both."

Shelby shook her head. "Promise me you'll never do that again. If I think you might be hiding something from me—for whatever reason—I'll never be able to trust you. It's important for me to trust you."

"I'm sorry."

"I mean it, Fran. I need someone who'll always tell me the truth."

Fran looked at her. "You never told me that."

"I know." She raked her hand through her hair. She was feeling very earnest, though she wasn't sure why this had suddenly become so urgent. "I realize we haven't known each other all that long, but it feels long. I mean, it feels like I've known you forever." She laughed. "Here I am saying these things, and I don't even know if you like me."

"I like you," Fran said.

"It's easy to be honest with you. That matters a lot to me. But I have to know you feel the same way. Please. I need a friend like you."

Fran squeezed her hand. "I don't think you have to worry about that."

Shelby realized she was blushing. "I feel silly. People don't say things like this."

"Well, that's too bad for people. Look, Shelby, I need an honest friend, too. But I've been places, and known people—it hasn't always been safe to be open, that's all. I'll do my best. But old habits die hard."

"Especially old *stupid* habits?"

"Especially that kind."

Shelby put the car in gear. She was confused. She hadn't intended to say all that. She hadn't even known she felt those things. Something was slipping out of control.

Glancing over at Fran, she grew calm. Fran was solid, comfortable. She'd been through things—probably things Shelby couldn't even imagine, everyone's life was so surprising and different—but she hadn't lost her openness. Fran might not always know who she was, Shelby thought, but she always *was* who she was.

"What places?" she asked.

"I grew up," Fran said. "I went to college. I had to drop out of college. I spent six years in the Army. Add that to just plain having lived, and I'm bound to have been a few places and had a few experiences. Haven't you?"

Shelby shrugged. "Not really. I mean, I did the college and graduate school thing, but my life hardly makes for an exciting story."

"Well," Fran said, "consider yourself lucky. Although, keeping in mind that you have brain-splitting headaches of no organic origin, don't sleep, and have nightmares when you do sleep—I think your life may be just a bit more interesting than you like to think."

She didn't know what to say to that.

Fran smiled. "You're the one who wanted me to tell you what I think."

"Yeah," Shelby said. "I've created a monster."

Instead of turning right out of the parking lot, the way they'd come in, she took a left.

"Where are we going?"

"Playing hooky. There's a Dairy Queen in East Sayer. That's about all there is, a Dairy Queen. I'm treating you to the biggest Brazier Burger and fries we can get."

Fran sighed. "I owe you. Forever."

"I owe you, too," Shelby said seriously.

"Another opening, another show…" The song ran through her head as she waited for Ray to come around to her side of the car and open the door.

Well, it *was* like a piece of theater. With the Country Club as the stage, and evening clothes as costumes—her off-the-shoulder cocktail dress was a rich lilac verging on purple, to match the irises Libby had ordered by the hundreds and placed on every flat surface in the room. The Country Club was going to look like a funeral parlor.

"Huh?" Ray said as he reached the open car window.

She'd said it out loud. "I was just talking to myself." She smiled up at him. "It comes from living alone."

He opened the door and helped her out, gathering her crinolines over his arm so they wouldn't be crushed. "In a year, you'll have me to talk to," he said. "Forever and forever." He helped her from the car, then put his hand around her elbow and led her toward the club.

Shelby hesitated.

This was it, the big moment. Time to stand up in front of witnesses and say, "This is what I intend to do." Going public. Not quite taking out an ad in the newspaper, but Libby had seen to an engagement announcement in the *Globe* and the *Times*. No turning back.

She was supposed to be thrilled. She was supposed to look glamorous. She didn't. Her clothes felt as if they belonged to someone else, some girl in a movie, someone cute and perky who could act like a lady if she had to. She thought of Doris Day, June Allyson, Debbie Reynolds…

Shelby herself felt simultaneously dumpy and scrawny. Nothing fit right. Shoes too small, bra too tight, waist too loose. Her corsage threatened to jump ship.

She felt about fifteen, much too young for this.

"What's wrong?" Ray asked.

"I need a minute." She took a deep breath to steady herself and fussed with her corsage pin.

Ray grinned. "Cold feet?"

She nodded. "A little. All this hoopla. It's not as if we won the Nobel Prize or anything. Doesn't it strike you as ridiculous?"

"Sure, it does. It's supposed to be ridiculous. It's wedding stuff."

"I think you enjoy it." She straightened his bow tie.

He took her shoulders in his hands. "I don't enjoy it, Shel. I hate it as much as you do."

"Impossible. No man could hate this as much as a woman."

"What makes you say that?"

"You don't have to wear girdles and long-line underwire bras."

Ray blushed slightly. "Well, I guess not. But neckties aren't exactly a day at the beach."

"What about stiff net stoles?" She rubbed hers against his face. "And high heels?"

He shuddered. "How about wool suits?"

"Hats and gloves."

"Men wear hats."

"Not like ours. Pins and veils, and you're always worrying about it coming off. Men dress for comfort. Women dress for…I'm not sure what we dress for, but it sure isn't comfort."

"I thought you dressed for men," Ray said.

"And how fair is that? Do men dress for women? No, they dress to impress other men. I'll make a deal with you. You wear my clothes for a day, and I'll wear yours, and we'll see who's suffering more by nightfall."

He looked up at the club house, then down at her, and grinned. "Let's do it. Tonight."

"What?"

"We'll slip into the locker rooms, and I'll put your clothes on and you put mine on. That should get things off to an interesting start."

She tried to picture him in her evening dress. Knobby knees poking out from beneath the skirt. Big, pale feet squashed into high heels. His broad, muscled chest stuffed in a Merry Widow. He'd look like a sausage. She couldn't help laughing.

"What's so funny?"

"I just got a picture of you in my head. Now I know why men don't wear dresses."

"Some do." He took her arm again and started on toward the club house. "I did, once, in college. Wore a dress, that is. We were doing one of those satirical revues."

"Did you enjoy it?"

"It was terrible. I was terrible."

"Do you have pictures?"

Ray glanced down at her. "There are pictures, but you'll never see them."

"Come on."

"Never. I'll destroy them."

"I'll bet there are copies. I'll bet they're on file somewhere at Harvard. Harvard never throws anything away."

"Neither does Mt. Holyoke. I'll bet your nude posture pictures are available."

"You wouldn't!"

"I would."

They laughed and walked into the club house, arms around each other. The happy couple, making it official.

They were all there, more than a hundred of them. Her father, without the latest girlfriend, for which she was grateful. Her mother, reigning over it all like a Queen. Her father's friends and business buddies, her mother's friends, and, huddling together in a ghetto of the young, Ray's friends and hers. Except for Fran, and Ray's parents, who had decided to wait until the wedding to fly in from Seattle. Fran had begged off, saying she had to work the night shift. Shelby suspected Fran, knowing no one very well, really didn't feel comfortable in a setting like this—and who did, pray tell?—and had told a polite lie about it. To tell the truth, she was secretly glad Fran hadn't come. For reasons she didn't entirely understand, she sensed she'd be ill-at-ease doing this in front of Fran. Probably because she had to engage in some serious acting tonight, and she had the feeling Fran could see through it. All she had to do was look over and see those cornflower eyes and that knowing half smile, and she might as well toss in the towel. Theatrical careers had been destroyed by less.

They paused at the top of the stairs to the dining/ballroom. Lisa spotted them and let out a whoop, "It's *them!*" and everyone crowded around. Shelby took a deep breath, steeled herself. Be friendly, smile, shake hands, thank them for coming, and don't let on you haven't the vaguest idea who you're talking to. The hands and faces went by like an assembly line.

"Great party," Connie said. "Really, the greatest." And dragged Charlie onto the dance floor.

Jean embraced her. "Get me out of this," Shelby whispered to her.

"Want me to set off the fire alarm?"

"No, you'd be arrested and sent to jail."

"It would get me out of lunchtime bridge," Jean said.

Penny came up "oohing" and "aahing" and generally gushing with enthusiasm. Shelby was relieved. There'd been tension between them ever since the incident of the rejected story, but now it seemed Penny had finally decided to let bygones be bygones. "I'm *so* happy for you," Penny said.

"Thanks." She glanced into Penny's eyes and saw a flicker of coldness. So she hadn't put it behind her entirely. But this was a start. She decided to try to move it forward a step. "I was afraid you were still annoyed with me. You know, about…"

Penny tossed her head. "Don't be silly. If our friendship can't survive a little disagreement…"

"You're right." She leaned forward. "Who's the new guy?"

"Jeff. No, Mike. God, I have to get a grip on myself. One of these days I'm going to slip up at a really bad time." She looked around the room. "Where's your housemate?"

"Working."

Other people were pressing around, ready to meet and greet. "I'd better go," Penny said. "Don't want what's-his-name to feel neglected."

She melted away into the crowd.

Between the soup and the entree Ray leaned over close to her ear. "How did Libby manage to get the Country Club on such short notice?"

Shelby shrugged. She was beginning to be too aware of her clothes. Her stole was scratchy. The underwire bra dug into her rib cage. It hurt and made her irritable. "Who knows? She probably steamrolled it the way she steamrolls everything."

He slipped an arm across the back of her chair. "Well, her days of steamrolling you are just about over."

It should have given her a feeling of safety. Her own Sir Galahad keeping the dragon from her door. Some women married for that alone. Some didn't even get that. But it annoyed her. She didn't feel protected, she felt crippled. Shelby picked at her peas and sauteed mushrooms and veal something-or-other smothered in a peculiar-looking sauce which had an overtaste of one or more ingredients gone bad. She took a forkful and washed it down with wine.

"Are you OK, Shel?" Ray asked.

"Sure."

"You look kind of down."

"It's the food," she said quickly. "Does it taste all right to you?"

Ray laughed. "Babe, all I have to compare it to is the hospital cafeteria. Anything tastes all right."

A year from now, she thought, all your dinners will be lovingly prepared by Little Wifey.

By the time dessert was served she'd managed to drink enough wine to relax. Ray had gone beyond relaxed. He was cranked up. Shelby was glad. When Ray was in this kind of mood all she had to do was sit back and enjoy the show.

Toasts were happening. Best wishes to the bride and groom to be. Reminiscences and embarrassing stories about Shelby as a child. Champagne flowed. Ray's friends told obscure and slightly raunchy tales about Ray and his activities in the pathology lab. Ray offered a toast to the "girl of his dreams." Shelby offered one to "the East's most sought-after and soon-not-to-be-available bachelor." They pretended to fight about how and where they'd met.

Doing it right, Shelby thought, aware that she was a little high.

She stood and offered a toast to her mother, "without whom, etc." Nobody knew how true that was. Not just the party, but the whole engagement-wedding-marriage...

She lost her train of thought.

"Don't let me drink any more," she whispered in Ray's ear.

He patted her knee under the table.

Libby declared dinner over. The band came back into the room. Tables were pushed to the side.

Shelby saw Penny heading toward the stairs. Her face was tight. Something was wrong. "Dance with Libby," she said to Ray, and started after her.

"Hey." He caught her arm. "Where are you going, bride-to-be?"

"Ladies' room."

He let her go and stepped back. She saw her mother striding toward her with a look on her face that said Shelby had committed a transgression. Whether large or small, she wasn't sure. And it didn't matter. Libby would go to great lengths to point out and explain exactly what Shelby had done wrong. You might as well commit mayhem as use the wrong fork. Once Libby caught up to her...

"Dance with her, please" she mouthed silently to Ray. He went to flag down his future mother-in-law.

At first she thought Penny wasn't in the ladies' room. It felt hollow and smelled of damp concrete and old sneakers. A dripping faucet was creating a rusty ring around the sink drain. She heard a sniffling noise from one of the stalls. "Penny?"

"Go away," Penny said.

"It's Shelby. Is anything wrong?"

"I'm fine. I'm always fine. Leave me alone."

Shelby sat down on one of the vanity chairs. "You're not fine." She wished her head would stop spinning. "Talk to me."

"No."

"OK, but I'm not leaving until you do. It's going to be a long night, and my chair's more comfortable than yours."

"Fine."

There was a long silence. Shelby shivered a little in the dampness and wondered if she'd made a mistake, daring Penny like that. If she didn't get back to the ballroom in fifteen minutes, Libby was going to come looking for her.

"I can't do this, Penny," she said. "I have to get back upstairs."

"So go."

Shelby stood up and brushed the wrinkles from the back of her skirt. "I know you're upset, and I think it's me you're upset with, and I don't know why. But I care about you a lot, and I value your friendship. So I hope you'll be able to bring yourself to tell me what it is, because I'd like to do what I can to fix it."

The lock on the stall door clanked open. Penny came out, looking ashamed. "I'm sorry."

"For what?"

"It's not your fault."

"Maybe it is." She touched Penny's shoulder. "I wish you'd tell me."

Penny reached up and embraced her. "I hate feeling distant from you." She started to cry.

Shelby stroked her hair. "It's a nasty feeling. I hate it, too."

"You do?" She clung to her.

"Of course," Shelby said. It was definitely a mistake to do this on champagne. She'd lost track of the conversation.

Another long silence, then Penny let her go. "I'm so glad you said that," she said. "I was so afraid…"

"It's fine, Penny. Everything's fine."

Penny turned and examined her face in the dressing table mirror. "God, I look awful. What's-his-name will never ask me out again." She glanced at Shelby in the glass. "You better go make hostess noises." She poked at a trickle of runny mascara. "I'll be up as soon as I repair the ravages."

"You're sure you're OK?"

"I'm OK," Penny said as she took her lipstick case from her evening bag. "More than OK. Really. See you upstairs."

Shelby closed the door quietly behind her and started up the steps. So everything was back to normal. She was glad of that. The trouble was, she didn't know had just happened, or how it had been fixed so easily, or really what she'd done to upset Penny in the first place.

Chapter 10

She hadn't seen Fran in days—weeks, really, if you didn't count the short conversations they had in the hall. Fran asked how she was, she said fine. She asked how Fran was, Fran said fine. Fran asked how the wedding was going. Shelby sighed and rolled her eyes. Fran laughed. Fran was working the night shift at the Health Service—penance, she was sure, for some ancient, long-forgotten transgression. Shelby was trying to learn the language of weddings, and she'd never been very good at foreign languages. They commiserated briefly. They promised themselves they'd go camping, as soon as Fran got off the weekend shift. They agreed to get together over dinner. Soon.

The trouble was, Shelby missed her. And the longer she went without seeing her, the more she missed her. So, on a Saturday afternoon, when she knew Fran wasn't working, she decided to make good on a promise she'd made to herself, and went looking for her.

She tapped on the door. Someone called faintly from inside, she thought, but she wasn't sure. Maybe Fran was in the kitchen or the bedroom. She tried the door. It wasn't locked. "Hey," she said as she opened it and looked in. "It's just me. What's up with you? Are you hiding…"

The room was dark after the hallway. The sun had already crossed to the west. The light through the east-facing windows was pale and touched with the faint green of young leaves. The air felt old.

Fran lay curled up on the couch, a blanket wrapped tightly around her. Her face was the color of ashes, her lips slate blue. Her eyes glittered. She was shivering.

It looked as if there'd been a fire in the fireplace, but it had gone out. Singed paper and half-burned twigs lay in a sprawl on the hearth. And the room was as warm as late-June could be, certainly not chilly enough to need a fire.

"What's wrong?" Shelby asked, going to her.

Fran pulled the cover tighter. "Freezing," she said.

Close up, it was clear that she was very sick. Her skin was dry and brittle. Shelby felt her forehead. "You're burning up," she said.

"No. Cold."

"Cold *and* burning up. This isn't good."

"Tell me," Fran said.

Shelby reached for her. "Come on. You're going to bed. Now." She took her hand and tried to help her up. Fran was as limp as a rag doll. Bending down, she slipped an arm under her shoulders and eased her to a sitting position.

"Glad you're here," Fran murmured.

"How long have you been like this?"

"Last night. I think."

"With the chills, the fever?"

Fran nodded.

She started to scold her for not calling her, but that would be cruel. Fran was obviously in pain and fragile. She boosted her up with an arm around the shoulders, and led her into the bedroom.

"Bathroom," Fran said, and veered off in that direction.

Shelby turned her attention to the room. It was a mess. Half the bureau drawers were open, spilling socks and shirts and pajamas. Fran's clothes were strewn across the floor, as if she'd stripped them off and dropped them wherever she happened to be. The bed was rumpled as a rat's nest. It wasn't like Fran. There was still a spit-and-polish military air about her apartment, with things tidy and in their places at all times. Whatever was wrong with her, it must have attacked suddenly. Which gave her a pretty good idea of what it was. Especially since almost everyone she knew, including herself, had had it last winter. They called it the Killer Flu. It wasn't a term of endearment. Shelby herself had come down with it in the middle of the A & P, suddenly feeling weak and dizzy, and had madly grabbed a cart full of frozen TV dinners. Barely making it home, she'd just had time to shove them into the freezer compartment before the truly horrible part started. Now she picked up Fran's clothes and tidied the bed and closed the bureau drawers and closet door.

The kitchen and bathroom led off from the bedroom, an oddity brought about when the owners cut up the house and installed more plumbing. From the kitchen, she could tell if Fran left the bathroom. She went through the cupboards to see if there was anything which might be helpful in the current emergency.

There wasn't. Not much of anything at all, helpful or frivolous. Fran must have been about to shop when the bug struck her. Shelby decided she could probably put together what she needed from her own apartment, at least for now.

Fran came out of the bathroom and stumbled to the bed. Shelby helped her in and pulled the covers up around her. Fran's teeth were chattering. Shelby found a quilt on the closet shelf and spread it over her.

"Sorry," Fran said.

"I don't want to hear that. I wish you'd called me."

"Didn't want to bother you." She was having trouble breathing.

"That's idiocy." She went to the bathroom and checked out the medicine cabinet. It was no more useful than the kitchen. "Honestly," she said, "for someone in the medical business, you have the world's most poorly equipped medicine cabinet."

"Shoot me," Fran muttered. "I can cure a bullet wound."

"I'm going over to my place for supplies. Hang in there."

By the time she got back, Fran was sitting up, and coughing. Shelby recognized that cough only too well. It was a choking, bone-cracking, muscle-tearing, throat-ripping cough. Lying down made it worse, and after a few rounds of it you were too weak to sit up. "I'll be there in a minute," she said. She filled the tea kettle and set it on to boil and poured a glass of water.

She sat on the edge of the bed. "Rough, isn't it?"

Fran nodded. She started to say something, and another convulsion of coughing took her over. It sounded like brittle wood exploding. Her face turned red, then back to white, and red again. Tears came to her eyes. She tried to get control, but the harder she tried the more the struggle made her choke. Shelby remembered it, remembered choking until she couldn't breathe, remembered the knife-stabs of pain in her lungs. Remembered being alone, and terrified. She put her arms around Fran and pressed her head against her shoulder. "Lean on me," she said. "Try to let yourself relax."

Slowly, Fran stopped fighting. The cough subsided until finally she was able to take a few deep breaths. "Thanks," she said, and started to pull away.

Shelby held onto her. "Stay like this. Rest a minute. It'll help. Lying down makes it worse." She liked the feel of Fran's head on her shoulder, Fran's back under her hands. It made her feel, strong and protective and...

...she searched for the word, but when it came to her she didn't understand it...

...whole.

She stayed very still and listened as their breathing synchronized until their separate breaths became one breath.

"Don't catch this," Fran murmured.

"I've already had it, in February. I'm immune."

Shelby stroked Fran's back soothingly. "Don't talk," she said. Fran was still shivering. Her bathrobe lay across the bottom of the bed. Shelby reached back and grabbed it and draped it over her shoulders. "I can tell you from experience," she said, "this will pass. It's miserable while it's happening, and it won't necessarily make you a better person, but it really will pass."

Fran coughed a little in a huffing way and tensed against the next onslaught.

"Easy," Shelby said. "Let it flow through you." She loosened her hold a little, to give her more breathing space. "And don't be afraid. I know what to do. You'll feel like this for a couple of days..."

"Won't make it."

Shelby smiled. "You'll make it. Are they driving hot spikes into your head and joints yet?"

Fran nodded.

"Eyes hurt?"

She nodded again.

"Dizzy?"

"Yeah."

"What about throwing up?"

"No, thanks."

"Did you throw up?"

Fran nodded. She relaxed a little. Apparently, this coughing fit had passed her by and gone in search of bigger game.

"Did you throw up a lot?"

"None of your business," Fran said.

"You medical types," Shelby said. "You expect *us* to tell all, but when it come to yourselves..."

"I hate you."

"You're not in a position to hate me. Besides, I took orders from you on our camping trip. It's your turn to take orders from me."

"I have a merit badge in camping."

"Well," Shelby said, "I have one in misery."

"Yes, I threw up a lot. I didn't have a good time. Does it make you happy knowing that?"

"Ah, pissiness," she said, "you're still among the living."

"If I'm not, I sure didn't go to Heaven." She was silent for a moment, then she said softly, "Thank you."

"Don't thank me. You're going to be sick of the sight of me. I'm going to force you to do things you don't want to do, and eat things you don't want to eat, and generally make a nuisance of myself."

Weakly, Fran raised one arm and touched Shelby's back in gratitude. Her hand fell back to the bed.

"You're going to be exhausted, once you get through the worst of this," Shelby recalled. "Your mind'll be fine, but your body will feel as if you're dragging lead weights. You have to be really careful not to overdo it. I forced myself to go out one evening, and relapsed for another two weeks. If you can stand it, just recline on the couch and watch soap operas on television."

"I don't have television," Fran said.

"My television. You'll need a change of scenery."

The water was beginning to hiss. "Time to lie down," Shelby said. "You're on your own for a minute." She arranged the pillows to support her and eased Fran back onto them and placed the thermometer in her mouth. Fran closed her eyes.

"OK," Shelby said, brushing Fran's hair away from her face. "I'm going to make you something to drink. You probably won't like it." She pulled the covers up around her.

She opened the box of lemon Jello and dropped it into a bowl, added a cup of boiling water, then enough cold water to make it drinkable. Pouring some into a mug, she noticed her hands were shaking. It was a scary thing, this flu. Almost as bad for the people around as the people who had it. It made them feel helpless, and sometimes annoyed because of that helpless feeling. She was glad she'd had it because she'd know what to do and what not to do, because she could do what needed to be done, because her knowing would make it easier for Fran.

Not that there was any such thing as "easy" with this monster, she thought as she handed the mug to Fran and took the thermometer. It registered high. Not life-threatening, exactly, but worth worrying about.

"A little over 103," she said. "If it doesn't go any higher, we're all right."

"Maybe you are," Fran muttered.

"If it does, we might have to make some decisions."

"Put me in the garbage."

Shelby smiled. "What I had in mind was calling a doctor."

Fran looked down at her drink. "What is this?"

"Jello."

"You're out of your mind."

"It's protein, glucose, and water," Shelby said. "All of which you need. Drink it." She could tell Fran was weak and only wanted to sleep, but she was dehydrating. The fever locked inside her had to be brought to the surface and released, and that wasn't going to happen that unless she could get fluids into her. She took the mug and sat beside her and held it to her lips, steadying her with her free arm. "Come on, Fran. It really isn't bad. Don't make me fight you every step of the way."

She drank. "Tastes like hot Lemonette."

"A lot like it, I guess. When you finish this, I'll let you sleep."

"Promises, promises."

She had finished the drink. Shelby took the mug away. She should probably get her to drink another, but she didn't have the heart to force it on her now. In a while, when she'd rested. She probably only had a few minutes before the congestion in her chest built up again, anyway. Shelby helped her lie down. She was almost asleep before Shelby had even finished straightening her covers.

"Shelby," Fran said as she was leaving the room.

"I'm right here."

"I hate this."

Shelby turned and went to her and rested her hand against the side of Fran's face. "Go to sleep."

The cough exploded like rifle shot. Shelby put down her book and ran to the bedroom. This one was worse than the last. Much worse. Fran's whole body was wracked with it. Her face was nearly purple.

I should have gotten a doctor, Shelby thought. I shouldn't have let it go this far.

Fran struggled for breath, struggled not to gag. Shelby sat next to her. "Remember, don't tense up," she said, and hoped she said it in a calm and matter-of-fact way that hid her panic. "It'll be all right."

But it was several helpless minutes before Fran got the spasm under control. Tears ran down her face. Shelby took a tissue from the box beside the bed and wiped them away. "Do you want to see a doctor?"

"Am I dying?"

"Of course not. I just thought you might feel more—well, secure."

"You think I don't trust you?"

"It would be OK if you didn't. I wouldn't take it personally."

"Well, I do." She took a deep breath and grimaced. "Jesus, that hurts."

"I know it does. I'll try to make you more comfortable."

Fran fell back against her pillows. "You must be God."

"If you'll drink the rest of the Jello…assuming it hasn't set…"

"Say it," Fran said, her words slurring from exhaustion. "You mean congealed. It's disgusting." She took another deep breath and groaned.

"If you'll drink it, I'll give you some aspirin. I didn't want to do it until I was sure you could keep it down."

"I'm so lucky."

"If you don't stop this," Shelby said firmly, "I'm going to walk out of here and leave you to your own devices."

Fran didn't answer.

"I lied," Shelby said. "I wouldn't do that."

"You could."

"I won't."

The Jello hadn't congealed, but it was a little thick. All right, slimy. Shelby heated the water and added some to the glass. "If this works out," she said as she helped Fran drink, "we'll move up to ginger ale and bouillon. Then maybe toast or macaroni. The important thing is to keep you from dehydrating, and at the same time not to stress your system."

Fran moved her shoulders and winced. "I'm already stressed. I think I was run over by a fire truck."

"We can take care of that, too. One thing at a time."

"I'm really sorry about this."

"Don't be on my account." She opened the aspirin and poured out two. "Take these. If you can tolerate it, you can have another."

Fran swallowed the aspirin with the last of the Jello. She handed the glass to Shelby. "I'm glad that's over."

"Well, maybe it is, and maybe it isn't. Are you ready to go back to sleep?" Fran nodded.

"OK, squinch down." She made the pillows a little lower. "I'm going to rub some stuff on your chest. It'll help you breathe." She opened the top button on Fran's pajamas and gently pushed the cloth aside. "This should feel good." She unscrewed the top to the Vicks Vaporub jar and scooped up two fingers full. "Smells kind of funny," she said as she spread the ointment on Fran's chest, "but it beats the old mustard plasters. Did you ever have one of them?"

"Yes." She closed her eyes.

"I used to have really sensitive skin when I was a kid." She smoothed the ointment out with the flat of her hand, working it in. "But I couldn't make anyone believe those things really burned me. My mother said I was just being a baby. Well, one time…I think it was during the whooping cough…she left one on me too long and I got blisters." Shelby laughed. "She was so upset and guilt-ridden I thought she'd spend the rest of her life going to Mass and doing penance. Except we weren't Catholic. Are you Catholic?"

Fran shook her head.

"My mother," Shelby said as she slowly massaged the muscles of Fran's chest, warming them, "was born into a Catholic family, but she left the church as soon as she could. She thinks being Catholic would interfere with her social-climbing career."

Fran's breathing deepened. Good, she was drifting off. "My mother's family was French-Canadian," Shelby said, lowering her voice to a rhythmic drone. "I never understood why she was ashamed of that. They were honest working people, and way back there are even some ancestors who went out to the West, trapping. Some of them married Indians. They all expected to get rich, of course, but nobody did, also of course. But they had a good time. I met the son of one of them once, when I was just a kid. He told great stories about those times, things he'd seen and things he'd heard from his father and uncles. He'd even met Calamity Jane once. My mother claimed he was a dreamer and a liar just like all the rest of them. But that didn't matter to me. As long as a story's good, who cares if it's true?"

Fran took a deep breath and let it out carefully. The tension lines melted from her face. Shelby went on rubbing her silently.

It was only late afternoon, the sun angling sharply across the lawn from the front of the house. The air drifting through the window was fresh and clean. A car drove past slowly. Sparrows twittered lazily in the warmth of early summer. It felt good to be doing this, taking care of her friend. Good, and right, and more important than anything she could think of.

She let her touch grow slower. Fran seemed to be almost asleep, but little frown marks wrinkled her forehead. Shelby smoothed them. "What's this for?"

Fran half-opened her eyes, but glanced away.

"Come on," Shelby said.

"I'm...kind of scared. Could you stay with me tonight?"

"I already have my sleeping bag and stuff here. I can sleep on your spare bed, or on the couch in the living room if you want privacy."

"Spare. You don't have to use the sleeping bag."

"It's my sleeping bag," Shelby said, "and I'll use it if I want to."

Fran smiled. "Nut." Her eyes drifted shut.

"As soon as you're asleep, I have to go over to my place for a minute and make a phone call," Shelby said. "I'll leave our doors open so I can hear you if you need me."

Fran didn't answer.

Shelby sat by her for a while, then got up carefully and slipped out of the apartment. She called Jean. "Listen, I'm not coming in to work Monday."

"Is everything OK?"

"With me it is. But Fran's picked up that wretched bug we all had last winter."

"Oh, God, that was terrible. Is there anything I can do?"

"I don't think so. But I need to stay near her. Tell the others, would you?"

"Sure. If you need anything, call me. I can drop it off."

"Thanks. Wait a minute, you haven't had this thing."

"I've been exposed to it, remember? From all of you. All at once. I felt like an itinerant Jewish mother."

Shelby recalled all too well. Jean, as the only healthy one among them, had commuted from one apartment to another, spreading cheer, aspirin, and chicken soup. "I don't know why you didn't get it."

"I eat right," Jean said.

She laughed. "I'll let that pass. Anyway, it was a relief, knowing you were making the rounds. It meant a lot. Really."

"Well, that's what friends are for."

"That was more than friendship, it was salvation."

"Come on, Shelby, you're embarrassing me."

"I'm going to call in sick, say I have cramps or something. Would you back up that story?"

"Listen," Jean said, "why not claim a migraine? Everyone knows about your headaches, they'd believe it in a minute. And you might need to stretch a second day out of it."

"Good thinking."

"OK, I'll pass the word. You feel like dog food."

"Thanks, Jean. I really appreciate it."

"Don't forget, call me if you need anything. I can run to the grocery or the drug store and drop stuff by your place."

"I will." She heard coughing from Fran's room. "I better get back."

There wasn't much she could do this time, except hold her up and give her ginger ale and try to make her comfortable. But it was clear the joint-crackers had taken up residence. Fran couldn't lie still, twisting and stretching and curling, and she was still cold. Shelby offered to help her into a hot bath, but she was too weak for that. She tried reading to her, but Fran didn't seem able to concentrate. Finally, convinced she was only making things worse by trying to help, she gave her another two aspirins and tucked her in. She took Fran's hand.

She sat quietly for a moment. The silence in the room, on the street, was too brittle, anticipatory. It made her twitchy. She turned on the radio on Fran's bureau, found the local classical FM station, and lowered the volume. "That OK?" she asked.

Fran nodded.

"Try to sleep." She should probably make herself some dinner. It was past seven and she'd skipped lunch. But she wasn't hungry, and couldn't think of anything she needed. Or wanted.

She heard her phone and checked her watch. Eight o'clock. That would be Ray. She put her book aside and slipped into her loafers and trotted down the hall.

"Hey, babe."

"Hey, yourself."

"How's it going?"

"Fine. How's life in the emergency room?"

"I have it figured out," Ray said. "This residency isn't about learning anything, or being prepared to handle a crisis. It's a test of motivation. If you want it badly enough to go through a year of hell and humiliation, they let you join the club." He was calling from a pay phone in the hospital. She could hear the crackle of the intercom, the murmur of voices, clatterings and squeakings and unidentifiable hospital noises. "So how are you spending your weekend, he said enviously."

"Actually, it's a lot like yours. You remember Fran? The woman who lives down the hall? The one I went camping with?"

"I know who you mean," he said.

"She's come down with the flu…"

"At this time of year?"

"She works over at the Student Health Center and is exposed to everything that comes in the door. Anyway, she's pretty miserable. I'm doing what I can."

He switched to his professional voice. "Symptoms?"

"Fever 103. Dizziness, cold, exhaustion. Joint pain. Dry cough."

"Is she sweating?"

"Nope, she's dry as paper."

"That's not good," Ray said. "Keep an eye on that fever. If it doesn't break, or it goes much higher, or if she doesn't start perspiring, she could be in trouble."

"I know. I might have to take desperate measures."

"You mean The Cure?"

"It worked for me. I haven't had so much fun since then."

Ray laughed. "You should see some of my reefer junkies. They *really* have fun. She's not taking any medication like sleeping pills or antihistamines, is she?"

"Just aspirin. There's nothing in the medicine cabinet."

"Ask first."

"I will. I'd better get back there."

"OK," Ray said. "If things take a turn for the worse, or if you just get nervous, have me paged. Any time of night. I'll be at my apartment in the morning."

"Thanks, Ray." She felt relieved. "Talk to you later."

"Don't wait too long. That sucker's locked inside her. Love 'ya, babe," he said.

"Love you, too."

At midnight she decided it had gone on long enough. Things weren't improving on their own. In fact, they were getting worse. Rather than dropping, Fran's fever had crept over 103. "We have to do something," she said as she shook the mercury back down in the thermometer. "This isn't going to go away by itself."

"I want to sleep."

"I know. And you can, as soon as we get squared away here."

"Don't expect me to help."

Fran lay on her back with her eyes shut, her body limp with fatigue. She looked as if she'd been ironed into the sheets.

"I'm getting you something to drink," Shelby said. "It'll make you feel better."

"That's what they always say before they do something awful to you."

Shelby touched Fran's face with the backs of her fingers. "After you're dead, after they lower you into the ground, I'll bet you rise up long enough to make one last wisecrack."

"Yeah, and you'll try to top it."

Shelby went to the kitchen and put the water on to boil. She opened a can of nearly-defrosted lemonade and scooped two spoonfuls into a mug. When the tea kettle shrieked, she added water and topped it off with a shot of bourbon. She put the mug on the bedside table and slipped an arm under Fran's shoulders, supporting her against her own shoulder. "Are you taking anything that doesn't get along with alcohol?"

Fran shook her head and glowered into the steaming mug. "What is that vileness?"

"Hot lemonade and bourbon. It's an old folk remedy. Cures stuck fever, menstrual cramps, insomnia, colds, and writer's block. I learned it from a friend in college. She was from Tennessee. I told you about her, the one that went strange."

"Do I really have to do this?"

"Yes, you do."

"Why?"

"Because if your fever doesn't break, it'll go up to 105 and you'll have a convulsion and suffer permanent brain damage."

"You are such a comfort," Fran said. She sipped at the liquid, then drank and shuddered.

"Come on, it's not that bad."

"It is."

"God, you're even more stubborn than I am." Shelby held the drink to Fran's lips. "The quicker you do this, the quicker I'll leave you alone."

"What'll it do to me?"

"With any kind of luck, make you sweat. And that'll make your joints stop hurting. If it doesn't work, you can have another one, and then you won't care if your joints hurt or not." She offered her the mug again. Fran made a face. "I'm going to win this battle, Fran," she said gently. "Come hell or high water."

Fran reached for the drink and finished it off. "Sleep now?"

Shelby set the mug aside and lowered her onto the pillows. "Of course."

"Nothing more you want me to eat?"

"Nope."

"Drink?"

"Nope."

"You're sure about that?"

"I'm sure."

"Any measurements you need to take?"

"You're all set." She pulled the covers up around her. "I'll see you on the other side of night."

She spread her sleeping bag on the spare bed, flicked off the bedroom lamp, went to the kitchen, rinsed the dishes, and turned out the light. She groped her way into her pajamas.

"Shelby?" Fran whispered into the darkness.

"That's what they call me."

"I don't mean to be difficult. I really appreciate…"

"I know."

"You're doing so much for me."

"I'm having a good time," Shelby said, surprising herself as she realized she meant it.

A series of muffled ear-cracking coughs woke her. There was a line of light under the bathroom door. "You OK?" she asked.

"No," Fran said as she came back into the room. "I'm dying."

Shelby got up and went to her. Fran's pajamas were soaked. Perspiration glistened on her face. Her hair was wet and matted. "Hey," Shelby said. "It worked."

"I don't know what you're so damned cheerful about," Fran stumbled to the bed.

"Don't get in. Where are your spare pajamas?"

Fran gestured in the direction of the bureau. "Bottom drawer. May I lie down now?"

"No." She found fresh clothes. "Sit."

She unbuttoned Fran's pajama top and peeled away the damp clothing and dried her with a towel. "You'll catch cold in these wet things."

"Is that supposed to be a joke?"

"Nope." She helped Fran out of her soggy pajama pants and into fresh ones. "You don't have a cold, you have the flu. There's always room for more."

Fran groaned and started to slip beneath the covers.

"Go in the other bed." She stripped away her sleeping bag and pulled back the spread and pushed Fran toward it. "This one's sodden."

It was clear Fran wanted to argue, but didn't have the strength. She toppled onto the spare bed. Shelby pulled the covers up around her, then went to the kitchen and found an old, clean, soft dish towel in a drawer. She brought it back and gently wiped the perspiration from her face.

Fran took a deep breath. Her lungs sounded like boiling water. Shelby found the Vicks and gently massaged it into her chest.

"Shelby," Fran said.

"Yes?"

"I'm sorry I'm such a mess."

"It'll be all right, Fran," she said softly. "It's awful now, but everything's under control. There's nothing to be afraid of."

"How can I feel this bad and live?"

Shelby smiled and stroked her. "You will." She turned off the light and sat beside her for a while. Glancing at the clock on the bureau, she saw that it was a little after two. That meant Fran had slept for nearly an hour before the coughing fit. Not enough, but it was a start.

When Fran's breathing had smoothed to a soft rhythm, Shelby got up and pulled the damp sheets from the bed and tossed them into a corner. She'd put on fresh ones in the morning. She tossed her sleeping bag onto the bed and lay down. As she was drifting off to sleep, she wondered why she was so happy.

Sunday morning Fran was clearly better, though her face still had blotches of fever red and she inhaled in slow, shallow gulps. Sore throat, Shelby thought. The kind that hurts when you breathe. The kind that's too high in the back of your mouth for anything to help. The truly nasty kind. But at least Fran was still sleeping. She was going to sleep a lot in the next few days, Shelby remembered that vividly. She'd be going along, maybe reading a book or having a perfectly pleasant, light hearted telephone conversation with someone, and suddenly sleep would reach out of the ground and grab her around the ankle and pull her down onto the nearest flat surface. Even after she went back to work, she'd have those sleeping fits. Connie teased her about narcolepsy, and Lisa worried. Jean swore it'd pass.

She took the damp sheets and pajamas to the basement laundry room and started up the washer. She considered getting Fran's dirty clothes from the bathroom hamper, but was afraid Fran would think that too personal and an intrusion on her privacy. People were like that, she thought as she watched the washer tub fill. You never knew when you were going to bump your nose on their invisible jet-age plastic shields.

She dumped in the soap. She was probably going to form opinions about brands of soap, once she was ensconced in marriage. Ensconced. As in candles in sconces. Silver sconces, requiring polishing. Then brands of silver cream become important. And dish soap, window spray, scouring powder, toilet bowl cleaner, fabric softener, bluing, bleach—so much to learn, so many earth-shaking decisions to make.

We'll send the laundry out, she told herself. I refuse to learn about laundry soap. Absolute bottom line on the marriage contract. I get to send the laundry out. Even if I have to get a job to pay for it...

Get a job. She wouldn't have her job. Sooner or later Ray would have to go where his work was. Probably to a city. Certainly not to Bass Falls or West Sayer. Seattle, maybe. His father'd like that. Would she? She didn't know anything about Seattle, except that on the few days of the year that the sun shone, they gave the newspaper away free.

She didn't want to give up her life, to have it nested inside someone else's life. Libby was right, she shouldn't have waited so long to get married, she was too set in her ways now, like the Misses Young, her old maid ways. It'd be good for her to be married. It'd keep her flexible. It'd...

Think about it tomorrow, Scarlett. For today just think about today things, like life and death upstairs.

Fran was just waking when she got back. She sat up and swung her legs over the edge of the bed and stared at the floor.

"Dizzy?"

Fran nodded.

"I know you have a sore throat, so just point me toward your clean sheets."

She pointed to the bathroom closet. "How'd you know?"

"I know everything. Move." Fran shuffled toward the bathroom door. Shelby stripped the damp sheets from the bed.

"What's after sore throat?"

"Your sinuses turn to cement, I think. It's quite unpleasant." She pulled another set of pajamas from the bureau and tossed them in Fran's direction. "Change into these." She looked at her with her full attention for the first time. Fran definitely seemed better, no longer pale and blue-lipped. There was more energy in her. But she was wet, droopy, and bedraggled. Shelby smiled. "You look like a half-drowned kitten."

"It's your fault," Fran croaked.

"Are you still cold?"

"Are you kidding? Look at me." Her hair was clumped to her head. Beads of perspiration trickled down her face. "I hate myself. Going to try and take a shower."

"Leave the door open a little." She got more clean sheets and started to make the other bed. "So I can hear you hit the ground if you faint."

"You don't like me very much, do you?"

Shelby glanced at her. "I like you very, very much. Don't get in the shower until you do your temp."

It was down. Not much, just under 103, but heading in the right direction. She rolled up her sleeping bag and went to check the kitchen. Macaroni and cheese would do for lunch. Fran could probably handle that. She still wasn't hungry, herself, but knew she had to eat. She made a list of supplies they needed from the store. Better call Jean. It didn't feel safe to leave yet, and the only place that would be open on Sunday was the A&P.

"How are things?" Jean asked.

Shelby listened for sounds of trouble from the bathroom. The water was running, making a splashing sound as if there were a live body moving around beneath it.

"She had a bad night, but it's a little better today."

"Only one bad night? That woman has a guardian angel."

"At least so far. It was very bad. Can you pick up some stuff at the store for us?"

"No problem. Give me the list."

She did.

"Just out of curiosity, is Fran any better at being sick than you were?"

"I was OK at it," Shelby said.

"You were not, Miss Independent, Miss I Can Take Care of Myself. You were impossible. It's why you relapsed."

"Why are you yelling at me now?"

"Because you were too sick to yell at then."

Shelby laughed. "I still am. No, she's no better than I was."

"You deserve it," Jean said. "I'll see you later this afternoon."

"I think you're in the wrong career," Jean said. "You should go into nursing."

"What makes you say that?" Shelby asked as she took the bag of groceries from her.

"It suits you. You're glowing."

"It's probably just a sympathetic fever." She carried the groceries to Fran's kitchen, glancing over at her as she passed. Fran was still asleep, had been asleep for about two hours now.

"Come down to my place," she said quietly to Jean. "She's sleeping."

She gave Jean the food money. "I really, really appreciate this."

"Don't be silly," Jean said. "How is she doing?"

"Lunch went OK. She kept it down. She's at the sore throat stage."

Jean grimaced. "I hate that part."

It felt odd, suddenly, having someone there. Odd, and a little disconcerting, like coming out of a movie into bright afternoon sun.

"What?" Jean asked.

"I'm sorry. I was just thinking. It's kind of unsettling, talking to a real, live, healthy person. We've been communicating mostly in grunts and nods."

"I know what you mean." She touched Shelby's face. "You don't look great yourself."

"I thought you said I was glowing."

"Glowing, but exhausted. How much sleep have you had?"

"Enough."

"Take a nap." Jean picked up her shoulder bag. "Want me to tell the office about the migraine?"

"I can do it."

"Yeah, but you'll underplay it. You always do. By the time *I* finish, there won't be a dry eye in the place."

"Do it." She felt a sudden rush of warmth. "You're really a good friend, Jean."

"Don't embarrass me."

"Maybe I should have talked you into being maid of honor."

Jean made a strangling noise. "You hate me, I can tell."

Before she even realized she was doing it, Shelby grabbed her and hugged her hard.

"Wow," Jean said, "what was that for?"

Shelby was a little surprised by her own behavior. "I was just overwhelmed by how lucky I am to know you."

Jean smiled and shook her head. "There you go again. I don't know what to do with that." She trotted for the door.

"Thanks for everything," Shelby called after her. "Talk to you later."

If she were Fran, she'd hate her by now. She felt as if she were at her every waking moment, demanding that she eat, demanding that she drink, nagging, forcing aspirin on her. Rubbing Vicks into her chest whenever the coughing got bad. By nightfall they'd gone through macaroni and progressed to chicken, and at least two quarts of ginger ale. Her temperature had fallen another half degree. Things were looking up. The trouble was, Fran hurt. Her sinuses hurt with congestion. Her throat hurt when she breathed. Her chest and back hurt from her fits of coughing. Her joints hurt from fever. Around eight o'clock, Shelby couldn't take it any more. She couldn't read a book and glance up to see Fran tossing and turning, trying to get comfortable, only hurting herself more. She couldn't just sit there like an idiot, helpless.

"OK," she said as she put a glass of ice and water on the bedside table. "I don't know if this will work or not, but it's worth a try. Turn over, I'm going to rub your back."

"You don't have to do that," Fran said quickly. "You've done enough."

"I can't watch you like this. I have to do something."

"Go in the other room."

"Fran…" she said in a faintly menacing way.

"All right, all right."

Shelby unbuttoned Fran's pajama top and slipped it off and helped her turn onto her stomach. "You're much too weak to take me on in hand-to-hand combat," she said as she tucked one pillow under her hips, another beneath her chest.

Fran didn't answer. She seemed tense, as if waiting for something horrible to happen.

"I won't hurt you," Shelby said. "If I do, just say so. I won't take it personally."

She put her hand between Fran's shoulder blades. Fran started.

"I'm sorry. What did I do?"

"Cold hands," Fran said.

Shelby held her other hand up to her own face. It was warm. "Not really," she said. "It must be the fever."

"Yeah."

She sat beside her and touched both of Fran's shoulders and drew her hands down her back. Her skin was smooth and soft, the muscles beneath as hard as steel. "Either you work out three times a day, or you're awfully tense."

"You'd be tense, too," Fran said.

Shelby smiled. "I guess I would." She rubbed her for a while in silence. "I wish I had something like Ben-Gay or something. It would help."

"Place already smells like a locker room."

"Does not," Shelby said, massaging the muscles around Fran's shoulder blades. She was aware of the heat in her own hands, and the way Fran's skin lay warm beneath them. And an unfamiliar tingling in her own finger tips. "Is this making it worse?" she asked after a while.

Fran shook her head. "Better."

She worked on her neck and shoulders next, rubbing gently and with increasing pressure until Fran's skin turned pink from the blood and heat that rose to the surface. She massaged her arms, and her hands, one at a time, slowly. The joints of her fingers. Fran began to relax a little. She stroked her back, carefully, gently, lovingly.

There was a hum in her ears, and the room around them seemed very small and very warm and very personal. They were safe together in a dark cozy place. No one else existed. There was no time, only one long moment that went on forever. Shelby felt as if her whole body had turned to a single object, not separate muscles and bones and organs, but one entity that existed only for this. She was soft and strong. Vulnerable and solid. Living only for this one small act of comforting.

Fran was hit by a fit of coughing. Shelby gave her room, but kept her hand against her back, pressing just hard enough so Fran would know she was there. "Do you need water?"

"Huh-uh." She cleared her throat. It sounded dry.

"Sure, you do." She turned Fran over and gave her the ice water.

Fran wouldn't look at her. She held onto herself, as if she were holding something alive in her arms that might escape at any minute.

"You're beautiful," Shelby said.

"I'm a mess."

Shelby turned out the bedside light and went back to stroking her.

"I'm giving you a hard time, aren't I?" Fran said into her pillow.

"I've seen worse." She ran a hand through Fran's hair. "I've *been* worse."

"It's hard for me to let anyone take care of me."

"I've noticed."

"I'm sorry."

"I understand, Fran. I'm the same way. It's as if, if you let someone care for you or comfort you, it'll open up a bottomless pit of longing." She hadn't known she knew that until she heard herself say it.

"Yeah."

"Go to sleep." She could feel Fran slipping away. It was still and quiet in the room. She sat for a while longer, not thinking, only aware of the touch of her friend's back under her hands. Then she got up slowly, draped Fran's pajama top across her back and shoulders, and pulled the covers over her. She looked down at her for a moment, then leaned over and kissed her between the shoulder blades.

* * *

She woke to the sound of stifled crying. She sat up. "Fran?"

Fran made a low choking noise.

"Don't fight," Shelby said. "You'll just make it worse." She went to her.

Fran had hidden her face beneath the pillow. Shelby eased it away.

"Talk to me."

"Go away," Fran sobbed.

"No."

Shelby thought about turning on a light, but decided against it. Whatever was going on here, it was too private to be seen. She pulled Fran into her arms and held her.

This wasn't ordinary crying. These were hard tears, desperate tears, iron tears, helpless tears. They seemed to come from somewhere deep inside, an old hurt, a hurt that wouldn't go away, a hurt that must be a constant ache in Fran's heart.

She tried to think of comforting words to say. It would be wrong to be silent in the face of this horrible sadness. But the things people usually said— "It'll be all right," "It's OK"—weren't right. Because she didn't know if it would be all right, and it wasn't OK. This felt like something that would never be OK.

All she could say was what was in her heart. "I hope you can tell me what it is," she murmured gently. "I hope together we can make it better. I don't know who hurt you this way, but I'd like very much to kill them, if it's all right with you."

Fran clung to her. There was an emptiness below her tears that made Shelby think of deserted railroad platforms, and planes silently lifting off runways. A saying goodbye. More than sorrow, more than hurt. This was grieving. For things lost forever. She felt a terrible, hopeless sadness herself. It frightened her. Deeply. It made her heart pound, her head spin. Seeing Fran like this was more intimate than sex. She wanted to stop it, to run away from it, but knew she couldn't. Hang on, she told herself. Go through it. And held Fran tighter.

"I'm here," she said, stroking Fran's hair. She rocked her a little. "I'm not going to leave you."

Fran shook. She cried in huge and violent gasps.

Shelby wondered if morning would ever come. The night was black and still behind the windows. On top of the dresser, the dial of the alarm clock glowed green. She tried to hear the ticking over the sound of Fran's tears, but couldn't. She's going to turn herself inside out, Shelby thought. There must be something she could do to ease that pain. But sitting here like this, holding her, was really the best thing, she knew it instinctively. Let her go. Let it run its course. Make it safe for her. Let your arms be strength and protection and comfort. Try to draw the pain into yourself and take it away from her.

The emptiness was the worst. The hollow, black emptiness. Wind blew through it and made a groaning sound. It was cold, so cold.

Oh, God, Shelby thought. To carry that cold inside you all the time.

She kissed the top of Fran's head. "I love you," she said softly. She wondered if Fran even heard, if she even knew Shelby was there.

But there was still a thread between them. She could feel it. Hang on, hang on. Shelby focused her attention on that thread. Don't let it break. Something terrible will happen if it breaks.

If I hold her any tighter, I'll choke her.

She tried to ease up, but then she'd feel that awful crying, shaking them both, and her arms would pull Fran closer. She wanted to draw Fran inside her where she could be warm, where she wouldn't be alone. "I love you," she said over and over, with her words, with her arms, with her hands, with her heart. She kept on rocking.

After a time Fran's sobbing grew lighter. Shelby reached for the tissues and gave her a handful.

"I got you wet," Fran said.

"I'll survive. I'll steal one of your tee shirts." She brushed Fran's hair from her forehead. "Want to tell me about this?"

Fran shook her head. She seemed so tired, but she still hung onto Shelby with one arm.

Shelby let her rest against her. "I'm not leaving," she repeated, and held her until she felt her start to go soft. She helped her lie down. Fran groped for her hand. Shelby ran her thumb across Fran's knuckles and gave her hand a squeeze.

She peeled out of her wet pajama top and crawled into a tee-shirt. It was soft, and smelled like ironed cotton and Fran. The water in the glass was still cool. She gave Fran a drink. "Better?"

"Shaky," Fran said.

Light was about to come. She could tell by the silence, like the second of silence before a thunder clap.

Fran lay down on her side, facing away. Hesitating only a moment, Shelby slipped in bed beside her and slid one arm under Fran's neck, and wrapped the other around her. She pulled her close.

"Shelby," Fran mumbled.

"That's what they call me."

"I never want to do anything to make us not be friends."

"I can't imagine it."

She could make out the outlines of the furniture, and the white woodwork. Shelby closed her eyes.

She didn't care whether she slept or not.

Fran was stirring. Shelby put down the story she was editing and went to sit on the side of the bed.

"Hey," she said, and touched her hand to Fran's forehead. It felt cooler.

Fran slipped a hand out from beneath the covers and fumbled for Shelby's hand. Shelby took it. "Hey," she said again, softly. "Sleepy head."

Fran's eyelids fluttered open. Her eyes were red-rimmed and swollen and sore. Her forehead wrinkled into a frown. She struggled to focus.

As if she had suddenly touched something sharp, her hand jerked, pulling away.

Shelby held on tighter. "It's OK," she said, and stroked Fran's hair.

Fran scrunched her eyes shut and shook her head. "Don't."

"I'm sorry." She sat back a little. She knew how it felt, having a fever. Sometimes your skin was so sensitive you thought you'd been burned. "Want some water?"

"I guess so," Fran said, her eyes still closed, her head turned away.

The water in her glass was warm. Shelby went to the kitchen to freshen it. Glancing up as she passed the bureau, she could see the bed and Fran, reflected in the mirror. She was trying to sit up. "Wait a minute," she said. "I'll help you."

As she filled the glass, she noticed her hands were trembling again.

Fran had managed on her own, with her legs pulled up and her head resting on her knees. Shelby sat beside her and put an arm around her. "Here," she said, and offered the water.

She took it and drank, not looking at Shelby. "Last night…," she began.

"Yes."

"Forget it, please?"

Shelby placed her hand against the side of Fran's face and turned her head toward her. "Fran."

She pulled away. "Please. It was the fever."

Shelby knew that wasn't true. She knew Fran knew it, too. "You were very upset last night. I think we should talk about it."

"I need to go to the bathroom," Fran said, and struggled out of bed.

Shelby waited for her to come back, then tucked her beneath the covers. "Fran."

"Please," Fran said, "let it go for now."

"All right." She felt helpless. "What do you want for breakfast?"

"I'm not hungry."

"That's irrelevant."

"I can fend for myself. Really."

It was clear she felt better. But she had a long way to go.

"Right," Shelby said ironically. "You can take care of yourself, but you're not hungry. When were you planning to eat?"

Fran glanced at her. "This isn't fair to you."

"I intend to suffer with you," Shelby said as she got up and started for the bathroom. "Every inch of the way."

"You're crazy."

"That's what lonely people do…" She ran cold water and soaked a washcloth in it and wrung it out. "…with other lonely people. They suffer together." She came back and put the cloth across Fran's eyes and pressed it against her eyelids and temples. "There. Now you don't have to keep your head turned away. You can't see me."

"I'm sorry."

"It's all right." In fact, it was all right. Whatever Fran wanted to say or not say, it was all right. It made her feel gentle, and free.

She sat for a while looking at the floor, at the threadbare pattern on the rug. Something was happening between them, had happened between them. It was like being swept down a river on a raft. She didn't know where she was going, or how long it would take to get there, or what was at the other end. Her head told her to get off now, to push her way to shore or swim if she had to, just get off the river. Her heart told her to float.

She floated.

"You don't have to sit with me," Fran said. Her voice was shaky. "I'm OK."

"You are not. You are, as you so succinctly put it last night, a mess."

"It's my mess. If you have things to do…"

"I'm doing the things I have to do," Shelby said.

"You have to go to work."

"Do not. I called in sick."

"I really can take care of myself."

"At the moment, maybe," Shelby said. "But it comes and goes in waves. You could fall down in a dead faint on the linoleum, and that would be really uncomfortable."

"Not for me."

"Look, I know you want me to get the hell out of here and give you back your privacy…"

"I don't," Fran said quickly.

"…but trying to do anything at this point is asking for trouble. Let me take care of you today, then we'll see how you feel."

Fran was silent. "I really didn't mean to do that," she said at last.

"What?"

"Last night."

"Nothing happened that anyone should be sorry for."

"I don't know why I acted that way. The flu gremlins must have gotten to my emotions."

"That had nothing to do with gremlins," Shelby said, and took her hand. Her hand was lifeless.

"What made you cry was something that hurt you. We both know that."

Fran didn't answer.

"Please, Fran. You don't have to talk about it. But just say you don't want to. Or can't. Don't ask me to swallow lies."

"You're lucky. You can swallow." She hesitated. "I'm sorry. It wasn't just fever, it was…old things. Really old things."

"I wish you could tell me."

"Not now."

"Any time."

"I can't think…. I want to…but…I mean, it sounds silly but…it's just too sore right now."

"That was clear last night," Shelby said softly.

"I'm really embarrassed."

"You shouldn't be." She got up and went to the bathroom to cool the wash cloth. She wiped Fran's face and covered her eyes again.

"Thank you," Fran said.

"I don't know what you're talking about, but you're welcome."

"For what you did. For understanding."

"I'm not sure I do understand, but it doesn't matter." She fussed with the blankets. "Rest now. And stop worrying."

"I feel like garbage."

"I know."

Fran looked soft, and small, and vulnerable. The emptiness was still there, hovering behind her face like a hungry ghost.

It hurt her, to see Fran broken and know there was no way she could help.

To realize that this woman, this friend she cared so much about, had been deeply damaged, and all she could do was be strong and patient, and try not to hurt her more.

Shelby felt an ache in her chest, an emotion too huge to bear and too precious to let go.

Something had happened to her, too, last night. She had the feeling she'd crossed an invisible boundary, and things would never be the same again.

Chapter 11

Shelby froze in the doorway to the lounge, a deer stunned in the headlights of a poacher's truck.

They were all there. The whole lunch bunch, and Charlotte, and three women from the advertising department whom she recognized but whose names she didn't know. The medical reporter, with his buddies from layout. Even the travel editor was here, on one of his rare appearances at the stateside office.

Women's voices sounded shrill as mating cats. Men rumbled like empty freight trains on trestle bridges. There was too much motion, people crossing the room, back and forth, doing things at the coffee urn, shaking out newspapers, rearranging the coat closet, wandering for the sake of wandering. Movement blended into sound into light and melted in confusion. Sunlight glared through the windows. The orange vinyl sofas shimmered. Black and white squares of checkered linoleum seemed to rise and fall in three dimensions.

Connie spotted her first, and let out a whoop. Shelby cringed.

She wished she hadn't come in here. She wished she'd gone directly to her office, do not pass "Go," do not collect two-hundred dollars. But eyebrows would be raised, questions would be asked. Someone might get the idea she was avoiding them.

Maybe she was.

No, not really. She didn't want to avoid anyone, exactly. She only wanted to come back slowly. To decompress.

Instead, she pasted on a smile and went to greet her friends.

"How's the headache?" Jean asked.

"It comes and goes."

"I hear you're working short days this week," Penny said. "For doctors' appointments."

Jean had done a good job. She'd even found a way for her to leave the office early. "You have untapped talents," Shelby said in a low voice.

"I suspect I do."

"You might be a natural psychopath."

Jean laughed. "If I were a psychopath, I'd be rich by now."

Connie moved closer to her. "How are things, really?"

A feeling like guilt washed over her. "Shaky. It was a monster."

Miss Myers had come into the room and was pouring herself a cup of coffee. Not in a styrofoam cup, not Miss Myers. Miss Myers had brought her very own stoneware mug with daisies painted on it, which she undoubtedly washed out every time she used it.

Miss Myers glanced up and caught them looking her way.

Penny detached herself from the group and trotted over to the coffee urn, pausing next to Miss Myers for an exchange of "good mornings" and a quick smile.

"Penny knows how to brown-nose," Connie said. "I'll bet she sets a new record for making assistant editor."

"Not until somebody dies or gets married and quits," Lisa said. She looked slyly at Shelby. "What do you think are the chances of that?"

"I might die," Shelby said. "But at the moment I'm not planning to quit."

"Not even after you're married?" Lisa asked.

"Not even then."

"You must be out of your mind."

"Not quite," Shelby said. But any minute now she would be. The conversation was beginning to get on her nerves. It was shallow and forced and she could do it in her sleep. It made her want to lie down.

Maybe she had come back to work too soon. Maybe she wasn't ready. Fran was comfortable enough, fever down, convalescing in front of Shelby's television set with a pitcher of lemonade and a copy of *The Group*. She'd promised to behave in an adult and responsible manner, sleep when she needed to sleep, drink the lemonade and as much water as she could, and turn the heat on under the pan of canned vegetable soup Shelby'd left behind.

Fran was fine. It was Shelby who wasn't doing so well.

The last three days had been easy, straightforward. Do what's needed. Be spontaneous. Follow where the heart goes and trust its judgment. A leads to B leads to C. What feels right is, miraculously, correct. Now she was back in the land of the obscure, the subtle, the duplicitous. Now it wasn't how things felt that mattered, it was how things looked. And she wasn't prepared for it.

"You're really out of it," Connie commented.

Shelby forced herself to concentrate. "I'm just tired. Didn't get much sleep. I should probably get to work before I turn completely useless." She picked up her pocketbook and started for the door.

"Save enough energy for bridge," Connie called after her.

Miss Myers flagged her down at the entrance to the lounge. "Miss Camden!"

She stopped.

"I hope you're feeling better," Miss Myers said.

Shelby was surprised. "Somewhat, thank you."

Miss Myers tapped her arm. "Now, don't do anything foolish. Take as much time as you need to get well." She strode off toward her office.

Shelby glanced over at her friends. They were staring at her, open-mouthed. She shrugged and raised her hands in a "beats me" gesture. Of all the things Miss Myers was known for, concern wasn't one of them.

Before she got down to work she called her apartment. Fran answered on the first ring.

"Hi," Shelby said. "How you doing?"

"OK. How about you?"

"I'm fine, but I wasn't sick to begin with."

"This is true," Fran said. "I was about to make up that soup you left."

"So soon?"

"Hunger hurts."

"Can you manage?"

"I think so."

"There's more in the cupboard if you want it. I'm checking out of here at three," Shelby said. "See you around three-thirty."

"Great. We can watch *Young Doctor Malone*."

Things seemed normal enough on the surface, but there was a stiff, distant tone in Fran's voice that made her sound forced.

Don't be silly, she told herself. Fran's still sick. This is her telephone voice. Her *sick* telephone voice. "Don't wash any dishes," she said, trying not to sound stiff or distant herself. "Rest. You don't want to have a relapse."

Fran laughed a little. "I won't have a relapse."

"*I* did. And all I did was go out for a few hours with Ray."

"I'm not likely to go out with Ray. Even for a few hours. You probably got yourself overly excited."

"Well, don't get *your*self overly excited."

"On game shows? Fat chance. 'Queen for a Day' doesn't set my heart to pounding."

Shelby tried to think of something else to say, small talk, news of the day, gossip, even. "When you feel better, we'll go to a movie, OK?"

"As long as it's not overly exciting," Fran said.

That made her smile. That sounded like Fran. "OK. Go lie down."

"I'm not a dog, and I *am* lying down."

"So lie down flatter. I…" She caught herself, realizing she was about to say "I miss you," which would sound ridiculous. "…I'll see you later." She started to hang up.

"Ice cream!" Fran said.

"What?"

"Get ice cream."

"OK, what kind?"

"I don't care, as long as it's not too exciting."

Shelby sighed and shook her head. "All right, Fran."

"Sorry."

"Clearly," Shelby said, "you're feeling better. Good-bye."

She hung up the phone and wondered why she felt a small jolt of disappointment, then shrugged it off and picked up the nearest folder.

By the end of lunch she really wished she hadn't come to work. Not that the day had been particularly hard, or that anyone had asked questions she couldn't answer. In fact, everyone behaved normally, and that was the problem. Shelby didn't feel normal. She felt turned in on herself, as if the outside world existed only as an echo. She had to force herself to listen. The slightest conversation was exhausting. She kept looking at the clock, and wondering how Fran was doing at home. During post-lunch bridge, she mis-bid three consecutive hands, and finally begged off the game entirely, claiming fatigue. The lunch bunch clucked and muttered over her like a clutch of worried hens. There were times when she'd have secretly enjoyed that kind of attention. This wasn't one of those times. It annoyed her and made her feel trapped and uncomfortable and...once more...guilty.

At least Libby was out of town again. It was almost a semi-monthly occurrence during the cooler times of year. Libby prided herself on her always-fresh "just a touch of tan." During the fall and winter months, she went where she could get it. Puerto Rico, Cuba before Castro took over, Jamaica, the Virgin Islands. "This darned old tan is fading," she'd pout, and before you could count to twenty she was winging her way south. Then Shelby could relax, knowing she was safe for at least a week. Libby tended to be nicer when she was out of the country. Instead of the usual predictable letters of complaint and reminder, scotch-taped shut for privacy, she sent cheerful post cards. If Shelby did anything Libby didn't approve of, it would never be mentioned on a post card for All the World to See. Meaning The Mail Man. Libby thought all Mail Men were Voyeurs and Perverts, who deliberately snooped into people's private business and reported immediately to those awful, trashy newspapers they carried in the supermarkets for Ignorant People to read. For which the Mail Men were undoubtedly paid unwholesome amounts of Money.

If she'd had to deal with Libby on Monday, if she'd had to choose between leaving Fran for the evening, or taking the risk of cancelling their dinner meeting...

She wondered what she'd have done.

Focus, damn it, she told herself roughly. She glanced at the clock. Another hour and she could leave for that bogus doctor's appointment. She'd better get some work done.

Easy to say.

She slapped a folder against the desk. It was one thing to whip through a pile of submissions when she was still a reader. All she had to do then was separate the obviously bad from the obviously good, and leave the shades of gray for the assistant editors. And now she was one of the gray-sorters. If she ever made associate editor, she'd have to use a microscope to tell the difference between shades.

Who was she kidding? She'd never make associate editor. Not at The Magazine. Because she'd either be a) married and have to quit to follow her husband wherever he ended up, or b) married and be expected to quit any minute to...etc., etc. It wasn't fair. Just because she was a woman, she couldn't move up in this job. Not unless she was willing to be like Miss Myers and have no personal life at all.

Assuming Miss Myers really had no personal life. How would anyone know? No one ever saw her outside the office, so apparently she didn't shop, eat out, frequent the grocery or liquor stores, or go to movies—not even foreign films and other unintelligible cultural events. Nor had she been spotted in any of the local churches. So Miss Myers was either a heathen or a pagan, or a figment of their collective imagination. She was in the phone book, and lived in an apartment in downtown West Sayer. At least that was the address. Whether anyone actually lived there was open to debate. Once, when they'd all had a little too much to drink and had regressed to the age of giggling ten, Connie had called her number. But the phone only rang. So they didn't know any more than they had before.

She was embarrassed now, remembering how juvenile they'd been that night. At one point they'd even piled into Lisa's car and driven up and down the street past her building, trying to catch a glimpse of Miss Myers. The shade was pulled, yellow light behind it. There were no shadows, and no sign of movement. They'd gone around the block a few times, then given up and gone home.

Not only immature, cruel. Miss Myers had never done anything to them to merit the way they giggled about her. Miss Myers' only sin was being different.

Suddenly she remembered how she'd been in grade school, always kind to the girls who weren't well dressed, or had funny teeth, or couldn't see the blackboard, or were "slower" than the rest. She never laughed at people who were different back then, when almost everyone did. The other kids teased her when she took her books and went to sit beside the outcasts. Her mother called her "the Angel of Mercy," her voice acid with sarcasm and disgust. Libby made a point of filling Shelby's weekends with outings with the "right" people. But she couldn't control who Shelby sat beside in school.

Shelby wondered when and why she'd changed. It was as if something had happened when she wasn't paying attention. Something that made her nasty. After all, why should she judge Miss Myers? Miss Myers was probably lonely, had nothing but her job to care about, and knew she'd risen as high as she'd ever go. While Shelby was on the way to being a success in her life. She could afford to be a little more generous.

She cringed. She hated the way that sounded, self-righteous and condescending. That wasn't how she felt at all. How she felt—really felt—was that she owed Miss Myers an apology. But she couldn't just go up to her and say, "I'm sorry for making fun of you." How sensitive was *that*?

Well, according to Libby, *that* was her problem—she was too sensitive. Libby made it quite clear that they lived in a world in which your feelings were going to be hurt sooner or later, and the sooner she stopped with her "bleeding wound routine," the better off she'd be. And while she was at it she could lose five pounds, and "Do Something with your Hair," and try to develop a Sense of Style, because, "You'd be rather lovely, Shelby, if only…"

There were a lot of "if onlys…" They tended to increase exponentially. In fact, the wedding had brought a veritable plague of "if onlys…"

Two-thirty. She could leave in half an hour. Not that she was likely to accomplish much in that half hour. Or all day, as a matter of fact. She'd been useless, cocooning in on herself, unable to generate a coherent thought—much less a cogent, rational opinion. She'd left her soul back in her apartment. Without it she was a robot.

The weekend had been quiet and intense. It wasn't easy to come back from that. People who led monastic lives, or went on long retreats, or into the rain forest or out on the desert for weeks at a time must suffer terrible culture shock. They must feel as if they were walking around without any skin. It really wasn't pleasant.

And she hadn't been able to get Fran off her mind. Nothing in particular, just images and snapshot memories. Always circling back to Sunday night, when Fran had cried and...

See, she was doing it again. She ran her hands through her hair roughly. She had a half hour. In that time she could certainly concentrate enough to get through one story.

Shelby picked up a folder and opened it.

Maybe she could find a way to do something nice for Miss Myers, to make up for things. Maybe bring her a little gift—flowers or a plate of cookies—in a casual way, as if it was just such a lovely day she'd felt expansive and wanted to brighten up the world.

Two forty-five.

Come on, come on, do the story. Trouble was, it was one of those clearly borderline jobs, the kind you maybe put in the file for a really slow month. Not that they ever had a really slow month. She should probably reject it outright, with an encouraging note about "not meeting our editorial needs at the present time." Which brought her to problem number two: it was one Penny had passed on. If she rejected it, they could find themselves back in one of those strange and uncomfortable tensions. But if she accepted it just to avoid trouble, it was blackmail. Also cowardly and unprofessional.

"Fiddle-dee-dee," she muttered to the empty office as the clock hands edged toward three. "I'll think about it tomorrow."

Shelby opened the door to her apartment quietly. Fran was sprawled on the couch, asleep. She'd kicked the blankets into a heap on the floor. The sheets were twisted into a skein of white. There was a damp gloss on her face.

Closing the door, Shelby put her things down and went to her and rested her hand on Fran's forehead. A little fever, not much. One of those low-grade, "you're not going out until it's been normal for twenty-four hours" fevers that leaves you bored, irritable, cranky, exhausted and not a whole lot of fun.

She opened the window a little wider to let fresh air into the room, and draped one of the blankets over Fran.

Fran stirred a little in her sleep.

Shelby tiptoed out of the room to put away the groceries and change into her home clothes. She sat at the kitchen table to open her mail, alert for sounds from the living room. Fran was all right, she told herself. It was all going to be fine. Nothing to worry about.

An advertisement for a new magazine. She tossed the envelope into the waste basket without opening it.

But it was in her nature to worry. It was what she did best.

United Fund, request for money. She'd given at the office.

She wished Fran would wake up.

Newsweek magazine. She wondered why she got it. She hardly ever had time to read it.

No "Time" to read "Newsweek." Get it? Ha-ha.

Date with Ray this weekend. It seemed as if she hadn't seen him in years.

A post card from Libby, who was Having a Fabulous Time in Martinique, and had she remembered to look at the new *Bride?*

She'd remembered. Wedding gowns, bridesmaids' dresses, silver place settings, china patterns, floral arrangements…a world so strange she might as well be reading *National Geographic*.

Floral arrangements. For everyday events you had flowers. For weddings you had Floral Arrangements.

What was this whole wedding business, anyway? Who thought it up? Some women built their whole lives around their wedding day—planning from the time they were children, keeping scrapbooks and photo albums and home movies of people dressed the way they never dressed, acting the way they never acted. What for? To feel important and the center of attention for one day of their lives, she supposed. But if you wanted to be a Star for a day, why not take the money and rent a theater?

Not a bad idea. They could find some silly, romantic play to do. Some Noel Coward thing, where people chased each other in and out of elegant hotel bedrooms.

A catalogue. Cheap clothing, ugly ceramic *objets d'art*. She wondered how she got on that particular mailing list. She wondered if Fran was waking up yet. She wondered if their friendship would change after her marriage.

Of course it would change. She wouldn't be living down the hall from her, for one thing. Or have the free time she was accustomed to. Fran might even have finished school in a year, and gone on to other adventures. This was it, this year, their time together.

It made her stomach hard to think about that.

She got up and went to the living room and looked down at her friend. One year. She fiddled with the blanket, pulling it up across Fran's shoulders. The gesture had become a familiar one after these four days. As had saying "good night" to her as she turned out the light, and listening for her in the shower to be sure she was all right, and leaving their doors open when she had to go to her own apartment to make a phone call. Cooking for her, being concerned. She touched Fran's hair, marvelled at its softness, traced a wave with one finger.

Fran moved and muttered a little.

Shelby sat down on the coffee table by the couch.

Fran's eyelids eased open, catching the light in those gorgeous cornflower…

"Hi," Shelby said.

Fran pulled herself up so her head rested on the arm of the couch. "Hi." She scrubbed at her face with her hands. "What time is it?"

"Nearly four."

"Wouldn't want to miss 'Young Doctor Malone.' If I miss it three days in a row, it takes forever to catch up."

"God forbid." Shelby smiled. She touched the backs of her fingers to Fran's face. "Have you been running this fever all day?"

Fran shook her head. "Only since around two-thirty. I think it happens every day around that time, doesn't it?"

"It does, and you're not going back to work until it doesn't."

"I'll die of boredom and self-pity."

"Can't be helped," Shelby said. "I'm making the rules." She glanced down at the floor. The paper bag she'd left beside the couch for trash was filled with bunched-up tissues. Either Fran's flu had taken a major turn toward the respiratory, or she'd been crying. "Are you really OK?" she asked.

"Sure, considering I've been at death's door," Fran said. Her eyes were red-rimmed and puffy. She caught Shelby studying her and looked away.

"You were crying, weren't you?"

"Not really."

"A little?" Fran was silent. Shelby took her hand. "I wish you could talk to me."

"Well, I can't," Fran said, sad and angry at the same time. "So can we just get off it?"

"I'm sorry. I shouldn't have pushed."

"I'd hate it if you weren't concerned about me." Fran smiled ruefully. "Guess I'm hard to please."

Shelby laughed. "You're not hard to please. I've dealt with professionals."

"Ah, yes, the famous Libby. I don't want to make you feel unexceptional, but my mother had her moments, too."

"Had? Isn't your mother alive?"

"She's alive," Fran said, and took a sip of water. "I'm the one who's dead, in her opinion."

"Really?"

"Really." She looked in the general direction of the north window, avoiding Shelby's eyes. "She gave away or burned all my stuff. When people ask her how many kids she has, she says 'one.' According to my brother, anyway, and he has no reason to lie."

"I never heard of anything like that," Shelby said. "It must be awful."

"Not so awful, considering the alternatives." She shot Shelby a quick glance. "Libby, for instance."

"What about your father?"

"He does what Mom says." Fran shrugged. "It's no big deal. I mean, it's no big deal now. It was at the time but it's in the past."

"But what happened?" Shelby was having a hard time wrapping her mind around this. "To make her like that, I mean. Toward you."

"We didn't get along."

"That's a pretty big 'not getting along.'"

"We *really* didn't get along."

"Is that what…the other night…I'm sorry, you asked me not to bring it up."

Fran smiled and squeezed her hand. "It's all right. And, no, it has very little to do with the other night. OK?"

"OK."

"Are you going to turn on the TV, or do I have to drag my fevered, beaten body inch by agonizing inch across the room?"

If she thought going back to the office was strange, seeing Ray again was even stranger. He came to her apartment, banged on the door, and when she opened it swooped her up in an embrace and a mighty kiss. "Babe," he murmured into her ear. "I missed you."

"Me, too," she said, glad he couldn't see her face.

"Bad news, though. I have to go on duty at six a.m. tomorrow. OK with you if we just have dinner in West Sayer and come back here and fool around?"

"OK with me." The dinner part was OK. She wasn't so certain about the fooling around. Which struck her as odd. After not seeing her fiancé for two weeks, even though they'd talked on the phone every night, she should be up for some major fooling around. But his gestures felt rough, his size and strength frightened her...

"Come on, then. Put on your old gray bonnet and let's hit the trail."

It grew even worse over dinner. She picked at her lobster and tried to listen to him, but all she could hear were the voices in her head, shouting at him, "Go away, go away, go away."

At one point she even thought she'd said it out loud, but Ray didn't break stride in his talking. There were more and more cases of drug overdose every week, he said, especially among the college students. It disturbed him. He thought he should do something. He didn't know what to do. He'd talked with administration officials from both Harvard and M.I.T., but they either refused to recognize the problem, or refused to admit it was a problem, and muttered platitudes about "learning experiences" and "academic freedom."

Shelby nodded sympathetically, and reminded herself that Ray was a caring, compassionate man, a person of honor, all too rare in today's world. On the brink of extinction, really. She was grateful he cared so deeply about his work, especially since it kept him from noticing that she felt as odd as a three-dollar bill.

The restaurant wasn't crowded, but the edges of things were blurred as if the room were filled with smoke or fog. People, Ray, the waiters, the kitchen with the gray metal swinging doors, seemed very far away. She might be watching it in a movie. An old movie. Colors seemed washed out, barely there. She didn't like this feeling. Connect, she told herself sharply.

They drove back to the apartment. Ray wanted to come in. Shelby pleaded exhaustion. It wasn't a lie. She hadn't slept since Thursday, when Fran had declared herself out of danger and into convalescence, and no longer in need of round-the-clock supervision. She was genuinely glad Fran felt better, but sleeping in her own apartment, no longer listening for Fran's cough or wheeze, or just restless tossing, was a lonely and useless feeling. She'd begun to feel the lack of sleep, too. There was a gray headache overhead. Still distant and faint as faraway thunder but she knew it was only a matter of time until it rolled over the horizon. Maybe, if she took a sleeping pill and got caught up, it would go away.

"You do look bushed," Ray said. "Get in bed. Right now. Doctor's orders."

She told Ray she'd call him first thing in the morning, and that he was the most understanding man in the world, and she was the luckiest woman alive and terribly in love. He kissed her outside her door, and let himself out. Shelby stood for a moment, listening. There was music in the hall, coming from behind Fran's door. Classical music. Brahms.

She thought about going to Fran's apartment, asking her if there was anything wrong, if there was anything she could do. But she didn't want to be pushy. If there *was* something wrong, she had to trust Fran to tell her sooner or later. That was the mature, responsible, respectful way to handle it. She hated it.

Because something *was* wrong. The past few days Fran had been withdrawn, pulled into herself. Ever since that night. It made Shelby feel crazy, wanting to know. It wasn't like her, to feel so…so *stuck* with something. If one of her friends was troubled, she made a point of noticing. If they wanted to talk, she was there to listen. She never took their reticence personally. If they wanted to be left alone, she left them alone. But this was different. She couldn't solve it, and she couldn't let it go. And worst of all, she was convinced it had something to do with her.

She hung her dress in the closet and slipped into pajamas. Take a sleeping pill. Go to bed. Things will look different in the morning. Maybe worse, maybe better, but different.

The last thing she did before she got into bed was slip out into the hall and listen for Fran's music.

It was still playing.

It was still Brahms.

Chapter 12

Jean's birthday was the middle of July. It required a party, another back yard barbecue. Summer had settled in to stay, and they were in the throes of their annual week-long breath-choking heat wave. The air was spongy with humidity. Pictures curled inside their frames. Charcoal was reluctant to catch fire, and so much starter fluid was used the town looked like an oil refinery every evening from five to seven. The touch of air against skin was unpleasant, clammy and warm. Maple leaves drooped darkly. There was a powder of mildew on the lilac bushes. The grass stopped growing. Every time Shelby saw a road crew, she wanted to take them gallons of lemonade. Dogs lay panting on their sides, their tongues lolling in the dust. There were no visible cats. The only creatures moving were the sparrows, taking dust baths in wilting gardens.

The whole lunch bunch was there, of course, with their assorted escorts. And Libby, who had breezed in at the last minute to drop off magazines with possible bridesmaids' dresses. She'd invited herself to stay. At Jean's request, she'd invited Fran. "Too much boy-girl, boy-girl," Jean had said. Her "relationship" with Greg had never gotten off the ground. "I'll feel like a leper. Besides, I haven't seen her in a while."

Fran accepted. "I like Jean," she said. "I'd like to know her better." Still with that touch of formality, and not looking Shelby in the eye.

"Great," Shelby said, covering her own uneasiness with enthusiasm. "And we'd better sit down and plan our camping trip, before the summer gets away from us."

"As soon as I get off the weekend shift." She smiled and shrugged helplessly. "You know how it is."

No, she wanted to say, I don't know how it is. I don't know how anything is, or what it is, or where we stand. "Sure," she said. It wasn't that she was just frustrated, she was hurt. Fran had brought something into her life, and now she was taking it away.

I didn't do anything wrong, Shelby thought, and felt as if she were going to cry.

If she hadn't had the sleeping pills to fall back on for the past couple of weeks, she probably would never have slept.

Shelby wondered if they should move the party inside, where it was cooler. It might even be worthwhile dragging her bedroom air conditioner out of the storage space in the basement. Every year she tried to get through the summer without it. The humming bothered her; it made her feel cut off from the world. The cold air made her sleepy so she went around in a comfortable but unproductive daze. And when it cycled on and off during the night it did so with a "clunk" loud enough to wake the neighbors three houses over. But, try as hard as she could, she couldn't make it through the July heat wave. The inversion layer, they called it on the radio. Dampness from the river combining with industrial smog and pollen and trapped by a high-pressure system, or a low-pressure system, or some kind of system that didn't move much. It might be time to give in to it.

She went over to where Fran was drinking a beer and chatting with Jean. "Do you think we should bring the air conditioner up?"

"You couldn't tell by me," Fran said. "I've been living in Tex-ass. In weather like this, we go south to get warm."

Jean laughed. "You wouldn't want to spoil the boys' fun, would you?"

For reasons no one really understood, human beings of the male persuasion seemed to have a compulsion, during killer heat, to go outside and hurl objects through the air and catch them. They were at it now. Charlie and Ray and Lisa's Wayne and yet another man they'd never met who'd come with Penny, tossing a tiny rubber football that the baby upstairs had thrown out of his playpen on the patio.

"Male energy," Jean said, "is incomprehensible."

"I'll drink to that." Fran drained her bottle. "Whatever happened with Greg?"

"Greg?"

"That boy you were dating when I met you."

"That's ancient history," Jean said. "Doesn't Shelby keep you up on the news?"

Fran glanced up at Shelby. "Usually. I haven't been well."

"How are you now?"

"Fine. Except for the occasional sleeping fits."

"Oh, God," Jean groaned. "The narcolepsy."

"I'm afraid every time she drives," Shelby said lightly, and rested a deliberate hand casually on Fran's shoulder. It was a childish and silly thing to do, but she hadn't touched her in so long...

Fran laughed. "She thinks I'm going to fall asleep at the wheel," she said. She slipped out from under Shelby's hand. "I need another beer. How about you two?"

"Thanks," Jean said.

Shelby shook her head. She could feel the redness in her face, the embarrassment. Then she got mad. Damn it, what was the big stinking deal about putting her hand on Fran's shoulder? It was a perfectly normal, friendly gesture. Fran didn't have to act as though she...She didn't know what. As though she...something. Something rude. Something nasty.

"I really like her," Jean was saying. "I'll bet you two have a lot of fun."

Oh, yes, tons of fun. Every day another thrill, every minute another laugh. "Sometimes," she said. "I don't see her a lot. She works funny hours."

"That's what she said. She doesn't see as much of you as she'd like because of her work schedule."

Did she mention the evenings she's spent shut up in her room listening to

Brahms? Did she mention we were going to go camping again and didn't? And did she happen to mention what the hell is really going on? Because I certainly would be interested in knowing.

Fran came toward them, carrying three beers. "I got you one," she said, handing it to Shelby. She didn't make eye contact. "You looked hot."

"Thank you." Shelby turned to Jean and lifted her beer. "Here's to you. Many happy returns."

"Jean!" Libby called from across the patio. "Come here and let me give you a big birthday kiss."

Jean waved to her. Under her breath, she said, "Do I have to?"

"Of course you don't," Shelby said.

Libby was calling and making "come here" gestures.

"Yes, I do." Jean smiled grimly. "Might as well get in over with."

Shelby leaned against the stone wall and watched Connie join them. General expressions of jollity all around. She really ought to go and rescue her.

"Shelby," Fran said.

"Yeah?"

"I'm sorry."

Shelby looked at her. "What for?"

"What I did just now."

Shelby felt tight-lipped and unforgiving. "I don't have a contagious disease, you know."

"I know. It was…complicated. I don't expect you to understand."

"Clearly."

Fran was silent for a moment. "We're losing each other, aren't we?"

She could feel herself begin to melt. "Are we?"

"I think so. And it's my fault. I'm in kind of a stuck place right now. I thought I could handle it, but I guess I can't."

"I don't know what's going on, Fran."

"I know you don't." She sighed. "I think we have to talk."

"That sounds like a good idea. Whenever you have the time."

"I'll make the time." Fran looked down at the ground. "I really miss you, Shelby."

She rested her hand against the side of Fran's face. "I miss you, too."

Fran cleared her throat. "Look, this has nothing to do with you, but I don't feel real comfortable with…"

Shelby smiled, because Fran looked so lovely. She took her hand away. "I know. You don't like public displays of affection."

"That's sort of it."

"Are you afraid people will think we're having an affair?" She laughed and felt a little giddy. "I wish they would. It would make for some very interesting lunch table conversation."

Fran glanced over to where Libby and Connie and Jean were standing, looking their way. "Be careful what you wish for. You might get it."

Time to serve dinner. Ray tried to make himself scarce, so he wouldn't have to help. Shelby told him he could be as lazy as a slug after they were married, but as far as she was concerned the courtship was still in session and she expected to be treated like a queen. He grinned and came to help, but after ten minutes of his bungling she declared him untrainable and told him to get out and send her someone more competent. Someone like Lisa.

After he left, pretending to feel rejected, she realized in the pit of her stomach what had happened. They'd fallen into the classic Dagwood-and-Blondie scenario—dominant, harried wife; incompetent husband. They'd never played that game before. It had happened so easily.

She made herself a gin and tonic.

"If you're a closet lush," Lisa said as she bounced through the door, "I'd suggest something with a less distinctive odor. Something that goes better with beer."

Shelby put her glass in the sink. "You're right."

"I'm not saying I blame you." Lisa opened the refrigerator and began tossing lettuce and tomatoes and onions and carrots and peppers randomly onto the drain board.

"What do you mean?"

"The tension's so thick you can cut it with a knife." She bent down and rummaged through the crisper.

"It is?"

"I'm not certain," she found a bunch of radishes and added them to the pile, "but I suspect your mother isn't exactly fond of your housemate."

"Oh, for God's sake." Shelby found a large bowl and started ripping up the lettuce.

"She keeps giving her surreptitious, nasty glances. They were talking a little while ago. I wonder what set her off.'"

"It doesn't take anything to set Libby off," Shelby said roughly. "She's in a constant state of 'off.' "

"Maybe she needs a boyfriend."

"When have you ever known Libby to be without a boyfriend?"

Lisa discovered a jar of olives. "Well, maybe she needs to get married."

"She'll never get married. She'd lose her alimony."

"Hey, go easy on the lettuce. You're beating it into submission."

"Yeah, I am." She stopped.

"It's a *tossed* salad, not a *mauled* salad."

"I got carried away." She found a paring knife and started cutting up vegetables.

"I can do that," Lisa said. "I'm supposed to be helping you."

Shelby smiled at her. "Lisa, I love you dearly, but your bloody fingertips in the salad we do not need."

"Croutons!" Lisa said, and started looking through the cupboards. She found a box of lemon Jello. "You made Fran drink this stuff, didn't you?"

"Yep. Did she tell you that?"

Lisa nodded. "She said you probably saved her life, but it wasn't much of a blast."

"Things that are good for you seldom *are* much of a blast." She got a larger knife and sliced the onions translucent-thin.

"You sound like my mother," Lisa said with a giggle.

"As long as I don't sound like mine." She stacked the onion slices and attacked them vertically.

Lisa finished tearing up the lettuce and took the smaller knife and started in on a pepper. "Something bothering you, Shel?"

Surprised, she looked up. "No. Why?"

"You seem kind of P.O.'d."

"I'm fine. I guess I shouldn't talk about my mother while I'm slicing onions. Remind me of that next time."

Lisa ran the pepper under water. "Libby's OK."

"She's OK around you. She likes you."

"She likes you, too."

"Not very much."

As soon as she said it she realized it was true. Her mother didn't like her very much.

"Don't be silly," Lisa said. "Of course she does."

"No, really, she doesn't." This was big. This was a major realization. Maybe even a Major Realization. It frightened her. And excited her. "She really doesn't. Hardly at all."

She didn't know what to think about this. Didn't even know *how* to think about it.

Lisa gave an uncertain little laugh. "You know that's not true. You're trying to shock me."

"No, I'm serious. I…" One glance at Lisa's face told her to back off. This was shocking stuff to Lisa. Hell, it'd be shocking to anyone. She was even a mite shocked, herself. She'd better get off this before Lisa died of embarrassment. Lisa had the look of someone caught eavesdropping. Lisa was worried, and wouldn't meet her eyes. "Of course I'm not serious," she said. "I'm annoyed with her tonight, that's all."

"That happens," Lisa said uncomfortably, and went back to slicing peppers.

You're not supposed to talk about things like that, Shelby reminded herself. Taboo topics. Fratricide, matricide, patricide, incest, and the possibility that your mother doesn't like you. Mothers love their children. They can't help it, it's something that happens to them when they're pregnant. Some hormonal thing. And children love their mothers. They can't help it, either. Probably the same hormonal thing. And in spite of all the tension and squabbling and things that seem to go wrong, when it comes right down to the bottom line, your mother's your mother and she'll do the motherly thing.

A nurse at camp had told her that, when she'd been moping with homesickness and hurt that her parents wouldn't call her and they'd sent her to the nurse because she wouldn't eat and was losing weight. "Next to the Lord Jesus Christ," the nurse had said in a there-there, off-handed kind of way, "your mother's your best friend."

That had impressed her, being at an age when she was apt to be impressed by anything Biblical. She'd thought about it and thought about it, trying to figure out what was being a "best friend" about refusing to talk to her on the phone. She finally gave up, and decided it was probably one of those things she'd understand once she was older. Once she was a mother, maybe, and wise. She'd asked her mother if it was true, though, just to be on the safe side. "Of course it is," Libby had said. She took a strand of Shelby's hair in her hand and stroked it between her fingers. "I wonder if you'd look better with a perm."

Mothers. Study up, kiddo, she reminded herself. You'll be one some day.

She wondered if she'd be a good mother, whatever that meant. She hoped so. When she thought of "good mother," she thought of someone you could run to when you were hurt, who'd pick you up and hold you no matter what the problem was and whether it was your own fault or not. Someone who'd stand by you even when you made a mistake. Someone...

"Parsley?" Lisa asked.

"Parsley?"

"Do you have any parsley."

"Oh, yeah, sure." She waved toward the back door. "In that little herb garden, right next to the garage wall. If the heat hasn't done it in."

Lisa slipped out the door.

Thank God, a minute to be alone, to think, to...

"Shelby, what in the world *are* you doing in there?" Libby was annoyed. You could tell by the way the ice chattered in her Tom Collins.

"Getting dinner on," Shelby said, trying not to sound defensive and nearly succeeding.

"Well, how complicated can that be, for heaven's sake?"

"I'm almost done. Make yourself a drink."

Libby bustled noisily between the refrigerator and the sink. Despite the clatter, her verbal silence made Shelby apprehensive. You never could tell what would come at the end of one of those silences. "I noticed you met Fran," she said, to make small talk.

"Yes, I did." Libby found the gin and poured herself a healthy shot. The silence came back.

"What did you think of her?"

Her mother opened a fresh bottle of mixer and slopped some into her drink. She put one finger over her lips thoughtfully. "An odd child."

"Child?" Shelby said. "She's older than me."

"Compared to me, who's soon to be older than Methuselah, she's a child. And so are you." She took Shelby's chin between her thumb and forefinger. "And you'll always be a child to your old Mom."

Shelby pulled away. "I'm cutting off your booze, Libby," she said lightly. "You're becoming maudlin."

"God forbid!" She leaned against the sink and sipped her drink. "Kind of a diamond-in-the-rough, maybe?"

"Who?"

"Nan...Jan..."

"Fran."

"She tells me she was in the Army."

"That's right."

"Well, that's what I mean by odd."

This time she couldn't keep the defensiveness from her voice. "Being in the Army isn't illegal, immoral, or fattening."

"No," said Libby smoothly. "Just odd."

This was becoming distressingly familiar. Next Libby would say she

163

thought Fran didn't like her. Then it would be Libby didn't like Fran, which was the real truth of it all along. It had happened with college friends. It had happened with graduate school friends. It hadn't happened yet with Jean, though it was bound to. Jean had probably escaped so far by always being in Libby's presence with Connie and Lisa and Penny, who were much more acceptable, being much more noisy. But it was coming. She could tell by the way Libby looked at Jean, her face as expressionless as a mannequin's.

To hell with it, Shelby thought. There was nothing she could do about it except try not to give a damn. Which would be a lot easier if Libby were less persistently vocal about her likes and dislikes.

Lisa was back with the parsley. It was a little pathetic but not too bad. Shelby wouldn't have cared if it looked like straw or dried moss. It was the excuse she needed to gear up into a flurry of activity that left no room for conversation.

Fran left early, pleading a morning shift at the Health Service. Shelby wondered if it really was that. Fran had seemed to grow more and more uncomfortable as the evening wore on. She probably sensed Libby's antipathy, which increased every time Shelby sent a word or look in Fran's direction.

It made Shelby angry. This was Fran's home…well, almost, the house, anyway, more than it was Libby's…Shelby's home, at any rate. And if she wanted her here, it was Libby's business to adjust, not glower over the place like a Rottweiler with a fresh bone.

She wished they'd leave, so she could catch Fran before she went to bed, so they could talk. Not anything big or heavy. She just needed to be reassured Libby hadn't run her off.

There was no way that was going to happen, though. They'd barely started on cake and coffee and presents. That would take at least another hour. Then the obligatory drive with Ray to the all-night diner. Shelby sighed. Her whole life was cemented in routine. She wished she had the nerve to break the rules. If there were a Shelby Black, Shelby Black would break the rules. Shelby Black would stand up, clap her hands, and announce, "Party's over, folks. It was swell. Thanks for coming. Ray, take someone else to the diner. You smell of beer and I have better things to do." But Shelby Black didn't exist. Just good old agreeable, cowardly Shelby Camden.

Sometimes she thought everyone in the world was going insane, and she was leading the way.

She asked Connie to be her maid of honor. Connie just looked at her as if she'd lost her mind to ask. As if Everyone, Connie's favorite group of people, had known for months that Connie would be the maid of honor. As if, the minute she'd agreed to marry Ray, a billboard had gone up somewhere reading, "Connie Thurmond, maid of honor."

The lunch bunch had taken to sudden, embarrassed silences whenever Shelby entered the room. Even Jean. Shelby had tried to sound her out about it, but Jean assured her they were just discussing wedding gifts. She would have believed her if Jean hadn't looked so guilty.

At least Penny was still behaving as usual, blowing hot and cold for no apparent reason.

Libby had worked herself into a frenzy of activity around the wedding. Every weekend, and sometimes on weeknights, she summoned Shelby to Boston to make yet another decision, choose another china or silver or linen pattern, register at yet another department store. The material out of which the bridesmaids' shoes would be made assumed an importance equal to the decision to drop the atomic bomb. If Ray hadn't lived in Cambridge and been able to meet her for dinner, she would have forgotten what he looked like.

She supposed this was normal mother-of-the-bride behavior. Most of the married women around the office declared it was hell on wheels. Some even claimed they'd never recovered, and at least one woman swore it had permanently damaged her relationship with her mother.

Then why are we doing this? she kept wanting to ask. If you hated it, and your mother probably hated it just as much when *her* mother arranged her wedding, and her mother before her…

Weddings, she decided, are a primitive ritual more deeply embedded in the human psyche than deathbed promises and last rites.

"Sorry about running out on you at Jean's party," Fran said when they had finally bumped into each other by the mailboxes. "Your mother made me nervous."

"I thought so."

"She's so *watchful*. Reminds me of why I left home."

"You left because your mother was watchful?"

"The reasons were many and multifarious," Fran said. "But that was one of them."

"Damn."

"Damn what?"

"I was hoping it would be reason enough."

Fran smiled. "Feel like flying the coop?"

Shelby kneaded her face. "How fast can you teach me wilderness survival skills?"

"Depends on how you feel about cannibalism."

"Some of my best friends are cannibals," Shelby said. "But I wouldn't want my sister to marry one."

Fran leaned against the wall, junk mail clutched beneath one arm, and looked at her. "I'm worried about you," she said.

Shelby was startled. "About me?"

"You're still getting headaches. I can tell by looking at you. And I don't think you're sleeping well, either."

"In other words," Shelby said lightly, "I look like something the cat dragged in and wouldn't eat."

"Are you taking the sleeping pills?"

Shelby shrugged, feeling caught and cared for. She liked it. "Occasionally."

"What else are you doing for yourself?"

Trying to get you to tell me what's wrong with you, she thought. "I'm OK. It's all a little hectic, that's all. How about yourself?"

It was Fran's turn to glance at the floor. "What about myself?"

"What's going on with you, Fran?" she heard herself ask.

Fran blushed. "Nothing. I'm fine."

"Back at Jean's party, I thought we were going to talk about things."

Fran's laugh was insincere. "You have a memory like a steel trap. Once in, you have to gnaw off a leg to get out."

"Stop that."

"I'm fine," Fran said roughly. "Everything's fine."

"Everything is not fine," Shelby said. "It hasn't been fine since you were sick. Will you please tell me what the hell's happening with us?"

"Nothing's happening with us. There's nothing *to* happen with us."

"Fran..."

"Look, just...just let it go, will you?" She started to turn away. Magazines and junk mail cascaded from under her arm. She swore and knelt to pick them up.

Shelby knew she should help, but she was too angry. Not speaking, she went into her apartment and slammed the door.

She couldn't have slept that night if her life depended on it. Even a sleeping pill didn't help. Neither did the second. She didn't dare risk a third; it would leave her stupid and near-comatose the next day. Instead, she climbed onto an emotional carousel and gave the horses their heads.

It wasn't fair, what Fran was doing. She wouldn't let *Shelby* get away with it. If it was obvious something was bothering Shelby, she'd insist she talk. She wouldn't let Shelby leave her in the dark, tied up in knots, lonely.

The loneliness was terrible. She'd thought she was lonely in the past, but that was before Fran had made her feel less alone. Never knowing understanding was one thing. Knowing it and having it taken away was something else. To feel so close to another person, to feel so open and safe...And Fran had closed the door in her face. Fran had cheated on their friendship.

Wait a minute, she scolded herself. She let you see something she didn't want you to see, because she was sick and couldn't help it. Now she can't take it back, and she's trying to restore her privacy.

But it isn't as if I laughed at her, or turned away from her. I saw how much she hurt, and I handled it with gentleness and love. And she pays me back with silence. And withdrawal. She might as well call me names, or spit in my face.

Damn it, it wasn't easy to sit through that, but I'm glad I did. It was an honor.

Maybe she can't help herself. Maybe she hates it, too. Maybe I should approach it differently. Don't demand answers, but don't ignore it. Be persistent but not pushy. Firm but not rigid.

Or maybe she should learn to be more patient. If she trusted the feeling that had passed between them, Fran would come to her when she was ready. She was in pain, confused, and working it out on her own.

Assuming she *was* really working it out. What if what she really wanted was to end the friendship, and was trying to figure out how to do it gently? That would be like Fran, to want to be gentle.

Shelby sat up and turned on the light. How did she know that was like Fran? She hardly knew the woman. Had only met her in March. April, May, June, July—four and a half months ago. She couldn't know all the different sides of her. There could be a hundred Frans, flying in all directions like tiddly-winks.

But I trust her, damn it. Something in my heart trusts her.

You have to stop this, she told herself. This road leads straight to the funny farm.

She gave up on sleep and wandered out into the living room. Nothing but test patterns on television. Too late even for Jack Paar, the insomniac's friend. She could learn a lot from Jack Paar. He could conduct an entire conversation without letting it slip into anything meaningful. Fran would probably like that.

She was tempted to peek out into the hall and see if Fran's light was on. Forget it. She was tired of running after her like an abandoned puppy. She had enough on her mind, she didn't need this. Just get over it.

Get over what? What exactly was she trying to get over? This friendship that was maybe a friendship and maybe not? Big deal, big stinking deal. It was ridiculous to thrash around this way over someone you've known for four and a half months.

She decided to try the warm milk trick. As she stood watching the pan heat, she thought of the times she'd sat in this kitchen with Fran, talking, laughing, simply being comfortable in each other's presence.

Ten and a half months left of their year.

She turned off the stove and began to cry.

The first person on the staff to notice there was something wrong and to speak about it was Harry Rosen, one of her associate editors. Harry was a quiet, gentle, middle-aged man, whose instinct for good fiction was legendary. He could probably have made editor if he'd wanted, but he was happy in his current position and had no aspirations to power. It took courage and skill for him to stay where he was. A woman would have been fired, on the grounds that she lacked ambition and the competitive spirit. Another man might have given in to pressure and the promise of a higher salary. But Harry said he wanted to keep on doing what he did best, and moving up in the world could only distance him from his first love, reading and editing fiction.

He tended to avoid talking on a personal level with his subordinates. Not out of lack of interest or caring, but because he was a deeply shy man. So it surprised her when he asked her into his office and closed the door. "Miss Camden," he said in the abrupt way people said things they were afraid to say, "You look terrible."

Shelby didn't know how to respond. She knew she looked like death warmed over. Her skin was papery and dry. Her eyes were puffy and smudged from lack of sleep. Her friends had noticed, of course, but she had laughed it off as headaches and wedding anxiety. Connie and Lisa clucked. Penny hovered. Jean looked at her skeptically. They'd let it drop.

"Miss Camden?"

"I'm sorry. I have a thousand things running through my head."

"I understand you're to be married in the spring."

"June, actually."

Harry raked his thinning hair. "Excuse my bluntness, but you look as if you're going through a divorce, not a marriage."

"I do?"

"And your work lately…" He picked up a folder of stories she had passed on to him. "Frankly, you seem to have lost your edge."

"I'm sorry."

He took a story from the folder and studied it. "Is there anything I can do to help?"

Shelby bit her lip. Lately, when anyone showed her even the most casual concern, she felt as if she might crack wide open. Maybe she'd know something if she did. Maybe something would come flying out, some nugget of truth in a cyclone of words and tears. "There are just so many things…decisions to make, plans, you know."

"My daughter was married last year," he said with a sympathetic nod. "I thought she and her mother would kill each other before it was over."

"I guess that's part of the ritual."

He glanced at her. "At no time did she look as *strained* as you do."

Shelby couldn't think of anything to say, so she said, "I'm sorry," again.

"How much vacation time do you have?"

"A week."

"Maybe you should take it. Go somewhere quiet and relax."

"My mother and her *Bride* magazines would find me."

He smiled. "It really will pass, you know." He sat forward and cleared his throat. "Meanwhile, I think you should take time off, while it's still summer. Go to the beach. Go to the mountains. Go anywhere there are no telephones, no mothers, and no bridal magazines." He closed her folder in a 'well, that's done' way and folded his hands.

Shelby stood. "Thanks for your concern. I'll try to keep my focus better." She didn't like the way that sounded, cold and formal. "I really appreciate your understanding. You may be right about getting away."

He nodded abruptly and immersed himself in a report.

By the time she got back to her office, she realized she was uneasy about the conversation, knowing that her tension was visible. She didn't want people thinking her wedding was making a wreck of her. Shelby Camden handled things better than that.

Besides, it wasn't the truth, not the entire truth. It was Fran as much as the wedding. Or the wedding wouldn't be so hard if it weren't for Fran, or the trouble with Fran wouldn't be so hard if it weren't for the wedding…

Whatever it was, she had to stop letting it show. She could do that. Pay more attention to her make-up. Focus on her work more. Concentrate. Like right now. Start acting like a woman with a career.

By quitting time, she had actually read and critiqued four stories—rather brilliantly, she thought—and met with three readers who'd been trying to get an appointment with her all week. She called an author whose work she had rejected with great reluctance, and encouraged her to submit again. They discussed *The Magazine's* editorial needs and standards. The author was flattered and grateful. It made Shelby feel a little more like a card-carrying member of the human race. As she cleared the worst of the clutter from the top of her desk, she thought about the evening ahead. Maybe she'd go to a movie, but there really wasn't anything she wanted to see, or anyone she wanted to see it with. So it was go alone, or sit in her apartment listening to Fran's damn stereo down the hall.

Maybe she should stop by the Army Surplus store and pick up a machete, kick her way into Fran's room and threaten to decapitate her if she didn't open up.

God, she was sick of this. She had to do something to get her mind off it. She felt stuck, as if she were trapped in a deep pit, in mud up to her knees. She had to climb, but she couldn't stop looking down, peering into the sludge as if she could find a key that would get her out.

OK, she told herself, time to put the present behind you and think about the future. She reached for the phone and dialled Ray's apartment.

He was delighted to come, glad she'd called him, pleased she thought of him as a cure for "the blues." He'd be there by seven. If there was a concert at the University, they could eat before or after. He loved her.

She showered and slipped into an off-the-shoulder, off-the-back, nearly off-the-front item her mother had brought her from Guadeloupe. This was what women did, wasn't it? If you're depressed, go shopping, dress up, take in a musical, have fun. In other words, do exactly what you don't feel like doing. The effort will perk you right up. Well, it was better than spending another evening brooding. And it certainly made Ray happy. That ought to help, making the man she loved happy. That was what was important. Not the strange and bewildering behavior of a neighbor she'd only known for four and a half months and would probably never see again.

When Ray picked her up, she ran to greet him in the hall, loudly. If Fran were home, she couldn't help but hear. It was tacky of her. She didn't care. She was sick of caring.

There were no concerts of interest. They went to dinner, then to a student bar where some local folksingers were performing. It was dark and not too noisy, a good place to relax and talk. The incense of marijuana hung in the air.

Ray wrinkled his nose. "Jesus, I hate that stuff."

"I kind of like the smell," Shelby said. "Have you ever tried it?"

"Once. It made me feel like mashed potatoes."

Shelby thought it might be pleasant, to feel like mashed potatoes. It would be warm and relaxing. Mashed potatoes probably slept very well. Mashed potatoes probably weren't torn apart by baked potatoes' peculiar behaviors.

Ray was looking at her with a puzzled expression. "Would you rather go somewhere else?"

"Not at all. This is fine." He held her chair for her. "I was just wool-gathering."

"It's much too hot," he said as he took off his madras jacket, "to have anything to do with wool."

Shelby envied him. In his short-sleeved white shirt and chinos, he looked cool, comfortable, and at peace with the world. She told him so.

Ray laughed. "Cool, no. Comfortable, yes. At peace with the world?" He shrugged. "What's not to be at peace?"

She found that amazing. "Nothing, I guess."

He signalled the waitress and ordered himself a bourbon-and-water. Shelby considered having a glass of wine. But she felt like drinking. Serious drinking. "Scotch and soda," she said.

When they had their drinks, Ray leaned toward her over the table. "You've seemed kind of strung out lately, Shel. Want to tell me about it?"

"It's nothing. I'm just not sleeping well."

"You didn't tell me that."

She laughed it off. "So what else is new? Same old stuff."

"Look," he said, and took her hand. "It may be old news to you, but you're the woman I love. Are you going to keep things from me after we're married, just because it's nothing new?"

He was right. In another ten months, Ray would be her husband, her lover, her best friend.

"To tell you the truth," she said, "I'm pretty upset about Fran. She's been acting strangely."

Ray smiled. "She's one of the strangest people I've ever met."

She looked at him. "What makes you say that?"

"I don't know, just strange."

Shelby waited him out.

"All right, intense, I guess. Really intense."

"How can you tell that?"

"It's a feeling, a hunch. Hey, don't glare at me. I'm not the only one who thinks that."

"I'm not glaring," Shelby said, and tried not to glare. She made her voice calm. "Who else thinks it?"

He stared down at the table and looked guilty. "Well...Connie, for one, and your mother..."

"You were discussing Fran with my mother?"

His ears reddened. "I wasn't *discussing* her. It was a quick, casual conversation. Connie said, 'She's intense, isn't she?,' and I said 'Yes,' and Libby said, 'She certainly is.' And that was it. End of conversation."

Shelby shook her head. "I hate that, Ray."

"What?"

"Talking about me behind my back."

"I wasn't talking about you, and it wasn't behind your back. I'd have said the same thing to you. In fact, I just did. Look where it got me." He forced a smile. "I can't say I'll never do it again, but I sure as hell won't tell you about it."

"Well, that's great," Shelby said. "That's just great."

"I was making a joke."

"It wasn't funny." She downed her drink and caught the waitress's eye and ordered another.

Ray pretended to mop his brow. "My God, it's prickly in here. Is it the heat, or that time of month?"

She gripped the empty glass in her hand and wanted to throw it at him. "Men," she muttered. "You're all stuffed with righteous indignation for yourselves, but let a woman complain, and it's 'that time of month.'"

"Shel..."

"Well, it isn't 'that time of month,' and this happens to be something that really matters to me, and I resent that condescending tone."

"I'm not condescending."

"Yes, you are." The waitress arrived with her drink. She waited until she'd left. "You are," she repeated.

"For God's sake," Ray said, annoyed, "what the hell is wrong with you?"

"Fran is wrong with me. She's…was…my friend, and she's treating me like a stranger, and that makes me very, very unhappy."

He shook his head. "Shel, you've only known her a few months."

"So what? I probably know her better than I know you. I certainly know her better than you know me."

"If that's the case," Ray snapped, "maybe you should marry *her*."

"That's really *cute*," she said.

He held out his hands. "Look, I'm sorry. I know you're strung out. I don't want us to fight. I'm sorry your friend hurt your feelings. I'm sorry I put my foot in it. If you want to talk about it…"

"I don't want to talk about it." She looked toward the tiny, makeshift stage where a young man with a blonde crew cut was tuning his guitar. With his button-down collared, vertical-striped-short-sleeved shirt, he reminded her of one of the Chad Mitchell Trio.

"Then we'll talk about something else."

"I don't want to talk."

"Fine," Ray said stiffly. "We'll just sit here quietly until you get over your fit of pique."

She didn't let herself respond to him. She couldn't. The way her mind was spinning, there was no telling what would come out. She ordered another drink, stared at the singer, and learned more than she'd ever wanted to know about guitar tuning.

"Has it ever occurred to you," she said, calmer and wanting to make up but still feeling fragile, "that there are an awful lot of really boring jobs in the world?"

"I guess there are," he said. He nodded toward the stage. "Like his?"

"Like his. And like waitressing. Even tending bar must be boring most of the time."

"Probably not as bad as driving a bus."

"Especially a school bus," she said.

Ray laughed. "Please, not a school bus."

"Is your job boring?"

"When it's not terrifying. How about yours?"

"Not usually." She thought about it. "Sometimes, when we get a run on truly terrible stories, but mostly they're filtered out before they get to me."

He tapped his fingers on the table top as if he were playing bongo drums. "Will you miss it?"

Shelby felt herself go cold. "Miss my job?"

Ray nodded.

"I haven't decided what to do about it."

He took a swallow of his drink. "Maybe you'll find another magazine to work for, wherever we end up."

"Maybe."

"Not for a while, of course. I'm going to need all your help building my practice." He grinned. "You'll be great at playing Doctor's Wife."

She wasn't sure what to say, so she said, "Thank you."

"And then there'll be kids. But in a bunch of years…"

In a bunch of years, I'll have forgotten everything I ever knew. The language will have changed. I'll have the vocabulary of a kindergartner. I'll be unemployable. We'll live in the suburbs and entertain on our patio, and I'll drink too much, and Ray will start coming home later and later, which will cause me to drink more. When the kids have finally gone off to college, I won't have anything to do except drink. I'll have a sordid affair with the Electrolux man, or the Fuller Brush man, or the college student who sells encyclopedias. This'll go on until one day Ray comes home and catches us and someone puts a bullet in someone's head. If it's not my head, I'll live out my declining years in a state of shame and disgrace, and die of a painful and terrible disease which causes me to lose my mind and control of all my bodily functions. In other words, I'll have a perfectly normal life.

Ten and a half months.

Ray was looking at her quizzically. "Hey, where'd you go?"

Shelby forced a laugh. "I was just contemplating married life in the sixties."

"Yeah? What do you think of it?"

"I don't know what to think. I mean, we don't know what's going to happen in the future. Everything could change overnight."

He squeezed her hand. "Sure. You're going to drop out of society and go on the road with the Beatniks."

"I might. You shouldn't take me for granted."

"Babe, I'll never take you for granted." He leaned across the table and kissed her. "Let's bust out of here," he whispered in her ear.

She knew what that meant, and felt herself pull around herself until she was nothing but a hard knot. But she couldn't let him know…

She looked at him in what she hoped was a thrilled—or at least pleased—way. "Let's."

Ray went in search of the waitress and the check.

When she was a child they'd had her tested for allergies. Every week they drove into Boston, and the doctor stuck needles under the skin of her back and the soft parts of her arms. Every week she was paralyzed with fear, watching the scenery go by out the car window, knowing she was going to be hurt, no matter how much the doctor smiled and twinkled at her and called the needles "the kitty-cat." There was nothing she could do to stop it, no way to turn the car around, no one who'd take her in their arms and stand between them and her, demand that they stop this cruelty immediately. She wanted to cry, but she knew they'd make fun of her and maybe punish her, and it wouldn't make the slightest difference, the needles would happen anyway. So she watched the scenery and turned her fears and tears to ice, and kept them deep inside where no one would ever know.

Sometimes she felt like that now. But now it wasn't doctors and needles that terrified her, but Life. There was no one to stand between her and Life.

Wasn't that what the husband-wife thing was supposed to be about? The two of them, hand in hand, beating the dragon from the door, standing side by side against the winds of adversity or some damn thing? A shared solitude.

She liked that one, the shared solitude. It was so wonderfully depressing.

So existential. So filled with *angst* and futility. Two solitudes in their own separate plastic bubbles, engaging in parallel play.

It was probably a good thing they were leaving. She'd had more than enough to drink. Her mind was surging and plummeting like ocean waves in a storm. It seemed that Ray had been gone forever. Or was her sense of time distorted? Warped, like wet paper. Like tell-tale white rings left on the coffee table where the drinking glass used to be. White rings making holes in time.

Maybe she was mistaken, wanting someone to stand between her and Life. Maybe what she really needed was someone to stand between her and time. Time with its white rings. Saturn time.

Shelby rubbed her forehead. God, she thought, I'm really snockered. She glanced up and saw Ray coming from the men's room. That explained it. It wasn't that time was distorted. Ray had been in there a long time, "climbing into his diving suit," as he called it.

He had sex on his mind. Oh, please, not that. Not tonight.

Not that she had anything against sex, or even sex before marriage. Lots of people were having sex before marriage these days. At least, they said they were. She'd already had sex before marriage herself. On more than one occasion. She ought to be getting used to it. Maybe someday she'd really enjoy it. Maybe someday she wouldn't be aware of the roughness of his five o'clock shadow, or the sweat-dewed hairs on his arms, or how hard and heavy his body was pressed against hers. How he seemed to forget who she was once he was into the rhythm of his love-making. How she felt like furniture beneath him. Maybe someday she'd know he was making love to her, not just enjoying himself.

Maybe someday she'd be able to make love to him without having her mind go somewhere else.

He was grinning at her across the room, standing by the door. His little-boy, puppy-dog grin.

Shelby got up and started toward him.

I'm too young for this, she thought.

Chapter 13

There was a knock on the apartment door. Shelby put down the story she was evaluating and went to open it. Fran looked as if she'd ironed everything she was wearing, right down to her underwear. Military.

Except for her eyes. Her eyes were uneasy.

"May I talk to you?" Fran asked softly.

"Of course." She forced a smile. "Come on in. I won't bite."

Fran sat on the edge of the couch, stiff and uncomfortable.

"Want something to drink? Coffee? Anything?"

"No, thanks. I just have to tell you…" She shrugged in that endearingly helpless way of hers.

They were finally getting to it. Shelby pushed aside some papers and sat beside her, feeling her own excitement—and apprehension—rise. "Talk."

"I wanted to tell you…I didn't want you to hear…" Fran took a deep breath. In the yellow light from the reading lamp there were purple shadows on her eyes. "I'm moving."

The blood drained from her face. "What?"

"I have to move. I need to find a place before the students come back. Before the end of the summer. I wanted you to know…"

"I don't understand."

Fran glanced at her quickly. "I need to live closer to work…"

She's lying, Shelby thought. "It's a ten minute drive." Her voice slipped to a higher, tighter range. "You have a car."

"Yeah, but in the winter…"

"Plenty of people make it through winter here. This is New England. We make it through winter." She told herself this wasn't happening. It was all a joke. Any minute now, Fran would look at her with those cornflower eyes, and laugh, and run a hand through her wavy bangs, and say, "I'm a jerk." And tell her what was really going on, and they'd sit down together over coffee at the kitchen table and fix it, and…

Fran stood up. "I'm sorry. I have to go."

Close to panic, Shelby caught her by the shoulder. "Fran…"

"I have to go," Fran said again.

"This doesn't make sense."

"I'm sorry."

"Something really strange is…"

Fran turned to her. "I have to move. That's it."

"Please, what's it all about?"

"Nothing."

"I can't accept that," Shelby said, shaking her head vehemently. "We were friends. We understood each other, we had great times together."

"Shelby…"

She was beginning to feel desperate. "Now all of a sudden we're not friends any more, and you're leaving, and I don't know what I did…"

"You didn't do anything. It's my stuff."

Shelby looked at Fran and felt the now-familiar yearning. She wanted to tell her about the hurt she felt. About the confusion. About the fear. Something in her reached out to Fran and wanted to touch her and be held by her, and comforted by her…

Fran stood stiffly at attention and said in a formal voice, "I didn't mean it to affect you. I'm sorry."

"That's it? You're sorry?"

"Yes, I'm sorry."

Shelby swallowed. Anger replaced yearning. "That's not good enough," she said coldly. "I want to know what's going on."

Fran turned away from her. "What's going on is that I have to move. You can accept my reasons or not, I can't help that."

"I think your reasons are bogus."

"Thank you." She stepped toward the door.

Shelby stopped her. "Fran…" She took a deep breath and forced herself to calm down. "We're not doing this right." Fran was staring at the floor. Shelby touched her. "Look at me. Please."

Fran shook her head. Shelby put her hand under Fran's chin and tilted her face upward. Tears were quivering in her eyes. One spilled over and cut a silvery trail down her cheek. Shelby melted. "Fran," she said gently.

Fran's face closed over. "I can't do this," she said, and turned to the door.

"Please, tell me what's wrong." It was almost too late. "You can't just walk out this way."

"I have to."

One last try. One final plea. "There's some huge awful secret in you. Every time we start getting close, or even just talking about ourselves, I run into it."

Fran reached for the door knob.

"When you were sick, you cried yourself inside out, and then tried to tell me it was nothing. And ever since then you've treated me as if I had some contagious disease. You're so damn polite, and distant. I miss you, and I feel cut off from you, and I don't know what to do." She grasped Fran's arm and spun her around. "At least look at me, damn it."

Fran pulled away.

"I trusted you. I've let you know parts of me no one's ever known. I thought you trusted me. I guess I was wrong."

"Please," Fran said, "don't think like that." Her voice had turned soft, but still she wouldn't look at her.

"I cherish your friendship. I've missed you so much it's like a hole in my heart. Just tell me what happened. We can't leave it like this."

"Stop it!" Fran whirled and punched her fist against the door. "For God's sake, leave me alone." She turned back to face Shelby. Her expression was angry. "I don't want your friendship."

"I need you."

"You don't need me."

"You can't..."

"And you don't own me. We're not married, Shelby."

That did it. Now she was insulted, and coldly angry. She turned away so she wouldn't have to look at her. So she wouldn't feel the hurt. "You should be branded, you know that? 'Dangerous. Heart smasher.'"

"I didn't mean to."

Suddenly, coldly, she wanted Fran out of her life. Forever. She wanted her never to have existed. She wanted..."I don't know you," she heard herself say evenly. "You don't know me. Everything I ever told you about myself was a lie. There's nothing between us now, and there never was."

"There was, Shelby."

"I made it up. None of it was real. It was all a game."

"I don't believe that," Fran said.

"Don't believe it, then. Have a nice life. Don't slam the door on your way out."

Fran left, slamming the door.

She made a drink and sat at the kitchen table and waited for the numbness to wear off. It'd hurt then, like a serious burn that you can't feel at first because your nerves are shocked. But as the shock wears off, the pain sets in, and builds, and won't stop, won't ever stop.

Maybe, if she sat here very quietly, hardly breathing, never moving, maybe she wouldn't have to feel again. If she didn't move, maybe time would stand still, encasing her in a pastless, futureless, insensate present.

I'm not going to survive this, she thought calmly. It was all right, though. This particular moment was all right. If she could stretch it out into the next, and the next...

She decided to think about something neutral. Something that wouldn't make her feel, or remind her of...

The phone rang. She glanced at her watch, and time began again.

It was Libby, of course. Only Libby would call at this hour unless it was an emergency. For Libby, everything was an emergency. Running out of ice was an emergency. Being five minutes late for an open house was an emergency. One of these days, Libby was going to wake up and realize she was over fifty, and that would be a *real* emergency.

"Shelby," Libby barked before she'd even had a chance to finish hello, "What did you do with the swatches for the bridesmaids' dresses?"

"I have them." Fran was leaving. Oh, God, Fran was leaving.

"Well, what did you think? The peach is nice, but it might make Connie look too washed out. She'd be stunning in light green, but that wouldn't go well with Jean's mousy hair. I thought the pale blue, but I don't feel comfortable with what that particular shade does to the texture. It seems rather...well, casual."

"I haven't really looked at them yet."

A brief shocked silence. Then, disbelieving, "You haven't looked."

"There hasn't been time."

"Time," Libby said with a dismissive snort. "Well, I suggest you find the

176

time. We have to move the wedding up to Easter."

"Huh?" Shelby said.

"We have to move the wedding up to Easter," her mother said slowly and distinctly.

Shelby was confused. "Libby…"

"Your Aunt Harriet's going to Europe in June."

Inwardly, Shelby groaned. Harriet Camden was Shelby's great-aunt, her father's aunt, the only one she knew from that generation, which she never regretted. Harriet was the self-proclaimed Dowager Queen of the family. She kept newspaper clippings of the actions—legal and otherwise—of the family members. She knew the dates of birth, marriage, and death of every Camden in their branch of the family. She had extensive photo albums of important Camden occasions, though she never took a picture herself but expected to be presented with copies of whatever had been made. These she collected and pasted and labeled in her shaky, spidery old lady handwriting. At family functions, Harriet Camden placed herself in a wing-backed chair and observed. The rest of the family fed her beverages, snacks, and compliments. It made Shelby want to throw up, though she smiled and kissed the powdery cheek and kow-towed like the rest of them. The thought of the wedding *sans* Aunt Harriet Camden was too delicious for words. The thought of it happening two months sooner than they'd planned made her head pound with anxiety. "We can just have it without her," she said hopefully.

"Don't be ridiculous," her mother said.

"There's no law…"

"There's good manners, and common sense, and respect for family," Libby said sharply. "You know that."

This is definitely not a good night to do this, she thought and wanted to say. See, I've just gotten some really, really bad news. The wedding is the last thing I care about. "But we have everything underway," she managed to argue.

"Nonsense. I rescheduled the Country Club. We were lucky. The invitations haven't even been printed yet. We'll just have to work a little harder, that's all."

Panic was clearly setting in. "I'm giving it all the time I have as it is, Libby."

"And just what do you do with all that precious time? Every time I call you, you're off somewhere with that girl down the hall."

"That's not true."

"At least twice, in the last two weeks."

Shelby felt her face begin to redden. She'd used that excuse. When she'd known Libby was going to call, and she'd felt too exhausted or nervous or depressed or… Instead of answering the phone, she'd let it ring, and later said she'd been at Fran's. "Twice," she said.

"And what about Ray?"

"What about him?"

"On at least four occasions…"

"For God's sake, I was only out for a minute. Do the two of you get together and compare notes?"

"It just strikes us as rather strange."

A wave of fury swept through her. "It strikes me as a little strange that my mother and my fiancé see fit to discuss me behind my back."

"When do we get a chance to talk to you to your face?"

"I have a job, Libby. And I have a fiancé who likes a certain amount of my personal and unchaperoned attention. Lots of it, as a matter of fact, no matter what he says about feeling neglected. I have friends in addition to Fran." She stopped herself before she could add, "and I have you calling at all hours of the day and night to talk at me about this…*wedding thing*."

"I'm delighted you're so popular. Next time I need to talk to you, I'll go directly through Miss Jarvis. Now, can you see your way clear to meeting with me tomorrow for dinner? So we can plan *your* wedding?"

She wanted to scream. More than that, she wanted to end this particular discussion. "Fine. Tomorrow night."

"I'll call and let you know the time. Please make some sort of decision about the bridesmaids' dresses before then, and we can discuss it, if it's not *too* much of an inconvenience."

Shelby realized she was gripping the phone tightly in her hand. A drop of perspiration rolled out of her palm and down her wrist.

"I'll do it tonight." She was shaking. Badly. She leaned against the wall and wrapped the telephone cord around her free hand.

"That would be nice," Libby said with acid in her voice. "And try to come up with some ideas about fabric, if you can spare the time from your housemate."

Shelby clenched her teeth. "You don't have to worry about that. She's moving."

"It can't be any too soon. Honestly, you'd think she means more to you than your own wedding."

Something in her boiled over. "It's a wedding, for Christ's sake, not a coronation."

"Excuse *me*, Miss…"

"I'd like to have a life, too, if it's all right with you."

"It's fine with me, just fine," Libby said coldly. "In fact, I'll wash my hands of the whole affair. You make all the plans, and you can have any kind of wedding you damn well want. Elope to Gretna Green, for all I care."

This was getting out of hand. "I'm sorry," Shelby said. "I didn't mean all that."

"You've been behaving very strangely. Ever since that girl moved into your apartment house. I don't know what it's all about, and I don't want to know. But you'd better take yourself in hand, my friend, if you know what's good for you."

Shelby slammed down the receiver and made herself another drink. The phone rang. Libby hadn't exhausted the things she wanted to say.

To hell with it.

She let it ring.

You've really done it this time, she thought as she downed her refill and poured another. Maligning The Wedding, Arguing with The Mother, Slamming down The Phone, not Answering.

Forgetting to choose a Color for The Bridesmaids' Dresses paled by comparison.

She wished there was someone she could talk to. But it was late. And she didn't know how to explain what was happening. Maybe, by the time she saw her friends in the morning, she'd have it sorted out enough to talk. At least to Jean.

Jean. Wait, she could call Jean tonight. Jean stayed up and read late. And Jean could understand things without a lot of explanation. She reached for the phone.

And stopped. If she talked to Jean, it would make everything real. If she talked to Jean, the emotions she was barely keeping in check would come unglued at the first sympathetic sound. She couldn't do that.

Wash the dishes. Such as they were. A plate, a pot, a glass…It took almost five minutes. She dried them and put them away.

Maybe a snack would help. She opened the cupboard door.

Wheat thins. Too crunchy.

Triscuits. They must be stale. They'd gone through July opened.

Lemon Jello.

An icy fist twisted her stomach.

No, she told herself.

She sipped her drink while she changed into pajamas.

Beddy-bye.

Heading for the bathroom, she collided with the corner of the bureau. It sent a sharp pain through her hip and threw her off balance.

Shit!

That'll be a lovely shade of teal blue in the am.

Maybe that would be the right color for the bridesmaids' dresses.

She reached for her drink and took a swallow and then another and thought about another but it was obvious she was already a little stewed. She set the rest on the edge of the bathroom sink. "Sorry, pal," she said to her reflection in the mirror, "scotch and toothpaste don't mix."

Basically still on top of things, though. In control.

Except for the hard, expanding feeling in her chest.

She looked at herself again and didn't like what she saw. Her hair was limp, her eyes dull. Her skin had the papery texture of a hornets' nest. She looked old and sick.

Good night's sleep will take care of that, she told herself briskly.

Pop right into that old bed and close your eyes and it's "All aboard the Slumberland Express."

Who was she kidding? It was going to take her hours to get to sleep. If she ever did. If she ever got to sleep again.

"When I'm worried and I can't sleep, I count my blessings instead of sheep…" The old Rosemary Clooney song drifted through her mind.

Good advice.

She took her toothbrush from its holder and uncapped the toothpaste.

OK, first blessing is the job. Great job. Perfect job. Excellent working environment. Better than I ever dreamed of. Of course, I won't be able to keep it more than a year. Excuse me, move that termination date up a couple of months.

She squeezed a little too much toothpaste onto the bristles. Top heavy, it slipped off and landed in the basin. She scooped it up with the brush.

Second blessing, great husband-to-be. No doubt about that.

Third, a wise and devoted mother.

She grimaced at herself in the mirror. And don't forget your finely-honed sense of irony.

And friendly friends.

Whatever was growing in her chest was swelling.

Friendly friends.

And some ex-friends.

She scrubbed furiously at her teeth.

Look on the bright side. You got your very own sleeping bag out of it.

Shelby gripped the sides of the sink.

She was shaking so hard the aspirin bottle jumped.

I'm not going to make it, she thought wildly. She was going to split apart, and what came out would be hot, and dark, and burn like acid. The future stopped there, black and solid. Beyond it there was nothing.

Have to sleep. Get through this night. If you can get through this one, maybe you can get through the next. She found her sleeping pills and took one, washing it down with scotch and melted ice water from her glass.

One wasn't going to do it. One never did it.

She took another.

OK. She put the cap back on the bottle. Two's enough, what with the couple of drinks I had. I should sleep like a baby.

And wake up to what?

Everything exactly, identically, the same.

Christ!

Her stomach was so twisted she could hardly move. Anxiety bored into her. The tightness in her chest kept growing. All around her was a gray vacuum, sucking her down into nothing.

I can't do this.

She felt trapped, in a place too small to move. She wanted to strike out. There was nothing to strike out at.

When I wake up in the morning, there'll be that moment of disorientation, just lying there in bed, not knowing what's out there, running through the schedule for the day. And then, suddenly, it'll all come rushing in on me...the wedding, the job, my mother, Fran...

I can't live it.

She snatched up the rest of the pills and emptied them into the palm of her hand and put them in her mouth and washed them down.

She closed her eyes, held her breath and waited, waited for her heart to stop pounding, her skin to stop crawling. Waited for the terror to subside.

After few minutes she opened her eyes. Same old canary yellow towels hanging neatly on the rod behind her. Same old silhouette cut-out framed and hanging on the wall, a house warming gift from Libby. Same old laundry hamper, and bath mat, and soap dish and shampoo bottle and...

Same old Shelby.

God DAMN it! She hurled the heavy drinking glass at the mirror. It shattered into a million stars.

All right, she thought with some satisfaction. All right.

She slid down the wall to the floor, circled by broken glass, broken inside.

Everything broken, she thought. Finally and forever broken.

I'm going to die. All I have to do is wait.

A feeling of deep calm swept over her. The tile was cool against her back. It felt good to let go.

Someone knocked at the apartment door.

Sorry, she thought languidly, no Girl Scout cookies this year.

Or bridesmaids' dresses.

Now the visitor was pounding and shouting her name.

How rude, middle of the night. Some people have no consideration. She really should get up and answer it before they woke everyone in the house. She should reach out and grasp the lip of the sink and pull herself up and go deal with that.

Later.

The door slammed open.

Shelby winced.

Probably dented the plaster. Landlord wasn't going to like that.

Footsteps crossing the living room. Then Fran was standing over her, looking at all the mess. "Jesus, Shelby," she said.

"Not me. Must be some other guy."

Fran found the empty pill bottle and shoved it at her roughly. "Is this what you took?"

Shelby shrugged.

"How many?"

She shrugged again.

Fran grabbed her arm and twisted it. "HOW MANY?"

"How should I know?" she mumbled. "I didn't count them, I just took them. Leave me alone."

"Damn," Fran said. She ran from the bathroom, made rummaging through cupboards noises in kitchen, then water running and spoon-against-glass stirring sounds in the sink.

Everything was getting very soft and warm. She tried to remember what she'd been upset about, but the thoughts floated away like truant balloons.

"Drink this," Fran said, and held out a glass.

Shelby gazed at the yellowish, musty-looking liquid. It spun in a whirlpool in the glass. Mustard. She looked at Fran's bare feet. "You should have shoes on," she said. "You'll get cut."

"Drink it."

"It looks nasty. Not at all like lemon Jello."

"Drink it."

Shelby shook her head. She knew what would happen if she drank it. She'd throw up. And if she did that everything would cycle back to the beginning.

"Look, either you drink this right now, or I'm calling an ambulance."

"I want to die," Shelby said.

"Not tonight, you won't. What's it going to be?"

"It took me a long time to get those pills. Expensive, too." She grinned idiotically.

Fran swept aside some mirror shards and knelt beside her. She took Shelby's wrist firmly in her free hand. Her grip was like a vise. "If you don't drink this right now, I'm going to break your arm."

Shelby looked away.

Fran twisted her hand behind her back and yanked. It felt as if someone had stabbed a knife into her shoulder blade. "I mean it, Shelby. I'll cripple you before I let you die."

Her shoulder burning, she reached for the glass and drank. The mustard was bitter and sharp in her mouth. It burned her tongue. Her stomach churned.

"Is that all of it?" Fran asked when she had stopped vomiting.

"I think so." She slumped against the toilet, too weak to get up. Her skin was clammy, her arms and legs trembled. Her stomach felt as if it had been ripped out of her.

Fran rinsed a cloth in cool water and held it to her face. "You did fine."

Shelby grunted.

Fran stroked her back for a moment. "I'm sorry I had to hurt you."

Shelby flapped her hand in a weak, dismissing motion.

"Come on."

Shakily, she let herself be pulled up.

Fran brushed the shards of glass from her pajamas with a towel. "Go change your clothes. I'll take care of this and make coffee. We have a long night ahead of us."

She stumbled to the bedroom. She wanted to lie down. Plodding exhaustion, as if she'd been climbing a mountain. For days, for weeks, forever. Her body felt like lead. She could hardly bear the weight of her head. Her arm and back and stomach muscles were screaming. She knew what came next—she'd have to drink a swimming pool of coffee, and Fran would yell at her and demand an explanation.

And then Fran would leave, as soon as it was safe. Fran wouldn't leave during a crisis. Fran was a good soldier.

There weren't any explanations, not even for herself. Too much to drink, too much tension, too many disappointments. Not good enough. The truth was, she was tired. That was all, tired. Tired down to the marrow in her bones.

She sat on the edge of the bed and buttoned her pajama top. Fran was probably furious with her. She had every right to be. It was a childish thing to do. Stupid and childish. She should have made sure no one could stop her.

"No sitting down," Fran said from the doorway.

Shelby nodded submissively and got up, humiliated to have shown her pain in front of Fran. "I'm sorry," she muttered, and started past her to the kitchen.

Fran blocked her way. "No," she said softly, "I am." She put her arms around her and held her tight. It felt good.

"This isn't your fault," Shelby said.

"Maybe not. Maybe."

Her head was spinning. She felt dizzy, didn't want to talk. She dropped her head onto Fran's shoulder. She wanted to lean against her and sleep. There was only the tiniest string between herself and darkness. If she let it go…

Fran shook her. "Coffee," she said. "Stay with me."

182

Just before dawn Fran declared her out of danger and no longer "funny in the eyes."

Maybe not, but she still felt funny in the head. Everything was stuffed with cotton, thoughts either refused to come or dropped in and sped away before she could catch them. It was nice, in a way, not being able to think. She just wished she didn't have a pounding headache to go with it. Her stomach felt as if it had been struck repeatedly with a sledge hammer. Her insides were dry and shaky. The muscles in her arms and back were cramped, and her legs were on fire from walking and standing and walking and standing.

"Think you can sleep now?" Fran asked.

Shelby nodded.

Fran led her to the bed and helped her lie down and tucked her in. She sat beside her and held her hand. "We're going to have to talk about this, you know," she said softly.

"Not tonight," Shelby said.

"It's almost tomorrow."

Shelby groaned. "I'm having dinner with Libby tonight."

"I don't think so."

"We have to pick the colors for the bridesmaids' dresses." She felt as if her eyes were rolling in her head. "Or the material. Or both."

Fran touched her face. Her hand was cool. "I don't think you'll make that meeting. You're going to feel like road kill." She stroked her forehead, brushing back her matted hair. "Look, I know it's in your nature to make light of this..." Fran said gently. "But you really tried to kill yourself tonight, Shelby. That's no small thing."

"It just happened."

"No. Maybe you didn't plan it, but something in you reached out and took those pills."

"I only wanted to sleep."

"Forever."

"If I can't sleep forever, can I at least sleep tonight?"

Fran smiled. "Want me to stay by you?"

"It'd be nice." It was safe for now, with Fran holding her hand. At least Fran was here right now. If she could hold onto this...

"It'd be very nice," Fran said. Her voice seemed far away. "Go to sleep now."

"Hey."

Something touched her. Terrified, she struck out, flailing. She felt her arm held...

"Wake up, Shelby."

She opened her eyes. The bedside lamp was on. Fran sat on the bed, leaning over her, resting her hands lightly on Shelby's arms. "Bad dream?"

Shelby tried to focus. She couldn't remember it. "I guess so." She felt confused. Something was wrong. Really, really wrong.

"It'll be OK." Fran stroked her face with the back of her hand.

She struggled to remember. "I tried to kill...," she said suddenly, startled into wakefulness.

"Unlike your usually smooth and competent self, you failed."

The awfulness of everything came to her. Her life. What she'd done. What she'd have to do now. She was blind and drowning in mud. She grabbed for Fran's hand.

"It'll be OK," Fran said again. "There's nothing here that can't be fixed, and nothing we can fix tonight."

Shelby clutched her hand. She felt disoriented, as if she had left her body and couldn't get back. She was floating, drifting, all of her cells separating from one another. She could see the stars through her dissolving arm. She was evaporating into the Universe.

"Shelby. Come on, kid."

Fran's voice reached her like a silver cord, gathering her up and pulling her back to earth. She wanted to resist. Earth was hard. Earth was pain. "Help me," she said.

"I'm right here."

She felt Fran touch her face again, firmly, holding her attention.

"Hang on," Fran said.

She was in a town she'd seen before, on a vacation with friends from college. Somewhere between Connecticut and Kentucky, she remembered that much. The town center was a large circle, like a compass, with roads leading in from the four directions. A nice town. A good place to stay...

"Shelby!"

She didn't want Fran to pull her back this time. If she stayed there, none of what was happening now would go on. No Ray or Libby or weddings or bridesmaids or Fran. If she just stepped to the side, into another dimension, she could be someone else with a different life.

All she had to do was let go.

But Fran was holding on too tightly. She couldn't ignore the ache in her wrist where Fran's fingers squeezed.

Reluctantly, she let herself slide back on that ribbon of pain.

"I thought you were going into a coma," Fran said as she opened her eyes.

Shelby shook her head. "It was the oddest thing. I was somewhere else."

"You certainly were."

"But this was strange, real..." She tried to find the words but couldn't.

"Your hand went dead, Shelby."

She flexed her fingers. "Feels OK now. Maybe it was asleep, the way you were gripping."

"Maybe. But I never saw anything like that."

"Well, how many people have you done that to?" She rubbed her wrist.

"I'm sorry. It just scared me."

"I don't think you broke anything."

"Where did you go?"

"I'm not sure," Shelby said.

"Can I get you anything?"

"How about a drink? And a sleeping pill?"

"There's nothing funny about this," Fran said sharply.

"I know. I'm sorry." She let herself feel what she really felt. "It scared me, too. What happened to me, Fran?"

"Like you said, you went somewhere." She stroked Shelby's hair. "Your emotions are all fer-hoodled. It's probably a perfectly normal reaction to anxiety or something. Or maybe those pills took you on a little trip to the Twilight Zone. Anyway, you're here now. And you need rest. So what do you say you try to go back to sleep?"

Suddenly her stomach was churning. Her breath was short. The trapped and lonely feeling was back. "I'll try," she said. She hadn't meant for her voice to come out as small as it did.

"Want me to crawl in with you? Think that'll help?"

"It might."

Fran reached over and turned out the light and slipped into the bed beside her, and put one arm around her. "How come you rate a double bed? My apartment came with twins."

"Libby's idea." It felt good, her back against Fran's chest, her hips cradled in her lap, Fran's arm across her shoulder, her hand holding Fran's. Being with her felt the way it used to, soft and easy and safe. "All up-and-coming young career-until-they-marry girls have double beds. For sex."

Fran was still and silent for a moment. "Shelby?" she said at last.

"What?"

"I don't really think I needed to know that."

Chapter 14

"Of course you have a killer headache," Fran said. "It's probably a hang-over."

"Don't pick on me." Shelby pulled her knees up to her chest and wrapped her robe more tightly around her. She was cold in spite of the hot August air, and the chair was hard, and her head and stomach hurt, and she was embarrassed and generally miserable. "I feel awful."

"I know."

"You don't know," Shelby insisted. "I'll bet you never tried to kill yourself."

Fran slipped two pieces of buttered toast onto a plate and placed it in front of her. "This is true. And if I had, booze and pills wouldn't be my style." She poured Shelby a glass of milk. "I'm more the leaping off tall edifices, or blowing my brains out type. Messier, but less chance for error."

"That's not funny." She nibbled on a bit of toast and waited for it to hit her stomach. She hoped it wouldn't bounce.

"It wasn't intended to be funny. Nothing that happened here in the last twelve hours is funny in any way." Fran brought her coffee to the table and sat. "Are you ready to talk about it?"

Shelby felt as if all the energy had been sucked out of her. "I don't want to talk about it."

"I'm sure you don't." Fran stirred sugar into her coffee. "But you have to. If not with me, with someone else."

"I knew that was coming," Shelby said bitterly. She took a swallow of milk. She thought it might stay down. "Shelby Camden's finally gone off the deep end. Ship her to a shrink."

"I didn't say that."

"You're thinking it."

"No, I'm not. But I'm scared for you."

Shelby shrugged. "I'll be OK." Don't let me do this, something in her begged. She was moving on the surface of things, staying away from her life, staying away from Fran. "Things got to be too much, I pitched a fit."

"Shelby…"

"I'm sorry. You were good to me last night. I guess you saved my life. I'm grateful—I think. I apologize for my behavior."

"Stop it," Fran said roughly. She got up and walked to the window, her back to Shelby's back. "Look, I know I haven't treated you well lately, and I'm not trying to mind your business. I don't have that right…"

"That's not true."

Fran ignored her. "I have to tell you what I think." She took a breath. "There's something really screwy and dangerous going on with you, and I don't know if you don't know what it is, or if you know and can't say. But it's eating you up."

"So that makes two of us, doesn't it?" Shelby toyed with a crust of toast. Her head was pounding, and little knife-pricks ran through it. She wanted to forget. Pretend it hadn't happened. She didn't want to look at it, it was too big and too ugly...

"Last night wasn't amateur night," Fran said, ignoring her remark. She came back and sat down. "You meant it."

"I guess."

"You'd rather die than live your life. It's that simple."

She shrugged again.

"So tell me what's wrong."

"My life is uninhabitable."

Fran shot her a sharp look.

"I don't *know.*"

"You do know," Fran said. "You just don't want to know."

Shelby felt annoyed. For weeks this woman had treated her like furniture, and now she wanted to play Freud. "My current situation," she said, "leaves something to be desired."

"What? What do you need?"

Everything inside felt like a large, gray mass of fog. "I can't think. I have a hangover."

"You can change things." Fran's voice was soft and sympathetic.

"If I knew what I wanted to change things *to,* or *what* things I wanted to change, or *how* to change them, don't you think I would?" Her throat caught. She felt a burning in her eyes and nose, and stared at the table and choked back tears.

Fran touched her hand. Shelby glanced up at her. Fran's face was spotted with red blotches, as if she were coming down with something. "You know what you want, Shelby. And you know what you don't want. It's just a matter of letting it out."

The truth was, when she looked at what she'd done, she was embarrassed and ashamed. Fran had seen too much, had seen her raw, had seen her give up. Fran had been a witness.

Shelby made herself hard and laughed. "You're very good at this."

"It won't work," Fran said. "I won't let you provoke me."

The worst of it was, she wanted to have last night back. Not to die, but to bring back those late-night hours when the pain and desperation were out in the open, and she didn't have to do anything but be taken care of. Taken care of. The words felt like a miracle.

"Sorry," she said.

But Fran was leaving, and she'd never have the chance again.

"Shelby..."

"What?"

"Are you listening?"

"Always."

"Do you understand what I'm talking about?"

"Yes, Mother."

"Stop that." Fran squeezed her hand. "This is deadly serious." She tried to look intent and severe.

Fran leaned back in her chair and watched her. "You're going to do it again," she said at last.

"I haven't decided. I'm a little short on supplies, thanks to you."

"Goddamn it!" Fran slapped the palm of her hand against the table and winced.

"Please," Shelby said, her heart pounding, "I haven't been well."

Fran kneaded her face with her fingertips. "Can't we drop this? Please? You're in big trouble. It scares me. I don't want anything to happen to you."

"What do you care? You won't be around to see." She felt mean, saying that. It was good to be mean. Better than wanting to be taken care of. Better than that no-ground-beneath-her-feet feeling whenever she thought of Fran going away.

"OK," Fran said in a low voice. Her eyes had faded to palest slate. She looked beaten. "You're right about everything." She got up and walked over to the window again and stared out at the garbage cans in the driveway. "It's none of my business what you do."

"That's right."

"Just do me one favor. Try to be honest with yourself."

Now she was really angry. "Don't you dare lecture me about honesty," she said, turning in her seat to look at Fran's back. "You haven't been honest with me since the day we met."

"What?" She glanced around.

"You know what I'm talking about."

Fran leaned her forehead against the window pane.

"At least look at me."

"This is about you," Fran said. "You're the one who's desperate. Leave me out of it."

"I can't leave you out of it. It *is* about you." She got up and went to stand behind her. "Some of it is." Her head was spinning, blood rushing past her ears. She felt reckless, and slightly deranged. "I was handling my life all right," she said in a rush. "It was do-able. Especially after…after you moved in. But then you went and spit in my face…" She realized that sounded unnecessarily harsh, and regretted it. "I'm sorry," she said, and rested one hand lightly on Fran's shoulder.

She heard her catch her breath and felt her stiffen, and suddenly she was back at the camping trip, when she had made the same casual gesture, and Fran had reacted the same way.

The pieces fell together.

Oh.

Reflexively, she felt herself withdraw.

But she had stepped into a place she couldn't back out of. Not unless she could manage not to know what she knew, and she knew she couldn't do that.

It was a dangerous place, and one where everything made sense. She forced herself to stay.

"Fran."

Fran didn't answer.

Shelby waited in silence for a while. Humidity formed drops of water and dripped from the rain spout. The sound was as regular as a clock.

"Say it."

Fran shook her head.

Shelby rested her hand on Fran's shoulder and squeezed. Her muscles were hard as steel beneath Shelby's hand. "It's all right. You can say it."

"Everything'll be ruined."

"It's already on the way to ruined. Say it." She knew she was right, doing it like this. But even the air was so very fragile. What she did now could mean the difference between everything and nothing. She was invading Fran's most private self, and if she heard what she knew she'd hear, she wasn't sure how she'd feel, afterward. Or how Fran would feel. If they'd be able to have a friendship. Maybe it was already too late. But they were in it now, and there was nothing she could do but see it through to the end. Make it all right, she prayed silently. I don't do a whole lot of praying, but this is really important. "Please, Fran?"

Fran took a deep breath, still not looking at her. Sunlight pouring through the window glistened like sparks in her hair. It caught the light tips of her eyelashes. "When I left the Army," she said quietly, "it wasn't just because I wanted to finish school."

Shelby waited, not daring to breathe.

"I didn't have a choice. It was leave or face a Court Martial."

"Why?"

"Because they found out I'm..." She couldn't go on.

Shelby slipped her arm around Fran's shoulders. It felt all right, the way it always had. "Don't be afraid. Say the word."

Fran's body was so stiff Shelby thought it would snap like a frozen tree limb if she moved. "I'm a lesbian," Fran said.

"I know."

Fran turned to her. Her eyes were dark and questioning.

"I just figured it out," Shelby said with a shrug. "I mean, what else could you have such a hard time saying? 'I'm a serial killer?' 'I poison puppies for kicks?'"

"What do you...think?"

"I think I've never felt closer to you than I do right now." She touched Fran's hair. "Why couldn't you tell me?"

Fran laughed harshly. "It's easy to see you've never been there."

"I really want to know. What you've been through. What it's like. Why it's so hard."

"I hope you never find out."

"Does your moving out have anything to do with this?"

Fran looked at the floor and nodded.

She felt like laughing, or cheering. "I can't believe this. You were *moving out* just so I wouldn't find out you're a *lesbian*?"

"Look," Fran said, "there are people upstairs. Would you mind not shouting?"

"You broke my heart so you could keep a secret?"

"I broke your heart to keep mine from breaking."

Shelby looked at her. The silence between them was deep. "What do you mean?"

"This is all screwed up." Fran pushed away from the window and crossed the kitchen. "You're the one who tried to kill herself, not me."

"All *right*." So nothing was going to be solved, after all. There was still something unspoken between them. Her head was spinning and her whole body hurt. She wanted to lie down. She slumped against the window sill. "Fran, please. I've had a rough night. I feel like the bottom of a bird cage. Can't you just tell me what's wrong so I can go back to bed?"

Fran glanced her way, then went to the table and sat, not looking at her. She stared down at her hands. "I tried not to fall in love with you," she said.

Shelby felt her stomach tighten defensively, as if someone had threatened to punch her. "What?"

"You heard me."

She didn't know what to say. There was a low buzzing in her ears, and a fog in her head that obscured the shape of things. "Did you...Did you succeed? In not?"

"No," Fran said.

"But why?"

"Because I knew it would be like this."

"I mean...why did you fall in love with me?"

"God's punishing me."

Shelby felt something like hysterics welling up inside her. "Well, that's very flattering."

"I didn't mean it like that."

There were tears slipping down Fran's face. Slow and silent. "I swear I tried not to let it happen. For months I convinced myself we could be friends, that those other feelings wouldn't happen. But then I got sick, and you were so good to me, so kind...You touched me. It'd been so long since anyone...I couldn't help it, I couldn't fool myself any more. I hated this thing inside me, but it was there. It'd been there from the day I met you, I think. I loved you." Shelby handed her a tissue. Fran mopped her eyes and blew her nose. "I knew I'd lose your friendship."

"You haven't lost my friendship."

Fran looked up at her, her face tight with anxiety and sadness. "For God's sake, Shelby, tell me what's going on inside you."

This was the hardest part, Shelby thought. She wanted to be able to say, "Everything's all right, you silly thing," or something light like that. But she didn't know if everything was all right. She didn't know if *anything* was all right. The one thing she did know was that she had to do this very carefully. A wrong word or gesture...She wished her brain weren't so soupy.

She knew what she was expected to feel. She'd heard all the ugly names and cruel jokes and snickering. And she had to admit she was a little afraid of...well, of someone so *different* from everyone she knew.

But Fran wasn't different, not really. Other than being the most understanding, most comfortable person Shelby had ever met. She'd loved her, not in the way Fran meant, maybe, but like a dear friend, a sister. She still did, in spite of the hurt in her heart these past weeks. It was her head that made her want to run, with its library of nasty whispers.

"I can't believe I'm doing this," Fran said. She started to get up. "You're having a horrible time, and I'm just adding to it. Telling you this stuff, asking you to…"

"No." Shelby leaned over and stared at the linoleum. She felt the chipping paint of the window sill beneath her hands. Speak the truth, she told herself. "I don't know what's going on inside me. A lot of things. Contradictions."

"If you want me to leave…"

"Of course not." She made herself look into Fran's face. She was still Fran, after all. "I don't know what I think or feel," she said. She sorted among her thoughts. "But I know you're important to me and I want it to be OK, and I'll do whatever I have to to make it OK."

One thing she knew for certain. She couldn't be—mustn't be, wasn't—afraid to touch her. It would be horrible if she couldn't touch her. Her body wanted to stay where it was, unmoving, a statue. Because of the whispers. But to pull away from her that way…it was the cruelest thing she could do. This woman wasn't a monster. She was smart, and fun, and warm, and gentle…

She was on the brink of giddiness again. She could feel it. This wasn't the right time for humor. Shelby forced herself to go over to Fran, and rested her hand against her friend's face. To do it felt the same as it had so many times before. When it was a gesture of pleasure and affection. But it couldn't really be the same. Because now there was maybe this thing between them, and gestures of affection might never be simple again. "I wish I could make it OK with you. I hope I can make it OK with me. God, Fran, if I can't make it OK with me…if all the nasty stuff I've been fed all my life is bigger than me, bigger than us…I don't think I can bear that."

"You're too weird to live in this world," Fran said, and leaned against Shelby's hand. "I know, I know, speak for myself." She sighed. "Everything I've ever cared about I've lost because of what I am. I've tried to not be like this. It never works."

"It's OK, Fran."

"I don't want to do anything to hurt you."

"Too late for that," Shelby said. "But at least it can't be any worse than the silent treatment."

Fran covered her face with her hands.

"Hey, I'm sorry." Shelby took her in her arms. "I'm nervous. It makes me say tactless things."

"It certainly does," Fran said.

She wished she'd relax. Her body was still tight and hard. It was like holding a log. "Will you please loosen up? It's going to be OK."

Tentatively, Fran softened a little.

"What are you afraid of?" Shelby asked.

"Your eyes. I'm afraid I'll see that blank, cold look. It happens every time I tell."

Shelby knew that look very well. Libby had perfected it. It meant you were disgusting, lower than low, and to even acknowledge your existence would be to degrade oneself.

It made you feel like something scraped off the bottom of someone's shoe. "No blank, cold looks," she said. "Try me."

Fran glanced up at her. "Oh, God," she said, and turned away.

"What? Did I do blank-cold?"

"You're just so incredible."

Her heart felt as if it wanted to reach out and physically wrap around her. "What I am," she said, "is exhausted, and feeling like nothing that should be allowed to live."

"I haven't freaked you out?"

"The only time you freaked me out, as you so delicately put it, was the day I met you. "

"I freaked you out?"

"You sneaked up and spied on me just when I was chopping wood and being…well, tough."

"Butch," Fran said. "You were being butch."

"I can see it now. I'm going to have to learn a whole new vocabulary. Lying down would be nice."

"Do you want to lie down on the floor, or can you make it to the bedroom?"

"Don't go off duty. I may need help."

She managed to get there on her own. She flopped on the bed, grateful for the soft support of the mattress beneath her, for not having to hold herself up any more.

Fran sat on the edge of the bed, tentatively. "Is it OK?" she asked.

"Is what OK?"

"If I sit here."

"For God's sake, Fran." She looked at her. "You're still you. I'm still me. We just have this…minor complication."

"*Minor complication?*" Fran's eyes widened. "This is no minor complication, Shelby. A whole lot of people don't like what I am, and if I get linked to you, they're going to think the same things about you."

"Do you really think I care about that?"

Fran looked at her for a long time, solemnly. "Yes, Shelby, I think you do care about that. I think that's part of the problem."

Shelby groaned. "If you're going to sit there and psychoanalyze me, I'll throw up on you. I can do it, too. I'm right on the verge, and it's milk."

"Get some sleep," Fran said with a little smile. "I'll call your office and then hang out in the kitchen."

"Oh, shit," Shelby said. "My mother."

"I couldn't have put it better myself. Time to have one of your handy headaches." She pulled up the cotton spread and tucked it around her. "Deal with her later." She started to go to the other room.

"Fran."

"Yep?"

"Please don't move out. Of the house."

"I won't." She turned back and looked at Shelby. "It wouldn't have solved anything, anyway. I was kidding myself."

"Will it be hard for you? Being around me? Feeling…you know…like you

192

couldn't not…" She laughed, embarrassed. "I sound so damned arrogant."

"It'll be hard. Not as hard as never seeing you. But you have to promise not to pity me."

"Why would I pity you?"

"Because of my proclivity for impossible loves."

"You have your impossible loves. I have my impossible situations." She remembered something she'd said last night. "I can't believe what I said to you. About the bed and sex."

"That was a little awkward, but I'll live. I haven't *completely* lost touch with reality. I don't think." Fran smiled down at her. Her face was soft and open, the way it hadn't been for weeks. "Thanks for everything, Shelby."

Shelby dismissed it with a wave of her hand. "Oh, please…"

"I'll call your office now, OK?"

"OK." She wanted to ask her to come back and lie beside her the way she had before, or sit with her. But that was ridiculous. She wasn't a baby.

Shelby turned on her side and invited sleep.

It was Fran who ended up talking to Libby. Three times in a half hour Shelby had reached for the phone, then frozen with anxiety and decided to wait another few minutes.

"Maybe I shouldn't cancel the dinner. Maybe I should just meet her."

Fran shook her head. "You're worn out. To say nothing of barfing up your socks half the night."

"I'll make it a quick dinner and an early night."

"You'd rather do that than change your plans?"

"It'd be less awkward."

"Are you trying to cover up what happened?"

"I guess so," Shelby said with a shrug.

"Well, it won't work. You look like death warmed over. Even your usually unobservant mother would know something's up."

"My mother's observant. All *too* observant."

"Then you definitely shouldn't go. Shelby, do you *really* think you could handle that."

She shook her head. She didn't know what to do.

She felt trapped again, the way she had last night. Even if she got over this hurdle, Libby wasn't going to go away. There'd always be another problem, and another…

Halfway through her third period of procrastination, the phone rang.

Shelby felt herself go cold. She knew it was Libby. Libby had undoubtedly called her at work with some minor detail to remind her of, and been told she was at home. She stared at the phone.

"Aren't you going to answer it?" Fran asked.

"It's my mother."

"Great. We can get it over with." She picked up the receiver.

"I can't do it," Shelby mouthed silently.

Fran nodded. "Hello?" she said into the mouthpiece.

Shelby didn't even want to listen to this. She wanted to leave the room. She wanted to find a nice, safe place where the Libbies couldn't get her. She started to stand up.

Fran put a firm hand on her shoulder and pushed her back down. "Oh, yeah, hi, Mrs. Camden," she said warmly into the phone. "This is Fran Jarvis...uh-huh, that one. How're you today?"

In spite of her anxiety, Shelby had to smile. Fran was doing her San Antonio charm routine. She'd performed it for her one evening when they were sitting around swapping life stories. Fran claimed it had oiled a thousand wheels and gotten her out of a hundred scrapes, and even though those Texans knew it was as phony as a three-dollar bill, they were too polite not to play along.

"Yes, Ma'am, I have given some thought to moving closer to campus.... No, I'm still looking.... I'll certainly do that. The minute I'm moved in I'll have you all over for a drink." She looked at Shelby and rolled her eyes. "'Scuse me? Yes, Shelby's here, except she's asleep right now... I know, she felt terrible this morning. But I think it's just one of those twenty-four hour things.... I really would hate to wake her, she was up all night...you know, throwing up and stuff....Yeah, it just came on her like a bolt of lightning.... No, I really don't think I should disturb her.... Wait, I think I heard something."

She covered the mouthpiece with her hand and looked questioningly at Shelby.

Shelby shook her head.

"Sorry, I guess I was wrong. She's out like a light. I'm not surprised, the way she was throwing up. It was really bad...Well, from the looks of it, she won't be up to calling you back tonight, but I can give her a message. Hang on a minute." She pretended to look for pencil and paper. "OK, sorry to keep you. The message is...."

She mimed writing very slowly.

"'Think...about...the...pink fabric...in...' could you repeat that? 'Aqua.' That's it? And call you when she feels better....Yes, ma'am, it was nice to talk to you, too. You have a good evening."

She hung up the phone and flashed Shelby a Cheshire cat grin. "Your mother likes me today. Must be because she thinks I'm moving."

"I'm sure it helps."

"She's a cold one, isn't she?"

"Cold?"

"I tell her you're feeling lousy, and all she can talk about is bridesmaids' dresses. Eat that." Fran handed her the half of the peanut butter sandwich she'd let sit and go stale, hoping Fran wouldn't notice.

Shelby frowned at it. "I haven't eaten this much since last Thanksgiving."

"You've probably never thrown up that much in your *life*." She was silent for a moment. "Your mother really doesn't like me, does she?"

"Not a whole lot. It's nothing personal. She doesn't like most of the people I like."

"Well, if she knew what you know, she *really* wouldn't like me."

"You better believe it." Shelby took a bite of the sandwich. The bread was dry and brittle on the outside, too soft and kind of spongy on the inside. It reminded her of railroad food.

"People like your mother can be dangerous."

"Don't worry. I can take care of her."

Fran laughed. "Sure, you can. Shelby, you can't even answer the phone when you think she's calling."

What little taste there was went out of the peanut butter. "You're right. I'm a fool and a coward and undeserving of your love." She realized what she'd said and rubbed her face with her hands. "Oh, God, this is going to be one of those *things* where I try not to say things and end up doing it constantly like when you go to a funeral and keep saying stuff like, 'Well, I thought I'd *die* laughing.'"

"I guess it will be, for a while." Fran perched on the back of the couch and smiled down at her. "Don't worry about it."

Shelby let herself take in the warmth of the moment. "You look tired."

"It was a long night for me, too. You really scared me."

"I'm sorry."

"You still do."

Shelby looked away from her. "I know. I'm scared, too. It's all a big mess and I don't know what to do. I mean, everything's just awful." She felt like crying. "I really don't like myself very much, and I don't know why anyone else does."

Fran reached toward her, hesitated.

Shelby took her hand. "I know it's crazy," she went on, "but I thought I could handle it, as long as I had you to make me feel sane. Then things went weird between us, and you said you were leaving, and it was as if…as if everything that was holding me together was gone."

"I couldn't believe I could be that important to you. I really was stupid about that." Fran laughed a little. "Was stupid, am stupid, probably always will be stupid."

Shelby shook her head. "I didn't know it, either. Honestly. Until last night." She hesitated. "I knew I liked you. I didn't know how much I needed you."

"I knew I needed you," Fran said. "But at least I was only going to leave the house, not the world." She looked at her quickly. "Was that insensitive?"

"No." She squeezed Fran's hand. Even that slight exertion made her head pound. Her muscles ached. In spite of drowsing away most of the afternoon, she felt so tired she could fall asleep in the middle of a sentence. But it didn't matter. They were together.

There were a million things she wanted to tell Fran. A lifetime of things—about the first time she saw a robin's egg shell, in the grass by the driveway. About the night she went walking on the beach in Cape May, and the sand was littered with jelly fish, glowing in the moonlight. The time she took a pine cone apart and discovered it wasn't a seed itself, but full of seeds. About the kid at camp who yelled at her for being homesick. And her secret feeling of power and pleasure the day the kid stepped in a yellow jacket's nest. College. The first time she tried pot and got so silly she and her graduate school friends had wandered around The Village until dawn, having mystical experiences and composing Beat poetry.

But mostly she wanted to stay here, the way they were, absorbing the quiet, the clear and gentle air after the weeks of murkiness.

"Hey," Fran said, "where'd you go this time?"

"Nowhere. This is good, isn't it?"

Fran smiled. "Very good. I really missed you."

"Know what we are?" Shelby picked up her glass of water from the coffee table and took a sip.

"I'm afraid to ask. What?"

"Idiots."

"Well, this country needs a few good idiots."

"We can't tiptoe around what's going on. Neither of us. We should have just talked about it, instead of making ourselves miserable."

"Twenty-twenty hindsight," Fran said. "It isn't that easy."

Shelby squeezed her hand. "I know. There's something I have to ask you," she went on. She wondered how to phrase it. "Is it really hard being around me...I mean...you know...feeling how you do and not wanting to?"

"Do you mean is there a huge ache in my heart from unrequited love? There's an ache, but it's not a huge one."

"It's not unrequited love," Shelby said. "Just dissimilar."

Fran frowned at her. "Thank you, Professor."

"Anyway, I hope you'll tell me if I do anything that bothers you. Like talk about Ray too much or something."

"You hardly talk about Ray at all," Fran said. "A fact which I find interesting, by the way. Most of the girls I've known can't talk about anything *but* their boyfriends, even if they only met them last night."

"I know what you mean."

"Why don't you?"

Shelby shrugged. "I always thought it was boring. I try very hard not to be boring."

"I don't think there's much danger of that."

She was beginning to feel even more exhausted. Her mind was still functional in a slow and plodding way, but her body was weak to the point of collapse, as if there were wet sandbags piled on top of her.

Fran noticed it. "You should get back to bed," she said.

"I can't believe how sleepy I am. Maybe that stuff's still in me."

"Trust me, it isn't. I was there."

"But it's so good to be talking."

"There'll be plenty of time for talking." She hopped down from the back of the couch. "I'll whip you up something less horrible than peanut butter to eat. You..." She leaned over and ruffled Shelby's hair., "...scamper off and get flat."

She pulled herself up from the couch. "You're a hard woman, Fran Jarvis," she grumbled.

"Yeah, yeah." She put an arm around Shelby's shoulders and propelled her toward the bedroom. "Know what I think?"

"Seldom." She let herself take in the feel of Fran's arm, the clean sun-and-air smell of her, the sound of her voice.

"I think it's time to go camping," Fran said.

Chapter 15

The day she went back to work was easier than she'd expected. She looked terrible, but not much worse than she usually did following a sleepless, headache-filled night. She wasn't exactly productive at work, but was able to fake it enough so her officemate didn't grow suspicious. Not that Charlotte May was especially prone to suspicion. Charlotte did what she had to do, and assumed everyone else did, too. If she saw someone loafing, she ignored it, believing their sins would catch up with them sooner or later. Charlotte's motto was, "Leave 'em to the angels."

Even Libby wasn't too difficult, once Shelby'd apologized profusely and explained that she had behaved strangely because of the bug she was coming down with. "It attacks the central nervous system," she said, "and makes you peculiar."

Libby wasn't the least bit interested in bugs, peculiar or otherwise. She was interested in apologies, and she was interested in the wedding.

Following Fran's suggestion, Shelby had told her she thought the pink fabric in aqua was a stroke of brilliance. "Since you don't really give a damn about the bridesmaids' dresses," Fran had said, "why not butter her up a little? You never know when brownie points might come in handy."

It had worked. It left Libby pleased with herself, which made her pleased with Shelby.

The next challenge was the invitations. Shelby suggested they split the work. She'd look at paper, calligraphy, and type, while Libby drew up the guest list. On her own, Libby offered to spend one day of the weekend with Ray planning "groom goodies." Unfortunately, Ray had only one day off this weekend. It would mean he couldn't spend it with Shelby. Shelby sighed and said she'd try to survive, and as long as Libby was declaring this "ancillary personnel" weekend, why not let the mother of the bride spend Sunday with the bridesmaids herself, planning shoes and showers and whatever it was bridesmaids planned?

She had enough to do, she said, to keep her miserably busy. Work had piled up while she was out nursing her whatever-it-was, and if she caught up now she'd have more time to think about the wedding in the days to come. She was going to hole up in her office or at home, take the phone off the hook, and force herself to get through it no matter how much fun she was missing.

Fran said Shelby was turning into a skillful liar and manipulator, and could have had a great career as a con artist if she hadn't started so late in life.

Shelby doubted it. She was a nervous wreck every step of the way.

She didn't care, though. She was getting away with it. It made her feel mildly euphoric. As a matter of fact, she'd been mildly euphoric ever since that night. Looking death in the face, no doubt. Gives you a real rush. But it wasn't really that. It was because she'd finally done something. It wasn't a particularly brilliant something, and she hadn't done it very well, but at least it was action.

And Fran was back.

"Damn." Fran pulled her flaming marshmallow from the fire and blew it out.

"I like them burnt," Shelby said. "They taste interesting."

"Take it, then." Fran handed her the stick and took Shelby's and threaded another marshmallow.

Shelby pulled the charred, gooey shell away from the sticky insides and chewed on it. She stuck the rest back into the fire.

"What's it like?"

"What's what like?"

"Having sex with a woman."

Fran's face was already golden pink from the firelight. It deepened three shades and she dropped her marshmallow. "For God's sake, Shelby."

Shelby tried not to smile. She didn't want Fran to think she was laughing at her. The thing was, recently just the sight of Fran's face made her want to smile. "We agreed to talk about things if we had questions about them, didn't we?"

"But this is personal."

"OK." She shrugged indifference.

"All right," Fran said after a moment. "But first you tell me, what's it like having sex with a man?"

"It's like having sex," Shelby said. "What's it like with a woman?"

"Like making love."

Shelby smiled. "Are you being devious and provocative?"

"I hope not."

"Then tell me."

Fran gave a resigned sigh. "OK." Her face glowed cardinal red with self-consciousness. "When you make love with a woman you…feel stuff, and then you feel more stuff, and then you feel a whole lot of stuff all at once, and then you feel warm and close. Is that what it's like with a man?"

"I guess."

"You don't know? You mean you've never done it?"

"I've done it," Shelby said. "A couple of times. I just don't remember very well what it was like. I'd had a few drinks."

"It's *supposed* to be the peak experience of a lifetime. The '1812 Overture' with cannons, bells and fireworks."

She knew that. She'd talked about it enough with her friends, comparing experiences. Trouble was, what she felt was a long way from the cannons and bells they described. But she'd pretended to agree. She wondered if the rest of them were pretending, too. "I think," she said, "it's a little overrated."

"The more I know you," Fran said, "the more you scare me."

"What about with women? Are there fireworks?"

"Only if you get caught."

"Is this still hard for you to talk about?"

"Of course it is."

Shelby watched the fire consume Fran's marshmallow. "How come?"

"How *come*?" Fran said wildly. "Why do you think how come?"

"Hey, I'm sorry."

Fran shook her head. "No, I am. I really want to be honest with you. But we just don't…talk about it."

"Even with your lovers?"

"I haven't had that many lovers, and, no, we didn't talk about it." She was silent for a moment. "When I told you, that was the first time I've ever said the word out loud to someone who mattered."

Shelby was stunned. "You're kidding."

"No, I'm not."

"You think being a lesbian is that awful?"

"Me and everyone else."

"I don't."

"Yeah. But you're probably not in your right mind."

Shelby felt tremendously sad. She took a marshmallow and held it over the fire, away from the flames, so it would toast without burning. "Do you wish you were different?"

Fran tapped her stick rhythmically against one of the rocks with which she'd ringed the fire. "I guess most of us feel that way, sometimes. Much of the time. Most of the time. It's hard, living in a world that thinks you're garbage. Sometimes you start believing it yourself." She glanced over, then away. "But, to be perfectly honest with you, most of the time I enjoy loving women. Not the sex, that's OK but it's not the most important thing. It's loving them in my heart. Women are just…well, just neat." She laughed. "You probably don't have the vaguest idea what I'm talking about."

"I do," Shelby said. "Really." She rotated the marshmallow to tan the other side. "I enjoy women more than men, actually. A few of my friends, from college and graduate school. And Jean, and Lisa and even Connie. And Penny, I guess. And you. It's easier to be around them, especially if I'm feeling a little low. Women understand things. And they're softer than men."

Fran tossed her stick into the fire and watched it burn.

The marshmallow looked about right. She passed it to Fran. "Have room for one more?"

"Me?" She took the stick. "Thank you."

"My mother doesn't like women," Shelby said.

"Then she ought to be crazy about me."

Shelby looked at her.

"I'm not a real woman," Fran explained. "Not by most people's standards."

"That's nuts, Fran. If a woman who loves women isn't a woman, who is? A woman who doesn't love women? Is that the definition of a woman?"

Fran shrugged and bit into the marshmallow. She chewed silently for a moment.

In the fire light, Shelby could see Fran was crying. Not hard crying, just a few small trickling tears. She moved over and sat next to her.

"I'm sorry," Fran said after a while. "This is no way to spend a camping trip."

"It's a perfectly fine way." She reached into the pocket of her shorts and pulled out a clean, rumpled Kleenex.

"Jesus," Fran said as she wiped her eyes. "I haven't cried this often in six years."

"I know," Shelby said, gently teasing. "You're so extraordinarily tough."

"I didn't mean to go on about this stuff. I really don't think about it all the time. It's your fault, for taking the lids off things I thought were sealed."

"How rude of me." She slipped an arm around Fran's shoulders.

Fran made a move as if to lean her head against Shelby's arm. She stopped herself. "A week ago I thought I had it figured out. What I should do about you, how I should live. Now it's all upside down."

"Sorry," Shelby said.

"Until you made me say it, I never realized how much I wanted to tell someone. I was so afraid you'd pull away."

"So was I. I must say I'm deeply impressed by my behavior."

Fran swatted her on the knee.

They sat quietly, watching the fire.

"Shelby," Fran said at last, "what happened to you the other night?"

She felt herself pull inward. "Kind of lost my grip, I guess."

"But why? I mean, what triggered it? When I left, you were angry and cold as ice. But not suicidal. Or maybe you were, I don't know. And I know you were drinking…" She glanced over. "Do you mind me talking about this?"

Shelby shook her head, even though her stomach was hard as a rock. She wanted to talk about it, she really did. But she didn't know what to say, or how to start, or where it would end up. It was like driving a car blindfolded. But worse than that, because it was about *knowing* things, and she wasn't sure knowing things was something she wanted to do.

"After you left," she said, "I sat around kind of numb for a while. Then Libby called to tell me we had to have the wedding at Easter instead of in June, and I felt…well, empty and trapped. Trapped in emptiness."

Fran took a breath, about to say something, then changed her mind.

"It's OK," Shelby said. "I know what you're thinking, it's a strange way to think about marriage and makes you want to scream." She pondered for a moment. "But it's not about being married. It's Libby. The wedding means Libby, and Libby means misery. I can't sort it out."

"If you could get married without the wedding, would you?"

"Are you kidding? No bridesmaids' dresses, no mother, no relatives, no theatrics, no maid of honor I'm not even sure I like a whole lot at the moment but I can't find a good reason not to have her and everyone expects me…"

"Everyone expects you," Fran said flatly.

"Everyone but you. Do you?"

"Hardly." She didn't say anything for a minute. "And that's it?"

"It?"

"The only problem with the wedding?"

"That and nerves."

It was getting dark, but she could tell Fran was looking at her. Waiting for something more.

"Sounds like a flimsy reason to kill myself, doesn't it?"

"I've heard better."

"I've thought about it, over and over. It's all I can come up with." She hugged herself. "Honestly."

"That scares me."

Shelby fell silent. It scared her, too. Because, if it was true, what kept her hanging onto life was a very fragile thread. When she forced herself to look at that night…which she couldn't do unless she forced herself…she knew there was something terribly wrong. But whatever had pushed her over that final edge was still inside her, still unknown, and still very, very dangerous.

She hated feeling this way. It was like living between two layers of herself. Nothing could come in from the outside, and nothing could reach out from the center. Except for Fran. Fran got in sometimes, unexpectedly, unpredictably. There'd be a sudden flash of empathy between them, as if they vibrated to the same single plucked string on a guitar. Sometimes she'd glance up, and see Fran looking at her, and know Fran was really, really seeing her. Seeing her all the way to the center. She'd see Fran at the same time, all the way to *her* center. And for just the smallest instant she'd know what it was like not to be lonely.

Then the moment would pass, like the shutter of a camera closing, and she'd be left with a longing so deep it was nearly unbearable, and a memory that faded like morning fog under a hot sun.

She couldn't force those moments to happen. She suspected Fran couldn't, either. They were accidents. Gifts. Blessings.

"I don't want to want to die," she said.

"I'm glad to hear that."

"But sometimes living seems…I don't know…complicated. Too hard."

"It's a challenge," Fran agreed. "Life doesn't come with an owner's manual."

"If it did, it'd be written in Japanese or Swahili or Sanskrit."

"Unless your only language was Japanese or Swahili or Sanskrit, in which case it'd be written in English."

"I've always been glad I was born in an English-speaking culture," Shelby said. "I don't think I could ever learn it."

"You think you're proficient in English? Come with me to Texas. They won't understand a word you say, and vice versa."

But that wouldn't happen, ever, because she'd never go to Texas with Fran. Because she was getting married, and married women didn't take trips to Texas with lesbians.

"What language do they speak in California?" she asked.

"All of them. Simultaneously."

"You know, I don't think I've ever heard a California accent. Is there one?"

"As you so graciously put it the day we met, no one's from California. Sometimes they come *back* from California, but they never start out there. Except for movie stars' children and me. But that's all we have in common."

"I really doubt that."

"Well, we did have a swimming pool…"

"That's not what I meant."

Fran laughed. "If that's true, that movie stars' children are...different...it's one of the best-kept secrets in the universe." She glanced over at Shelby in the near-darkness. "You don't want to talk about you any more, do you?"

Shelby brushed her hair back with both hands. "I really can't think of anything to say." She sighed. "Maybe I need professional help."

"Maybe you do."

"I can just imagine what Libby would say to that. Camdens don't air their dirty linen in front of strangers."

"Don't tell her."

"She'd find out. She has spies. Some of them are my friends."

"So what if she finds out? It's your life."

"Is it?"

Fran was silent for a minute. "Well," she said, "that was a pregnant statement."

"I guess it was." She forced a laugh. "I will be, too, one day. Pregnant."

"Are you looking forward to having kids?" Fran asked.

"I haven't thought about it much."

"Do you like them?"

"I don't know. I haven't known many, except myself, and I didn't like that one much. Do you?"

"Yeah, I do."

"I'll bet you'd make a good mother."

Fran picked up a stone and rubbed it between her thumb and index finger. "Not much chance of that."

"I'm no expert on being a lesbian," Shelby said, and noticed that Fran winced slightly at the word, "but I never heard it made you infertile."

"Not infertile, but unfeasible." Fran transferred the stone to her other hand. "If I had a kid, my family would sweep down on it like locusts on a wheat field. They'd go to court, if they had to, to get it away from me. And they'd win, and I'd just be eccentric Aunt Francis who sends cards and gifts but never visits. The irony is, I'd probably be a good mother."

"I know you would," Shelby said.

"Better than mine, anyway." Fran snorted. "Hell, Medea was better than mine."

"I don't know how they could shut you out like this."

Fran tossed the stone away, into the shadows. She looked over at Shelby. "What do you think Libby would do in the same situation?"

"She wouldn't shut me out." She thought about it. "She'd lock me up. And probably make them give me electroshock treatments."

Fran shuddered. "That actually happened to a woman I knew in college. I'd rather be shut out, thank you. Are you serious?"

"I suspect maybe I am." She contemplated the fire. "It seems so hard, Fran. Being you. Being different. Isn't there anything that makes up for all the unhappiness?"

"Yeah," Fran said. "Women." She stood up and stretched. "I've had enough of my *angst* for one night. And you seem reluctant to talk about yours."

Shelby felt caught and a little embarrassed. "I guess I am."

"Then let's get into our pajamas and I'll teach you to play gin rummy."

She lay silently and listened for the night sounds. The dull flutter of leaves where a bird stirred. Water dripping. The quick scratching of a small animal scurrying across the forest floor. A night hawk called once and fell silent. She tried to hear the trees breathing, tried to hear a breeze. But it was still. A heavy, oppressive stillness that made her want to shout, to break it, but sapped her of the energy.

In movies, the night was portrayed as uneasy, filled with animal shrieks and stealthy creeping sounds and buzzing insects. They had it all wrong. It was the silence that was uneasy. The silence was like a held breath.

Her sleeping bag felt vaguely damp. Humidity. Rain tomorrow, she thought. She pushed back the top layer, leaving only her feet covered. The wilted cotton of her pajamas had an oily feel. Not terrible, but unpleasant.

The dusty odor of tent canvas hung heavily in the air.

Beside her, Fran's breathing was shallow. If she slept, it wasn't deeply. Shelby had the feeling she wasn't sleeping, and looked over at her. Fran lay on her back, arms stiffly at her sides, eyes closed against the faint light from the moon. The shadows of a frown cut furrows in her forehead. She looked frightened, or troubled; it was hard to tell in the ashy light.

Shelby reached over and took her hand. Fran wrapped her fingers around Shelby's thumb, lightly. Shelby looked up at the tent roof and thought, I'm holding her hand. I'm holding Fran's hand and it was all my idea and she didn't pull away. I'm holding Fran's hand, and she's a lesbian. I'm holding a lesbian's hand.

I'm holding hands with a lesbian.

She waited, probing for what she might feel. Disgust, fear, withdrawal. But her body felt warm, and her heart felt safe, and her busy-body mind, with all its nettling and nagging, had gone somewhere it couldn't bother her.

"Tell me one thing," Fran said into the darkness. "How much of what you do is because it's expected?"

"Most of it."

Fran was silent for a long time. "What's wrong with this picture?" she said at last.

"I'm tired of me. Good night." Shelby gave Fran's hand a squeeze, and closed her eyes.

She came fully awake out of a dream. She didn't remember any details. Familiar feelings of comfort and apprehension were still there. A clear thought followed them.

She rolled onto her side and shook Fran by the shoulder.

"What?" Fran said.

The tent was filled with a gray light, the steely glow of pre-dawn.

"I have to tell you something."

Fran wriggled to a sitting position. She rubbed her eyes. "Go ahead."

Shelby took a deep breath. "I don't think I want to get married."

Fran stared at her in amazement. "You woke me up to tell me that?"

"Yeah."

She flopped back onto the sleeping bag and groaned. "Shelby, I've known that as long as I've known you. What time is it?"

Shelby ignored her. "But that's it. That's what's wrong with this picture. I don't think I want to get married."

Fran pushed herself up again. "You sound awfully cheerful about it."

"I finally understand."

"I think we're awake for good," Fran muttered. She pulled on a pair of shorts over the boxer shorts she slept in. "I better make coffee."

Shelby's euphoria lasted another two seconds. "Fran!" she shouted. "What do I do now?"

"Don't panic. Stay loose. Have coffee."

She changed into her shorts and t-shirt, crammed her feet into the ratty sneakers, and spread both their sleeping bags out to air.

She stumbled her way out of the tent.

"Just because I don't want to do it doesn't mean I have to not do it, does it?"

"No, it doesn't," Fran said, "but you might want to start thinking along those lines."

The enormity of it all stifled her. "Call it off, explain, deal with my family, my friends..." Shelby kneaded her face. "You should have let me die."

"Sorry," Fran said. "That's not an option." She came over to Shelby and took her by the shoulder and led her to the sitting log. "Look, you don't have to do everything right now. In fact, you don't have to do *anything* right now. Sit with it, and if you want to talk, I'm here."

"I can't believe what a mess this is."

Fran looked down at her. "It's a mess. But it's not World War III. Relax, Shelby. We're out here in the middle of the woods, nobody knows where you are, there's no telephone, so catch your breath. You don't have to go off half-cocked."

"You're right," Shelby said with a firm and insincere nod. "Absolutely." There was plenty of time to figure out what to do. Plenty of time to do it. The wedding wasn't until Easter, for crying out loud. They hadn't even sent the invitations, or fitted the bridesmaids' dresses, or...

Maybe by Easter she'd be used to the idea.

Get used to it? Get *used* to it? There was no way she was going to get used to marriage.

And no way she could get out of it.

"Shelby," Fran said sharply. She stood in front of her with a tin plate of eggs and bacon and tomatoes. "Eat." She handed it to her, and put the mug of coffee on the ground beside her, and sat down on the log with her own breakfast. "Once you come out of your coma, you're not going to run away, are you?"

"Maybe I could," she said hopefully.

"You'd hate yourself for the rest of your life." Fran salted and peppered her eggs. "Believe me. I know you. Eat."

She forced herself to swallow a forkful of scrambled eggs. Fran made the best scrambled eggs in the world. These tasted like talcum powder.

"Bacon next," Fran said.

That was a little better.

"Coffee."

She'd have to be dead not to taste that. "OK," she said, "I think I'm capable of feeding myself now."

"How about rational thought? Are you capable of that?"

"Not yet."

Fran smiled. "Look, Shelby…"

It made her calmer to hear Fran say her name.

"There's nothing going on here that you have to go through alone. I'm with you. Whatever it takes."

Nobody'd ever said anything like that to her before. It made a salty lump in the back of her throat.

"That's a promise," Fran said.

Shelby struggled not to say something flippant, like "then be my maid of honor." The way she felt wasn't flippant. It was terrifyingly serious.

She was accustomed to going it alone. She was the doer, the care-taker, the one who waded in and straightened out the mess. Or tried to. There'd been more than a few failures along the way. Failures that had left her helpless and angry, failures that had shown her she could never do it right.

She shook herself.

"What?" Fran asked.

"Sorry. I was thinking. About my failures."

"Failures." Fran drew a circle in the dust. "Like what?"

"Well, like that friend in college that went strange. I never could do anything about that. I tried, but I couldn't."

Fran placed her plate on the ground and folded her hands and leaned her elbows on her knees. "Did it ever occur to you," she asked, "that she might have been in love with you?"

"*What?*" But it had occurred to her, not in a flash of understanding, but in a niggling, nagging kind of way. Like mice in the attic. Mice she couldn't get rid of and tried to ignore, except sometimes their little mouse claws ticked across her dreams. "Everything doesn't have to be about love," she said irritably. "People do things, lots of things, all the time, for years at a time, that have absolutely nothing to do with love."

"This is true."

"Even marriage doesn't have to be about love."

Fran simply raised one eyebrow.

It made her want to throw something at her. "God," she said, "is that all you think about, love?"

"I'm sorry I upset you."

"You didn't *upset* me, it annoys me. You *perseverate* on that subject, and it's really, really boring."

"I'm sorry," Fran said again.

The conversation made her skin feel sticky, as if something slimy and green and unpleasant had attached itself to her. Something that lived in ponds. Something that had nothing to do with her but was going along creating new and unattractive life forms just under her skin.

She brushed at her forearms as if she could brush it off.

"Do you have bugs on you?"

"I thought I did," she covered. "Ants or spiders, I don't know."

"Find any?"

"Nope."

"Must have been the conversation, then." Fran grinned and held her hands up protectively. "Don't hit me."

"You drive me crazy," Shelby said.

"That's not a drive, it's a short putt."

What was she doing? She didn't want to fight with Fran. Fran hadn't done anything. "I apologize for being so touchy."

"You have every right, I'm the one who's perseverating," Fran said. "*Mea culpa.*" She crossed herself.

Shelby got up and poured another mug of coffee. "Are you Catholic?" She took Fran's mug and filled it.

"Good God, no! Do you know what the Church says about people like me?"

"People like you." Shelby straddled the log. "Meaning lesbians."

Fran grimaced. "You're certainly fond of that word."

"I keep testing myself. To see if I can say it. To see if it scares me." She glanced over at Fran. "I don't mean *you* scare me. You don't. And it doesn't. But the word…"

"Don't explain to me," Fran said. "You know how I am about it."

"You do get a little peculiar on the subject."

"You mean 'queer' on the subject."

Shelby shrugged. "Peculiar, queer. It doesn't matter. But you sure are cute when you're embarrassed."

Fran covered her head with her arms.

"I shouldn't have said that." Shelby touched her shoulder.

"Can we just start the day over?" Fran mumbled.

"I doubt it."

"I'm still half asleep. How can I follow your twists and turns when I'm half asleep?" Fran looked at her. "We were talking about *you.*"

"An unfortunate choice of topics."

"And the marriage."

"Even more unfortunate."

"Shelby…"

She ran her hand through the front of her hair. "I know, I'm impossible." This was going to be harder than she'd realized. She knew she wanted to be honest with Fran, with herself, that much was obvious. What she didn't know was if she'd be able to. Or if her wonderful jet-age plastic protective shield had become welded to her.

"I just don't know how I feel," she said. "I'm all mixed up about this."

"Relax," Fran said. "Rome wasn't built in a day."

Shelby had declared rest hour. Fran could sleep, or read, or write postcards home or do woodland crafts, but there was to be no talking. The army had been fine, she was sure, and Fran had learned many useful things no doubt, but Shelby wanted her to see a little of what a real summer camp was like when you weren't getting ready for war. The good parts. The quiet, the aroma of pine and dark earth. The restfulness and sense that there was all the time in the world and nothing really terrible could happen. She'd felt those things at camp, even through the misery and homesickness and loneliness. They had nothing to do with the people who were there. The quiet and the trees and the sky and clouds and sparkling lake were there. Rest hour had been one of the magic times at camp, when everything was silent except the breeze, and she could lie on her cot and smell the rough pine boards the cabin was built of, and daydream that some day she and a friend would have a magic place like this.

She glanced over at Fran. She'd been reading and had gone to sleep, her book open on her chest, rising and falling with her breath. Shelby looked at her, just looked at her, and everything went warm inside her.

If she went ahead with the wedding... They wouldn't be like this again. Most of the things she did, she'd do with Ray. Most of her friendships would be with couples.

Of course, if Fran happened to find her knight in shining armor—in her case it would be a princess, of course—then she'd be part of a couple.

Though that would hardly qualify her for membership in the country club.

Fran opened her eyes, leaned over to her knapsack and started rummaging through it. She found pencil and paper. "I don't know what you're thinking about," she wrote, "but it's keeping me awake."

Shelby smiled and mouthed "Sorry." She slipped into her sneakers and left the tent.

She sat on the log by the cold ashes of their campfire. The day was sticky, the humidity still building, the edges of things watery and blurred. The kind of day when you can barely stand the feel of your own skin. Tonight would be muggy, too, but chilly. Her sleeping bag would feel as if it had been washed and not quite dried. Drops of dew would form on the tips of pine needles and drip, rhythmically, all night.

Even the children playing on the beach by the lake were subdued as the heat pressed down and made them tired and whiney. Many of the mothers were in various stages of pregnancy.

Don't laugh, she reminded herself. Someday that could be you trying to wallow your way out of a beach chair with a magazine in one hand and a screaming child in the other.

She couldn't imagine it.

A woman was jogging on the road by the lake. In the heat. Out of her mind.

She thought she must be seeing things, but she wasn't. It was Penny, coming toward their tent. She stopped, wide-eyed, when she spotted Shelby.

"Hi," Shelby said.

Penny trotted up to her. "I don't believe this. I thought you were back at the office, slaving over a hot manuscript."

"I was," Shelby said, feeling only a little guilty. "But I decided I could slave just as well outdoors. What about yourself?"

"Getting some exercise." Penny ran a few steps in place. "I wanted real air for a change. You know, full of moldspores and pollen."

Shelby laughed. "Wait a couple of weeks. The ragweed will be at the height of loveliness."

"I still can't believe it. Running into you all the way out here. Is this neat, or what?"

She wasn't quite sure she thought it was neat, but said it was. "Want a cup of coffee or anything?"

"No, thanks. I…" Penny glanced around, spotted the two coffee mugs drying on the fireplace. "Yeah, heck, why not?"

"It's terrible coffee," Shelby said as she poured her some. "But it's hot and wards off sleep. Just the thing for slaving."

"I see." Penny took the mug, tasted it, grimaced. "God! Is Jean with you or something?"

"She's doing the bridesmaid thing with Libby. That's Fran's cooking magic."

A little smile tickled the corners of Penny's mouth. It made Shelby uncomfortable.

"So where is she?"

"In the tent. Having a nap."

"Oops!" Penny covered her mouth with her hand. Irrelevantly, Shelby noticed she was wearing nail polish. "Better not wake her," Penny whispered.

"It's all right." Shelby raised her voice. "Jarvis, front and center."

Fran poked her head out through the tent flap, "Hi, Penny."

"Hello," Penny said. "I was enjoying some of your fabulous coffee."

"Don't let me interrupt." Fran straddled the sitting log. She was wearing shorts, a tee-shirt, and no shoes or bra. Not that she needed a bra. Fran was, as she herself said, as flat as a pond.

She saw Penny notice, and quickly look away.

"So you guys are playing hooky."

"Not exactly," Shelby said. "I brought my work with me."

Behind Penny's back, Fran grinned.

"It's too nice out to work," Penny said.

"That's why I'm not working at the moment."

There was a brief, not entirely comfortable moment of silence.

"So," Penny asked, "what's happening?"

Fran smiled. "Not much."

"That's how it is in the woods," Shelby said. "Not much happens."

"Hardly anything at all," Fran said. "At least not at breakneck speed. Time doesn't fly out here, it oozes."

Penny sipped her coffee. Fran got up and poured herself a mug, took a swallow, shuddered the way she always did, and sat down.

"Have you gotten to my stuff yet?" Penny asked Shelby. Her voice had an edge.

Shelby nodded. She wished she hadn't read Penny's submissions, or had thought to lie. It was going to be another of those conversations.

"What did you think?"

"I have to go over them again…"

"Just off the top of your head."

"If you don't mind," Shelby said, "I'd rather talk about it back at the office. We need to set some time aside to go over them in detail, so we're both thinking in the same direction."

"I take it that means you didn't like my choices."

"It doesn't mean that. It means we need to talk about it at work."

Penny's lower lip jutted out just a bit. "I thought this was a working trip."

"It is."

"So I'm work, aren't I?"

You certainly are, Shelby thought, and smiled a little at her own joke. She widened her smile to a semblance of affection. "Not exactly, Penny."

"Ah, work," Fran said cheerily. "Can't live with it, can't live without it. Let's play gin."

"She wants to play gin," Shelby explained, "because I've never played before last night, and she thinks she can beat me for the twenty-fifth consecutive time."

"If we had a fourth," Penny said, "we could play bridge."

"Me, playing bridge, is a terrible sight," Fran said. "I think you might be too young for it."

Penny ignored her. "If there's a problem about those stories," she said to Shelby, "we could talk about it now."

"Not now," Shelby said firmly. "I don't have them with me, and I'd have to refer…"

"I thought you brought your work."

"I *did*. I just didn't happen to bring *your* stories."

Penny tossed her head. "Well, if it's not really important enough…"

"It's important." She was beginning to feel very tired.

"Think I'll hit the latrine," Fran said. She stood up and dusted off her shorts. "Anyone care to join me?"

Shelby noticed Penny watching her. "What?" she asked.

"Go ahead. I'll wait."

"I don't have to…"

"Hit the latrine," Penny said, and smiled.

Shelby shook her head.

"Suit yourself," Fran said. "You don't know what you're missing." She strolled off down the road.

"Look," Shelby said. "I don't know what I did to offend you, but I apologize. Now can we drop it?"

"Sure." Penny grinned.

Shelby wondered what she was grinning about. Needing a moment to find her balance, she took Fran's cup and rinsed it out.

"What's this?"

She turned. Penny was holding up a piece of wood Fran had been whittling on.

"Nothing yet."

"What's it going to be?"

"She doesn't know."

"She?"

"Fran."

"Oh." Penny got up and wandered around the campsite. Shelby watched her, feeling invaded, and annoyed with herself for feeling that way.

"What's that?" She pointed to the pile of sticks and string Shelby had stashed away at the tent corner.

"I'm making a camp stool. Lashing it. With string."

"Wow." Penny stared down at the heap. "Can you really do that?"

"Not to brag about. Not yet, anyway. I may master it by the time I'm fifty."

"Do you have a book or something?"

"Fran's teaching me." She gestured toward the dish shelf Fran had strung between two trees. "See that? Not a nail in it, and when we leave we just take it apart and leave the sticks for the next person to use for firewood."

"At least this isn't an all-work-no-play holiday," Penny said with a smile. She perused the camp site. "Fran's quite a Girl Scout, isn't she?"

Shelby had to laugh at that. She could hardly see Fran making pot holders and sit-upons, which was all Shelby could recall doing in the one year she'd spent with the Scouts as a kid. And make-up. She remembered learning to put on make-up. But maybe the Girl Scouts were different outside the North Shore. Maybe they actually engaged in scouting activities, like building campfires and finding lost children.

She'd felt very much like a lost child, herself, at that age. The other girls liked making sit-upons, but Shelby had pestered her mother to let her join the scouts because she thought they'd go camping. She'd read it in a book somewhere. Girl Scouts went camping, and learned how to build fires and use a compass and a knife, and how to read maps and other useful things. But the First Congregational Church Girl Scouts of Troop 240 didn't want to do those things. Which was just as well, since none of the leaders knew how to do them, either.

She told that to Penny, who laughed and said she'd never belonged to the Girl Scouts, though she'd joined the Girl Guides once when they were living in England, but they'd made fun of her accent and pretended they couldn't understand her.

They spent a couple of minutes contemplating the unnecessary cruelty of the young.

Fran reappeared, shaking water out of her hair with one hand. "That was truly inspirational," she said. "What're you two up to?"

"Shelby was showing me the stuff you built," Penny said cheerfully. "You're really great."

"Aw, shucks," Fran said.

"Did you wash your hair?" Shelby asked.

"I tried." She tossed her head with a vigorous shake, spraying them with drops.

"Hey," Shelby said.

"A little trick I learned from the company dog."

Penny said, "Oh" again in her non-committal way, but the sharp, jerky motions with which she brushed the water droplets from her tee-shirt were clearly not expressions of amusement.

Shelby tossed Fran a towel. "Behave yourself," she said.

"Yes, Mother." She rubbed at her hair, then formed the towel into a turban.

"You look like something out of *South Pacific*," Shelby said.

"Luther Billis?"

"I was thinking of Nellie Forbush." She grabbed the towel from Fran's head and ruffled her damp hair.

Penny was watching them hard.

"Penny," Fran said, pulling away, "how about more of my excellent coffee?"

"No thanks." Penny tucked her tee-shirt into her shorts. "I have to get the show on the road." She turned away. "See you at the salt mine, Shel."

Fran looked after her. "I have to agree with Connie," she said when Penny was out of hearing. "The lady has a crush on you."

"Don't be silly. She's too old for that."

"One is never," Fran said, "too old for that."

"Well, maybe she did, but she must be over it."

Fran shook her head. "Not by a long shot."

"How do you know?"

"Her energy. Toward me. If she were a dog, the hair on the back of her neck would be stiff as a porcupine's quills."

"I didn't notice," Shelby said. "I mean, I wasn't sure what I was seeing."

"That's why I went to the john. I figured if I didn't give her some time alone with you there'd be big trouble."

"I hope it wasn't awkward for you."

"Hey, I understand what she's going through. I, myself, have found you desirable on more than one occasion."

Shelby felt herself blush.

"Could she be dangerous?"

"I doubt it," Shelby said. "Besides, if she's so crazy about me, she wouldn't do anything to hurt me, would she?"

Fran shook her head. "Oh, my friend, I do worry about you."

"Well, would she?"

"Never underestimate the power of love to cause trouble."

It one of those little glimpses at the scars on Fran's heart. She'd been through things she hadn't even told Shelby, that much she acknowledged. Things that had hurt her, things that had taken pieces of her spirit. She'd been hurt for something that wasn't her fault. Not anybody's fault, really. Not a fault at all, just a difference. Sometimes the hurts weren't even intentional. Sometimes, she suspected, they were self-inflicted. Like the unhappiness Fran had gone through because she was afraid to tell Shelby who she really was. She must have loved many people, and been afraid to let them know.

She looked over at Fran, and wanted to take her in her arms. To hold her. To protect her from the world. She wanted her to feel safe, to let go, to put herself in Shelby's hands and rest, if only for a minute. But she knew it couldn't happen. One touch and Fran would draw back deep into herself like a turtle into its shell. She'd felt it last night, when she'd taken Fran's hand, that light return touch that said, "I want you here but I can't let it be real."

"Something wrong?" Fran asked.

Shelby shook her head. "I was off on my own trajectory." She was tempted to say, "Love doesn't always hurt." But she wasn't absolutely sure that for Fran it didn't. Instead she said, "Let's take a walk."

Chapter 16

By the time they'd circled the lake the sun was going behind storm clouds. Very dark, nasty storm clouds. They discussed packing up and leaving, but didn't really want to. Fran told of camping in Glacier National Park one August. As soon as the tent went up, the snow and rain began. She and her "friend"—a euphemism, Shelby was sure—thought of leaving, but there was nowhere to go, no motels or hotels, only wilderness and grizzly bears. They decided to wait it out, give the storm time to pass and let the sun dry the tent. Three days later, cold, wet, exhausted and coughing up their lungs with bronchitis, they gave up. They loaded the soggy tent and soggy sleeping bags into the car and headed for the Continental Divide. On the other side, the air was as hot and dry as the desert. Their gear dried in half an hour at the Bozeman hotel. Their lungs took several days.

The last straw came when they told their sad story to the local pharmacist. Instead of sympathizing over freak storms, he'd placed their filled penicillin prescriptions on the counter and said, "Hell, girls, winter starts up there on August 15."

"There's nothing worse," Fran said, "than surviving a natural disaster and then finding out you were stupid to be there in the first place."

"I don't care," Shelby said. "I've never been in a tent in a thunderstorm before. Please?"

They stowed their gear under tarps and in the car, took the sandwich makings into the tent, and cozied in. A wind came up, fluttering the tent flaps. The temperature plummeted. The first big drops of rain hit the roof as Fran zipped the canvas door. "If it gets bad," she said, "remember it was your idea."

"Leave if you want." Shelby smeared mayonnaise on a slice of bread and rummaged in the cooler for the pickle and pimento loaf. "I'm staying."

Fran pulled an Army sweat shirt over her head. She found another, with a picture of the Alamo, and tossed it over. "Don't freeze."

She finished making her sandwich and one for Fran, replaced her shorts with jeans, and pulled the shirt over her head. It felt warm and soft and smelled of Fran. The touch of it was like a caress on her skin. She smoothed it against her body.

Fran pulled a bag of potato chips from their supplies and tore it open. "Better eat these fast," she said, plopping down to sit cross-legged on her sleeping bag and smiling up at Shelby. "They'll go limp in seconds."

In the wooly darkness, her eyes were cobalt blue. Shelby couldn't stop staring at her.

"What?"

"Your eyes. They're...gorgeous."

Fran laughed self-consciously and looked down at the floor. "They change," she said. "Depending on my mood."

"What does deep blue mean?"

Fran hesitated. Then, not meeting Shelby's eyes, she said, "No one should be allowed to be this happy."

Shelby reached down and placed her hand on top of Fran's head. "Yes," she said, "you should."

It was an angry storm. Lightning as sharp as razors and silver as minnows. Thunder like an artillery barrage. Their campsite was too low to catch the worst of the wind, but water poured down on the tent with the force of a fire hose. Lying on her back, her arm cradling Fran's head, Shelby watched it through the net window in the rear of the tent.

"We don't usually get a lot of storms like this in late August," she said, running her hand through Fran's hair. "I guess this one has to make up for it."

Fran nodded against her shoulder.

"Does it remind you of war games?"

"Being snuggled by a friend while the world blows up around me? Hardly."

Shelby smiled and pressed her cheek against the top of Fran's head. Her hair was warm and soft. It reminded her of milkweed silk. "Feels good, doesn't it?"

"Do you have to ask?"

"No." She wanted to make promises to her. To be there, whenever Fran needed her. To hold her and be a place of comfort and safety. To love her.

But she couldn't make those promises.

A sharp hiss and crack, the sound of a falling tree, crushing branches.

Fran sat up. "That was close."

"You know what they say," Shelby said. "The one to worry about is the one you *don't* hear. As long as you're up, get me a Coke?"

"Whenever I think of camping in Massachusetts," Fran said as she pawed through the cooler, "I'll think of rain."

Shelby laughed. "Whenever you think of doing *anything* in Massachusetts, think of rain."

Fran handed her the open bottle. She hesitated only a moment, then climbed back onto the sleeping bag and lay down with her head resting back against Shelby's shoulder.

"That's more like it," Shelby said.

"Like what?"

"I was beginning to think I smelled bad, you seem so reluctant to touch me."

"I'm not reluctant."

"Not if I touch you first."

Fran pushed herself up on one elbow. "I don't want to do anything to offend you, or scare you."

"Your withdrawal offends and scares me." She ran one finger down Fran's cheek. "It's kind of ironic, you know. You were afraid to tell me about yourself because you were afraid I'd withdraw. But you told me, and now *you're* the one who's withdrawing."

"Yeah." Fran reached for the Coke and took a swallow. "Kind of dumb, huh?"

"Very dumb."

A flash of distant lightning sparked. They waited, counting the seconds, until the thunder growled.

"Moving away," Shelby said.

Fran lay back down in the dark. "I don't know what's wrong with me. I act like an adolescent. I *feel* like an adolescent. Insecurities are running wild."

Shelby tightened her arm around her. "It's OK. I won't tell."

"You always say and do the right thing."

"I don't think so."

"Where I'm concerned, you do. I think you know me as well as I know myself."

"Do you mind?"

"I admit I'm messed up," Fran said, "but I'm not crazy."

Shelby smiled to herself. It was true. If she followed her instincts with Fran, she was usually right. Before the storm broke, she'd had to go down by the lake to the bathroom. When she'd come back Fran had not only tidied up, but had straightened the sleeping bags and was getting out the cards. She could tell, by the strained, sad look beneath Fran's smile, that she was trying desperately to pretend everything was all right. Before she'd even thought about what she was doing, Shelby'd taken the cards away from her and pulled her down next to her on the sleeping bag. "This is my storm, no card playing allowed," she'd said, and put her arms around her.

It had been the right thing to do. She could tell by the way Fran had sighed, then relaxed, and finally said, "Thank you."

"Well," Shelby said softly, "you may be messed up, but knowing you is a privilege and a pleasure."

Fran sighed again. "Ray's a lucky man."

"How so?"

"After you're married, he gets to come home every night so someone as gentle and loving as you."

Shelby laughed. "Don't be silly. I don't feel that way about Ray."

Someone opened the door of a jet plane and shoved her out.

They looked at each other.

"Uh-oh," Fran said.

* * *

Penny popped her head in the door. There was no other way to describe it, she popped her head in like a jack-in-the-box. Sudden and grinning. "Hey, boss, ready for me?"

"Good Morning, Merry Sunshine." No, she wasn't ready for Penny. She wasn't ready for anyone. Wasn't even sure why or how she'd come to work. She was going through the motions. Eating and sleeping and brushing her teeth and driving her car and saying "Hello" to people, even talking to Libby on the phone last night, being enthusiastic, going through the motions.

Inside, she was as cold and hard as a stalactite, frozen into place on her way somewhere, anywhere. She'd been that way since Saturday night.

"It's OK," Fran had said when she'd apologized. "Do what you have to do."

What she had to do was walk. All day Sunday. On the steepest, roughest, buggiest trails she could find. And chop wood. And do most of the packing up. Because she had to keep busy. If she didn't keep busy, if she stopped for a moment and realized what had happened to her, she'd run away.

Fran had stayed on the periphery, watchful, keeping out of her way but not letting her out of sight, making sure she ate and didn't cut herself with the axe or wander off into the woods. Which could have happened, because she wasn't sure where she was but she sure wasn't here.

When she stopped for a second, and let a little bit of awareness creep in, it came in the form of words—oh, my God; oh, my God—repeated over and over like a chant.

Fran left her at her door, but only when she promised that she wouldn't go for the pills and liquor. "At least until the mud has settled a little, OK?"

She'd nodded.

"I'm going to leave my door open," Fran said. "I want you to leave yours open, too."

"Don't you trust me?"

"Not entirely. But the main reason is I want you to remember you're not in this alone. I'm going to put some music on to remind you. Any requests?"

"Not Brahms," Shelby managed to say.

Fran smiled. "Definitely not Brahms." She took Shelby's shoulders in her hands. "I mean this, give yourself time. I'm going to check in on you every now and then to be sure you're OK. For my peace of mind, not yours."

"OK."

"Now, put on your best party persona and call Libby before she calls you."

She nodded again.

Fran started to leave, then turned back. "I'm trusting you, Shelby. Am I a fool?"

Shelby shook her head.

"Hey," Penny was saying, "you need coffee or something?"

It snapped her back to where she was. "Just got some," she said, and showed Penny her mug. "Thanks, anyway."

Penny smiled. "That must have been some weekend."

"What?"

"You look wiped out."

"I guess I am," Shelby said quickly. "I indulged myself and ended up having to work almost all night last night."

"That's rough. You want to postpone this for another time?"

"Definitely not. I've kept you hanging long enough." She was glad to have something to do, actually. It might keep her mind off…things. She pulled Penny's folder from her desk drawer. "Let's begin at the beginning and go on until we come to the end."

Penny hopped up onto the desk, facing Shelby and a little above her. She pulled out a low drawer for Penny to put her feet on. Penny's blood red circle skirt made her look as if she were being born from a hollyhock. "This first one isn't too bad, actually. Most of what you like in it, I like, too. I just think it's too borderline for the Mag."

"I like it," Penny said.

"I don't *dis*like it, exactly. I guess it just needs work. Can you send it back and ask for a rewrite?"

Penny sighed. "I suppose so." She held out her hand for the story.

"Now, on this next one—we're about as far apart on it as Republicans and Democrats. I suggest we go over it point by point." She glanced down to review her notes.

"She wasn't wearing a bra," Penny said.

"What?"

"She wasn't wearing a bra."

Shelby leafed through the story. "I don't remember a bra being mentioned, present or absent."

"Not in the story," Penny said in an annoyed tone. "Fran."

"She goes without when she's relaxing. She doesn't really need one."

"How do you come by that bit of information?"

"You can tell by looking at her."

"Personally," Penny said casually, with a smile, "I don't go around looking at women's breasts."

"That's probably just as well," Shelby said, and forced herself to attend to the story.

"It looks cheap."

"I thought you didn't look. If you *had* looked, you'd have noticed that Fran doesn't need to wear a bra."

"I suppose, if it was a hundred degrees in here, you'd think it was all right to come to work naked."

Shelby shook her head. "We were *camping*, Penny. She wasn't expecting anyone."

"You're someone."

She was becoming really annoyed. "But I don't care what Fran Jarvis wears. I don't care what you wear. I don't care what *anyone* wears. This is a ridiculous conversation, and I don't know why we're having it."

"It doesn't look good, going around without a bra."

Shelby tossed the folder of stories on the desk. "We're not here to discuss Fran's fashion sense, Penny. If you want to talk about what the well-dressed career girl wears, make an appointment with Charlotte."

Penny crossed her legs and swung one foot perilously close to Shelby's knee. "Well, excuse me. I don't mean to waste your valuable time."

Shelby took a deep breath and forced herself to remain calm. "You're not wasting my time, Penny. I just have a lot to do."

"Right. You didn't get much done last weekend."

Oh, God, Fran's right, she thought. Penny's jealous. She ought to be especially kind to her now. Jealousy was a painful, horrible feeling. But she really, really didn't have the energy. "Penny," she said as gently as she could, "I think I know what you're going through, and I sympathize, I really do. But we have to do this."

Penny swung her foot and shrugged. "Then let's do it."

OK, Camden, she told herself, ignore her mood. Say what you have to say.

"Look, this isn't about this latest batch of stories. Not entirely. It's all your work. You know how well you were doing when you started, but lately your judgment...well, it's not as sharp as it was." She forced herself to look Penny in the eye and speak in a concerned voice. "Is something bothering you? Getting in the way? I hope you know you can always talk to me..."

"There's nothing wrong with me. You're more particular than you were."

"I really don't think so."

"You are. It's unconscious. No one could live up to your standards. You're afraid Spurl will judge you by my work."

"You're not the only reader I supervise, Penny."

"Yeah, but I'm your particular responsibility. I'll bet you're not as hard on the others. It isn't fair."

Her temper flared. "File a grievance with the union."

"We don't have a union," Penny said calmly. She looked down at the floor and swung her feet and pouted. "You're cranky all the time, too."

"I have a lot on my mind."

"Like what?"

She'd never seen Penny chew gum, but her attitude and behavior cried out for gum-cracking. "Like the wedding, for one thing. I mean, you don't just snap your fingers and have it appear."

"According to your mother, that's what you think."

Shelby looked at her.

Penny looked back, big-eyed and innocent. "Well, that's what Connie says, anyway."

This was a mistake. Everything was a mistake. Being born was a mistake. She felt trapped, frozen...

The phone rang. She jumped to answer it. "Miss Camden."

"Hey, Miss Camden."

Her heart started up again. "Fran. Hi."

"Am I interrupting you?"

More like saving my life, she thought. "No."

"I'm checking up on you. Actually, I just wanted to hear your voice. No, to tell you the truth, I'm calling to see if you'd pick me up a couple of things from the supermarket on your way home."

"Sure." She got out a paper and pencil. "Let me have it."

Penny tapped her shoulder.

"Oh, wait a minute," she said into the phone.

Penny shook her head. "Don't stop. I have to get back to work. We can finish this later."

"Thanks."

Grinning from ear to ear, Penny left the room. She closed the door softly and tightly behind her.

"Sorry about that. It was just Penny, leaving."

"Did she say anything about Saturday?"

"She noticed you weren't wearing a bra."

Fran gasped. "Why, that dirty girl. You're doing OK?"

"I'm doing," Shelby said. "OK or not is open to debate. What do you need?"

Fran gave her the list. "You know where to find me if you need me. You have my work number, don't you?"

"Yep. I'll have you paged all over the Student Health Center and embarrass the pants off of you."

Fran laughed. "First no bra, now no pants. What next?"

"God, it's good to hear your voice."

"Not as good as it is to hear yours. You take care of yourself."

"I will. You, too. Don't pick up any incurable diseases."

"The only diseases around a college campus," Fran said, "are hormonal."

"Well, look out for them. See you tonight."

She ought to go find Penny now, and finish their conversation. That idea held all the charm of a trip to the dentist. Still, it had to be done...

No, what she really ought to do was figure out what the hell she was going to do with her life. Marrying Ray was definitely out of the question now. If she didn't love him, love him completely and without hesitation, she couldn't in good conscience go through with the wedding. So Ray would have to be told, before anyone else. Then her mother, and her friends. And she'd better do it soon before the arrangements went any further. So she had to start with Ray, probably tonight.

She didn't want to do this. She felt tired and weak and frightened. The thought of picking up the phone, telling Ray she needed to see him, explaining it—explain it how? "Gee, Ray, I hate to disappoint you, but I just found out I feel more for my friends than I do for you. Have a nice life."

The idea of it made her stomach churn. This was no little thing she was about to do. Not some minor inconvenience like rain on a picnic. This was going to cause major, irreversible destruction. Her parents, their friends, her friends, Ray's friends, the whole damn Camden clan...There'd be a thousand questions, and no acceptable answers. A thousand arguments while they tried to talk her out of it, or they'd laugh at her feelings or say it was "just wedding nerves." She'd already tried the "just wedding nerves" bit on herself. It hadn't worked.

She might as well have herself staked out on an ant hill.

When she looked at it, really looked at it, she knew it was impossible to change everything now. She just couldn't do it. All she wanted was to crawl down a hole and stay there until everyone had forgotten her.

But there were three good reasons she couldn't do that. One, she knew what she knew and she couldn't unknow it. Two, she couldn't spend the rest of her life married to a man she didn't love. She'd been pretending for years, and all it had done was give her headaches. And three, it would be just plain immoral.

They were going to eat her alive.

Oh, God. She doubled over to curl around her burning stomach. I want everything to just change. To blink my eyes and have it all be easy. To never have gotten myself to this point. I did what people wanted. I did what they expected me to do. And now it's going to blow up in my face, and all I did was try to do the right thing.

This couldn't really be happening. It was too much like a movie or a story...or a terrible nightmare. But she'd never had a nightmare this bad. This was the A Number One, Olympic sized, World's Record of Nightmares.

What was she going to tell people? "I woke up one morning and decided it had all been a mistake?" That might work for some people. People who were known for blowing in the wind. Like Lisa. Penny probably changed course in midstream without even thinking about it. And even Connie had been known to be stricken by a terminal case of attitude about some minor thing and completely changed her plans, indifferent to anyone else's inconvenience.

But not Shelby Camden. Shelby Camden did what she said she was going to do, and she'd never say she was going to do it unless she was certain, so you could absolutely, positively count on her to know what she was doing and why.

She'd always been like that. Even as a child. Teachers called her responsible. Her friends—even people who weren't really her friends but needed something from her—knew they could count on her. Shelby was the rock, the one person you could hang on to in an unpredictable world. It was universally assumed that Shelby knew herself and her word was as good as a contract.

Nobody ever guessed she had been running on fear. Fear of displeasing. Fear of being different. Fear of being found out. You name it, Shelby was afraid of it.

And look where it got you, she told herself. There was a poetic irony in the situation. After years of compromising and avoiding, years of doing her dance of balance, here she was face to face with a no-win situation.

It made her feel like a child.

She should have gone ahead and killed herself. But she couldn't do that to Fran. She loved Fran, too, in her way. A way that felt good and right, and like a true expression of herself. She was happy with Fran. Happier and less lonely than she'd been in a long time. She couldn't turn her back on that friendship. She wanted to bask in it, to feel the warm, safe feeling of being around her. Wanted to go camping, and hiking, and play gin rummy or just do nothing at all with Fran.

Maybe she was jumping to conclusions. Maybe the difference between what she felt for Fran and what she felt for Ray wasn't really that strange at all. Maybe loving a friend and loving a husband just *were* different feelings and it didn't mean anything. Maybe she'd grow to…

Get real, she told herself roughly. The truth of the matter is, you're not in love with Ray and you can't face it. So pick up the phone and call the man, and your mother…

Her hands were shaking so badly she couldn't dial. She slammed the receiver back on the cradle.

You know it's not going to get any easier, she reminded herself. Pull yourself together and do it.

She could feel her blood pounding through her veins. Suddenly she had to get out of here. Before she suffocated. Before her heart burst.

She reached for the phone again, and dialled Jean's desk. "I have to talk to someone," she said. "Can you meet me in the lounge?"

Just the sight of a friend made her feel better. Jean poured them each a cup of coffee and sat beside her on the couch. "Wow," Jean said, "you look awful."

"I have the willies," Shelby said. She tried to steady her cup. "Very large willies."

"Wedding willies?"

"You can't imagine."

Jean smiled. "No, I can't say I can."

Shelby took a sip of coffee. "I don't think…"

Jean waited for her to go on. She couldn't. "Neither do I," Jean said at last, "unless I absolutely have to."

"I don't think…I want to do it."

"The wedding?"

Shelby nodded miserably.

"OK," Jean said.

"*OK?*" She stared at her. "This isn't *OK*. No way is it *OK*. This is a disaster."

"I'd feel the same way in your place. Anyone would."

"I don't think so." Jean didn't get it. "I mean, I really have serious doubts about this. I'm not even sure I love Ray."

Jean turned thoughtful for a moment. "Where's this coming from, Shel? Did something happen?"

"Not really."

"Has Ray been a cad? We have a cure for men like that, you know. We send them on all-day excursions on school buses loaded with third graders singing 'one-hundred bottles of beer on the wall.'"

Shelby had to laugh. It felt good. "It kind of fell on me," she said. Her voice caught. "Over the weekend."

Jean took her hand and held it.

"I could be wrong. It could be more jitters, or something I don't even understand. Maybe it'll pass." She ran her free hand over her face. "Sometimes I think that was just a silly passing thing, why am I getting so shook up? And then I think the fact that I'm so shook up means it wasn't a silly passing thing…"

"What happened?" Jean asked softly.

"Nothing, really." Penny would certainly have spilled the beans by now. Shelby looked down at Jean's hand cupped around hers. "It suddenly hit me. I don't feel about Ray the way I do about my friends."

"Of course you don't," Jean said with a laugh.

"You don't understand. I don't feel as…open or…close with him."

"From what my mother tells me, it's always like that. The difference between men and women."

"But this is a very large difference."

Jean ran her thumb across Shelby's knuckles as she thought. It felt good. Disturbingly good…

"Look," Jean said, "maybe Ray's just not the right guy for you. Maybe you need to take a step back and check the whole thing out again."

"Maybe. Do you know what kind of a mess this could be?"

Jean nodded. "Not as big a mess as marrying the man and realizing later when you find yourself in a wild, compulsive affair with the pool boy."

Shelby had to laugh. "You've read too many bad stories."

"Maybe." She was silent for a moment. "Look maybe you *should* call it off, feeling the way you do."

Shelby forced herself to look at her. "What would you think? Of me?"

"We're talking about changing your mind," Jean said softly, "not committing murder."

"I guess."

"At least give yourself time. Meanwhile, try not to get pregnant."

That made her smile. "If I get pregnant, I might as well shoot myself right here."

"Here?" Jean looked around the room. "Shelby, listen to me. No matter how bad things are, they're never bad enough to justify shooting yourself on an orange vinyl sofa." She squeezed Shelby's hand. "Mind if I give you some advice?"

"I wish you would."

"If you do decide to call it off, wait until after your family Labor Day picnic."

"Oh, God!" She'd forgotten about the Camden reunion. The annual command performance, where she'd go and be paraded in front of various aunts and uncles and cousins for their disapproval. This would be her twenty-fifth, if you didn't count the one she'd attended *in utero*, which she was sure had warped her for life. In good years, it was painful. During her adolescent years, when she had been prone to attacks of shyness and insecurity, alternating with fits of rage—which she had managed to keep hidden—the Camden family reunion was a day in hell.

There was nothing wrong with the Camdens, exactly. They were just proud, old, and critical.

Even Libby, who really didn't like them, curried their favor.

They expected it. The main course at all Camden family dinners, Shelby thought, was curried favor.

Only blood Camdens were welcomed at those reunions. In-laws were expected to attend and observe, but were discouraged from participating. Mostly they were ignored. Unless they were absent, in which case they were discussed. Once, in a fit of collegiate rebellion and compassion, Shelby had tried to make one of the Camden-in-law wives feel at home by chatting with her. It had made the woman so uncomfortable she'd twitched and shifted for ten minutes, then announced she really had to see if they needed her help in the kitchen.

For years, Shelby had been the only child at the dinners. Camdens who had children tended to avoid them. This was encouraged, as children at Camden reunions were considered disruptive and made the older folks nervous. Not Shelby. Shelby was a *good* child, quiet and polite and invisible. Shelby had *good manners* for a child. No one ever wondered if there might be something troubling a child with such good manners.

"Hello," Jean said.

Shelby shook herself. Her mind was wandering, straying from The Problem. "You're right, I don't want to drop any bomb shells before the reunion." She laughed. "Who knows? In two weeks I may be over this fit of pique and wonder why I made such a federal case of it."

"Well, if you're not, I'll man the trenches with you."

"Thank you," Shelby said. She was genuinely moved. She decided to take a chance. "I'm really scared about this, Jean. If I do go through with...not going through with it…you know it's going to be terrible."

"I know. But look at it this way. You have friends you can count on, and a job that's great and destined to get better. So your mother cuts holes in the ceiling with her head. You're not alone in the world."

"And Ray?"

"Ray will be hurt. And Ray will recover. He's a big boy, Shel."

"I guess."

"And so will you."

She glanced up at the clock. "I'd better get back to work." Instead she broke bits of styrofoam from the rim of her cup and dropped them inside. She counted them. Jean smiled at her and waited. "Don't tell the others about this, OK?" she said at last. "I couldn't bear trying to explain."

"Your secret's my secret. Listen," Jean said as she gathered up their used and broken cups, "we're all going to a movie tonight. Why don't you forget this mess and come with us?"

"I'd better not. I have a million things to do, and I haven't talked to Ray since Friday. How was my revered maternal parent, by the way?"

"Libby? In rare form. Manic."

Shelby groaned and got up. "Thanks for the sympathy. I really mean that, Jean. It matters a lot. See you at lunch?"

"You might want to think twice about lunch. There's going to be a lot of wedding talk."

Shelby shook her head. "I don't want to let on anything's amiss. Just don't let me put my foot in it, OK?"

"Of course." Jean looked at her fondly. "Saving you from yourself is what I do best."

Later, back in her office after lunch, she had a sudden feeling that it could be all right. She had friends who cared about her. Really, genuinely cared about her. Jean was behind her. And Connie, who would rather be a mother hen than a maid of honor any day, would ride to her rescue. Lisa would do whatever Connie did. Even Penny would probably jump on the band wagon.

And there was Fran.

Chapter 17

They stood in the office doorway, the three of them, looking like the three weird sisters from Macbeth. Connie and Lisa, grim. Jean a little embarrassed and...ashamed?

She felt a moment of apprehension, and shot Jean a questioning look. Jean shook her head slightly. She looked guilty.

"Come on in," Shelby said to the *troika*.

Connie strode into the room, the others shuffling behind. "Close the door," Connie ordered Jean, last in. She turned to Shelby. "We need to talk to you."

Shelby didn't like the way this felt. She turned wary. "What's this? Before-lunch bridge? Where's Penny?"

"This doesn't concern Penny," Connie said. Lisa nodded agreement. Jean walked over and pretended to look out the window. It put her on Shelby's side of the desk, opposite Jean and Connie.

Shelby's apprehension increased. Jean was protecting her. From what? "So what's up?" she asked in a cheerful and innocent tone of voice.

"Well..." Connie made herself comfortable in Charlotte's chair behind Charlotte's desk. She took one of Charlotte's paper clips from Charlotte's ceramic desk tray and twisted it out of shape. "Look, we know you're strung out about the wedding and all..."

She didn't dare turn to look at Jean.

"I mean," Connie went on, "it must be really frantic, and there must be times when you want to get as far away from it as possible..."

Shelby almost laughed.

"But, frankly, we miss you."

"It seems like, any more," Lisa picked up, "you're always working, or doing wedding stuff, or with...well, with Fran. It's been weeks since you've done anything with us." She giggled nervously. "I guess we feel kind of neglected."

They were right. It had been weeks. The time was going by so fast she hadn't noticed. What with suicide attempts and all. "I'm really sorry," she said. "It's nothing personal. Everything's hectic."

"Maybe it's time to take a deep breath and restructure your priorities," Connie said as she doodled on Charlotte's pristine note pad with Charlotte's freshly sharpened pencil.

"Don't do that," Shelby said. "Charlotte will have a fit."

"Oops. Sorry." Connie tossed the pencil down, breaking the point. "So what do you think?"

"About what?"

"Priorities."

Shelby felt a little like an eight-year old standing in front of a tall, cold-faced teacher. Her mind went blank. "Well, sure," she said.

"Sure what?"

She was having trouble breathing. She wanted to open the door. She wanted to leave through it. "Priorities. Good idea, priorities."

"And how about us?" Lisa asked.

"How about you?"

"Are we a priority?"

Shelby forced a laugh. "Of course you are. For Heaven's sake, don't you know that?"

"Apparently not," Jean muttered.

Jean wasn't in favor of this whatever-it-was they were doing. All too reminiscent of their own "little chat" back in March, no doubt. Shelby looked over at her and hoped she conveyed both gratitude and apology.

"Then why haven't we seen more of you?" Connie plodded on.

"Time got away, that's all."

"It's not just a matter of us feeling neglected," Connie said. She stared at Shelby expressionlessly, as if challenging her.

Shelby made her face go blank in return. "I see."

"It's not healthy for you."

"It's not right," Lisa added.

Shelby felt her face redden, and didn't know why.

"You shouldn't cut yourself off from your friends. You need us at times like this, Camden."

"I know that."

"To help you relax and have fun."

Oh, yes, fun is exactly what I need right now. Tons and tons of FUN. "I appreciate your concern," she said.

"Well, can we do something together? For a change?"

It was impossible to miss Connie's tone, sarcasm laced with disapproval. It reminded her of Libby. Play dumb, she told herself, and smiled. "I'd love to."

"Not just *one* something," Connie said firmly. "Let's make this a part of a whole change of behavior."

Anger bubbled up in her. "What's the matter?" she heard herself say. "Are you jealous?"

Connie raised her eyebrows. "Of what?"

"My time with Ray, the wedding?"

"Hardly." Connie smiled.

Lines of music came into Shelby's head. From "Mac the Knife." Something about sharks and pearly white teeth...

"It doesn't have anything to do with us," Connie went on. "We're concerned about you."

Things suddenly fell into place. "It's Fran. You resent my friendship with her."

Connie laughed. "Be real, Camden."

It felt as if someone had poured acid into her stomach. Fear and rage went a few rounds. Rage won. "Penny told you about the weekend," she said flatly, her face cold as marble.

Lisa and Connie exchanged a look. "What about the weekend?" Lisa asked, innocent as a dog caught chewing the furniture.

"Yes," Jean broke in firmly. "She did."

"Jean…" Connie warned.

"She said she'd run into you. Camping. In the state park."

"After you told everyone you had to work," Lisa added.

"I was working. I explained it to Penny." Don't make excuses for yourself, she thought. It's none of their business how you spend your time.

"It really hurts us," Connie said. "That you'd lie to us. That's not like you."

Shelby felt a tingling sensation around her lips. "I ran into Fran. I told her I was working. She suggested taking the work up to the lake…" She hated herself for being defensive. She couldn't stop. "It was just as easy to work up there. Easier, really. I needed a change of scenery."

Jean sighed.

I should have told her. I don't blame her for being hurt. I would be. "It's very complicated," she said to Jean, touching her, hoping she'd realize the touch was a promise to clear it up later, when they were alone.

"I know," Jean said.

It gave her a tremendous feeling of relief, as if someone had just blessed her.

Connie glared at her.

"I told you it was a mix-up," Jean said.

"I still think it's indicative…"

"For God's sake," Shelby exploded. "I did one little thing not quite the way I said I would. You don't have to make a Federal case out of it. What is this? Communist Russia?"

Lisa had gone white and trembly, and seemed about to bolt.

"It's just a mistake," Jean said. "Nobody meant anything by anything."

Shelby was still angry. "I'm sorry," she said tightly. "I didn't mean to hurt your feelings. It just happened, OK?"

"A lot of things seem to be just happening," Connie began.

Jean cut her off. "Do you know how ridiculous we all sound? This is worse than high school."

"True," Connie said with a sudden smile. "We came in here to touch base, not to fight."

For some reason, that smile was even more unsettling. She was tempted to claim a need for the ladies' room, just to get out of there. But that wouldn't work. They'd come in the ladies' room after her. The ladies' room was only a refuge from men.

"So let's forget this business," Jean went on, "and do something ."

"Suits me," Shelby said quickly. "What do you have in mind?"

"We're all going to a movie tonight," Lisa said tentatively.

"Come with us," Connie demanded.

Shelby wanted to tell her where she could store her movie, one reel at a time. "No can do. I have a date to see Ray tonight." She smiled in what she hoped was a sheepish way. "How about Wednesday?"

"OK," Connie said.

"We can go to a movie then," Shelby said. "Unless you're tired of movies. What's on?"

Connie shrugged. "Who cares? Let's hit the early show and have a late supper after."

"Terrific." It wasn't terrific.

"We'll meet at my place. Six-thirty."

"Fine." It wasn't even fine.

They filed out, Jean going last again and turning back to throw her a look of apology.

* * *

The evening wasn't going well. Ray was tired and petulant. Shelby responded, out of habit, by turning relentlessly cheerful. It exhausted her, and didn't help the situation. She finally suggested they make an early night of it, since they were both a little cranky. Ray seemed surprised at this, and wanted her to explain exactly what he had done to make her think he was cranky. She said it wasn't any *thing* so much as a feeling. Which caused him to smile in a condescending, "women-and-their-little-intuitions" way. Which made her want to kill him. She didn't dare say anything. She might say too much.

She'd already decided not to bring up her doubts. Not until she was clear.

"Looks to me," Ray said, "as if someone's doing a little projecting."

"Projecting" had been Ray's favorite concept since he'd done his psychiatric quarter.

Shelby thought about "projecting" him into the next county.

He slipped an arm around her and gave her shoulders a little squeeze. "Tell you what," he said, "let's take your suggestion and call it an early evening." He yawned. "You obviously need a good night's sleep."

She gritted her teeth. If she got into an argument with him now—which she wanted to do with every fiber of her being—this could go on all night. If she played along, she'd get to go home soon.

Get to go home. A great way to feel about your beloved betrothed.

"You're probably right," she said. "If you don't mind…"

Ray laughed. "How many times do I have to say it, Shel? There'll be all the time in the world when we're married."

The list of things they could postpone until after they were married and had eternities together was growing longer every day. It was beginning to feel like a prison sentence.

A half hour of obligatory grope and fondle, and they were on their way to her house. Shelby glanced over at Ray in the dash board light. He was smiling, happy they were going to be together, happy to be taking care of her now. Guilt swept over her. This man really loved her, had loved her almost from their first date. She wondered what the rest of her life would be if she didn't marry him.

He didn't even ask to come in, for which she was grateful. Between the guilt and the fear and the mist, she wouldn't have the strength to refuse him. Instead he walked her to the front door, took her in his arms gently, and kissed her. "Good night, wife," he murmured in her ear.

She pretended she hadn't heard.

226

* * *

Fran's door was open. It meant she might be up for company, if Shelby were so inclined. Shelby decided she'd be very much inclined once she changed into her pajamas. She peeked into Fran's apartment. "Oh, God, you're playing solitaire."

Fran looked up at her and grinned. "But no Brahms."

"Does that mean you're only half depressed?"

"It means I know I won't be able to get to sleep if I go to bed now."

Shelby leaned against the door jamb. "Want to borrow *America as a Civilization* ?"

"No, thanks." She moved over to make room on the couch. "Join me?"

"In a minute. I want to change from a girl to a woman."

"Ah," Fran said.

"Sure you don't mind company?"

"Why? How many rowdy people do you have with you?"

"Only me."

"Good thing you don't want a party. I just ran out of onion dip."

Shelby laughed. She laughed a lot around Fran, she realized. Simply because it was so easy being together. "Need anything from down my way?"

"Nope. Just your gorgeous face."

She decided to make tea, anyway, while she shed her linen suit and heels and climbed into pajamas. With a sigh of relief, she reached for her brush and broke the stickiness of her sprayed hair. The teakettle whistled, she poured boiling water over the tea leaves. Living here, with Fran just down the hall where they could visit all times of the day or night without having to make an Event out of it…it was a little like being back in college. A lot like it, she thought as she waited for the tea to steep and decided her bare feet would survive a run down the carpeted hallway. A lot like it.

Maybe that was her problem. Maybe she wanted to hang onto the old, safe, carefree days of college. Except they hadn't been carefree, exactly. It seemed as if she was always putting things off to the last minute, so was usually in a panic of studying or paper writing, pulling all-nighters and subsisting on stale coffee and Hershey bars. She'd even begun to think that grainy eyes and a metallic taste in her mouth was her natural state. Once, her junior year, she'd taken a large amount of No-Doz during a pre-exam cram session. It kept her awake, all right, but her hands shook so badly she couldn't read her own writing on the exam.

There'd been a litany of things to worry about. Would she be liked? Had she said the wrong thing in a just-finished conversation? Had she made a fool of herself in chem lab?

By the end of her sophomore year, she'd pretty much eliminated that self-consciousness by collecting a pool of friends she could feel comfortable with. Well, almost comfortable. She was never really deep, down in her bones, comfortable. Not while there were mistakes to be made. And there were always mistakes to be made. But she knew they liked her, and that was a step forward.

She'd had a pretty normal college life, actually. Contributed her ten pounds of gained weight to the Freshman Ton, agonized through and survived Sophomore Slump. Read *Catcher in the Rye* her junior year, and declared war on "phonies." Even languished around the bridge table enjoying a case of Senioritis.

She gathered up the tea things and trotted down the hall to Fran's apartment.

"How'd it go tonight?"

"I got through it."

Fran smiled. "What makes me think it wasn't much fun?"

"Ray was in a foul mood, but he insisted it was me."

"Uh-huh," Fran said. "Feel any clearer on the marriage?"

Shelby shook her head. "Not tonight. I'm still waiting for enlightenment." She rested her head against the back of Fran's couch. "I wish I could go to sleep and it would be all over when I wake up." She looked over at Fran. "I'm really scared. I feel as if I'm holding the fuse on a mountain of dynamite, and sooner or later I'll have to set it off."

Fran merely nodded.

"Sometimes the whole thing seems unreal. I mean, I just don't get myself into messes like this. I've always tried so hard not to make mistakes. Even when it meant hurting myself." Tears welled up in her eyes. "It's not fair."

"I guess this was a mistake that happened when you weren't looking. It *is* going to be awful. I can't think of any way around that. But please remember you're not alone in this."

"I am," Shelby said. "Ultimately. I'm the one who has to break the news. And I have to do it soon. I even feel guilty talking to you about it, before I tell Ray. I mentioned to Jean that I was having doubts, and I feel guilty about that." She sighed. "Oh, Fran, I've made such a terrible mess."

Fran squeezed her hand. "You haven't. You've done what seemed best at the time. Maybe it was even all you *could* do at the time." She was silent for a moment. "You look worn out."

"I am. I can't sleep worth a darn."

"Stay here tonight. Maybe it'll be better if you're not alone."

She was about to resist when she realized she really, really wanted to be with Fran.

"If you're worried about tossing and turning and keeping me awake," Fran said, "we'll leave a light on out here. Then you can come out and read. I can't offer you *America as a Civilization*, but I find *Bleak House* to be pretty effective."

"Thank you," Shelby said. "I think I'd like that."

She only woke up once during the night. It had turned colder, and Fran was covering her with another blanket. Only half awake, she turned on her side and snuggled deeper into the bed. She felt a soft, warm breeze, and realized Fran was stroking her hair.

She pretended to be asleep, so she wouldn't stop.

"Hey," Fran called from the living room, "I don't hear sounds of dressing in there."

"I don't want to do this," Shelby called back.

"You're the one who said you had to, not me."

Shelby went to the living room. "I know."

Fran was curled in one corner of the couch, a medical reference book in her lap. "You also know you have a deadline. About six days from now."

"I know. Maybe I'll just skip the Labor Day reunion."

"If you want to face the Wrath of Libby."

"It's going to come down, sooner or later."

Fran looked at her with deep seriousness. "You don't have to blow the whole thing out of the water. Just let him know what you're thinking."

"That's not so easy. Even I don't know what I'm thinking."

"So tell him that. We'll cross other bridges if we come to them."

"We?"

Fran blushed a little. "I'm butting in. But isn't that what friends are for?"

Great, Shelby thought. I'm supposed to be getting ready for a date with my fiancé, so I can tell him I don't think I want to marry him, and all I can think of is staying home and talking with this woman.

And touching her, she realized. She yearned to feel Fran's arms around her, to lean her head against Fran's shoulder, to know how safe it was with her.

She picked up Fran's book. "Why are you reading about sports medicine?"

"I work in a university. It's nearly September. The jocks are coming. Get dressed."

"I think I'll go like this." Shelby looked down at her jeans and sneakers. "Isn't this what all up-and-coming young career women wear to break their boyfriends' hearts?"

"No," Fran said firmly. "It is not. Now, git."

She didn't hear him drive up, or come through the main door. Fran answered his knock. He seemed surprised, his eyes narrowing slightly, his pupils contracting, the hint of a frown. "Well," he said over Fran's shoulder to Shelby, "what are you girls up to?"

Fran went back to her seat and book. ""I'm trying to learn how to think again."

"Army rots the brain, huh?" He lifted her coat from the hook on the back of the door and held it out for her to slip into.

"Serious gangrene," Fran said. "We may have to amputate."

Shelby shrugged her arms into the coat sleeves. She flipped her hair from beneath her collar and looked around for her purse.

Her mad money was safely tucked in its little hidden pocket. She'd never needed the two dollars and ten cents for a phone call and a taxi. But this could be the night. She felt shaky inside. Brittle.

"OK," she said to Fran. "We're off like a herd of pregnant turtles." She wanted to stay home. More than she'd ever wanted anything.

"I'll leave a light on when I go," Fran said. "Thanks for letting me use the TV. Have a nice night, you two."

As soon as they were in the hall, Ray pulled her to him. "Hello there, bride," he said, and kissed her.

She felt herself stiffen.

"What's up?" he asked.

"Nothing." She led the way down the hall. "Could we go to the Steak House tonight? They have booths, and we need to talk."

To be precise, she thought as he eased her into the car and closed the door,

I need to talk. Ray has absolutely no need to talk about this particular topic. She smiled over at him as he started the car. A little tremble-lipped. She hoped he didn't notice.

The Steak House smelled of cigarette smoke, beer, and cooking meat. Too cool to turn on the air conditioning, and too warm to light the massive gray fieldstone fireplace at the far end of the room. So the air just hovered, unvented. Oil lamps on each table, with red glass potbellies and red shades, cast a slightly satanic glow and added the heavy odor of burning kerosene to the atmosphere.

They slid into the red plastic-cushioned booth and Ray dove for the menu. "This was a great idea, hon. I could eat a musk ox."

The condemned man ate a hearty meal, she thought.

She decided to wait until after they'd ordered. Then she decided to wait until they were served. Or maybe it would be better to wait until they'd eaten a little before she ruined the night.

Finally, she ran out of excuses.

"Ray," she said, putting her fork down, "there's something we need to discuss. Seriously."

He scooped a forkfull of baked potato with sour cream into his mouth. "Mmmmm?"

Shelby took a sip of her gin and tonic and a deep breath. "You know how I've talked about...well, being unsure about the wedding?"

"Uh-huh." He abandoned the potato and tasted the salad, imploding bits of crisp lettuce between his teeth.

"Well, I'm afraid I haven't gotten any surer."

Chewing, he waved one hand in a gesture of dismissal. "S'OK. It'll pass."

"No, Ray, that's what I keep trying to tell you. It isn't passing. It won't pass. I really think I don't want to..."

He dropped his fork onto his plate and turned his attention to her with an impatient sigh. "Look, Shel, I understand how you feel. It's the wedding jits. But I've told you a dozen times it'll be all right. It's getting kind of stale. How about you let go of it?"

"I've tried to." She felt a little irritated herself. He wasn't making this any easier. But, on the other hand, she didn't deserve to have it be easier. "I think," she said evenly, "I want to call off the wedding."

For a second he went pale. "You what?"

"I think I want to call off the wedding."

He picked up the fork and knife and did injury to his slab of prime rib. Impaling, sawing, pushing, chewing, battering the meat, swallowing.

Then he laughed. "I've seen a lot of nervous Nellies, but you beat them all. Maybe I should get you some Miltown."

"I don't need Miltown," Shelby said tightly.

"It's the latest thing, y'know. More than half a doctor's practice these days is dealing with disgruntled housewives with low back pain. Miltown works."

"I don't want to *be* a disgruntled housewife. I don't want to be a housewife at all. I'm too young, I'm too old, I don't know what it is. All I really know is this wedding is looking more and more like a disaster."

"Well, hell," Ray said around the wad of beef in his mouth, "if you're worried about the new time frame, we'll just change it. How much extra time do you think you need?"

A bubble of frustration popped in her brain. "Extra time isn't what it's about. I want out."

He picked up a spoon and scraped around the inside of his potato. "Eat something," he suggested, glancing at her barely touched plate. "It'll make you feel better."

"I don't want to feel better, I want you to listen to me."

Ray put down his spoon deliberately and folded his hands over his meal. "OK, hon, I'm all ears."

"I don't think I want to get married. Not now, not at Easter, not next summer. Never."

He was thoughtful for a while. "Your friend's coming to visit, isn't it?"

"What?"

"Your monthly friend."

Shelby began to fume. "I am *not* premenstrual. This has nothing to do with menstruation."

Ray winced a little at the bluntness of her language. "Then explain to me what it is."

"It's…it's…" She fumbled for clarity. "I don't *know* what it is. All I know is, this marriage is a bad idea."

"Hey," Ray said, "you're really strung out, aren't you? Want to elope?"

"Ray, I don't want to do it at all. Any of it."

He only gazed at her, silent and worried.

"This is really upsetting for me," she went on. "I mean, I'm in so deep, and I don't know how to…" She caught herself as tears puddled into her eyes.

Ray leaned across the table and took her hand. "I hate seeing you like this, Shel. It hurts me, down deep."

Did he understand? A little? Was he willing to…

"So why don't you stop dwelling on it? Put it out of your mind. Someday you'll look back on this and laugh."

Some day, Shelby thought, I'll look back on this and scream.

The tiny flicker of hope that had winked to light, died. She felt tired. Exhausted. Tired in every cell and muscle in her body. Even her bones felt tired. "Tell me," she said quietly, "why doesn't anyone ever take me seriously?"

Ray seemed surprised. "Everyone takes you seriously. Where's all this coming from, baby?"

She found enough energy to be angry. "It's coming from the fact that you refuse to listen to me. I have deep, troubling doubts about us, Ray. And you seem to think it's no worse than drinking too much coffee."

His expression was puzzled. "I don't know what to do for you, doll. Want me to make an appointment with the doc who supervised my psychiatric quarter?"

She'd never felt so sad or helpless. "Let's just go," she said.

But he insisted on dessert. She didn't even try to keep up her end of the conversation. Ray rambled on about work. And about all the things they'd do after they were married and had all the time in the world.

He leaned back in his chair, wiped his mouth, and tossed his napkin onto the table beside his plate. "I think I know what the problem is."

Shelby looked at him.

"It's those women's magazines you read. I've seen the articles. If you're not neurotic when you start, you are by the time you're half way through."

"That's very interesting," Shelby said, cold inside.

"So stay away from them until after the wedding."

"I work for one." Her lips felt like untanned leather.

"Yeah, that is a problem. Well, stick to your fiction department."

"Fiction's risky, too, you know." She wondered if the sarcasm she felt had crept into her voice. "Some of those stories are pretty whiney."

"Don't take them seriously. It's just imagination."

Thank you, Ray. Whatever ambivalence I felt about our marriage is totally resolved.

Without speaking, she got up and went to get her coat.

He had paid the bill when she got back. She thought about adding her two dollars of mad money to the tip.

But he'd probably think they were sharing a moment. Like the thousands of moments they'd share when they were married and had all the time in the world.

She was out of the car before Ray could even work his way around to open her door. She managed to avoid giving him a kiss, and started up the path.

"Shel," he called softly.

She stopped, not turning to him.

"I'll send you some Miltown," he said. "Try it. You don't have anything to lose."

Fran had left a note. "*Twilight Zone* was great. Hope you're likewise."

She thought about going to Fran's apartment to report on the evening. But she was too tired and too disappointed. She decided to sit with it for tonight.

"How'd it go?" Fran asked over coffee.

"Great," Shelby said wryly. "Fine."

"He didn't get mad?"

"He didn't get the point. He didn't get what I was saying."

"What do you mean?"

"He didn't believe me. He insists on thinking it's all nerves, or some little idea I picked up from a magazine. He's sending me Miltown."

"Not enough to kill yourself with, I hope."

"I'm not interested in that any more."

"You're not?" Fran's eyes were hopeful.

"No. There have to be better ways of handling this mess." She grinned. "Ways that don't leave you feeling so God-awful in the morning."

"Good idea," Fran said. "Hey, do you want breakfast? Orange juice?" She got up and went to the refrigerator.

"Sure."

A stifling, end-of-August day. She wanted to play hooky from work and spirit Fran away to the beach.

"So what did happen?" Fran put the juice in front of her and turned to light the stove.

"Just what I said. Nothing. He really didn't take it seriously."

Fran glanced over at her hand. "You didn't give back the ring?"

Shelby shook her head.

"It's usually done, when a woman breaks up with a man. It helps them get the point."

She took off her engagement ring and looked at it. It hadn't even occurred to her last night. In fact, she hardly ever thought about the ring at all. She'd blocked out any awareness of it, like a wound that only hurts when you pay attention. "Maybe I'm still a little ambivalent."

"Of course you're ambivalent," Fran said as she put a plate of buttered toast in front of her. "The only real question is: what are the dimensions of your ambivalence?"

Shelby bit into a corner of toast. "Pretty big, but with a definite slant toward breaking it. I just don't know if I can handle the fall-out."

Fran placed some strips of bacon in a broiler pan and shoved them under the fire. She held up a carton of eggs. "Scrambled OK?"

"Fine. Anything."

"In the Army," Fran said as she broke several into a bowl and tossed in a splash of milk, "the only scrambled eggs we got were the powdered kind. I think I'll always consider real scrambled eggs a gift from God."

"How about omelets?"

"Heaven."

"Next time we have breakfast together," Shelby said as she got up to refill her coffee cup, "we'll do it at my place, and I'll make you an omelet beyond your wildest dreams."

"Really?"

"Really." She gave Fran's shoulder a squeeze as she went back to her chair. "Just because I don't want to marry Ray, that doesn't mean I'm going to give up all housewifely arts."

Fran was awfully quiet. The kind of quiet that felt as if she wasn't just thinking, but had left the room.

"Is something wrong?" Shelby asked.

Fran shook her head and took a deep breath. "No. Everything's fine."

"Come on, Fran. Let's not do this again, OK?"

"Yeah, you're right." She rested against the edge of the sink, staring at the floor. "Just give me a minute to put it into words."

Shelby waited. The bacon began to pop and spatter. She got up and pulled it out from under the broiler and turned the meat and pushed it back in. Leaning with Fran against the sink, she let their fingers touch. "Speak," she said.

"I want you to have what you want," Fran said slowly, "but some-times...the thought of you getting married...well, it's hard." She looked up at Shelby. "And you will get married, someday. The problem is, when I told you...about me...I was afraid it would turn you away. And when it didn't— I really never expected us to be friends, but we are. And the real miracle is, you're the best friend I ever had." She laughed a little, humorlessly. "It scares me, Shelby. When I think of not seeing you again—I know this sounds silly, but— it feels like something in me's dying."

Shelby wrapped her fingers around Fran's hand. "I feel the same way. As

233

you might recall if you look back on our fairly recent history."

She smelled bacon burning and grabbed a pot holder and pulled it out of the oven just in time. "Fran," she said, standing in front of the stove holding the smoldering pan of bacon, "it isn't happening. And it won't happen in the immediate future. So, please, let's not worry and just go with this."

Fran nodded, a little uncertainly.

"Are we going to have eggs?" Shelby asked. She tore a paper towel from the roller to drain the bacon. "Or should I make us disgusting, exotic bacon sandwiches?"

Fran went back to her cooking. "Hey, are you free to do something tonight?"

"Darn, I'm not. I promised to go to a movie with the work gang." She sipped her coffee and sat down. "I'd cancel, but they all have their noses out of joint."

Fran glanced at her. "Yeah?"

"I guess I can't really blame them. They're jealous of the amount of time I'm spending with you."

Spatula half way to the frying pan, Fran froze.

"What's wrong?" Shelby asked.

"You have to go with them tonight." Fran spoke urgently. "You have to see more of them. This can't happen."

"What can't happen?"

"Don't let them get jealous of the time we spend together."

"It's my time. I can spend it any way I like."

Fran spun around to face her. Her knuckles stood out white. "No. Not in this case. Look," she said seriously, "you're a trusting person, and I love that in you. But you have to understand, when we're dealing with this particular issue, there's no such thing as being too paranoid."

It was an old building, an opera house from the 1890s. Jenny Lind had sung there, or so the framed, browning newspaper articles in the lobby proclaimed. The carpet was a dark crimson, like blood, or rubies in dim light. Dark hardwood molding framed deep green flocked velvet-paneled walls. A white wicker pedestal stood by the center aisle door to the auditorium, topped with the early '60s version of the rubber tree plant, a plastic fern. New movies opened in the shiny chrome theater down the street. This one didn't sell popcorn, and specialized in films worthy of a second look.

She'd never seen *The Children's Hour*, or even read the play. She knew it was by Lillian Hellman, had caused quite a stir when it was released two years ago, and dealt with two school teachers whose lives were ruined when they were accused of sexual deviancy by a nasty school child. The play had been considered shocking in the '30s, and had been made into a movie called "We Three," which had very little to do with the original. This version starred Audrey Hepburn and the new actress Shirley MacLaine. A potentially interesting combination. At least, she thought as Penny came scampering toward them with their tickets, it wouldn't be boring.

For the first fifteen minutes she enjoyed it. She and Connie—her fellow boarding-school parolee—nudged each other in recognition of familiar sights.

Uniforms, fiddle-backed chairs, drinking glasses as thick and swollen as beer barrels. Lawn parties and agonizing student piano recitals. Kids sneaking dirty books.

Then, without being aware of it, she forgot where she was, caught up in the movie. Intrigued, and a little frightened. Something was going on, below the action on screen. A tension that reached out to her and pulled her in. She felt part of it, yet not part of it. She was absorbed and uncomfortable, and felt an odd knowing, like the first tentative roots of a new plant coming to life.

It kept getting worse, on the screen and inside her. Karen told Martha she was getting married, and Martha blew up. Shelby understood that. She could feel herself sinking deeper and deeper into quicksand. The looks that passed between them—such tenderness and fear on Martha's face, such blithe ignorance on Karen's. The climactic scene—when Martha admitted her love for Karen and was overwhelmed with shame and guilt, was one of the most painful moments she had ever sat through. When Martha went to her room Shelby knew what was going to happen, knew why, felt the dead-end, no-other-choice-ness of it. She clenched her teeth to keep from shouting out loud, "Don't do it. Please, don't do it." By the end, she was stunned. In shock. She didn't even know what had happened in the final minutes, after the suicide.

The lights came up. Shelby sat, mindless and frozen until Connie grabbed her by the elbow and said with a laugh, "Come on, Camden. They won't let you sleep here."

Afterward, they went across the street for sandwiches and ice cream. Shelby didn't want to, hated the idea of the lights and other people in the soda shop. She wanted to get away, go home, be alone, be in darkness.

But the postmortem was part of their routine. They settled down in a dark wood booth, leaned on the sticky table. The air was heavy with the odor of cream and coffee. The jukebox was too loud.

The rest ordered supper. Shelby wanted to throw up, because of the smell and the noise and the way the air seemed to pound in her ears, because of whatever was crawling around inside her. She settled on a dish of sherbet. She doubted she could eat even that.

Inevitably, they discussed it. Connie opened by declaring she thought Audrey Hepburn was gorgeous as Karen. Lisa was totally smitten with James Garner. Jean thought Shirley MacLaine had a lot of courage to play Martha. Penny remarked on the "interesting chemistry" between the two women. Shelby muttered something about "good casting."

"Terrific casting," Jean said, "until they went and ruined it with that child."

"Mary?" Connie asked.

Jean nodded. "She was terrible. She overacted, she mugged... I think she must have been the director's niece."

They all had a laugh about that.

When the food arrived, they got down to content.

It was Jean's opinion that Martha had always been "that way" but didn't really want to know it.

Lisa thought she really wasn't, but had gotten the idea somewhere and believed it.

Penny found the whole thing depressing.

Connie seemed to be watching Shelby to see what she thought.

Shelby didn't think anything. She could feel, though. She knew where her body touched the seat, the floor, the table. It was as if she were melting in those spots, coming apart into molecules, sinking into and between the other molecules of physical things. Electricity prowled her back and face and hands, just under the skin. The outside world, the conversation, took on an unreal quality. There but not there, like a half-attended-to television program.

She wanted again to go off by herself and relive parts of the movie over and over, until she had it—the something—figured out.

She was furious with Karen, but she wasn't sure why.

Jean, who had read the play, thought the movie ending was stronger than the play's. "In the play," she said, "Martha kills herself off-stage, with a gun. You don't get the same rising tension you do with the movie."

"I never knew you were such an *aficionado*," Lisa said.

Jean laughed. "I'm just opinionated."

"Well," said Lisa, "I don't know a lot about *movies* but I think Martha was disgraceful."

Shelby looked at her. "You do?"

"She ruined Karen's life," Lisa said.

"She loved her."

"That was really great love," Connie put in sarcastically. "One of the all-time great loves."

"How can being loved ruin your life?"

"If she really loved her," Lisa insisted, "she'd have gone away before anything happened."

"She didn't know about herself," Shelby said. Her voice surprised her. It sounded a little like whining.

"But she suspected," Connie put in. "Remember what she said in that confession scene? 'I've always known something was wrong...' She should have known enough to stay out of it."

"Then there wouldn't have been a movie," Jean pointed out reasonably.

"Is it really so awful," Shelby heard herself asking, "what or who she was? I mean, she seemed like a smart, caring person..."

"Rattlesnakes are attractive, too. In their own way." Connie said.

"It was only a movie," Jean pointed out.

"But based on a real story," Penny said. "It happened up in New Hampshire or somewhere."

"Well," Jean said, "anything can happen in New Hampshire. There are some pretty scary folks up there."

Penny just shrugged.

"Well, I think the whole thing was disgusting," Lisa said angrily. "It belongs in one of those porn houses where oily old men go alone in trench coats."

"Ooooo," Connie cooed, "sounds like something struck a nerve. Is there anything you'd like to tell us, Lisa?"

"Don't be ridiculous. You think I'm like *that*?" Lisa made a face.

"Are you?" Penny asked coyly.

"Oh, for God's sake."

"I don't think I'd recognize one of those people," Lisa huffed, "if I fell over it."

"Hey," Connie said to the group in general, "have any of you guys ever known someone like that?" She leaned toward Shelby. "Camden?"

"What?"

"Did you ever know anyone like that?"

"Like what?"

"Queer," Connie said, and they all waited.

"I think so," Shelby forced herself to say. "One woman. Back in college. But I didn't know it at the time."

"When'd you find out?" Penny asked.

"I didn't, really. It just seems that way now."

"What was she like?" Lisa asked eagerly.

"She was a very nice person. I liked her."

"Uh-oh," Lisa sang. "Birds of a feather, you know."

She wanted to get up and storm out. She knew it was the worst thing she could possibly do.

"I knew a queer woman once," Penny said. "In France, of course, where else?"

All attention was turned toward her.

"It was at some party at the embassy. She was at least ten years older than me, and dressed in men's clothes and smoked a cigar, and kept looking at me over the top of her martini."

Lisa shivered. "What happened?"

"When my folks saw what was going on, they took me home. I was livid. It was a nice party until that woman ruined it for everyone."

"My God," Lisa said, "that is *just* disgusting."

Suddenly everything seemed to be speeding up. Something was pressing her, burning. She didn't know what it was, but knew she had to leave, leave immediately.

The others were still talking. She couldn't even hear them. "Get out of here," said a voice in her head. "Get out now. RIGHT NOW!"

She jumped to her feet, nearly knocking over her water glass. "I'm sorry," she said, her voice carrying her along. "I have to go. It's been swell." She pulled two dollars from her wallet and tossed it on the table. The others looked at her with blank, dull expressions. "This should cover mine, and the tip. If not, tell me tomorrow and I'll pay you back."

Turning before they could answer, she ran.

The phone was ringing when she walked through her apartment door. One of her friends, no doubt. Or Ray. Or her mother. She couldn't deal with that tonight. Couldn't deal with anything tonight. Tonight she just wanted to get out of these damned starchy, scratchy clothes. Her feet were damp and clammy inside her leather pumps. She kicked off her shoes and stripped away the nylon stockings. Fresh air poured over her feet and legs like balm. She peeled off her dress and half-slip and bra and garter belt. God, so many clothes. Every piece uncomfortable, stiff or tight and leaving a mark where it had dug into her. She stood in the middle of the room in only her underpants, raised her fist, and shouted in fine Scarlett O'Hara fashion, "With God as my witness, I'll never be uncomfortable again."

No full set of clean pajamas. One bottom, no top. Plenty of nightgowns, though. Filmy, lacy Libby-approved nightgowns. She was damned if she'd wear one of them. She grabbed the bottoms and an old sprung tee-shirt, and got herself ready for bed.

The phone was ringing again. She waited until it stopped, then took the receiver off the hook. No talking to anyone tonight, not even Fran. Just get into bed, turn out the lights, and wait for whatever's churning inside to surface.

She reran the movie in her head, in the darkness and safety of her bed. When she got to the break-down scene, she started to cry.

It was early, an hour before the alarm was set to go off. Still black beyond the windows. Dusk came earlier and earlier now, dawn later and later. Days dwindling down to a precious few, she thought. Dwindle, dwindle, dwindle.

It was clear she wasn't going back to sleep, so she might as well make herself useful.

She made a cup of coffee and settled, still in her pajama bottoms and tee-shirt, at the kitchen table to draw up a list. "Unpleasant Things I Have To Do."

Ray.

Family reunion.

Libby.

Cancel wedding.

Tell friends.

She frowned at the list. It was a garden of earthly horrors. She was glad she'd awakened early. Hate to miss one golden moment of a day like this, no indeed. All right, prioritize. Ray first, that went without saying. Good manners demanded it. Family picnic. She could opt out of that, no excuses given; it would all be clear later.

Libby. Oh, God, Libby. Jesus, Mary, and Joseph and all the Saints in Heaven, as her Junior year roommate used to say. Libby, Libby, Libby. Hey, Libby, you old can of peas, guess what? I'm going to bring your world smashing down around you.

Libby wouldn't kill her. That'd be too easy. Libby'd launch a campaign to fix her, to harass her until she felt like a cigarette ash on the carpet. It gave her a sick, lost feeling. She wanted to tear up her list and make everything go back to normal.

And get married and ruin her life, and Ray's life, because she was afraid of her mother?

You are twenty-five years old, she told herself firmly. You have a job, a career, even. You've been on your own for years. Surely you have the right to the life you want.

"I also have the right to be afraid of my mother," she muttered out loud. "I've earned it."

Let's get the worst of it over with before I'm fully awake and lose my momentum and false courage.

She found a padded envelope and a matchbox and some cotton, and couldn't remember where she'd left her engagement ring. Usually, she wore it to bed. That was what you were supposed to do, wasn't it? When you were madly in love?

She came across it on the edge of the bathroom sink, scene of previous acts of desperation. She'd replaced the mirror right away, before anyone could see it and ask questions. But there were still deep gouges in the linoleum where the glass had flown and she'd crushed it into the floor. A chip of porcelain was missing from the sink.

That was months ago, she reminded herself. You have other issues now. She picked up the ring and went back to the kitchen.

It seemed like a tacky way to do it. But she didn't have time to try to get him to take her seriously. She couldn't do any more pleading to be understood. If he wanted to talk after this, she'd talk. Right now all that mattered was putting an end to it.

She scribbled a note. "Dear Ray, I'm sorry to have to do this, especially this way. But our marriage definitely wouldn't work for me, and ultimately it wouldn't work for you, either. I hate to hurt you. And I hate doing it this way, but there's a real urgency about this. I don't want to drag it out, and only get in deeper into the wedding. You're a wonderful man, the best I've ever met. If you need to talk, just let me know. I'd be more than happy."

She wondered if she should sign it, "I love you." Or, "All my love." Or something like that. She decided just to sign her name.

The envelope was sealed, addressed, and ready to go.

Next, Libby.

Her mother wouldn't be up by this time, but she could leave a message with the maid. The Rubicon had to be crossed, and it had to be crossed right now.

As she'd expected, Edith answered the phone on the fourth ring.

"Hi, Edith," Shelby said. "It's Shelby. Is my mother up yet?"

"No, she's not," the maid said, keeping her voice low even though there were probably five rooms and a flight of stairs between her and the sleeping Libby. "Would you like me to wake her?"

God, no. We're taking the coward's way out here. "It's not necessary. Just tell her something's happened and I won't be able to make the Labor Day picnic. No big deal."

No big deal. That almost made her laugh out loud. It was going to be a huge deal. Not just because it Wasn't Done, but because Shelby legitimized Libby's non-Camden presence at the Camden reunion.

Knowing Libby, she'd probably go anyway, at least this time. As for the future…

It was finally time to get ready for work. No appointments today. She threw on a skirt and blouse, no stockings, and loafers. It'd have to do.

She dashed off a note to leave in Fran's mailbox. "Can we get together tonight? The compost has hit the air conditioning. S."

If she got out of here fast, and the traffic wasn't bad, she could get to the post office before she went to work.

I might be able to handle this, she thought.

Chapter 18

She'd have bet money Libby wouldn't wait until after work to call her, and she was right. The ring was in the mail, properly insured and certified, and she had managed to get to her office without anyone noticing the untanned mark on her finger. Charlotte was there, but engrossed in proofing copy for her article on the amazing comeback of the pillbox hat since Jackie Kennedy had taken to wearing one.

Shelby nodded a "good morning," and hung her coat on the rack. Charlotte glanced up. "You look in fine fettle today, Miss Camden."

"I guess I am," Shelby said. "I don't know why, though."

Her desk phone rang. She agonized through three rings, then picked up the receiver. "Shelby Camden," she said.

"This is your mother."

She glanced at her watch. Only nine o'clock. Libby must be calling between her first and second cups of coffee.

"I've just heard some very upsetting news from Edith," Libby said. "I hope you can tell me it's a mistake."

"I won't know until you tell me what it is." Her stomach turned over.

"You're not coming to the family reunion."

"That's right."

"Just like that. No discussion, no 'by your leave,' nothing."

"That's right."

"And may I ask you what on God's green earth you think you're doing?"

She wrapped the phone cord around her hand. "Not coming to the re-union."

"Have you gone stark, raving mad?"

She noticed Charlotte watching her with an inquisitive look. Placing her hand over the mouthpiece, she mouthed "mother."

Charlotte rolled her eyes and nodded and gestured toward the door in an offer to leave the room.

Shelby shook her head.

"I'm perfectly sane. I'm just not coming to the reunion. Is it against the law?"

"Don't get sarcastic with me. I assume you have an excuse?"

If she'd ever wanted to lie, now was the time. But she wouldn't. Starting today, she was through being Libby's doormat, and Libby could like it or lump it. "No excuse. Personal reasons."

There was a brief, shocked silence on the other end. "Something very strange and disturbing is happening to you," her mother said. "And I don't like it."

Shelby couldn't think of anything to say.

"Are you listening?"

"I'm here."

"I want an explanation for your behavior, and I want it right now."

She settled on the edge of her desk. "I don't have an explanation. I'm passing up one Labor Day picnic in twenty-five years. Say 'hi' to everyone for me."

Libby hung up.

Shelby shook her head and muttered, "I'm in for it."

"Mothers," Charlotte grunted in agreement.

Shelby had forgotten the older woman was there. "She talks funny, kind of stiff and antiquated," she said irrelevantly. "Like the way people write, but not the way they talk."

Charlotte plopped her eye glasses on top of her head and scrutinized her. "There's definitely something different about you today."

She was tempted to brush it off, but the thought of talking to someone, anyone, was too appealing. Charlotte wouldn't tell, not in the next twenty-four hours, and that was all she needed. "I just broke my engagement," she said, and waited for Charlotte's gasp of dismay.

"Seems to have done wonders for you," Charlotte said.

"I guess it has. To be perfectly honest, though, I feel a little reckless."

"Good for you."

"I just did it. On my way to work. I don't want a whole bunch of people finding out before Ray does. Could you keep it a secret for the next day or so?"

"Have you ever known me to gossip?"

Shelby shook her head.

"So." Charlotte crossed her arms over her chest. "Your young man doesn't know?"

"I tried to tell him, but he just can't hear it. So this morning I sent the ring back."

"Did you insure it?"

"I insured it."

"Well," said Charlotte, "I'm glad you finally saw the light. You've been moping around here ever since you announced your engagement."

"I have?"

"Your business is your business. But I just kept thinking, 'That girl doesn't want to get married.'"

Shelby sat in her desk chair. "You did?"

"It wasn't that obvious to everyone," Charlotte poked her pencil into her bun. "But I'm an expert on not wanting to get married, did so three times before I wised up enough to listen to that little voice inside."

"I know that voice."

"Never doubt your doubts," Charlotte said. "They're the only truth you can count on."

What a strange conversation. She wasn't sure where it had come from or what to do with it. In their months of sharing an office, they'd seldom spoken personally.

"Get to your business there." Charlotte's voice was surprisingly gentle, given the work years of cigarettes and whiskey had done on her vocal cords. She cleared her throat. "And by the way, when things get rough—and, believe me, they will—remember I'm behind you all the way." She turned to her proofreading with a finality that made it clear they were through talking for the morning.

That scared her a little. Because Charlotte had been there, and obviously knew things Shelby didn't. But she couldn't see what the problem would be, beyond her immediate family. She wasn't the first woman in history to break an engagement.

She got home late, reluctantly, exhausted from playing the "old Shelby" in public. One more day. Hang in for one more day.

There was a note from Fran under her door. "What do you mean, the manure's hitting the air conditioning? Come to my place immediately!"

She did.

"Congratulate me," she said when Fran opened the door. "I'm a free woman."

Fran went pale. "You broke the engagement?"

"I did." She held out her left hand. "See? No more ring in this bull's nose."

"I don't believe it."

"I mailed it to him. Insured and certified."

"Something's wrong with you," Fran said, standing aside and pulling her into the apartment. "What's happened?"

Shelby threw herself on the couch and stretched. "I decided to get it over with. I feel great." She laughed. "I'm going to feel lousy tomorrow, but tonight I feel great."

"What happened?" Fran repeated.

"We went to a movie, the gang and I. The way I told you we were. We went out for something to eat. I came home and went to bed, and this morning I woke up knowing what I had to do so I did it."

"What was the movie?"

"*The Children's Hour.*"

Fran dropped into the chair across from her, beneath the pole lamp. "Oh, shit," she said.

"Have you seen it? It came out last year."

"Of *course* I've seen it. About seventy-five times. Why did *you* see it?"

Shelby shrugged. "I don't know. They'd all decided by the time I got there."

"I knew this was going to happen." Fran covered her face with her hands. "This is trouble, Shelby. Really, really trouble. And then you went and broke your engagement."

"You knew I wanted out of the marriage. It was even your idea to return the ring."

"Your timing leaves something to be desired."

She was confused and a little hurt. "I thought you'd be glad for me."

Fran looked directly at her. "They were giving you a warning."

"Fran..."

"To stay away from me." She leaned toward Shelby earnestly. "That's what

242

the movie was about."

"It was a *nice* movie. I liked it. The people were good people, most of them…"

"It wasn't nice." Fran was nearly shouting. "It was about two perfectly decent women, only one of them turns out to be in love with the other and it ruins their lives."

"But there was nothing about Martha to dislike."

"She *killed* herself! Get it? She had to die because of what she was!"

Shelby stood up and went toward the kitchen. "You're overwrought. I'm getting you a beer."

"Probably a good idea," Fran said. Her voice was shaky. "I kept seeing the movie," she called after her, "because they *were* decent people, and I don't get to see or read about many people like…lesbians who are decent people."

Shelby pulled two beers from the refrigerator, then spent three long, frustrating minutes looking for the bottle opener. She found it and popped the caps.

Fran hadn't moved from her chair, and was staring off into space. Shelby handed her the beer, then sat on the coffee table to be closer to her. "Fran," she said softly, "start at the beginning and tell me what you think is happening."

"They're upset with our friendship. The whole going-to-the-movies idea came about because they felt neglected. But there was nothing accidental in their choice. There are plenty of other movies around. I think they know what I am." She paused and took a swallow of beer. "It scares me. Not for me. They can't take me anywhere I haven't already been. But they can hurt you. I don't like what I see coming."

Shelby waited.

"They'll accuse you of being like me. You can deny it, but the rumors won't stop until we stop spending time together. I'll probably have to move out, or you will. Then they'll pressure you to make up with Ray, or find some other guy for you to marry." She drank again. "And that doesn't begin to spell out the horrors when Libby gets her manicured talons into you."

"And if I pretend I don't know what the hell they're talking about?"

"They won't buy that. There goes your job, and your friends. Our landlord will have grounds for eviction." She gave Shelby a wry smile. "We're not a very popular group of people."

Shelby rested the back of her hand against Fran's face. "That's a crazy idea."

"The world's a crazy place." Tears had seeped up in her eyes. She knuckled them away roughly. "Welcome to the true underbelly of life."

"It's not a pretty place."

"That's right." Fran got up and walked to the fireplace. "That's why I don't want it creeping into your world." She turned, looked at Shelby. "I thought I could keep you out of it." She laughed. It was a hard, sharp laugh. Like a slap. "And I accuse *you* of being naive." She started for the kitchen.

Shelby grabbed her as she passed. "I don't *want* you to keep me out of your world. I don't want you to protect me. I don't *care* about this other stuff. What happens, happens. I just want you to be my friend. I just want…" She hesitated. "…to love you."

Fran closed her eyes. The room was very still. Someone was running water in an apartment upstairs. It sounded far away.

Shelby let go of Fran's sleeve. "We have to stop this. I need you. But I can't have you feeling guilty every time something happens to me. I know it's upsetting. I understand, really I do. But for you to take everything on yourself, just because…it's like that movie. Martha didn't mean any harm, and you don't mean any harm. You are who you are. And who you are is my friend, someone I care about more than I've ever cared…"

"Don't," Fran said, pulling away. She went to the window. The night was still and heavy. "You're right," she said after a while. "I have to stop feeling sorry for myself." She wiped away tears with the heels of her hands.

I love this woman, Shelby thought as a wave of warm feeling broke over her. "OK," she said. She retrieved Fran's beer and handed it to her. "You haven't heard all of it."

Fran sat on the couch and stared at her fearfully. "What next?"

"I told Libby I wasn't going to the Labor Day picnic."

Fran was silent for a long time. Then she looked at her with those blue, blue eyes. "I have a suggestion."

"Great. What is it?"

"Arm yourself," Fran said.

Shelby laughed. "I thought you were an authority on these horrors, and the best you can come up with is 'Arm yourself'?"

"There has to be a better solution." Fran squeezed her eyebrows together and stared at the floor and thought.

"I have an idea," Shelby said. "Tomorrow I'll have a talk with Jean. See if she can shed light on what's really going on."

"Think she'll tell you the truth?"

"No one else will. Jean doesn't say much, but it's clear she's on my side." She put down her beer. "Listen, I'm jumping out of my skin. I keep waiting for the phone to ring. Want to get some dinner out?"

"Great." Fran got up. "Let me 'girl' myself up a little."

She was wearing Shelby's favorite Fran outfit. Blue jeans, an old Army shirt, and sneakers without socks. "Do you really have to?"

"Yes, I really have to."

Shelby sighed deeply.

While Fran was changing, she finished her beer and thought about how terrified she was, deep down inside. As long as she kept it away, it was fine. But it was still there, gnawing at her like fire ants. It made her feel dizzy, and a little sick. She reminded herself that she didn't have to go through it alone. But, ultimately, she did. She had to deal with Ray. She had to deal with her mother, and her friends, and probably the whole damn Camden clan. Nobody'd do it for her. Nobody *could* do it for her. She didn't want anyone to do it for her.

She wished today could be the middle of next week. At least she'd know…

"You look positively stricken," Fran said. She had changed into a wheat colored dress and loafers. Her suntan was like soft bronze.

"You look great."

"Thank you. What's up?"

"Same old stuff. I want to curl up in a ball and hide under the sofa."

"Yeah." Fran held out her hand.

Shelby took it. "Libby's capable of anything. She could call, or show up in the middle of the night. To trap me."

"Spend tonight here, then. Might as well have one good night's sleep."

She wanted Fran's company tonight. She had the feeling it was going to be a long time before she slept deeply again.

* * *

The park bench smelled of old wood and paint. It was one of those late summer days when nothing seems to fit together. The sun was golden, the shadows slanted. Weeds had gone hard. Leaves were turning leathery. The grass had become coarse. And yet the heat and humidity were stifling.

Shelby kicked off her shoes and felt the warm earth beneath her feet. She offered Jean her sandwich. She didn't feel like eating. Jean refused, and offered to share her lunch in return. It was made of limp, yarn-like things in green and eggshell white, covered with a brown liquid. Shelby was positive she saw it move.

"Thanks," she said, "but I'm really not hungry."

Jean looked at her with a sly smile that let her know Jean knew exactly why she'd turned it down. Disgusting her lunch partners had become Jean's signature.

She tried to think of how to open the conversation.

"So," Jean said, "spit it out."

"Am I paranoid, or is something going on with you guys?"

Jean twirled some of the cooked yarn around a plastic fork. "Not with me. But, yeah, the rest of them are kind of bent out of shape."

"Why?"

"Feeling rejected. At least that's how it started. I think it's turning into something else."

"What else?"

Jean put her lunch down and folded her hands and studied her knuckles. Shelby waited.

A squirrel came up to them, begging. Shelby tossed it a piece of crust. "That movie was planned, wasn't it?" she asked.

Jean nodded. "Connie'd seen it before. She knew what it was about. She wanted to see how you'd react." Jean looked up at her. "She thinks Fran is...you know...like Martha."

"A lesbian."

"Yeah. And she thinks she's trying to take you away from us, and sooner or later she'll come between you and Ray."

Shelby had a sinking feeling deep in her stomach and ran a hand through her hair in dismay.

"Is she? A lesbian?"

That was a hard one to answer. It wasn't hers to confirm or deny. If she confirmed it, she was taking that choice out of Fran's hands. That wasn't right. If she denied it, it was like agreeing with everyone that it was a terrible thing to be. Which would be not only disloyal but dishonest.

"I can't answer that," she settled on. "You'll have to ask her. Would it matter to you?"

245

"Only if it messed things up for you."

She took a deep breath. "Jean, I have to tell you something, and please believe me it has nothing to do with what we were talking about."

Jean watched her expectantly.

Jump in, she told herself, and jumped. "Yesterday, I broke my engagement to Ray. You know I've been having my doubts," she went on quickly. "And the headaches, and not sleeping, I think they were all part of it. I just realized it wasn't what I wanted. It wasn't right. Not at this time in my life."

Jean only nodded.

"I've tried to talk to him about my doubts, the things I'm afraid will happen to me, but he won't take me seriously."

"That's Ray, all right."

"So a couple of nights ago we went to dinner and I found myself going through it all again, begging him to understand. But he didn't. He didn't get it. He didn't believe me. Yesterday morning I sent his ring back."

Jean was silent for a moment. "Well," she said at last.

"That's all you have to say?"

"I hope you remembered to insure it."

She grinned. "Yes, I insured it."

"Not to upset you unnecessarily," Jean said, "but this is going to be a real monstrosity."

"My sentiments exactly." She wondered if Jean was saying what she honestly thought. It mattered. A lot. "Do you think I'm wrong to do this?"

Jean laughed. "Wrong? Of course not. What would be wrong would be marrying him when you don't love him."

"You really think so?"

"Absolutely." She capped her plastic box and opened a waxed paper bag of fried noodles. She passed them to Shelby. "But there'll be fallout."

Shelby crunched on a noodle. "I don't doubt that at all, but I can't imagine what kind."

Jean tossed a noodle to a squirrel. It sniffed at it suspiciously, then grabbed it and raced off.

"OK, what I'm really worried about," Shelby said, "is that they'll find some connection between that and my friendship with Fran."

"Over my dead body," Jean said. "Maybe you should lay low at my place until it all blows over and people get their heads straightened around."

She felt a tremendous rush of relief. "Thanks, but that'd probably make it worse."

Jean touched her hand. "You must be scared."

"I feel as if I'm frozen in the middle of the railroad tracks, and I don't know when the train'll come along."

"There's one thing you can count on. It will."

I might get through it, Shelby thought, with friends like this. "There's more. I cancelled out of the Labor Day picnic."

"Oh, my GOD!" Jean pulled at handfuls of her hair in mock horror. "The sky is falling! The end of the world is at hand!"

Shelby found herself laughing. Really and genuinely laughing. "Thanks, Jean. For everything."

Jean shrugged it off. "I'll keep my ear to the ground for gossip." She placed a hand on Shelby's shoulder. "And I expect you to let me know what you need. Anything. Someone to talk to, tickets out of town, phony passport." Her voice turned serious. "I mean it, Shelby. Anything, whatever you need. And I won't let the gleesome threesome bad-mouth you around the office. Promise you'll let me help."

"I promise." Shelby said gratefully. "I really, really promise."

OK, she thought back at the office. Jean, Charlotte, Fran, and me. A formidable bunch. Bring on the enemy.

The people she'd thought were her friends six months ago had become 'the enemy.' That was sad. It made her feel as if she'd lost something, not just her friends, but a piece of her soul.

Time to grow up.

Growing up meant giving up. Illusions, hopes, that glow that assured her everything would work out in the end. As soon as she found the right key to fit the right door.

Well, the doors were opening now, and the view wasn't pretty.

She glanced down at her desk, at the story she'd been editing. She hardly recognized it, even though she'd been working on it all morning. Her editorial comments barely made sense to her, and wouldn't make any at all to anyone else.

Now it was interfering with her work. This really had to stop. This would be a long weekend. She promised herself she'd start to see the light at the end of the tunnel before Tuesday.

Nobody phoned her in the afternoon. Ray would certainly have her letter by now, and it wasn't like Libby to leave a stone unthrown. She ought to be glad for the peace and quiet. It only made her nervous.

They'd probably get her tonight, as soon as she got home.

She called Fran at work, asked her to meet her at the diner for dinner, to postpone the inevitable.

Fran said she'd made a vocation out of postponing the inevitable.

After dinner she cruised slowly down her block, searching for familiar cars. It seemed clear. She pulled around into the alley, where their parking area was. Fran's apartment was dark. She was running an errand, grabbing them breakfast makings before the A&P closed.

Her own lights were out, of course. She crossed the lawn and let herself in the back door. The odor of cigarette smoke hung in the air. Some of the neighbors must have spent the evening enjoying the last of summer. She unlocked the door and stepped inside.

The cigarette smell was even heavier here. Halfway across the kitchen she realized it wasn't just cigarette smoke, it was Libby's cigarette smoke.

There was a light under the door between the kitchen and living room. She pushed it open.

"Well, it's about time," Libby said. She'd made herself at home. Shelby's mail was stacked neatly on the coffee table, the couch pillows had been plumped and rearranged. The bit of cold ash that she liked on the hearth had been swept into the fireplace.

Libby the Invader had made herself a Manhattan.

"Enjoying yourself?" Shelby asked sarcastically. She was angry, more angry than afraid.

"Not much," Libby said. "Where have you been?"

"More to the point, what are you doing here, how'd you get in, and what do you want?"

"I've been waiting for over an hour, since you're concerned enough to ask. The landlord let me in. And we need to talk."

Shelby went over and pulled up the blinds her mother had drawn. Very clever. There was no way Shelby would have seen her from the street. She had the element of surprise in her favor. Fresh air poured in.

"Where's your car?"

"A few blocks over. It was such a lovely night to walk." Libby stubbed out her cigarette. "And what were you up to?"

"Dinner out." She picked up the mail and sorted through it. Her heart was pounding like a snare drum.

"With whom?"

She felt stubbornness dig in its heels. "A friend."

"Anyone I know?"

"I doubt it."

"Well, that's a relief. I was sure you'd be out with that *woman*." She flapped her hand in the general direction of Fran's door.

"What's your agenda?" Shelby heard herself say. "I'm sure you have one." She glanced at her mother. "You always have one."

"Yes, tonight I do, as you so sweetly point out." She languished back in her chair and lit another cigarette and drew in her breath with a windy sucking sound. "Ray called me today." She waited for Shelby's response.

"How is he?" Shelby asked after a while.

"Wretched, as you might imagine. He received your package this morning."

"Good. I can throw away the insurance receipt."

"My, my," Libby said. "Aren't you the cold one?"

"If he talked to you," she said evenly, "then you know what I did. And why. I explained it very clearly in my letter, which I'm certain he read to you."

"He did. It was a very uncaring letter."

"At least it seems to have gotten his attention."

Her mother smiled in a nasty, "gotcha" way. "So that's what it's all about. Attention."

"No, I don't need more attention from Ray, I need less." She knew she was being provocative, and it was dangerous. But she didn't care. She enjoyed it. It made her feel powerful. She wanted to be downright nasty. "I really don't think we have anything to discuss."

Libby lit yet another cigarette, this time from the stub of the last one. "I don't think I remember you ever having a mean streak before."

"I get it from you," Shelby said.

"It's quite unattractive."

"Yeah, I noticed that."

Libby emptied her drink glass and cracked a piece of ice between her teeth.

Shelby had never seen her mother do anything like that before. It fascinated her.

"I've come to a decision," Libby said. "After talking it over with Ray."

"Have you? I'm so glad you two are collaborating. But you have all along, haven't you?"

Her mother ignored her. "You'll come home with me. Tonight. On Monday you will go with me to the Camden reunion. On Tuesday you will see a psychiatrist. We already have an appointment."

"We? Whoever 'we' are can certainly keep it."

Libby screwed her lips together in a grimace of disapproval. It made her look as if she were sucking a lemon. "*We* have every intention of keeping it. And that includes you."

"No, thanks," Shelby said.

"Excuse me?"

"I said 'no thanks.'"

"This is not an *invitation.*"

Shelby folded her arms and looked at her mother until Libby looked away. She felt as if she'd just won the Nobel Prize.

"And most of all…," Libby said, the cigarette dangling from the corner of her mouth now.

She's reverting to type, Shelby thought.

"…you will have nothing more to do with that woman. Ever. Do you understand?"

"No, I don't."

"That *creature* across the hall."

Her anger was building like steam in a pressure cooker. "Her name, in case you're interested, is Fran Jarvis."

"Ever since she arrived on the scene there's been nothing but trouble. She's bad for you, and bad for everyone around you."

Vapor hissed out through the seal. The pressure valve rattled. "This is none of your business."

"It certainly is. You're on the verge of making a disaster of your life. Your choice of friendships has deteriorated far beyond the acceptable…"

Shelby felt herself explode. "You stay out of my life, and away from my friendships, *Mother.* I'm twenty-five years old, which seems to be lost on you. I'll choose my friends, and when and how I see them."

"You have no idea what you're doing," Libby said, her voice rising shrilly. "You haven't been yourself since that woman. It's not healthy."

"She's my friend," Shelby shouted back. "She's going to go on being my friend. As far as healthy goes, she's a damn sight less toxic than you."

In the silence she realized how loudly she'd been yelling. Loud enough to wake the whole apartment house, and probably half the citizens of Bass Falls.

Libby's nostrils dilated. She let smoke drift from her mouth and drew it in through her nose. "You're asking for trouble, Shelby."

"I don't give a damn. I'm sick of people sneaking around with their snotty, fastidious attitudes."

"So now I'm snotty and fastidious," Libby snorted.

"You're a bunch of humorless, self-righteous prigs. All the Camdens. And all the in-laws. And my former fiancé and some of my so-called friends."

"Is that so?" Libby asked sarcastically.

"All my life I've tried to do the things you want. It's never good enough. I can't even take out the garbage without you criticizing the way I do it." She knew she was shrieking, but couldn't stop. "I want my own life, Libby. Not some dream world you've created where the flowers match your clothing and you can't take a leak without having a party at the Country Club to celebrate it."

"I know the kind of life you want. Down in the mud in your filthy clothes with that twisted, perverted…"

The door slammed open and Fran strode in. "If you have something to say to me, Mrs. Camden," she said, "have the decency to say it to my face."

Libby turned on her. "I hardly think 'decency' is something you're an authority on."

"Go on. Say it to her," Shelby shouted at her mother. "Say the word. Or do you want me to say it for you?"

"It's an ugly word, and I won't soil my lips with it."

"Shelby," Fran said, "you don't have to fight my battles."

"The word is 'lesbian'." Shelby said. "Three syllables. Begins with an 'l' and ends with an 'n'. Dictionary definition, a resident of the island of Lesbos. A female homosexual. Synonyms: queer, bulldyke…"

"Stop, Shelby," Fran said.

Libby smiled maliciously. "That's right, you tell her. She'll do whatever *you* say." She took a puff on her cigarette and blew smoke in Fran's direction as she talked. "It's the end of your reign, Miss Queen Bee. I know what you are and I know what you people are up to. So just stay out of my way and away from my daughter if you know what's good for you."

"Leave her alone, Libby," Shelby warned. She moved closer to Fran.

"I've met a lot of people in my life, Mrs. Camden," Fran said. "But I've never before met anyone as rude as you."

"It's charming," Libby said to Shelby, "the way she comes rushing to your side like a knight in shining armor. But I think you'd do well to rein in your pit bull."

She suddenly felt very calm and clear, direct. She knew what she wanted to do. It was right. She knew it was right. "I think *you'd* better clean up your mouth. Or maybe I'll change my mind about the reunion, after all. Don't you think…" She slipped her hand around Fran's. "…the whole clan would be interested in meeting the woman I love?"

Libby stared at her. Beneath her heavy make-up, her lips were nearly purple. "Are you saying what I think you're saying?"

"You got it." Shelby felt herself grinning. She wanted to jump up and touch the ceiling. Her head and chest were filled with helium. "And as far as Ray's concerned, I really don't think he'd be interested in joining a threesome."

She could feel Fran's hand trembling in hers. Her skin was stiff and clammy.

"Leave now. Go do whatever you do with bad news." She started to turn away.

Libby pulled herself up to her full height, all five feet four inches of her. Shelby hadn't realized her mother was so short. "You can't begin to imagine," Libby muttered as she gathered up her things.

"Take your butts with you." She indicated the ash tray.

Ignoring her, Libby went to the door. "You're going to regret it, Shelby. I suggest you reassess your position." She glanced at Fran and deliberately turned her head away.

"Have a nice evening," Fran said politely.

"You make me sick," Libby said, and marched out.

"Go to hell," Shelby called after her pleasantly, loud enough for her to hear. The front door slammed.

Fran and Shelby looked at each other, realization creeping in. "My God," Shelby said, "what have we done?"

"Sunk the Titanic, I'm afraid."

Shelby dropped onto the couch, exhilarated and terrified. "It was worth it. I think."

Fran opened all the windows as high as they'd go. "Your mother's cigarette smoke is bad enough, but add it to her perfume…Should I make us a drink?"

"Yes, please. I don't care what. Just throw anything over ice."

Beyond the fear she could feel something changing inside her. Shifting with a kind of silky, rustling sound. Like a pile of wheat kernels beginning to slide.

She nibbled off a hangnail and was surprised at herself. This wasn't something she ever, ever did. Probably the first signs of a nervous break down. Nail biting. It could only lead to kleptomania, hallucinations, and taking off her clothes in the middle of the A&P. Or the Bass Falls Inn, the two-hundred-year-old Colonial tourist attraction at the side of the town common. A lot classier than the A&P.

She heard herself giggle.

"What's so funny?" Fran asked. She handed Shelby a scotch.

"Nothing. I think I'm cracking up."

"In that case hang on a few minutes more." Fran sat down beside her with a bourbon and water. "We have to figure out what to do with this."

Shelby took a long swallow of her drink. The warmth from the alcohol began spreading through her stomach. Only a few more minutes and she'd relax. She willed it to hurry.

"OK," Fran said, "here's what I've come up with so far." Her face was very smooth and calm. "First, you need to back off from what you said to Libby about me. It's not true, you were angry, and you only wanted to upset her. She'll believe that."

"I won't do it."

"That's the easy part. As far as the rest of it goes, I don't see how you can yield without risking what you need to do."

"I won't do it," Shelby repeated.

Fran looked at her. "Won't do what?"

"Take back what I said. About the way I feel about you."

"You're out of your mind."

Shelby leaned forward. "I think it might be true."

Fran stared at her as if she'd just announced the Second Coming. "All right," she said in a placating way. "You care about me. But there are a lot of definitions for 'love.' You don't want people getting the wrong idea."

"Remember when we went camping and I said that thing about not feeling about Ray the way I felt about you?"

Fran nodded. "It shook you up at the time."

"Because it was my first realization that I didn't want to marry Ray. But it's not just Ray. I don't want to get married…"

"That's fine," Fran said. "You don't have to get married."

"…until I find someone I feel about the way I feel about *you*. Don't you understand? About *you*."

Stone-faced, Fran stared off into space and twirled the drink in her hand. The ice cubes made sleigh-bell sounds against the glass.

Shelby didn't know what she expected Fran to feel. Glad? She hoped she'd be glad, but she really didn't expect it. Frightened? That would make sense. Guilty? That would be Fran-like.

"Hey," she said at last, "what's going through your mind?"

"Even if what you say turns out to be true," Fran said softly, "you'd better deny it."

She was deeply disappointed. "I thought you'd be glad, at least, considering…"

Fran seemed to shrink into the couch. She was curled in on herself, her face pale. "I am," she said. "But I'm afraid to believe, and afraid for you. I guess I'm waiting."

"For what?"

"To be sure."

Shelby was annoyed. "That's really condescending."

"It is?"

"You think I'm not capable of knowing my own mind?"

There was a gap between them. Her heart ached. It wanted to open like a flower and draw Fran into her very center. Not sit here having this cold discussion.

Fran spread her hands. "I don't know what to say. I don't know what to do. I don't even know what to feel. I don't believe in miracles. Things like this just don't…"

Shelby cut her off. "They do."

"Shelby," Fran said gently and firmly, "you've been through a lot. It's all happening fast. Don't get yourself into something you'll regret later, *we'll* regret later." She looked up. "I'll survive a mess. I've survived before. But you…before you bring this down on yourself, please, please be certain."

She didn't know if this feeling was love or not. She'd never felt love for a woman before, not this way. Or a man, either. Not with every inch of her body and heart. If it *was* true…

They were facing something a little bigger than a family reunion.

And she was going somewhere she'd never even thought about. At least, she thought giddily, when you go to Europe you have an itinerary.

"All right," she said. "But I won't take it back. Not if it might be true."

Fran gave a quick sigh of exasperation. "Why?"

"Because I won't deny what I feel for you."

"Shelby…"

"No," she said firmly. She held out her hands. "Stand up."

Fran stood and took her hands.

Shelby pulled her forward and wrapped her arms around her. She made herself forget everything but the sensation of Fran's body against hers. Made herself stop thinking, stop looking at it from the outside. She wanted to take this moment out of time and know it.

It was like nothing she'd ever felt before.

Chapter 19

It was a quiet weekend. Shelby might have enjoyed it if she hadn't spent most of the time, heart pounding, adrenaline pumping, waiting for something terrible to happen.

Fran had to work the weekend days, which was all right. Each evening when she got home they wandered through the nearly empty town, feeling the velvet night and listening to the sound of their own footsteps and the occasional scratchy roar of laughter from a muffled television set. Smelling the next-to-last grass cutting of the summer. Crickets still called. Beetles and moths swirled in the lights of the street lamps. Bats hurled themselves through the light into darkness, feeding.

They talked about their days. Fran said they were gearing up for the influx of students at the college infirmary. Getting ready for bumps and scrapes and hangovers and impulsive pregnancies. They had just finished stock-piling clandestine cartons of condoms and uterine devices, thumbing their noses at church and state. Pregnancies were increasing from year to year. Boys were being boys and girls were being girls at an alarming rate. Some of the nurses were compiling secret "referral" lists of doctors willing to perform a dark-of-night abortion.

Now that it was confirmed that Ray had received the ring, it was time to call her maid of honor. Connie was surprisingly placid about the whole thing. She'd had the feeling something was up, she said. Shelby just hadn't been herself. She knew it was a hard decision, anything she could do?

As a matter of fact, there was. It would take a load off of Shelby's mind if Connie could call Lisa and Penny.

And Jean?

She'd call Jean herself.

She couldn't believe it had been that easy.

She watched her reactions with Fran. When it was getting near time for her to get home from work, she found herself growing restless and nervous. When Fran came into the room, it was as if something had disturbed an ant's nest in her stomach, with tiny nerve impulses scurrying madly. Fran always seemed glad to see her, returned her touches. But when she didn't know Shelby was watching, her face took on a pinched, worried look.

By Sunday night, she had become genuinely apprehensive, sure there would be repercussions once Libby hit the phone tree. She tried giving Jean a call. Jean hadn't heard anything, had tried to call Connie or Lisa or Penny, but there was nobody home. Fran suggested the three of them have a Labor Day cookout. She wouldn't be much help, having to work, but it would still be light enough by the time she got home. Jean thought it was a great idea.

They sat and watched the coals wink out. Jean taught them songs from Girl Scout camp. Fran shared slightly raunchy ditties she'd picked up in the Army. Shelby had some truly filthy numbers she'd learned as a child, eavesdropping on her parents' parties. They agreed that maturity and money contributed to a serious eroding of morals.

Clinking beer bottles, they congratulated themselves on the fact that they would never be rich enough to become totally degenerate. Shelby had come close, what with the Camden and fortune and Ray's future earning potential. But she figured, between cancelling the wedding and skipping the family reunion, she could kiss that fortune good-bye.

Jean found it hard to believe her father would cut her out of his will for something like that. Shelby assured her he'd told her on more than one occasion that it was all going to his alma mater if she didn't "work out." And she certainly wasn't working out.

They commiserated on the plight of the career woman in today's society. They represented a fringe group, they decided. A shadowy world living in the shadow of the real world. Double-shadowed. Fated to become spinsters if they didn't catch a man in the next five years.

"Catch a man?" Jean said. "How about 'settle for' a man?"

They all laughed at that.

Fran remarked that they were getting snockered.

They drank a toast to the end of summer.

They talked about the pros and cons of living in a college town, where the population dropped by half every June. And the culture shock that hit the day after Labor Day when the students came back.

After a while they didn't talk about anything, just leaned back in their lawn chairs and looked at the stars.

It grew late, and Jean announced she'd better get home. Fran invited her to stay with her, since she had two beds. Jean said she'd rather get home late than face the agony of driving home and dressing for work first thing in the morning. They told her to drive safely and look out for rabid raccoons.

Still no calls from anyone.

Fran had Tuesday off, in exchange for the weekend. She said she'd take care of the picnic mess.

Shelby went to work early. She wanted to get there before the rest of the lunch bunch, so she could be settled in before they arrived. It seemed easier than walking into the middle of what was bound to be a shriek and gossip session. Since Connie was the only one she'd talked to, she could imagine the hubbub when the others got there. There'd be plenty of talk, and excitement, and questions. Especially questions.

Instead of silence and solitude, there were flowers on her desk. Yellow roses and carnations in a deep blue vase. She recognized Penny's handwriting on the card. "We're with you. The Lunch Bunch."

She was touched and surprised. She went down to the readers' room.

They greeted her and enveloped her in a group embrace. "Welcome back to the society of spinsters," Lisa said.

"Gee, guys." She hugged them all. "I didn't expect this kind of reaction. Don't you like Ray?"

"Of course," Connie said. "We thought you might need a morale-booster."

Shelby laughed and shook her head. "You don't know the half of it. Ray's pouting in silence, and Libby's on a rampage. Fortunately, she's not speaking to me."

"She's rough," Lisa said, and gave her a quick kiss on the cheek. "It'll pass."

"Penny, thank you so much for the flowers. They were just what I needed."

"They're from all of us," Penny said.

"I know, and I thank you all, but I can tell you picked them out."

Penny turned the color of a pomegranate. "You like them?"

"My very favorites." She glanced around, looking for Jean.

"Jean's still in the lounge," Lisa said. "She wasn't really in on this. We couldn't find her last night."

"She was at my place. We had an impromptu picnic." She added, "I tried to reach you, but no one was home." It was close enough to the truth.

She thought she saw Connie and Lisa exchange glances.

Miss Myers hovered in the doorway.

"Cheese it," Connie whispered. "The cops."

They scurried back to their desks.

As it turned out, Miss Myers was only looking for one of the new readers. But it was an excellent excuse to go to her own office.

Charlotte came in later, with a brisk, "How's it going?"

Shelby said it was going fine.

Charlotte said Shelby wasn't worth beans as a liar.

"It's been too easy," Shelby said. "Have you heard anything?"

"They know better than to gossip around me. Besides, it's none of their damn business what you do with your free time. Don't forget that."

Shelby smiled wryly. It was nobody's damn business, but she had a hunch it was about to be everybody's damn business.

It was growing deep twilight by the time she got home. Night would come earlier and earlier now. By the time she knew it, she'd be getting up in the dark as well as going to bed in the dark. The leaves would turn and remind her once again why she lived in New England. Followed by winter, season of frozen slush, which would make her think she was crazy. Until spring, arriving first with the chatter of sparrows, deepening as the maple buds swelled in mahogany knobs. And then, one day, the hills would be tinged with palest green and the odor of soil would rise. And nobody would remember that it had been a bad winter at all.

At home, Fran had gathered up all the brides' magazines Libby had contributed to Shelby's apartment. She had them stacked by the outdoor fireplace, a fire laid, and a can of charcoal lighter near by. "I thought we might have a ritual burning," she said.

"Love it. Any calls?"

"Your phone rang once, but it stopped after the fourth ring. Probably a wrong number."

"Be back in a sec."

She went through her apartment to the mailboxes and grabbed her mail. A magazine. Flyers. Bills. The rest junk. She tossed it on the couch and went to change.

By the time the pyre had consumed the last of the magazines, she was covered with soot and starving. Fran threw together one of her gourmet forgettable meals. Afterward, they sat around chatting about nothing in particular until Shelby heard the phone in her apartment ring.

"Shit," she said, turning to ice.

"Want to ignore it?"

She shook her head. "This has to happen sooner or later." She trudged down the hall.

"Shel," Ray said, "I'm glad I caught you in."

She almost didn't recognize him. His voice sounded older. She put her fear on 'hold.' "Hello, Ray," she said as noncommittally as possible.

"Hon, I feel like a real ass for not getting back to you before now…"

"I heard you got the ring."

"Yes. And here's the point…"

Oh, no, she thought. Not another argument, not another of those terrible conversations.

"…I think you were absolutely right to do it."

"What?"

"You had it pegged all along," he said. "I know I treated you like shit, not understanding and all, but I think…well, I've thought about it a lot, and I think I didn't want to face the fact that it wasn't right for me, either."

"You did? Didn't?"

"I think so." He laughed. "Of course I reserve the right to change my mind a hundred times. But when I saw that ring—to be perfectly honest, my first reaction was relief. Couldn't get around that. The anger came later, but it didn't stay." He stopped and took a deep breath. "So here's what I think. I think we make pretty good friends, but we wouldn't make a good marriage."

She finally started breathing again. "Ray, this isn't a joke, is it? Because if it is, not that I blame you, but it's really not a good time in my life for jokes."

"It's not a joke. More like a scene from a really bad movie."

Shelby had to laugh.

"Look, I wanted to warn you, Libby's on the war path. She's making some pretty ugly statements. I don't know what she has planned. I'll try to hold her back on this end, but she's in her own orbit."

"I'm sure she is. Ray, can we get together and talk about this? I mean, I have to tell you how really, really grateful I am…"

"No need to talk about it, but let's get together soon. Are friends allowed to go dancing together? Or is that reserved for couples?"

"We'll pretend." It didn't matter if she wasn't in love with this man. She liked him. Truly and genuinely liked him. "Thanks for this. I really mean it."

"I'll give you a call soon. Or you can call me, now that we're not romantically involved."

"I'll do it," she said, "I promise."

When she told her, Fran was as stunned as Shelby had been. "He's one in

257

a million," she said. "Maybe you should rethink your decision."

"Not on your life. This is fine the way it is." She stretched. "God, I just realized how exhausted I am. Think I'll take a hot bath and hit the sack."

"Good idea. I have to be bright-eyed and bushy-tailed in the morning."

"See you after work." She started to reach out to embrace her, then realized there were streaks of oily soot all over her arms and hands. "I'm disgusting."

"Not to me," Fran said.

It was an old, claw-footed tub with porcelain handles and permanent rust stains. She filled it with steaming water and added double the recommended amount of bubble bath. She looked around for something to read, but everything she was reading was either too complicated, too heavy to hold in the tub, or *America as a Civilization*. She wanted something light and unenlightening. The mail would do, ads and all.

By the time she was down to the last piece of junk, she was ready to fall asleep in the tub. She thought about tossing it aside, but decided to read it, anyway, just to have a sense of closure.

She glanced at the envelope. The return address was barely legible, from some sort of copy store, it seemed. She couldn't make out the postmark. She tore it open.

It was a photocopy of a photocopy, about five pages long. Official-looking, if it hadn't been reproduced so hurriedly and carelessly. A cover sheet with a filled-out form, what looked like a report clipped to it. The kind of thing they sometimes got at the magazine, a home-based cottage industry trying to convince them they couldn't afford not to review this product, which would solve everyone's problems forever. She yawned. Too much for tonight. She was about to drop it to the floor when something caught her eye. A familiar name.

Frances Ellen Jarvis.

She read over the cover form, which told her nothing she didn't already know, except that Fran was born in a small town, and had achieved the rank of Corporal.

The report itself was from the Department of Defense. But they obviously hadn't sent it. She tried again to make out the postmark. No luck.

Maybe she shouldn't read it. It might be personal. But someone had gone out of their way to send it to her, and she wanted to know why. She could get Fran and they could read it together. But Fran had an early morning. She'd show it to her first thing tomorrow evening.

She started to read.

Ten minutes later she threw the report against the wall.

God damn it!

It was a summary of Fran's service record, including the fact that she had left the service "voluntarily" in exchange for an honorable discharge, and to avoid a Court Martial for "suspected sexual perversion."

Who had sent this stuff, and why? To make trouble, of course. Someone who thought she didn't know. Well, that was wasted effort.

Still, it was a very nasty thing to do. And a complicated one. They'd have to get hold of Fran's service record, which couldn't be an easy task. Not many people she knew had the malice or connections for that...

Libby.

Libby would think of a dirty trick like this. And her father would have connections through his law office. He probably had a dozen World War II buddies stashed away in the Pentagon.

Obviously, it was a warning. A hint as to how far Libby could go.

Enraged, she threw a towel around herself and went to the phone. Her mother answered.

"I want this stupid game to stop. Right now."

"Who is this?" her mother asked in a silken voice.

"You know who it is. I got your lousy letter today..."

"I'm sorry," Libby said sweetly. "You must have the wrong number." She hung up.

No point in calling back. Her mother'd done that one before. It was followed by her taking the phone off the hook for as long as necessary.

She wanted to find someone and yell, but this wasn't the kind of thing you could rant and rave over to anyone who didn't know. Which left Fran, repository of all her complaints. She deserved to sleep.

Fran was sitting on the front steps when she got home from work. Shelby waved to her, then pulled around to the back of the house. All the way home, she'd worried about how to tell her about the letter. Actually, she'd worried about it all day. When Penny dropped by to invite her to after-work cocktails, she'd turned her down with an abrupt, "I have to get home." She regretted it afterward. Penny had looked hurt, and Shelby really wanted to go out of her way not to annoy or disturb anyone these days.

She parked the car, grabbed her pocketbook, and started up the walk to the house. Fran met her half way.

"We have to talk," Shelby said. "Something's happened."

"I know." She pulled a wad of folded and crumpled papers from her pocket. "I got my own personal copy."

"Fran, I'm so terribly sorry."

"It's not your doing. Go put on something comfortable and take me to the seediest, most depressing bar in town. Somewhere we can get really down and suicidal."

It wasn't easy to find a bar that fit. Most of the local spots were jammed with students, even on a Tuesday. They created a raucous, optimistic atmosphere that was incompatible with true despair.

Finally she remembered Willy's across the street from the movie theater and hidden slightly behind the library. Willy's had been around since the Depression. There were two separate entrances—one in front and one in the shadows out by the garbage cans—and rooms upstairs that might or might not be hotel rooms. Inside, it was dark and fragrant with stale beer. Every booth and table was covered with cigarette burns and carved initials and mysterious dark stains. A jukebox, half its lights working, played only sad Country and Western music. Red curtains hung over the windows, making the place look from the outside like a brothel that had fallen on hard times. It was the kind of place none of the locals ever frequented and parents warned their children about.

259

"It'll do," Fran said.

"Looks pretty bad to me," Shelby said.

"You've never seen the bars in a town with an Army post nearby."

They slid into a particularly dark booth with stuffing coming out of the vinyl seats. Shelby wondered if the stuffing was being harvested by mice. "What'll it be?" Fran asked.

"Just beer, thanks. In a bottle."

"Right. At least we'll know what we're drinking." She went to the bar to get it.

Shelby wondered what Libby would think if she saw her now, sitting in a dark and seedy bar with a lesbian she was probably in love with.

In love with.

She looked toward the bar and watched Fran chat up the bartender. Fran was always chatting up bartenders and waitresses and clerk in stores. She said it made her feel like a human being, not just some anonymous being draining their energy.

Fran was wearing the soft beige corduroys and a well-worn white shirt and her loafers.

In love with.

Shelby was surprised at herself. It had come to her, and she hadn't become hysterical or depressed or disgusted. None of those things she was supposed to feel.

It felt right.

In the midst of all the chaos and turmoil and strange things happening or about to happen—this was all right.

Fran came back and put down the beer bottles. "You first," she said. "What do you think's going on?"

"Well, it's obviously a Libby thing. She could do this, and would. The reasons are obvious, too. What isn't clear is what we should do with it, what the message is, and what happens next."

"I know what the message is for me," Fran said, "I know what you are, and I can use it to wreck your life, so stay away from my daughter. Or words to that effect."

"What could she do to you?"

"Get me kicked out of my job, for one thing. Maybe out of school. And probably things I haven't even dreamed of yet. What's she likely to do?"

Shelby sat for a moment, thinking it over. "I'm not sure. I've never been through this with her. She probably wouldn't do much publicly. But there must be a lot of options between here and there."

Fran was peeling the label off her beer. "I really think we should avoid each other," she said without looking up. "There's an awful lot at risk here."

"No."

"Shelby…"

"I told you before. That's not an option. Unless it's for your safety."

"I don't know what to do." Fran leaned her back against the window and rested one foot on the bench. "Jesus, I hate this."

"I'm not real crazy about it, myself."

"No matter what I try to do, sooner or later my feelings get me in trouble.

Every time I promise myself I won't get involved, I'll just go along breezing through my life, with no baggage…It happens all over again. I wish I could kill my feelings."

"Fran…"

"I really didn't mean to hurt you with this."

"You haven't hurt me. Fran, *I'm* the one who broke the engagement. *I'm* the one who chickened out of the reunion. *I'm* the one who wanted to be around you every minute I could."

"They picked up something." Fran must have been crying. She wiped her eyes on her sleeve. "Something coming from me."

"And *me*. Will you please try to hear this? It was coming from me, too."

"Yeah, but you're innocent."

"No more innocent than you, and no more guilty." She leaned across the table. "Fran, this isn't something to feel guilty about. It's who you are."

Fran dug in her pocketbook for a tissue and blew her nose. Shelby couldn't tell if she was listening or not.

"I know people don't like it," she went on. "I saw the movie, I heard the remarks. But, for God's sake, there's got to be a way to live within this."

"You haven't been there." Fran took a drink. She still wouldn't look at her.

"No, I haven't." She covered Fran's wrist with her hand. "So maybe I'm not as beaten down as you. Maybe I can see things a little more optimistically, if not clearly."

Fran gestured toward the window with her beer bottle. "Yeah, and just look at the crowds of people out there, lining up to help."

"*I'm* lining up." She squeezed her wrist. "Christ," she said loudly, "will you get out of yourself for one minute and listen to me?"

Startled, Fran looked at her.

"I *love* you. The way you love me. I want to be with you forever. Whatever happens, I want to be there with you, going through it with you. Do you understand what I'm saying?"

Fran's face went white, then red. She nodded.

"And don't tell me I don't know what I'm getting into. I do know. I don't care what they do. I…" She felt herself choke up. "…I want to love you. I want you to love me."

Panic swept over her. She could feel her hands go clammy and begin to tremble. Fran started to say something. She stopped her.

"I'm scared," she said. "I'm scared of what people are going to do. But I'm more scared of what you're going to say." She laughed humorlessly. "I've never proposed to a woman before."

Fran smiled. It was the first time in weeks Shelby'd seen her smile like that. It came from somewhere deep inside and levitated the room.

"I love you," Fran said.

They looked at each other for a long minute. Finally Shelby cleared her throat. "What are we supposed to do now?"

"Beats me." Even in the dark shadows of the room, her eyes seemed to spark. "What do you *want* to do?"

"Get out of here, go home, and just be with you."

Back in college, their constant free time activity had been "Identity crisis." What am I doing here? What's it all about? Her whole generation had struggled with it. If I strip away the things I've learned from my parents and teachers, if I subtract my background, who am I? Magazines printed articles and cartoons about it. Sociologists studied it.

They knew they were more than the people they saw on TV. They weren't the nuclear family from the suburbs, with trimmed lawns and backyard barbecues and fake Hawaiian luaus. The culture of the '50s surrounded them, but it didn't define them. They began to look for answers, not from their parents, but from poets and writers and artists. The Beat Generation began to take shape.

Their parents didn't "get it," of course. They'd achieved the American Dream, why not just sit back and enjoy it? Now it seemed the "kids" were rejecting everything their fathers had risked their lives for.

But it wasn't enough for them. They felt an emptiness, a hollowness they couldn't really understand. A hope that there was more to life than going through the motions. A desire to find out who they were at the core.

Many of her friends and acquaintances had moved on from there, settling into the very world they'd once declared "inadequate" or "phony." Everyday reality reared its head, and they bowed to its demands.

Shelby'd never understood that, and she didn't understand it now. She didn't know why it had happened to them, but at least now she knew why it hadn't happened to her. That world wasn't her world. It pulled her, but there was no way of settling into a life that had so little to do with her.

She looked down at Fran, asleep beside her. She knew she ought to be afraid, and she was. It was a hard world. Terrible things were probably going to happen, things she hadn't even imagined. But whatever was coming her way was nothing compared to the sadness and loneliness that were gone.

Fran stirred a little. In the vague pewter light that came before dawn, Shelby saw her eyelids flutter and smiled.

"Are you awake?" Fran asked.

"Yes."

"What's wrong?"

"Nothing. I was just thinking." She pushed herself up on one elbow and moved a bit of Fran's hair from her forehead with her fingertip.

"About what?"

"Life. Stuff like that."

"Trivia."

Shelby smiled down at her. "That's right."

"Lie down." Fran placed one hand at the back of Shelby's neck and pulled her down. "Let me hold you."

She let her head rest on Fran's chest, and felt her arms around her. Her own pajama top annoyed her. It kept Fran's hands from her skin. She wanted to feel her, all the different parts of her body touching all the different parts of Fran's body...

"Fran," she whispered.

"Uh-huh?"

"Do you think we could...well, make love or something?"

There was a long silence, then Fran laughed affectionately. "I think that could be arranged."

Suddenly she felt terribly inadequate. "I don't know what to do."

Fran eased her onto her back, one arm beneath Shelby's neck. "Here's what we're going to do." She stroked Shelby's hair. "I'm going to make love to you, but you're not going to make love to me."

Shelby felt herself tighten with apprehension and anticipation.

"I don't want you to worry about pleasing me," Fran went on, running her fingers across Shelby's face, touching her lips. "It's scary enough, your first time. Are you afraid?"

"A little."

"It'll be all right," Fran said softly. She undid the buttons of Shelby's pajamas and moved her hand across her chest. "Anything you don't like, you say. Any time you want me to stop or slow down, tell me. I won't take it personally."

"You'd better," Shelby said. "This *is* personal."

Fran hushed her. Her hand was warm and gentle and strong. Shelby could feel the love coming through Fran's fingertips. She let herself relax, knowing it was safe, and warm.

Fran kissed the top of her head, like a mother kissing a child, then her eyelids and the smooth cavity between her eyes. She moved her hand across Shelby's breast.

Electricity coursed through her. She reached up and threw her arm around Fran, holding her tightly. Her legs gripped Fran's legs.

"No," Fran said, easing her back down. "Not yet."

She thought she was going to lose her mind. Fran undressed her, and rubbed her hands slowly over Shelby's body. She kissed her breasts. She turned her over and stroked her back. Her loving fingers touched her legs, her buttocks. She stroked Shelby's whole body front and back with her hands, her fingertips, with the soft flesh of the insides of her forearms, with her face and mouth, with her breasts.

One minute her skin was a million tiny pores opening and reaching to draw Fran inside. The next minute it was so sensitive she could barely stand to be touched. She wanted to pull away, to run, and she wanted to melt into Fran's body all at the same time. She was on fire one second, and caressed by a tropical breeze the next.

"Finish it," she whispered.

"No," Fran said again and went on touching her.

She wanted to run to the top of a mountain and throw herself off. She was going to die if this didn't stop. But she didn't want it to stop, not ever.

It went on and on. Her throat felt as if she'd been screaming, though she hadn't. Her eyes burned. She couldn't move. She tried to will herself to move, and couldn't. She started to cry. Fran kissed away her tears.

Fran was in complete control of her. Everything she felt, every sensation and emotion—her body was like a pipe organ, and Fran played the music. All kinds of music. Familiar music, strange music. She was completely helpless, her body responding to Fran's every move and touch. It was terrifying, and the most comforting thing she'd ever felt.

Then, when she was sure she was breaking into a million pieces, her body disintegrating into atoms, then sparks, Fran slipped her hand between her legs.

"Well," Fran said in the morning over breakfast preparations, "I guess we don't have to worry about you liking sex with women."

Shelby tossed ground coffee into the basket and filled the Pyrex pot. She laughed. "That's the understatement of the year." She felt off-balance, as if all the molecules in her body had gone into space and some of them hadn't gotten back yet. "Where did you learn that?"

Fran blushed a little. "It's a God-given gift."

"If God gives lesbians gifts like that, we must be the Chosen People."

"You're good for me," Fran said. She split an English muffin and toasted it, buttered each half, then topped each with a slice of tomato, a lightly fried egg, and grated cheese. She slid them under the broiler until the cheese ran. "You're the first woman I've ever met who thinks being a lesbian is fun."

"It *is* fun." She poured their coffee. She had to get her head together. She'd never be able to work today. Assuming she got there at all, assuming she didn't run the car off the road into a ditch. "I don't think I'm going to earn my keep at the magazine today."

"I'm not going to earn mine at the Health Service. Last night wasn't all one-way, you know."

"That's me," Shelby said with a grin. "Highly skilled at doing nothing."

"How're you holding up?" Connie asked as Shelby joined their lunch table.

"Not bad." She unwrapped her silver ware and unfolded her napkin.

"Have you heard from Ray?"

"Yes, I did. He agrees it's the best thing for us to be friends."

Connie leaned forward and rubbed her hands together greedily. "Does that mean he's available?" she teased.

Shelby was a little shocked at that. It seemed sort of tactless, even as a joke. She tried to play along. "I suppose so. What about Charlie?"

"Charlie has decided to join the Army." Connie rolled her eyes. "I mean, give me a break."

"Why?"

"He *says* he doesn't know what to do with his life, so he's going in the service to figure it out. Gawd, that is *so* inconsiderate. But he'll get bored and come crawling back."

"And if he crawls back and finds you with Ray?"

Connie grinned. "That'll be entertaining, won't it?"

That's so like Connie, Shelby thought. She treats Charlie like a character in a movie.

As a matter of fact, she treats herself like a character in a movie. "Are you OK with it?"

Connie smiled, a little too broadly. "Sure. The sun'll rise tomorrow, just the way it did yesterday."

"First Shelby and Ray," Lisa said with a sigh. "Now Connie and Charlie. This is shaping up to be a September to remember."

Penny giggled. "'September to remember?' Gee, Lisa, you're a poet and you don't know it."

"Your feet show it," Connie picked up.

"They're Longfellows!" Lisa said, and shrieked with laughter.

The rest of them joined her.

Shelby glanced over at Jean, who faked a yawn. Shelby smiled.

"I tried to call you last evening," Connie said. "You weren't home."

"I must've just missed you," Shelby said. "Fran and I went out for a drink at Willy's."

"*Willy's?*" Lisa said with a shudder.

"It was an appropriate place to celebrate my return to the single life."

"You should have called us," Penny said. "You could have celebrated with *all* your friends."

Now, *that* would have been something to behold. And they could have all gone back to her place afterward.

She caught herself before she laughed out loud. "This was a spur-of-the-moment thing," she said. "We'll do some real celebrating later."

"It doesn't seem right," Lisa said, "celebrating the death of something."

It's not a death for me, she thought. It's a beginning. But it does call for celebrating. Real celebrating. Maybe I could take Fran out for dinner tonight. Somewhere really special. Maybe the Andover Country Club.

She giggled.

"What's so funny?" Connie demanded.

"My mind is slippery as ice today."

"I'm not surprised," Connie said sympathetically. "You've been through a lot lately."

"It's been like a roller coaster that's gone out of control," Shelby said. "But I can see the light at the end of the tunnel."

"I think," Jean said, "we're dealing with serious mental illness here." She turned her soft eyes on Shelby. "Maybe you need to a vacation. Or a change in diet." Her eyes took on a mischievous sparkle. "I have some excellent recipes…"

It wasn't really very funny, but it sent her over the top. She started to laugh, tried to stop but couldn't. She put her face in her hands and laughed until her stomach ached. Then someone touched her, and she realized she was crying. Crying hard, as hard as she'd laughed.

An arm slipped around her shoulders. "It'll be OK," she heard Jean murmur. "Let's go to your office."

She nodded, and felt herself being led up from the table and toward the door. Jean tightened her arm around her.

"Don't worry about what anyone's thinking," Jean said quietly. "You just broke your engagement. It's perfectly normal."

No, it wasn't perfectly normal, not what she was crying about. And they weren't tears of sorrow. They were tears of relief. Relief that finally, after years of pushing and pulling herself, she'd come home.

Jean got her settled in her chair. The rest trailed in behind. "Somebody get a glass of water," Jean said.

Someone did. She drank it. Jean rubbed her back.

"Better?"

Shelby nodded.

"We're going to give you some privacy," Jean said in a voice of finality that

265

no one would dare argue with. "If you need anything, or want to talk, I'm as near as your phone."

"Me, too," Penny said.

Connie and Lisa "uh-huh-ed" in agreement.

"Thanks," Shelby said. "I just need to put myself together."

Jean herded them out the door, turning at the last minute to look back at her. "OK?"

"OK."

She leaned back in her chair, exhausted.

She should probably go tell Spurl her engagement was off. No doubt he knew, but he did like to think anything that might affect his employees was shared with him immediately if not sooner. Which was why they sometimes called him "Big Daddy."

He'd probably be in his office now. On the other hand, she no doubt looked like something that had been run over and left for dead. She reached for the phone instead.

"Mr. Spurl's office, Miss Myers speaking."

"Hi," Shelby said. "This is Shelby Camden. Is he in?"

"I'm afraid not, Miss Camden."

"Oh. Do you know when he'll be back?"

"He's meeting with the people from *Redbook*. It could be quite a while."

And that was quite a bit of information for Miss Myers to give out.

"OK, I'll try him later."

There was a polite cough on the other end of the line. "Miss Camden?"

"Yes?"

"Is it true that you've been…" She cleared her throat. "…forced to dissolve your engagement?"

Shelby smiled. "Well, yes and no. I mean, I broke the engagement, but no one forced me to. It was mutually agreeable, actually."

"I see." There was a long, strained silence. "Miss Camden, if there's anything I can do for you…" She didn't seem to know what to say next.

"Thank you," Shelby said. "I appreciate that."

"Try Mr. Spurl tomorrow," Miss Myers said abruptly, and hung up.

This was beginning to make her nervous. People were being too easy. Too nice. It made her think she must be missing something.

On the other hand, maybe people were generally nicer than she expected, and they were genuinely concerned about her.

That was a very strange thought.

She went to the ladies' room and washed her face. Her eyes were so puffy they looked as if someone had stuffed marbles under them. The successful young career woman…

It was getting late. Mid-afternoon already and she'd spent most of the day in one kind of state or another. The magazine was crazy if they paid her for this week's work. She decided to call Fran, see what time she got off, arrange for them to meet for an extraordinary dinner.

The receptionist at the Health Center paged her a number of times, and finally gave up. "She's either stepped out for a moment, or she's left for the day."

That was strange. Shelby knew she wasn't due to leave there until at least five, maybe even six or seven. Fran never left work early. She said there was always something to catch up with or plan ahead for. And extra half hour now would pay off later.

Still, she thought she'd give Fran's number a try.

The phone rang and rang. On the seventh ring she was about to give up when the connection went through.

"Hello?" Fran said. Her voice was tight and strange.

"Hi, it's Shelby. What are you doing home? Are you sick?"

"No."

"You sound funny."

"Sorry." There was music in the background. Classical music. Brahms.

"Fran, what's wrong?"

"I just got fired," Fran said.

Chapter 20

"What happened?" She tossed her pocketbook on Fran's couch.

Fran gathered up the remnants of her solitaire game. "They fired me," she said with a shrug.

"Why?"

"Three guesses."

Fran's face was pale and pinched and tired. She looked beaten. She was just sitting there, taking it. Shelby sat down across from her. "You can't let them do that. You have to fight it."

"Any suggestions?"

"They have to give you a reason."

"I'm a bad influence on students, and reflect negatively on the Health Service."

"For God's sake, you're not selling drugs or performing abortions."

Fran shook her head wearily. "You know the answer to that, Shelby."

Shelby picked up the deck of cards. She turned up the top one, looked at it, and slid it onto the bottom of the deck. She turned up the next one...

"It was your mother," Fran said softly. "She sent them one of those reports. They showed it to me."

"Bitch!" She slammed the cards down on the table. It was inadequate. "Fran, I'm..."

"It's not your fault. Look, these things happen. Inevitably."

Shelby dropped her head into her hands. "Shit, shit, shit."

"Indeed." Fran forced a smile. "It's not a total disaster. They agreed not to put it on my academic record, as long as I behave myself."

Her body was stiff. It reminded Shelby of a puppet without hinges.

"What can I do?" she asked.

"I'll survive. I always survive."

"I'll help you find another job," Shelby said.

"Thank you," Fran said with a tight little smile.

"This *is* my fault. If I hadn't..."

"If you hadn't met me, this wouldn't have happened. If I didn't love you, this wouldn't have happened. If you didn't love me...If I didn't live here. If you didn't live here. There are a thousand 'ifs'. But it happened, and that's all there is to that."

It was very still and quiet in the house. She could hear Fran's alarm clock ticking in the bedroom. A squirrel ran up a maple outside, its nails making tiny scratching, jittery, nervous stop-and-start sounds. She checked her watch.

Three o'clock. Dead time. Day or night, everything stops. Except the squirrels. If the universe stops for a moment of silent worship, it's worship of a God the squirrels don't believe in.

The shadows of the trees worked their way across the lawn and up the sides of the houses. The sun set in autumn yellow, the sky clear blue with trails of cloud near the horizon. Color followed the sun, first the reds and golds, then the blues, and finally even the grass and leaves. The gray went dark.

Shelby reached over and turned on the lamp. It sent pockets of light among the shadows.

They couldn't sit here forever, Fran staring at the floor, Shelby staring at Fran staring at the floor.

Libby did this, Shelby thought. Because I didn't do what she wanted. It's too late to take it back. This can't be undone.

We're not dead. You can always do something if you're not dead. We can't take the chance of provoking the serpent, but we can do something to prove we're not dead.

"Fran," she said, "get up."

Fran looked at her, dazed.

"We're going out to dinner."

"What?"

"I planned to take you out to dinner tonight, to celebrate. We're going to do it."

"After what's happened..."

"What my mother did has nothing to do with how we feel about one another, except in her dirty eyes. If I want to take you out to dinner, the only person who has a right to prevent it is you."

Fran blinked. "I don't get it."

Shelby leaned over and took her hands. "I spent my whole life up to now being afraid. I'm not going to do it any more. I don't want you to, either."

"I haven't..."

"They drove you out of your home," Shelby said. "They drove you out of college, and out of the Army, and now out of your job. Nasty little people did that. It has to stop." She pulled her up from her seat. "This is our world, too. And until they gun us down, I plan to enjoy it."

"You were right," Fran said. "I do feel better."

Shelby twirled a string of spaghetti around her fork. "We had to get out of that apartment."

"I just hope we don't run into anyone you know."

"That's why I wanted to come here," Shelby said. "If there's one spot in the county I'm likely to run into someone I know, it's this place."

The restaurant was cozy and a bit elegant, with brick walls and oak tables and real hanging plants. A little too expensive for the college crowd, a little too casual for West Sayer's "old money." It was well-lighted, and looked out onto the main street. Shelby had insisted they sit next to the plate-glass window.

The only person who came by was Connie's Charlie, who saw them through the window and joined them. He wanted to talk with Fran about the Army.

She told him it was easy time, as long as you forget you had desires, opinions, or a personality of your own.

Charlie said that'd be simple, he'd been doing it for years with Connie.

When they got back to Bass Falls, it was nearly eleven o'clock. Fran thanked her for the night out, it had lifted her spirits considerably, but she still had a little more pouting to do, and would really rather do it alone if that was all right. Shelby said it was fine with her. She was completely tired out, couldn't recall a single moment of sleep the night before, and needed to get some rest before tackling her undone work at the magazine in the morning.

She was exhausted, too, from trying to keep Fran from knowing how frightened she was.

* * *

Next morning there was a message on her desk. Mr. Spurl could see her as soon as she got in.

Barely stopping to run a comb through her hair, she climbed the stairs to Spurl's office. Miss Myers greeted her with a tight, grim face. Clearly, Miss Myers was recovering from a night of wild passion and debauchery. She looked at Shelby, shook her head in a way that told her nothing, and said, "You can go right in."

Spurl still had his jacket on and his tie straight. He must have just gotten in himself. He nodded her into the chair by his desk and placed his hand on a stack of folders as if he were about to take the oath of office.

"I'm glad you could see me," Shelby said. "I wanted to tell you before it's all over the office, I've broken my engagement."

"Yes," he said. "I've heard."

Shelby smiled. "You have to get up before the birds to keep any secrets around here."

"It must have been painful," he said.

"It's turned out OK. A mutual decision. We're still friends."

He cleared his throat.

"Anyway," she went on, "I want to apologize for letting my work slip the last few days. I promise I'll catch up before the weekend."

He cleared his throat again. "Actually, Miss Camden, that's what I wanted to talk to you about."

Her full attention shot into focus on him, like a dog's ears to a strange sound.

"It's not the quantity of your work that's troublesome. But there is a problem of diminished quality."

'Diminished quality'? It sounded like a condition that came on with senility. "My mind hasn't been on things the way it should," she said quickly, "but I've been having personal problems. It's fine now." She hated the way her voice sounded.

"It affects your work." He glanced down. "And your office relations."

"Office relations?"

He didn't seem able to meet her eye. "Your friends are concerned."

She couldn't believe she was hearing this. She stared at him.

"They think you may have fallen in with...the wrong sort of people."

"They came to you with this?"

He blushed. "They brought it to my attention. It appears to be damaging your work, and the morale of the fiction department as well. As I say, we're concerned."

She was trembling like quicksand inside. "Mr. Spurl," she said as evenly and calmly as she could, "I understand that my personal problems have hurt my work. But my life is my life, and nobody owns it but me."

Spurl looked at her straight and hard. "This is a family magazine, Miss Camden. The public expects certain standards of behavior from us. We have to live up to those standards. We are not a supermarket tabloid. We take as much pride in who we are as we do in our product."

"You make it sound as if the public cares what we have for breakfast."

"No, but they do care who we have it with."

If she didn't move in the next three seconds, she'd never be able to move again. She stood up. "I don't think you really give a damn what the public cares about. You're the one who's bothered by this."

"Yes, I am. And so are your co-workers." He stroked his tie. "You're young and talented, Miss Camden. You have your whole life ahead of you. Please don't let a temporary obsession..."

"Mr. Spurl..."

"Let me spell it out for you. I find it personally uncomfortable to have this sort of thing in my office. I'm afraid I have to ask you to choose between your position here and your...well, your after-hours entertainment."

She pivoted on her heel and strode out of the room, slamming the door behind her. Miss Myers gave a tiny jump and squeak.

She wanted to go down to the readers' room and scream her rage, and go on screaming until the plaster fell from the walls. She also wanted to climb under her desk and never come out, to lock herself behind drawn blinds pretending nothing existed that she couldn't see through a pinhole in the fabric.

She settled for calling Jean. At first she was hesitant, picturing the others sitting at their desks, pretending to work but knowing where she'd been and waiting for a phone to ring. And when it did, the looks of smug satisfaction passing among them. But she needed to talk to someone now. She dialled Jean's desk.

"Look," she said when Jean picked up, "there's some really nasty stuff going on here."

"I know," Jean said.

"You weren't in on it, were you?"

"Of course not. For God's sake. I only found out just now."

"I need to talk to you. Alone."

"Let's meet at Friendly's for lunch."

"Good. See you there."

She wasn't hungry, but she ordered a grilled cheese sandwich and coffee. Jean arrived, a little breathlessly, and asked for a hamburger and fries.

Shelby raised her eyebrows. "What's this?"

"Not a day to keep up appearances." She pulled a pillbox from her pocketbook and searched through the jumble of colors and sizes. "Vitamins," she explained. "Care for any?"

"Do you have anything for incipient nervous breakdowns?"

"B." Jean found a white, round pill and handed it to her. She looked at Shelby carefully. "Better take two," she said, and found another.

"Thanks." Shelby swallowed the pills and sipped her water. "Jean, what's going on at the office?"

Jean shook her head. "I wish I knew. Connie and Lisa and Penny met with Spurl yesterday. They kept me out of it. They've kept me out of most things lately."

"They know you'll come to me with anything you find out."

"Exactly. I've turned into the office snitch."

The waitress brought their food. They waited until she'd left. Shelby picked up her sandwich. "Do you have any idea what they're up to?"

Jean loaded her hamburger with catsup. "From what I can make out, they're upset about your friendship with Fran." She added a slice of onion, lettuce, her tomato, and a sprinkling of potato chips.

"That looks lethal," Shelby said.

"Yeah." Jean took a bite of her sandwich. "We live in desperate times."

"Why would my friendship with Fran upset them?"

"They think you're changing. They don't like the direction."

Shelby thought about it. "I guess I am. Bridge has lost its thrill."

"Not for me," Jean said. "It can't lose what it never had."

She felt a little more relaxed, having a moment of normal, everyday conversation about bridge with her normal, everyday friend. She managed to eat, and taste, a bite of sandwich. "I think that confab with Spurl was about Fran and me," she said.

Jean stared at her. "You're kidding."

"I'm not. He just told me I had to choose…" She took a deep breath. "Basically, between Fran and my job."

"He doesn't have any right to do that."

"I pointed that out. Just before I slammed the door. Scared the wits out of Miss Myers."

Jean grinned. "It was a crazy thing to do, but I'm glad you did it."

"The thing is…" Shelby poured a spoonful of sugar and stirred it into her coffee. "…this whole business is really dangerous. I know Libby's behind it. She got hold of some information about Fran from the Army, and she's been passing it around. Fran's already lost her job. I don't know what she wants, or how far she'll go."

Jean stared at her in shocked amazement. "You think she's working behind your back?"

"Yeah, I do. I think she's got the others working with her. The pressure is on to get me away from Fran, and I don't know what to do about it. Do you have any ideas at all?"

"Yep." Jean chewed another bite of hamburger. "Deny everything, for starters. Everything."

"Even if it's true?"

Jean put her sandwich down. She fingered the rim of the plate. "What's true?"

"Fran is a lesbian."

"I figured as much," Jean said. Her voice was a little shaky.

"That's OK with you, isn't it?"

"Sure." She said it too quickly.

"Isn't it?"

Jean looked as if she wanted to shrink to the size of a pin and crawl under a fry. "Well, yeah, it's OK. I mean, it's *OK*..."

"But?"

"It's OK."

Shelby leaned across the table and touched Jean's hand. "You have to be honest with me, Jean. It's getting rough. I need to be able to trust you."

"All right." She extricated her hand from Shelby's and wiped grease from her fingers. "I *want* it to be OK. For your sake, even for Fran's. I like her. I don't want anything bad to happen to her." She lowered her head. "But, no, it's not entirely OK." She glanced up for a second. "I hate feeling this way. It's wrong, and unfair, and I don't understand it. But it's how I feel."

"I see." She felt as if she'd turned to cement. Everything was cold and hard. Inside her, outside her, everywhere. "And what would you think if I told you Fran and I are lovers?"

"Are you?"

"Yes."

Jean was silent for a moment, then burst into tears.

Shelby watched her.

"I didn't want you to say that," Jean said.

"It's the truth." She wanted to feel compassion for Jean. She couldn't.

"Because it's not...it's not you." She began to cry harder. "You're not like that. I know you're not."

"Then I guess you don't know me as well as you thought you did."

"That isn't true." Jean was sobbing like a child now, stiff-faced, mouth wide open. "You've changed, that's all. You can change back."

Shelby felt nothing.

The waitress was hovering. She caught Shelby's eye. "Anything I can do?" she asked.

"I just told her I'm a lesbian," Shelby said loudly. "She's taking it badly."

The waitress looked at her blankly, then seemed to remember an emergency in the kitchen.

"What did you do that for?"

Anger burst out of its cage. "Because it's *true*. It's all true, and I'm sick of people telling me to pretend it isn't. And threatening me. And making snide little comments and innuendos. Even Fran wants me to pretend. But, damn it, this is the best thing that ever happened to me, and I won't pretend it isn't. And if everyone else in the whole narrow-minded world thinks this is a tragedy, they're welcome to, just don't put it on me."

"I'm sorry," Jean began.

"I don't want to hear it. For the first time in my life, I really, truly know who I am. I wish the people who say they care about me could be happy for me. But obviously they can't. So screw them, Jean. And screw you."

She got up and grabbed the check.

Jean took it from her. "I'll do this. I owe it to you."

She was too angry and hurt to argue. Without speaking, she picked up her pocketbook and left the restaurant.

"I can't help it," Fran said later. "I feel sorry for her."

Shelby grunted.

"I mean it. Jean really loves you. How would you feel if you loved someone, and one day just couldn't love them any more? It's a horrible feeling, Shelby."

"I guess so," she admitted. "But I'm still angry."

"Give yourself some time. But give Jean a little time, too."

Shelby picked a blade of grass from her jeans.

"I know it's Libby behind it. Maybe she didn't say anything to Spurl, but she said something to someone who did."

"Not necessarily," Fran said. "Sometimes a virus gets into the air, and everyone catches it at the same time."

Shelby looked over at her. "Do you have to argue with everything I say?"

"Probably." She reached out and touched Shelby's cheek with her hand. "I love you."

"I love you, too." She caught Fran's hand and held it.

Fran stroked her knuckles. "You don't want to throw away Jean's friendship, do you?"

"She seems to want to throw away mine."

"No, she doesn't. She doesn't know what to do with herself, that's all. If she does manage to get herself squared away, I hope you'll be able to forgive her."

She looked over at Fran, at the kindness in her face, and felt herself on the verge of tears. "It hurts," she said.

"Yeah."

They stared out at the yard for a moment.

"There must be some way to stop this," Shelby said.

Fran picked a flake of paint from the porch railing. "The only thing I can think of," she said, "is to try to reach your mother."

She rubbed the back of her neck. "She's determined to separate us. She wants me to marry Ray. She wants everything back to normal."

"Would it make any difference to talk to her?"

"I really don't know," Shelby said. She didn't want to do that, didn't want to see her mother, ever. Didn't want to face that anger and soul-searing sarcasm. Didn't want to feel like the less-than-worm she always felt like at times like this. "But it looks like my only choice, doesn't it?"

Fran didn't answer, just took her hand.

It was getting close to dark. A few remaining locusts buzzed dryly in the trees. Two crickets started up.

"It was kind of nice having such a dry summer," Fran said irrelevantly. "No mosquitoes."

"Are you as terrified as I am?" Shelby asked.

"At least."

"I certainly got you into a mess, didn't I?"

"I thought it was me who got you into a mess."

Shelby squeezed Fran's hand. "We make a great team."

Libby didn't hang up on her this time. She even sounded friendly. She agreed to meet her for dinner on Friday—wait, no can do, library committee meeting—Saturday at the Inn. Yes, they needed to talk, things had gotten out of hand, hadn't they? It was time to try and patch them up. Seven o'clock, Sweetie, kiss-kiss.

She hardly had time to think about it over the next couple of days. She was damned if she'd give Spurl her work as an excuse to nose into her personal life. If he wanted to fire her, let him do it. She got to the office early and left late. Charlotte was there, in and out, and wondered if there was something wrong which had sent Shelby into such a frenzy of activity. Shelby said she was trying to catch up, and shut off any further conversation.

On the first day, she did what she should have done the day before. She gathered up the flowers her friends had given her, and the card, and left them on Penny's desk before anyone got there. She hadn't expected to feel much when she saw Jean's desk, but she was wrong. It was like an iron fist around her heart. She got out of there as fast as she could.

No word from anyone. No questions about the flowers. Once she ran into Jean unexpectedly in the lounge. Jean buried her head in a magazine. Shelby turned away from her, poured herself a cup of coffee, and left. She forced herself to put all her attention on her work.

Fran found work easily, at the local bookstore. Once the college re-opened, the pool of cheap summer labor dried up and jobs were plentiful. She registered for her classes without a problem. At night, she studied. Shelby sat beside her with her own work.

They tried not to talk about Saturday.

But it was there all the time. Hanging in the air with a stillness like the stillness between lightning and thunder. Sometimes she found herself hoping Libby'd had a change of heart, that she'd apologize for what she'd done and Shelby'd apologize for provoking her, and it would be all right.

Then she'd realize that they'd never, in all of Shelby's life, been like that. And never would. She was annoyed with herself for being so pathetic.

Fran was quite clear on what she expected. It was a set-up.

Saturday night Fran insisted on driving her to the Inn, even though she could have walked the distance in twenty minutes. She was uneasy, she said, and wanted to be sure things started out all right. After that she'd go across the Common to the bookstore and try to learn something about the business. She'd feel better being near-by.

Shelby laughed and asked if Fran expected her mother to pull a pearl-handled ladies' pistol and shoot her down in the Inn's foyer, like something out of a '40s movie. Fran said she wasn't putting anything past anyone, and knew Shelby was capable of doing something equally insane.

Fran spent Saturday washing her convertible and getting the gas tank filled and checking the air in the tires. Shelby said it was beginning to feel as if she were preparing the get-away car.

Fran said that wasn't far from the truth, and took a small quivery breath. Shelby went back to worrying over what to wear.

One thing she knew for sure, she wasn't about to have a drink before she met her mother. She needed to have her wits about her.

She took out everything in her closet and spread it on the bed, looking for something that would keep Libby mellow, but wouldn't make her feel like a stranger to herself.

Easier said than done. She was struck by how many of her clothes were Libby-pleasers. Even the dresses she wore to work—Libby thought skirts and blouses were too casual—had been chosen by Libby's standards.

Shelby sat down on the floor. Her whole life had been like this, Libby-approved. Even the nights in the Village listening to Beat poets hadn't really been a rebellion. Libby found it "cute" in an artsy kind of way.

Living here in Bass Falls, working for *The Magazine for Women*. Libby really didn't disapprove. She'd have disapproved of Shelby moving to the midwest to work for a newspaper. Shelby hadn't done that.

Why? Because Libby was so intimidating? Well, she was. But there was more to it than that.

Sadness gushed up inside her.

And anger.

She hit her hand against the floor. Damn it!

She'd wanted Libby to love her.

A tear tickled down her face. Then another. She let them run. She felt about twelve years old, a skein of contradictions.

When you're twelve years old and confused, it's all right to cry. You can wipe your eyes on your sleeve, and you're not required to blow your nose.

Fran walked in on her that way. "Hey," she said, "what's up?"

"I'm just being maudlin," Shelby said. She searched for a tissue.

Fran handed her one. "What about?" she asked gently.

Shelby felt her eyes fill up again. "My mother. My stupid mother. I'm crying because I want my stupid mother to love me, and that makes me stupidest of all."

"It's not stupid." Fran sat down beside her. "The stories I could tell you." She stroked Shelby's hair. "The trouble is, they get us when we're very small, and after that there's no way to fight."

"Yeah." She felt a little better, just having someone there.

Fran stayed with her for a while, until she'd stopped crying. "You don't want to be late," she said gently.

"Good God, no." Shelby got up and straightened her hair. "But I can't figure out what to wear. Pick something."

Fran came up with a soft, plain beige dress and a matching cashmere cardigan. "There. It'll make you look like a matron and feel like Nancy Drew."

"Shucks," Shelby said, "if I'd thought of it I'd have polished my saddle shoes." She looked Fran over. "You look nice."

"Thank you."

"Want to come with me?"

Fran laughed. "My business with your mother is finished. She fired her best shot, I didn't go down. All that's left is to negotiate the terms of her surrender."

The nights were growing cooler. Shelby was glad Fran had suggested a sweater. Or maybe it was only fear that made her hands clammy and her breath tight.

They drove the mile to the Inn in silence.

"Well," Fran said, "here we are."

Shelby glanced toward the dining room windows, hoping she had gotten there first.

She hadn't. Libby was seated at a table, having a drink with a man Shelby'd never seen before. Probably a stranger to Libby, too. She was fond of having drinks with men she'd never met. She didn't pick them up, exactly. She met them and charmed them and went on her way. It was a harmless pastime, feeding her ego.

Shelby opened the car door. Her heart banged in her chest.

"Remember," Fran said, "I'm right across the street. Come over there when you've finished, no matter how it goes. And don't do anything rash."

"Right." She closed the car door and started up the walk. Only a few more yards…She could barely move her legs. Libby and the man were laughing together.

"Shelby!"

Fran ran toward her. She grabbed Shelby's arm. "Back in the car. "

"What's the matter?"

"Get in the car!" She shoved Shelby into the front seat and ran around to her side. The motor was still running. She slammed the car into gear and took off spewing gravel.

She saw Libby turn toward the window. She started to get up.

Shelby gripped the armrest for balance. "What's happening?"

Fran didn't answer. She skidded around one corner, then another.

"Where are we going?"

"Out of here."

They were in open country. The dirt road ambled between fields of corn. Dried stalks stood out against the moon. Fran slowed the car, stopped. The breeze they'd made rustled the corn. Dust settled, red in the rear lights of the car.

Fran's hands gripped the steering wheel. "I know that man," she said.

"What man?"

"The man with your mother. At the inn. Jesus, Shelby, you could be in real trouble."

"I don't know what you're talking about."

Fran took a deep breath and turned to face her. "He spoke at an orientation session at the Health Service. He's a psychiatrist. From Harvard. He runs a ward in one of the mental hospitals and claims to specialize in 'curing' homosexuality."

She still didn't get it. "I don't understand."

"Your mother set up this dinner with you so she could have you committed to a hospital. That's why she was so agreeable."

"A mental hospital?"

"That's right."

"Why?"

"To get you cured." Fran ran her hand through her hair. "I know it sounds crazy, but it's happened to friends of mine. It happens all the time. This guy's particular method is electroshock."

"My mother's trying to do that? To me?"

277

"Apparently."

"But she'd die of embarrassment if I went in a mental hospital."

"He's discreet," Fran said. "I guess she considers it worth the risk."

It was beginning to sink in. It made her feel all twisted inside. "What am I going to do?"

"You can't go home tonight, that's for sure. They're probably looking for you now. We can't go to a motel. Your mother knows my car. If we're both gone, they'll probably call the cops. I have to get back there and see what's happening."

"But what can I do?" she asked again, helpless.

"I have one idea," Fran said. "You won't like it."

"What?"

Fran started the motor and pulled away without speaking. She found a paved road, and turned toward the lights of West Sayer. There was a phone booth next to a bank at the corner of the state highway. She stopped the car and got out.

"What are we doing?" Shelby asked.

Fran motioned her from the car and into the phone booth. She put in a dime and dialled a number and handed the phone to Shelby.

"What's going on?" Shelby asked.

Fran walked away.

"Hello?" She recognized the voice on the other end. She started to hang up, but realized Fran was right.

"Jean? It's Shelby. I'm in trouble."

She heard Jean's quick intake of breath. "Where are you?"

"In the phone booth outside the First Bank on Route 12."

"Are you all right?"

"For now. I need somewhere to hide."

"Should I come for you, or can you get here?"

"I could get there…" She hesitated to say it, but she had to. "…but they might recognize Fran's car."

"Sounds intriguing."

"I'll explain when I see you."

"OK," Jean said. "Be there in ten minutes."

"We're parked behind the bank. You can't see us from the road."

"Got it. Hey, Shelby, I'm really, really sorry about the other day."

"So am I," Shelby said.

"We'll talk. See you soon." Jean hung up.

Shelby leaned against the side of the phone booth, weak with relief. She went around back to the car.

"Well?" Fran asked.

"She's on her way."

"I knew it."

She slipped into the passenger seat. "How?"

"I know Jean, and I know you. That snit couldn't last." Fran looked very pleased with herself.

"There's no need to be smug," Shelby said, slapping her playfully on the arm.

"There is, too."

She edged closer to Fran and leaned against her shoulder. "I'm getting more and more people involved in this."

"It's a worthy cause. Now, be quiet. We don't want to attract attention."

Shelby thought of the turn her life had taken. One day she was doing almost everything right, and less than a week later she was running from her mother who wanted to lock her up in a mental hospital. It was like the plot for a B movie. But it was real, and it was her life. If she had any doubts, the fear burning in her stomach assured her.

This must be how you get ulcers, she thought.

It wasn't safe to go to her apartment. Libby could easily track her down there. And at work? Would that be safe? What the hell was she going to do next?

The lights from Jean's car swept the parking lot. Fran blinked hers and Jean parked beside them. She got out and leaned in Fran's window. "What's happening?"

Fran explained as succinctly as she could. "She needs to find a place to hide out for a couple of days, until we figure out what to do."

"No problem. I have plenty of room. How about you?"

"Someone has to watch the house. We can't be missing together. I'll keep my head down and play dumb."

"What if they try to take you?" Jean asked.

"A woman I hardly know and a man I never met? Hell, I'll call the cops."

Jean leaned across to her. "How's it going, Shel?"

"OK."

"She's not OK," Fran corrected her. "A lot has happened. She has to sort it out."

Jean laughed. "I know how she feels."

Fran took Shelby's hand. "Trouble's her middle name," she said to Jean.

"Don't I know it." Jean's voice was warm and slightly teasing. "I'm glad it's you dating her, not me."

Shelby recognized that for what it was, Jean's attempt at apologizing to Fran and trying to make things easy. She felt enormously grateful.

"Go with her now," Fran said to Shelby. "I'll bring you some things in the morning. We need to plan what to do next."

She got out of the car, glad someone else was making the decisions. She stood by Jean and watched Fran's car disappear into the darkness.

Jean slipped an arm around her. "Welcome back," she said.

Chapter 21

Shelby stumbled into the living room next morning to find Fran already there, sharing coffee and a box of doughnuts with Jean. She yawned and said, "You should have called me," and rummaged through the plates and napkins and wrappers until she found a vanilla creme-filled.

"You needed sleep," Jean said.

Fran waved her away. "Make us another pot of coffee. And would you *please* try not to leak powdered sugar over everything?"

Shelby grumbled and went to the kitchen.

"Here's how it looks to us," Fran said as she came back in with the coffee, considerably more alert but wishing she were still asleep and not anxious.

"Uh," she said.

"We can't stay here. In the area. They were outside your apartment all night. They won't give up. We have to go somewhere your mother won't find us. Take as much as we need and start over. Leave your car and everything. That'll give us a little headway. It'll take them a few days to realize you've really gone."

"Go somewhere?"

"Give me your apartment keys," Jean picked up, "and I'll make it look as if you're around. Leave a light on occasionally, take in the mail. Maybe even burn something on the stove to fool the upstairs neighbors."

"Won't work," Fran said. "She never burns food. Do it in my place."

Shelby's head was spinning. Just pick up and go? "Wait a minute. Can we slow down here?"

"After you find out where you're settling," Jean told her, "I'll close your apartment, and sell whatever you want me to sell. You'll need the money at first. I'll keep the rest of your stuff until you decide what to do with it."

"Better give Jean power of attorney so she won't get arrested. And take all your money out of the bank. I'll do the same. We can arrange all that tomorrow. Personally, I think California's a good destination. Things are looser there, it's easier to get lost in the crowd. But we can decide that when we're ready. We'll drive across the country, and if we find a place we really like, we'll stop."

"No." Shelby said frantically. "This is my life you're talking about."

"That's right," Fran said. "It's your life and your mother wants it. One does not, under any circumstances, screw around with vampires."

"I have to change my whole way of thinking. About everything. You're asking me to do something that's never even occurred to me."

"I know that," Fran said earnestly. "But we do have to get out of here. You can think while we're driving. I'm sorry. I know it's hard, but…"

"Damn right it's hard. This could be a mistake."

Fran came over close and knelt beside her. "Look, nothing's written in stone here. If you decide it's not right for you—no matter where we are—I swear I'll get you back here. You can tell them I took you away at gun point."

She knew Fran was right, but it seemed unreal. It was like being jerked off your feet when you least expect it. It was…

"We have to do this," Fran said urgently. "It's really, really serious."

Shelby looked down into Fran's face, so open, so frightened.

She touched her. "I do see your point. I just…It's a big thing."

"It'll be OK," Fran said. "I promise."

"OK," Jean said efficiently. "Monday we'll go to the lawyer's and the bank. Then I'll go into the office and see if I can scrounge up a decent letter of reference for you. Think Charlotte's all right?"

Shelby nodded. "She seems pretty sympathetic, but I don't know about this…this…lesbian stuff."

"What's the matter?" Fran said with a grin. "Can't you say the word?"

"The matter is," Shelby answered huffily, "you two have had a lot more sugar and caffeine than I have, *and* you're enjoying this entirely too much." She swallowed some coffee. "In the first place, who says I have to leave? And who says you have to get involved in it?"

"Well," Fran said, "we've cussed it and discussed it, and it seems like the only way for you. You can't stay in Bass Falls or West Sayer, Libby'd be on you like a flock of buzzards. Things are looking rocky at your job—plus it would keep you stuck here—so maybe it's time to move on."

"Your mother wants to lock you up," Jean continued. "You aren't engaged any more. And your friends have turned against you. What would you stay for?"

"I don't know." Shelby rubbed her forehead with the heel of her hand. "It seems so extreme."

"Don't talk to me about extreme," Jean said. "You're engaged to be married, you break the engagement, and less than a week later you're sleeping with a woman. Unless you started that before."

"Not me," Fran said, raising one hand as if taking a Girl Scout oath. "I'm not a slut."

"Yeah, but…"

"The fact of the matter is," Fran said seriously, "you really don't have a choice. Trust me, I've met women who've been locked up in those places. They don't come out intact. One woman I know was lobotomized. And Herr Doktor that your mother was sharing a drink with isn't exactly against that as a 'treatment modality.'"

"I've never done anything like this. Running away…"

"At your age," Jean said, "you're overdue. Come on, you've been upright and uptight all your life. Time to spread your wings."

Shelby looked at Fran. "You shouldn't have to uproot your life for me."

"It would be my absolute pleasure." The sun touched her head. Her hair shimmered. Her eyes were bright. Her smile penetrated the deepest shadows.

"OK," Shelby said. "Let's do it. But let's do it before I have a chance to think any more."

She changed into the shirt and slacks Fran had brought. They spent most of the day making plans. When Fran brought out the road maps, she began to get excited. She'd always wanted to see the country. To drive across the plains and deserts and mountains. To go places she'd only read about. To see how other people lived. Sometimes her fantasies had taken the form of a bus trip to nowhere, stopping in small towns with coffee joints and laundromats along the way. Sometimes she'd thought about strapping on a knapsack and heading west along the railroad tracks.

She hadn't had those daydreams for a long time. She was glad to see them again. "My knapsack," she said to Fran, who was making a list of things to pack. "And my jackknife, and sleeping bag."

"Good idea. We might end up sleeping under tables in rest areas."

She could tell Fran was serious, and that made her even more excited. Going On the Road, like Kerouac and Steinbeck. To whatever they liked, whatever drew their interest. They could wander down dirt roads if they thought there might be something at the end. If they saw a place marked in little red letters on the tourist map, they could go there and see what it was. They could scavenge for nuts in pecan groves. And hang out at lunch counters where the locals dropped in at noon to gossip.

"One thing to remember," Fran said, "if anyone asks, we're sisters or school teachers. People don't seem surprised at sisters and school teachers travelling together without male company."

"You mean like nuns?"

"It's OK to say you're nuns," Jean said, "but don't get in the habit."

Fran rolled her eyes.

By evening they'd converted their escape into lists and plans. Jean went out and brought in buckets of Chinese food. They debated going to a movie. Jean suggested *The Children's Hour*. They threatened to strangle her. Fran said she'd better get back to the apartment house. She had a lot of packing to do under cover of darkness. When she got home, she called to tell them things seemed all right, there were no signs of forced entry.

Shelby realized they were treating this like a game. It was a good way to beat back fear. It was also a good way to get careless.

"What do you really think?" she asked Jean when they were both in pajamas.

"I think this is something you have to do," she said sadly. "But I'll miss you terribly."

"Me, too. You've been an awfully good friend to me, and I just…well, I just plain like you."

Jean was silent for a moment. Traffic going by on the street made a sound like wind in pines. "To tell you the truth," she said, "I love you." She glanced up quickly. "Not in the way you're in love with Fran. And she is with you." She smiled. "Brother has she got it bad. But I just…I don't know, you're part of my heart and you always will be."

"I feel the same about you," Shelby said.

"I'm sorry for the way I acted when you told me. I was confused."

"I understand that."

"I was afraid it would make you different. That you wouldn't be the Shelby I knew. It would be like you'd died, and someone who looks like you had taken your place."

"And I thought it had happened to you."

Jean rested her head on Shelby's shoulder. Shelby slipped an arm around her.

"It's going to be awfully lonely with you gone," Jean said.

"It'll be lonely for me, too, without you."

"Maybe some day I'll bust out of here and track you down."

"You'll always know where I am," Shelby said.

"That'll be unique. I don't always know where *I* am." Jean sat up. "If we don't stop this, I'll never be able to let you go. I'll fling myself in front of your car."

"Yeah. We have a lot of hard things to do tomorrow. I guess we should go to bed."

"I guess we should."

But they sat there for another hour, holding hands in silence.

The next day went like clockwork. Jean went to work early, and tracked down Charlotte May, who said she would not only write a letter of reference, but would go one better. Then she turned enigmatic and told Jean to check with her at the end of the day.

Shelby met Jean at the bank. Together they tracked down a lawyer who wasn't busy, and drew up a power of attorney for Jean.

Jean went back to the office.

Fran called and said Libby'd been snooping around, and had even dared to confront Fran in her apartment. Fran pretended not to have any idea what Libby was talking about.

"I think she drank some of your scotch," she said. "She sure smelled like it."

"Delightful," Shelby said. "I'll be ready to go by six. How about you?"

"Fine with me. I'll pick you up then."

"Fran, do you feel as if we're living in Nazi Germany?"

"We are," Fran said.

Jean came back with a glowing letter of recommendation from Charlotte, and one from Spurl. Shelby looked at it, puzzled. "How did you get this?"

"You won't believe it. Charlotte went to Myers, who wrote it and stuck it in with a bunch of letters Spurl was supposed to sign. He always does that without looking."

"Miss *Myers* did that?"

Jean nodded. "Charlotte said to tell you there's more to Grace Myers than meets the eye."

She couldn't keep herself from shrieking. "My God, Miss Myers? And I'll bet Charlotte is, too."

"Sure looked that way to me." Jean grinned. There was a knock on the door. Shelby's stomach sank.

"Time to go," Fran said. "Ready?"

"As ready as I'll ever be." She picked up her papers.

Jean looked as if she might fall apart any second. Shelby went over to her.

"Thank you," she said. "For all of it."

"Have a good…" Her voice broke.

Shelby took her in her arms and held her for a long time.

The night was solid darkness, broken only by the cones of light from her headlights. Now and then a pair of eyes, low to the ground, glinted from the roadside and disappeared. They were deep in night.

Shelby Camden, once soon-to-be-successful career woman, slinking through the Iowa darkness.

By Indiana, she had stopped looking in the rearview mirror, expecting to see a police car, or even Libby's Cadillac following them. By Illinois, the feeling of running from her life had changed to the feeling she was running toward her future. There'd be plenty of grieving to do down the road. Betrayals to be mourned. Missing Jean—and even her old friends, from when they had been friends. Missing Ray and the friendship they could have had.

But for now there was adventure ahead. With lots of blind alleys and hidden driveways. Beside her, Fran stirred. Her face was ghostly in the green dash light. "Shel?"

"Hmmm."

"You OK?"

"I guess. A little scared."

Fran reached over and touched her. "It'll be OK."

"I know," she said without conviction.

"And if it's not, we'll still be together."

Yes, she thought, we'll be together. Together.

"Hey, Shelby?"

"What?"

"Do you like dogs?"

Shelby smiled. "Tremendously."

"What kind?"

"Ratty mutts from the pound."

"Thank God. I was afraid I'd made a terrible mistake in judgment." She shifted, and rested her head against the window.

Shelby glanced over quickly, then focused her attention on her driving. After all, she was carrying precious cargo. She glanced in the rearview mirror, searching for signs of dawn. Only the red glow of her own tail lights tinted the darkness.

Safe here in the car. Outside of time and space. She pushed their speed beyond sixty-five, to seventy, seventy-five, carried along in the slip-stream of night. Tomorrow they'd start to look again, the way they had for two days. Is this town big enough to offer jobs? Are there too many conservative churches? What are the people like? What happens if they guess? Should we push on toward California? Questions. Observations. Wonderings.

But tonight there was only the road and the darkness. The low, comforting rumble of tires on asphalt. The glow of the dashboard lights.

The two of them, alone, together, safe in their cocoon of night.